THE
ABDUCTION
"Nonstop plot surprises.... One of the year's better thrillers."
—San Francisco Examiner
D0092401
UNITED STA
JAMES
GRIPPANDO
Bestselling author of Found Money, The Informant, and The Pardon

Harper
Paperbacks

U.S. $6.99
CAN. $8.99

ISBN 0-06-109748-9

9 780061 097485

50699

EAN

ACCLAIM FOR JAMES GRIPPANDO AND *THE ABDUCTION*

"Continually chilling intrigue. . . . Certain to become a bestseller. . . . A thriller within a mystery within a drama . . . that ensures readers stay on the edge of their seats."

—*Naples Daily News* (FL)

"Truly dirty politics and crime. . . . Hits a nerve . . . as timely as today's headlines."

—*San Francisco Chronicle*

"A gripping (and frightening) story about the Machiavellian world of American politics. . . . Genuinely surprising."

—*Booklist*

"Deftly plotted political fun."

—*Library Journal*

"Breathless."

—*Philadelphia Inquirer*

THE INFORMANT

"Spectacular effects . . . entertaining. . . . Grippando has done his homework on FBI forensics, criminal profiling and the internal protocol for backstabbing. . . . Plenty of blood is spilled on the rug."

—*New York Times Book Review*

"A breathlessly scary, unpredictable thriller . . . extravagantly plotted. . . . Grippando has produced a work that will deserve its place on bestseller lists."

—*Fort Lauderdale Sun Sentinel*

"Grippando meets the criteria for the genre. He thrills."

—*Houston Chronicle*

"A worthy addition to the genre. . . . Byzantine plot twists and close calls . . . an explosive climax."

—*Toronto Star*

"Intriguing . . . Grippando handles this unusual [plot] with ease."

—*Chicago Tribune*

"A thoroughly convincing edge-of-your-seat thriller, clearly on par with *The Silence of the Lambs*."

—John Douglas,
bestselling author of *Mind Hunter*

"It's not only titillating, but terrifying—indeed, terrorizing. . . . Takes the FBI—and [Grippando's] readers—through a series of bizarre twists and turns."

—*Naples Daily News* (FL)

"Surges with tension . . . an absorbing tale [written] with cool competence . . . and a nail-biter to boot."

—*Publishers Weekly*

"Edgy . . . keeps you tearing through the pages."
—*Kirkus Reviews*

THE PARDON

"Powerful. . . . I read *The Pardon* in one sitting—one exciting night of thrills and chills."

—James Patterson

"A gritty mystery that . . . rings true to the emotional realities of contemporary life. Readers will turn the pages of *The Pardon* faster than a bailiff can swear in a witness."

—*People* magazine

"A gripping mélange of courtroom drama and psychotic manipulation . . . possesses gritty veracity, genuine characters that elicit sympathy, and superb plotting and pacing. . . . A bona fide blockbuster."

—*Boston Herald*

"One of the best novels I've read in a long time. I was unable to put it down."

—F. Lee Bailey

"Takes us into the seamy side of Florida law, politics, and murder. . . . Grippando writes about what he knows and it's good."

—*Sunday Oklahoman*

"Sensationally effective. . . . It won't kill more than a few hours, but oh, what hours they'll be."

—*Kirkus Reviews*

"Chilling. . . . Grippando ratches up the suspense every few pages. . . . A promising, cleverly plotted, and taut first novel."

—*Booklist*

Books by James Grippando

The Pardon
The Informant
The Abduction
*Found Money**

Published by HarperCollins Publishers

*coming soon

THE Abduction

a novel

JAMES GRIPPANDO

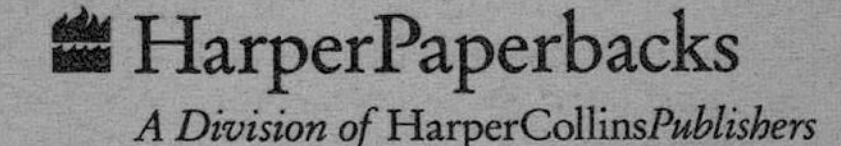

HarperPaperbacks
A Division of HarperCollins*Publishers*
10 East 53rd Street, New York, NY 10022-5299

This book contains an excerpt from *Found Money* by James Grippando. This excerpt has been set for this edition only and may not reflect the final content of the hardcover edition.

A hardcover edition of this book was published in 1998 by HarperCollins Publishers.

ISBN 0-06-109748-9

HarperCollins®, ®, and HarperPaperbacks™, are trademarks of HarperCollins Publishers, Inc.

Cover illustration © 1999 by Jon Paul

First HarperPaperbacks printing: February 1999

Printed in the United States of America

Visit HarperPaperbacks on the World Wide Web at
http://www.harpercollins.com

❖ 10 9 8 7 6 5 4 3 2 1

For Tiffany

Acknowledgments

Thank you . . .

To Tiffany. I don't say it enough, but I couldn't do it without you.

To Carolyn Marino, Robin Stamm, and the usual suspects with the unusual talent—Artie Pine, Richard Pine, and Joan Sanger.

And to Carlos Sires, Eleanor Raynor, Judy Russell, Nancy Lehner, Eric Helmers, Jim Hall, Terri Gavulic (once a Pepper, always a Pepper), Gayle DeJulio, Jennifer Stearns, and Jerry Houlihan.

The third time's a charm, even though we all know this is really the fourth.

Prologue: March 1992

At eleven o'clock, the screaming finally stopped.

It had started as a whimper, faint but steady. With each shaky breath it strengthened, growing more shrill by the minute, culminating in a desperate spate of primal pleas that defied the bounds of language, that barely sounded human.

Tonight, like every night, Allison Leahy could only cringe at the cries of her four-month-old daughter. That the pediatrician declared it "normal" didn't make it any softer on the ears. *Something* had to be bothering her baby, though Allison had the distinct and helpless feeling that little Emily would probably reach puberty by the time Mommy figured it out.

She did have a few theories—fears, actually, that tormented her in flashes of panic. It could be serious, a psychological sign that Emily was rejecting her adopted mother. Maybe it was one of those dreaded syndromes, the lasting legacy of an unknown teenage mother on a prenatal diet of vodka and cigarettes. Or was the problem just Allison? It was entirely possible her friends were right: It *was* crazy for a thirty-nine-year-old career woman to adopt a newborn when there was no father on the horizon.

Fortunately, her paranoia usually melted at the mere sight of that little face—the turned-up nose and perfect little mouth that prompted people to say she looked just like her mother. Not her biological mother. Her real mother. Allison relished the resemblance, even if it was mere coincidence.

"You asleep, pretty baby?" she whispered hopefully.

Emily slumped in her car seat, multiple chins on her chest. The silence was a clear "affirmative."

Allison switched off the clothes dryer. She couldn't recall where she'd picked up the helpful tip, but perching an infant in a car seat atop a warm, vibrating dryer was like mechanical Sominex. She bundled her baby in her arms and headed across the kitchen. They paused before the portable television that rested on the Corian countertop. Anthony Hopkins was happily thanking the academy for his Best Actor award. Emily's sleepy eyes popped open, as if she were somehow taken by the Hollywood magic.

Allison smiled and continued down the hall, speaking in a soft, gooey mommy voice as they entered the nursery. "That'll be you someday, sweetheart. Maybe by then even all those silly old men out in Hollywood will realize they don't give separate awards for 'best boy director' and 'best girl director,' so they don't need 'best actress' and 'best actor,' either. You'll be Emily Leahy, best *actor*. Better than all the boys and all the girls. Because you're just the best. Yes," she gushed, "that's what *you* are: *duh best*!"

She laid her little fourteen-pound prize atop the pink cotton sheets in the crib, thankful that her chronic inability to keep her convictions to herself hadn't in this instance rendered ninety minutes of standing over the dryer completely futile. Emily was sound asleep. Maybe she was getting used to a mother who wasn't afraid to air her views. *She'd better*, thought Allison.

Allison had been raised during the Eisenhower era in a small town north of Chicago, where at age nine she was kicked out of the Catholic school for fattening the lip of an old nun who'd said her mother was going to hell because she was divorced. She completed her education in public schools, graduating second in her class at the University of Illinois College of Law, class of '76. In just two years she gained national recognition as counsel for the Consumer Safety Defense Fund. Eleven infants thought to have died from sudden infant death syndrome were actually the victims of knock-off teddy bears stuffed with old rags that still bore the remnants of an odorless but highly toxic cleaning solvent. Allison paved the way for the government to bring slam-dunk criminal charges against the top executives who had approved the cost-cutting scheme. Her tenacity had caught the eye of the United States Attorney, who promptly hired her. In six years she'd never lost a case. After a four-year stint in Washington as the youngest-ever chief of the Justice Department's public integrity section, she came home to Chicago and entered the world of real politics. At age thirty-six she won the hotly contested race for Cook County State Attorney, with 60 percent of the vote. The female half of the electorate had clearly responded to her message that women were too often the victims of violent crime. Even her own pollsters, however, weren't sure whether male voters had been moved by the issues or by what her sexist opponent called the "Princess Grace factor." The burdens of three years in office hadn't robbed her of the look, though her long blond hair was now shoulder-length, and her big hazel eyes more often blinked with skepticism. She was a woman in transition, her mother had recently told her, from striking beauty to elegant self-assuredness.

"Good night, darling," she said as she planted a kiss on Emily's forehead. She placed the transmitter for the electronic baby monitor on the dresser beside the crib. The small cordless receiver fit easily into the deep pocket of her terry cloth robe. She switched on the volume. It was like eavesdropping on your own baby, a one-way wiretap of sorts that allowed worried parents to wander around the house or sleep in another room without missing a single coo or gurgle. Allison adjusted her receiver to clear the static, then switched off the Winnie the Pooh lamp on the dresser and headed for the master bedroom.

The phone rang, striking panic. She snatched up the cordless telephone and ran to the guest bedroom at the other end of the house, far away from the sleeping angel for whom there would be hell to pay if she woke up now.

"Hello," she answered in a husky whisper.

"Hi, it's Mitch."

She sighed. Mitch O'Brien, her ex-fiancé. Their engagement had lasted three years, until Allison finally admitted that her failure to set a wedding date wasn't mere procrastination. It had been nearly eight months since their amicable breakup, but ever since he'd called three months ago to congratulate her on the adoption, he'd made a habit of calling every Monday night. Allison didn't mind, though when she'd told him she hoped they could remain friends, she didn't exactly mean *best* friends.

"So how's little Miss America?" he asked.

"That was last week. This week she's best actor."

"You mean best actress."

"We'll see about that," she said coyly.

A happy gurgle crackled over the baby monitor. Emily seemed to concur.

Allison smiled. "Actually, she's so chatty lately I may groom her to replace Oprah in 2010. How's this for her first show? Michael Crichton and Martha Stewart jointly touting their delicious new cure for cancer."

Mitch laughed, then changed the subject. He was soon fishing to see how things were going in the dating department. She did have a new "significant other," though a long-distance relationship with a man who lived in New York hardly seemed significant compared to what was in the next room. Allison was tuning out, focusing instead on the happy sounds of her baby transmitted by the monitor. To all else she was nearly oblivious—to Mitch's words, to the passage of time.

To anything in the world that didn't revolve around Emily.

"The Taker" was getting interference. He'd been parked at the end of Royal Oak Court for over ninety minutes, where the radio signal had been strong and clear. A steady chorus of gurgles and sighs, followed by intermittent snorts—the infantile version of sawing logs. Now, the airwaves were filled with annoying static, peppered with an occasional lapse into inane conversation between Allison Leahy and Mitch O'Brien.

She's on a cordless phone, he realized. The

combined radio frequencies were screwing up the signal he'd intercepted from the Leahy's baby monitor.

He switched off the digital electronic scanner on the dashboard. The crackling stopped. The van was dark and silent. He cracked the driver-side window to release stale cigarette smoke, then crushed out his Camel in the overflowing ashtray. The blinking orange light on the console said the miniature cassette tape was still recording. He hit the stop button, then eject. He had all the recorded cooing and baby grunts he needed—nearly ninety minutes worth, counting the audiotape he'd made on last week's stakeout.

Thanks to his earlier handiwork, the streetlight was out on the corner, leaving the Leahy residence in a shroud of darkness. He removed his sport shirt and slipped the top half of a hooded Nomex body suit over his torso. It fit like a wet suit, a sleek and perfect nighttime complement to his black jeans and black sneakers. He checked himself in the rearview mirror and covered his face with black greasepaint. His camouflage complete, he wiped his hands and pulled on black rubber gloves. He never used leather. Animal skin left its own set of distinctive patterns, like fingerprints. Quietly, he stepped down from the van.

The ranch-style house sat toward the back of a heavily wooded quarter-acre lot. A thick, ten-foot-high hedge enclosed the yard for privacy. Beneath the twisted limbs of towering oak trees, a curved front walk stretched seventy-five feet from street to doorstep. He selected the tallest oak, the one closest to the house, then quietly broke through the hedge and started up the tree. In a matter of seconds he was stretched out on a long limb that hovered over the roof. Gently, he lowered himself onto the cedar shingles.

With three silent steps he reached the chimney. He knew from an earlier drive-by that the alarm box was fastened on the back of the chimney. It was the size of a large lunch box, painted gray. It was padlocked, but it had slats on the front that allowed the noise to escape when the alarm sounded. He zipped open his pouch and removed a spray can, then fastened a six-inch plastic straw to the nozzle. The straw fit perfectly between the slats on the alarm box. He pressed the nozzle, unleashing a stream of white foam insulation that expanded to fill the entire box. It hardened in seconds. The alarm was silenced without cutting a wire.

He stuck the spray can back in his pouch, zipped it up quickly, and climbed back down the oak tree. In thirty seconds he was crouched beneath the bedroom window in the rear of the house. The room was dark, but the little dancing bears on the curtains told him he was in the right place. He moved closer to inspect, almost touching the pane with the tip of his nose. No security bars or fancy locks here. Just the standard latch and filament that wired the window to the disabled alarm. It might be linked to a central alarm station, but he could count on them to take at least five or ten minutes to respond.

He smirked, as if it were too easy. *Sure doesn't take much to beat home security.*

It was almost midnight when Allison hung up the phone. Mitch didn't want to say good night, but she was tired and finally had to be almost rude about it. For the third week in a row their conversation had ended on an awkward note. This time he wanted to know if her single motherhood was causing any political backlash. To be sure, she was concerned about her continued electability. One newspaper had already raised questions about a system that allowed a certain state attorney to get in line for adoption before her wedding day and to stay on the list after her engagement fizzled. Nonetheless, she wanted a child. She didn't think she should have to marry the wrong man to get one. And she was convinced that—right or wrong—adoption by an unmarried woman wouldn't evoke the same moral judgments or create the same political baggage as a pregnancy out of wedlock.

Allison switched off the bedroom lamp and walked sleepily down the hall. The cordless receiver in her pocket continued to emit little Emily's normal nighttime sounds. A little baby noise was nothing to worry about. It was sustained silence that sent new mothers rushing to the crib to make sure all was well.

She smiled with anticipation as she neared the darkened nursery. She peeked through the doorway, then caught her breath. The baby was on her stomach. Allison *never* laid her on her stomach. The recommended SIDS position was on the side or back. She hurried to the crib and leaned over the rail.

Her scream pierced the darkness.

A doll lay in Emily's place. Allison frantically pitched it aside and unfurled the blanket, knocking something to the floor. She flipped on the light switch. It was a hand-held Dictaphone emitting the sounds of her baby.

She screamed louder and rushed to the window. The latch was unlocked. A round hole had been drilled through the glass—just big enough to allow a thin metal rod or a pointed stick to pass through and unlock the latch. Her horrified expression was reflected in the window.

"Emily!"

She raced from the nursery and down the hall, grabbing the portable phone. Without breaking stride she checked the kitchen, the bathroom, every room in the house, shouting her child's name. She was still running as she dialed 911, then stopped at the kitchen counter.

"Somebody's got my baby!" she told the operator.

"Just calm down, ma'am."

"Calm down! My four-month-old daughter's been snatched from her crib. Send a squad car right now. Nine-oh-one Royal Oak Court."

"Are they still there?"

"No. I don't know. I don't see anyone. They took my baby!"

"I'll dispatch a unit right now, ma'am. They're on their way. Just stay inside."

A car, thought Allison. *They must have a car!* She flew through the living room and out the front door.

"Emily!"

She checked the porch, the shrubs and the rose bed by the walkway. Thorny branches tore into her skin and shredded her robe. She sprinted to the street and checked for cars or pedestrians—*anyone* at all. Her chest heaved with a shortness of breath. A pain ripped her belly from the inside out, and a flood of tears warmed her cheeks. She glanced left, then right, toward both ends of the street. There was no sign of anyone.

"Ma'am," said the 911 operator, "are you still there?"

Allison couldn't answer. She fell to her knees at the end of the sidewalk, her shoulders heaving with great racking sobs. A crackling noise was coming from her pocket. Her hand shook as she reached inside her robe and pulled out the receiver.

A chill ran through her as she realized what it was. The baby monitor was still transmitting from the nursery. The Dictaphone was still on.

The recorded sounds of Emily were playing in her hand.

Part 1

October 2000

1

Allison could feel her heart pounding. Her lungs burned as she fought for air. The treadmill's digital display told her she was passing the two-mile mark. She punched the speed button to slow the pace and catch her breath. Perspiration soaked her, pasting the nylon sweat pants and extra-large T-shirt to her trim forty-eight-year-old body. It was her favorite T-shirt, white with bright red and blue lettering.

It read, "Leahy for President—A *New* Millennium."

After nearly four years as the United States attorney general, Allison was just fifteen days away from the historic date on which voters would decide whether the nation's "top cop" would become its first woman president. The race was wide-open and without an incumbent, as her boss—Democratic President Charlie Sires—was at the end of his second and final four-year term. Allison was his second-term attorney general, part of the president's shake-up of his own cabinet upon reelection in 1996. Eight months ago, Allison didn't consider herself a serious presidential contender. But when the Republicans nominated Lincoln Howe, the nation's most beloved black man, the polls made it clear that the only Democrat who could beat him was a charismatic white woman.

Ironically, thirty minutes of walking in place on the treadmill had actually put Allison thirty miles closer to her afternoon rally in Philadelphia. She was on the last leg of a two-day bus tour through Pennsylvania, a critical swing state with twenty-four electoral college votes. Her campaign bus had logged nearly ten thousand miles in the past six months. Now more than ever, it was showing the signs of a well-oiled political machine in the homestretch—which to the average organized human being looked remarkably like utter chaos. A dozen noisy staffers were busy at the fax machines and computer terminals. A scattered collection of bulging archive boxes blocked the bathroom entrance, as if strategically placed to trip up anyone desperate enough to use the on-board facilities. Thousands of campaign buttons, leaflets, and bumper stickers cluttered the rear storage area. Four small color television sets were suspended from the ceiling, each blaring a different broadcast for simultaneous multinetwork viewing. One set was electronically "padlocked," permanently tuned to CNN's virtually continuous coverage of Campaign 2000.

"That's about enough self-flagellation for one day," said Allison, groaning. She hit the stop button and stepped down from the treadmill.

Walking had been her chief source of exercise since the beginning of the New Hampshire Democratic primary in January. Whatever the town, she'd walk up and down Main Street, and people would join in and walk along with her. It provided great photo ops early in the primary, but after she won the Democratic nomination in August the crowds grew so large that she needed a parade permit. In the last week, time constraints and cold

Appalachian rains had forced her to confine her walking to the treadmill during bus-ride debriefings from her campaign strategist, David Wilcox.

"What else, David?" she said as she leaned over and stretched her calf muscles.

Wilcox was a tall and wiry fifty-one-year-old graduate of the Woodrow Wilson School of Public Affairs at Princeton. He had shone as a young White House Fellow under President Carter, but a bitter loss in a personal bid for Congress in 1982 convinced him he'd rather not be a candidate. In high school he was voted most likely to become a game show host, and he'd finally found his niche as a political strategist. Over seventeen years his list of satisfied clients included nine United States senators, seven congressmen, and five governors, and he'd masterminded Allison's upset victory over a sitting vice president in the Democratic primaries. In the last few weeks, however, he'd grown concerned about the growing influence of outside consultants, so he'd decided to glue himself to Allison's side for the bus tour. At the moment, he was reviewing his checklist, seemingly oblivious to Allison's sweaty exercise attire or to the blurred Pennsylvania countryside in the window behind her.

"The drug problem has reared its ugly head." He had an ominous voice for a thin man, part of an overall seriousness that was more suitable for a White House state dinner than the frenetic campaign trail. "I think our distinguished opposition is turning desperate. They're finally trying to make something out of your treatment for depression, back in ninety-two."

"That was eight years ago. Politically speaking, it's ancient history."

"They're saying you took Prozac."

"I told you I was in counseling."

"Are you splitting hairs on me?"

She flashed a sobering look. "My four-month-old daughter was taken right out of her crib, right from my own house. Yes, I was depressed. I was in group counseling. Eight of us. Parents who'd lost children. No, I didn't take Prozac. But if you ask the other members of my support group, they'll probably say I needed it. So don't expect me to apologize for having reached out for a little support. And don't sit there and act like this is news to you, either. I laid out all the skeletons the day I hired you."

He grimaced, thinking it through. "I just wish we could put the whole episode in more of a context."

Her look became a glare. "I won't make Emily's abduction part of this campaign, if that's what you mean."

"Allison, we can't just say you were depressed and leave it at that. We need a positive spin."

"Okay," she said sarcastically, "how about this? Depression is a good thing. It's what stimulates ideas. Every invention, every accomplishment stems from depression, not euphoria. Nobody ever said, 'Life's swell, let's invent fire.' It was the malcontent in the back of the cave who finally stood up and said, 'Hey, I'm freezing my ass off in here!' You want something to get done in Washington? By all means, elect the clinically depressed."

He was deadpan. "Please don't repeat that publicly. Or *I'll* be very depressed."

"Good," she said with a smirk. "We could use some new ideas around here." She took a deep breath. Wilcox didn't look amused, but she knew he wouldn't push it. Throughout the campaign she'd nipped every mention of the abduction with some brusque remark—sometimes pointed, sometimes flip—which immediately moved the agenda to less personal territory. "Anything else?" she asked.

"I hate to keep harping on this, but General Howe's wife has been stumping hard for him lately. Our polls show she's making inroads. A lot of voters—male and female, Democrat and Republican—are nostalgic about having a First Lady in the White House. We can't counteract those warm fuzzies unless we define the role of a First Husband. The election is two weeks away, and forty percent of the public still has no opinion on Peter Tunnello."

"Sorry, but the CEO of a publicly traded company can't duck out of a stockholders meeting for a rubber chicken luncheon at the VFW."

"That's kind of my point. I think he would, if you asked him."

"How do you know I haven't asked?"

"Your attitude, that's how. It started right after the convention, when Howe's camp floated those ugly rumors that you married Peter just to bankroll your political ambition. Ever since then, you've been on a one-woman crusade to shake more hands and raise more money than anybody in history. Don't get me wrong. The money's great. But the more you adopt this go-it-alone persona, the more you fuel suspicions about your marriage."

"This is not a buy-one, get-two presidency. My marriage is *my* business."

"It would still be nice if the American people could see you two together sometimes, especially as we get closer to election day. Just a few strategic public displays of affection, like Nancy and Ron Reagan."

"News flash!" shouted one of her aides. He pitched his cellular phone onto the seat beside him and spun around, facing Allison. "Howe's about to launch something in New Jersey. Check out CNN."

Allison moved closer to the main set. Her aides watched intently, straining to hear over the rumble of the bus's diesel engine. Wilcox raised the volume. General Howe was near the end of a short speech before the National Convention of the American Legion in Atlantic City.

On screen, a handsome African-American man stood tall behind a chest-high podium, facing an enthusiastic crowd. The American flag hung limply on the yellow wall of painted cinder block. A blue and white banner hung from the rafters, proclaiming the campaign slogan, "Lincoln Howe—Lincoln *Now!*" The house was packed, and the most enthusiastic supporters were strategically standing in the aisles to make the turnout seem even better than it was.

General Howe was an imposing figure, even when wearing a simple business suit and VFW cap. Army regulations prohibited him from wearing his uniform after his retirement, but the larger-than-life photograph in the background reminded voters of his distinguished forty-year career. It was a photo fit for history books: the triumphant general inspecting his troops, dressed in riding boots, bloused green trousers, and short-waisted jacket. His chest was decorated with an array of medals, including a Medal of Honor. Each shoulder bore four silver stars, indicating his rank. To his right was a photograph of Howe in another uniform, old number twenty-two, carrying a football for Army. He was a Heisman Trophy–winning running back in 1961. The best player in college football had given up a promising career as professional athlete to serve his country.

"The thing I remember most about my combat experience in Vietnam," he said in a commanding voice, "is the eerie feeling of fighting an invisible enemy. As we marched through the thick tropical jungle of the A Shau Valley, gunfire would quickly erupt, men would fall—and then all was quiet. The enemy was nowhere to be seen.

"This presidential campaign has been strangely reminiscent of that experience. Marching along the campaign trail, I get machine-gunned out of nowhere with a barrage of clever sound bites created by my Democratic opponent's high-paid advisers. When it comes time to stand and fight, however, Ms. Leahy is nowhere to be found."

A combination of light laughter and applause rolled across the auditorium.

General Howe flashed a serious expression straight into the camera, his voice growing louder. "The American people deserve better than that. So today I issue this challenge. Come out from your hiding place in the Washington jungle, Ms. Leahy. Debate me on the issues, one on one!"

The crowd cheered, but the general kept talking.

"I'm not talking about another round of sickeningly sweet question-and-answer sessions, like those so-called debates we held earlier this month. No more use of a single moderator who would sooner pick up a rattlesnake than ask a potentially embarrassing question. Forget the town-hall format, where the tough questions may or may not be asked. Let's have a panel of four independent experts. You pick two, I pick two. Let *them* ask the questions the American people are asking. And let *us* answer them!"

The crowd erupted into louder cheers. Balloons fell from the ceiling. Supporters clapped their hands and waved their red and blue cardboard signs, chanting, *"We want Lincoln! We want Lincoln!"*

The television coverage quickly shifted back to a stiff and serious anchorman fingering the small audio piece into his ear. "Joining me now from Washington is CNN political analyst Nick Beaugard. Nick, why does this challenge come now?"

The screen flashed a head-and-shoulders shot of a silver-haired reporter before a mock-up of the White House. "If you believe General Howe's campaign staff, they've been trying to persuade the nonpartisan Commission on Presidential Debates to approve another debate ever since the first round failed to produce a clear winner. But the real urgency for the Howe campaign stems from the painful reality of recent trends in public opinion polls. For the eight weeks following the August conventions, General Howe ran neck and neck with Attorney General Leahy. That's not surprising, since they're both moderates and, apart from the question of military spending, their stand on the issues is quite similar. Conservative Republicans have recently dubbed the general 'Lincoln Center,' an unflattering play on the native New Yorker's middle-of-the-road politics.

"In the past nine days we've seen a dramatic shift. The major polls show that an increasing number of previously undecided voters are now leaning toward Leahy. Today's CNN/*USA Today*/Gallup poll shows Leahy up by a whopping six points. A clear victory over Ms. Leahy in a no-holds-barred debate may be General Howe's only hope. Otherwise, when faced with the choice between a black man and a white woman on November seventh, the American people may well elect their first woman president."

The anchorman furrowed his brow inquisitively. "Has there been any response yet from the Leahy campaign?"

"None yet," said the correspondent. "Some say the attorney general is content to sit on her lead. But there are also reports of concern within the Leahy camp as to how their candidate would fare in a debate against General Howe in a format where, essentially, anything goes."

"All right, thank you. In other news today—"

Allison hit the mute button on her remote control. Her expression had fallen. "I'm already being cast as the chicken. We can't go another minute with no response to a challenge like that."

"Let's not be knee-jerk," said Wilcox. "We need to check things out, make sure it's the right thing to do."

"Of course it's the right thing. He's proposing a format that actually forces the candidates to think on their feet. If the previous debates showed anything about his speaking abilities, General Howe has more of the old college football jock in him than the commanding general."

"Careful, Allison. You're dealing with a military mentality. Howe wouldn't invite you to debate unless he were thinking ambush. Before we agree to anything, we need to have a very clear understanding of what he's proposing."

"Work out the details later," she said with a wave of her hand. "Set up a press conference before the rally in Philly. I want to make sure we air my response in time for the six o'clock news." Her mouth curled into a confident, almost imperceptible smile. "I'd love a good old-fashioned debate with Lincoln Howe. Anytime. Anyplace. Of course I'm accepting the challenge."

2

All four thousand red velvet seats at Atlanta's Fox Theatre were filled with partisan politicos. Signs and hats were prohibited inside the auditorium, but the political buttons fastened to lapels indicated an audience fairly evenly divided between Leahy and Howe supporters.

Immediately following Allison's Monday-night acceptance of General Howe's challenge, the Commission on Presidential Debates scheduled the debate in Atlanta on Thursday, twelve days before the election. Allison had spent the balance of Wednesday night and all of Thursday studying up on the issues, meeting with advisers, and gathering last-minute tips from her consultants.

Allison stood behind a mahogany podium to the audience's left. She wore a bright blue St. John suit, and her hair was up in a stylish twist that completed the serious but feminine look that had graced the cover of thousands of magazines. Lincoln Howe was to the right, dressed in a well-tailored suit with a light blue shirt, red tie, and gold cuff links. He'd campaigned in civilian clothes all along, of course, but he had somehow always looked like a soldier caught out of uniform. Tonight, he looked decidedly presidential.

"Good evening," said the moderator, "and welcome to the Campaign 2000 presidential debates.

We have an unusual format tonight. A panel of four distinguished journalists, two selected by each candidate, have absolute freedom to ask whatever questions they wish."

Allison scanned the audience as the moderator introduced the panel. She shared a subtle smile with her husband, who was seated in the second row. Peter Tunnello was, according to *Business Week* magazine, "a visionary self-made millionaire" who had pioneered the plastic recycling business—a highly profitable and politically correct line of work for a politician's spouse. At age fifty-six he was eight years older than Allison, with distinguished flecks of gray in his hair and dark eyes that could charm his wife or chill his enemies. They'd dated casually a few months before Emily's abduction. He'd never been gorgeous, but if the ensuing tragedy and endless search had proven anything, it was that Peter was that rare breed of man who came through in times of need.

Allison was no slave to intuition, but something in the air—the vibes, the setting—was suddenly making her feel as if tonight could be one of those times of need.

The moderator continued, "As this is the third debate, we will dispense with opening statements and move straight to questions."

Allison sipped her water, relieved that she wouldn't have to hear the general recite his résumé yet again. Certainly it was impressive. A Medal of Honor from Vietnam. His bold triumph as the four-star general in charge of the Special Operations Command that had liberated thirty-eight American hostages from heavily armed terrorists in Beirut. The well-earned reputation as a fearless hawk at the Pentagon. She wondered, however, when his strategists would finally realize that all the military machismo was making even his biggest fans nervous about electing a president who might be a little too eager to send their sons and daughters marching off to war.

The moderator turned to the panel. "Mr. Mahwani, we begin with you, sir."

Abdul Kahesh Mahwani was a radical but respected former president of the National Association of Black Journalists. He'd made a name for himself covering the civil rights movement in the sixties, then turned Muslim and changed his name. His dark shaved head glistened beneath the stage lights. His wrinkled hand shook as he slowly removed the folded handkerchief from his breast pocket and dabbed his moist forehead.

Mahwani was one of General Howe's selections. Of the four panelists, he made Allison most nervous.

"Mr. Mahwani, your question, please."

The distinguished old gentleman shuffled the note cards on the table before him, then laid them aside. He removed his reading glasses and held them in his hand, like a professor with his pointer.

"Congratulations!" he shouted, startling everyone. "Congratulations to both of you, for what will surely be a healthy discussion of important issues."

He leaned back in his chair, as if he were no longer speaking to the candidates, but to the world. His voice took on the rhythmic cadence of a southern preacher. "Come November seventh, however, the American people will do more than choose sides on issues. They will choose a leader. A *person* to lead them in this new millennium. A man or a woman who they will call their president.

"This campaign has been utterly bankrupt of any discussion of the character of either candidate. Yet I'm certain that millions of people watching at home tonight are asking themselves some fundamental questions. How can a president lead, if not by example? Is this man, or this woman, a model citizen for our children?"

Mahwani leaned forward for effect, then looked at each candidate—first at Howe, then at Allison. His voice took on a hushed tone, forcing everyone in the auditorium to listen more carefully. "My question to both candidates is simply this: Have you ever broken your marital vow of fidelity?"

The audience fell silent. After an uneasy pause, the moderator spoke up. "Ms. Leahy. Your response, please."

Allison swallowed hard. Going first always had risks, but responding first to a question like this one raised special concerns. She thought carefully about the question, measuring her response. She found Peter's eyes again in the second row. He seemed stoic but supportive. Finally she answered, speaking to the audience at large rather than directly to Mahwani or even her husband.

"First of all, let me say that while I respect Mr. Mahwani's right to ask whatever he likes, this character question is completely out of step with the tone of the issue-oriented campaign that both I and General Howe have waged so far. I'm proud of the fact that this presidential campaign—unlike many of those in the past—has been conducted in a civilized and informative manner. I'm proud that both candidates have refused to stoop to the character bashing, personal insults, and attacks on family members that have sadly become a trademark of American politics.

"Mr. Mahwani's question really raises a larger issue. Will we as Americans hold fast to this important step forward we've taken and talk about issues, rather than resorting to insults? Or will we move backward to a time when running for office meant open season on a candidate's most intimate and personal secrets, no matter how irrelevant to the issues in the election?

"Please understand what I'm saying. I can see circumstances where extremely personal questions might be relevant. If a candidate directly challenges the media and puts his or her marital fidelity at issue, that candidate should be prepared to answer some probing questions. If a credible third party comes forth with evidence that a candidate has engaged in immoral conduct, the public should expect a response. I do not think, however, that every candidate in every election should be forced as a matter of course to let the media look inside their bedroom."

She paused, but her voice remained resonant. "Therefore, in the interest of restoring a level of dignity to American political debate, I decline to answer the question simply as a matter of principle."

A hearty applause rose from the left side of the auditorium. She glanced once again at her husband in the second row. He too was applauding. She breathed a discreet sigh of relief.

"Quiet, please," said the moderator.

The applause slowly faded. Mahwani looked away, shaking his head in visible disgust.

"General Howe," said the moderator. "Same question. Your response, please."

All eyes turned to the general. Mahwani, in particular, shot him a steely glare—though Allison could swear she detected the silent exchange of an insider's smile between the two men.

Howe gripped the podium, squaring his shoulders to the center television camera.

"My fellow Americans," he said solemnly. "Nearly four decades ago, Dr. Martin Luther King, Jr., stood on the marble steps of the Lincoln Memorial and proclaimed to the American people, 'I have a dream.' He dreamed of a day when all people were judged not by the color of their skin, but by the content of their character.

"I share that dream. *All* people should be judged by the content of their character. That includes men; that includes women. That includes whites, blacks, and people of all races. And most of all, that includes candidates for public office—men and women who seek a public vote of trust and confidence.

"It would seem that my opponent and I hold a very different set of principles. While Ms. Leahy refuses to answer the question as a matter of principle, I *will* answer it—based on *my* principles."

Howe looked directly into the center camera. "No, I have *never* broken my vows of marital fidelity. And I would never stand silent on something that, in my view, is the most sacred test of character for any man." He paused, then shot a judgmental glare at Allison. "Or for any woman."

The Howe half of the auditorium erupted with a standing ovation. The moderator raised his arms. "Quiet, please. Quiet."

The cheers only grew louder.

Allison's heart thumped. The lights overhead suddenly seemed hotter. Her palms were sweating. She glanced at David Wilcox, who had warned her about an ambush from the very beginning. He was normally poker-faced in public. This time, however, his eyes said it all.

The rest of the night was irrelevant. She'd just been slaughtered.

3

LEAHY TAKES THE FIFTH ON ADULTERY, blazed Friday morning's headlines.

Last night, Allison had retired to her hotel room at the Ritz Carlton with a sick feeling in her stomach. She had hoped it would be gone when she woke in the morning.

It was only worse.

She tossed the *Atlanta Journal* on the unmade bed. The *New York Times* and *Washington Post* were less sensational in their headlines, but by 8:00 A.M. she'd seen and heard enough to know that even the most respected print and television media were raising the same damning questions about her character. Was she hiding something? If so, would the American people elect as president a woman who had cheated on her husband?

As the warm shower waters pelted her body, she recalled her mother's words eight years ago, when Emily was abducted—the Leahy creed that "everything happens for a reason." This morning, not even the creed made sense. Allison had come to terms with the loss of her daughter only by reasoning that she was destined to do something else with her life, something so great that it was beyond even motherhood. She immersed herself in volunteer work, eventually landing as executive director of the Benton Foundation and head of the Coalition for America's Children, where she became friends with the First Lady. The crusade continued as attorney general and Democratic nominee for the presidency. Losing Emily would never make sense, but she had tried to make as much sense of it as she possibly could.

The adultery scandal not only threatened her presidential hopes, but it shook the inner peace she'd built on the shaky bedrock of ambition.

"I told you so," she whispered to herself, staring at her wet reflection in the glass shower door. It was exactly what her mother would say if she were still living. Washington was fickle, she'd warned, especially about women. But Allison had been too busy climbing to worry about falling. "Women want to be her, men want to meet her," was the way *George* magazine had summed up the Leahy phenomenon four years ago. "The class of Jackie O., the charisma of JFK," the *Times* had proclaimed. She'd brought enthusiasm to her post, so much so that people had good-naturedly dubbed the Department of Justice the department of energy. Talented lawyers who ordinarily wouldn't think of leaving their lucrative private practice were flocking to her door for low-paying government positions, just to work with her. She could start a fashion trend by wearing a sweat suit into the office on Saturday morning, or make a local restaurant "chic" just by stopping in for a muffin on her way to work.

And now the slide—just eleven damn days before the election. *Okay, Mom, you were right again. Now get these bastards off my back.*

By eight-thirty Allison had taken breakfast in her room, her bags were packed, and she was ready for a full day of appearances in Atlanta. She and David Wilcox shared the backseat of a limo from the Buckhead Ritz Carlton to the downtown Five Points area. The FBI normally guarded the attorney general. As a presidential candidate, however, she also received Secret Service protection. A Plexiglas partition separated her and Wilcox from the agents in the front seat, giving them the privacy they desired. They said nothing on the ride down Peachtree Street, each deep in thought. The limo's interior blackened, then brightened in the intermittent shadows of glass office towers. Finally Wilcox broke the silence.

"I need to know, Allison."

Her head turned. "Need to know what?"

He raised an eyebrow, as if she had to be joking. "Why did you dodge the question?"

"Because it didn't deserve an answer."

He chuckled, but it was an angry chuckle. "Who do you think you are, Meryl Streep in *The Bridges of Madison County*? Maybe it plays in the movies, but extramarital sex is still a serious political liability."

"Is it?" she said in a voice that challenged. "I must say that I find this whole controversy very intriguing. Think of all the philandering *men* this country has elected president. But the minute there's the slightest possibility that a *woman* candidate may have been unfaithful to her husband, the old double standard kicks in. The entire nation is suddenly in a time warp. It's like a throwback to 1952, when the cover of *Look* magazine asked about Adlai Stevenson, can a divorced man be elected president?"

Wilcox was deadpan. "I would remind you that the answer to that question was no. And he lost to a respected national war hero, a general in the United States Army."

"Lincoln Howe is no Dwight Eisenhower."

They fell silent again, until the limo passed a towering cylinder that resembled a seventy-story silo.

"I think you should answer the question." He stared out the window as he spoke.

Allison shot him a look. "No."

"*Are* you hiding something? Is that why you won't answer?"

She grimaced. "I stood before fifty million viewers last night and refused to answer any questions about marital fidelity—based on principle. If I check the public opinion polls twelve hours later and decide I will answer, what would *that* say about my principles?"

His eyes were suddenly bulging. "It's not just *your* reputation that's at stake here, okay? I don't make a name for myself in this business by losing elections in the homestretch. A year of my life—eighteen-hour days, seven days a week—has gone into your campaign with one goal: getting you elected. I won't have it pissed away by some weekend romp with some nineteen-year-old campaign volunteer you won't tell me about."

"Is that really what you think of me?" she asked bitterly.

"I don't know what to think. I just deserve to know the truth."

"The only person who deserves to know anything is Peter. And you know what? Peter didn't even think to ask such a stupid question before he left the hotel this morning. But if you really must know, I'll tell you: No, I have never cheated on Peter. Now, would you like to know what positions I prefer?"

His cellular phone rang. He looked away and answered it. "Wilcox."

Allison took some deep breaths as he took the call. It surprised her that even her own strategist would question her integrity. It hadn't occurred to her until now, but maybe Peter could have used a little reassurance, too. Maybe it wasn't really "business" that made him check out of the Ritz earlier than expected.

Her glance shifted back to Wilcox. He was massaging his temple as he switched off the phone. She asked, "What is it?"

"The results of last night's Gallup poll are in. Your six-point lead is down to one and a half. With the statistical margin of error, you and Howe are in a dead heat." He blinked hard, then looked her in the eye. "You realize what this means, don't you?"

"Yeah," she said in disbelief. "It's 1952 all over again."

From a hotel suite fifteen stories above Atlanta, Lincoln Howe smiled down upon the scene of last night's rout. The old Fox Theatre was built like a mosque, complete with onion domes and minarets, a grandiose monument to America's passing fascination with "anything Egyptian" after the discovery of King Tut's tomb in 1922. The marquee above the main entrance on Peachtree Street still proclaimed, PRESIDENTIAL DEBATES, TONIGHT 9:00 P.M. The general's eyes lit up, wishing it *were* tonight, wishing he could live it all over again.

"Ironic, isn't it?" he said as he turned away from the window. But his campaign director wasn't listening. As usual, Buck LaBelle was on the telephone with five lines holding.

For years, General Howe had known the forty-four-year-old LaBelle by reputation as a cigar-chomping former Texas state legislator, a graduate of Texas A&M University, and a campaign spin doctor who could have made the Alamo sound like a resounding American victory. As chairman of the Republican National Party in the early nineties, he was a tenacious fund-raiser and a principal author of the Republican National Committee Campaign Handbook. Howe had personally recruited him to serve as his Texas state chairman in the Republican primary, seeing him as the perfect experienced complement to a candidate who'd never before run for public office. By Memorial Day, LaBelle had earned himself the top spot as national campaign director.

Howe shot a commanding look across the room. LaBelle dutifully hung up the phone, lending the general his full attention.

With a quick nod, Howe pointed out the window. "You see that fire escape on the side of the theater? Over there," he indicated. "On Ponce de Leon Avenue."

LaBelle walked to the window and gazed down. "Yes, sir. I see it."

"When I was a boy, my aunt brought me and my brother right here to the Fox to see a Saturday-afternoon matinee. I thought she was sneaking us in. I couldn't understand why we had to go in through the fire escape. But that was the only entrance for colored people. White people used that fancy entrance up the street. The one that looks like a shrine."

LaBelle blinked, embarrassed for his race. But he was suddenly all business. "I'm glad you didn't mention that in last night's debate, sir."

"Why?"

He grimaced, uncomfortable. "White people

will do a lot of things out of guilt. We'll smile at you. Invite you to our home. Even let you walk in the front door of the Fox Theatre. But so long as there are secret ballots in this country, guilt will never get a black man elected president."

"And character will?"

"You bet it will. The media is feasting on this already. Just wait until our local organizations turn up the heat. We'll have every preacher, priest, and rabbi talking about adultery this weekend. Talk radio and television will be flooded with phone calls. Concerned parents will barrage the local papers with letters to the editor. Teachers will be lecturing about morality in schools. The potential here is endless."

"What about me? What am I going to say?"

"I'll script something myself. I didn't like what our speechwriters came up with. They're a little timid, which is somewhat understandable. Lots of people have had affairs or have forgiven someone who's cheated on them. They're afraid we'll sound too judgmental—like we're condemning *them*, instead of Leahy."

"What do you think?"

"Sir, I firmly believe you should never underestimate the hypocrisy of the American people."

"You're a political genius, Buck."

"Just leave it to me, sir. Between now and the election, I'll have every man and woman in America talking about marital infidelity."

The general turned to the window, glancing again toward the Fox marquee heralding last night's debate. "Everyone," he said smugly, "except Allison Leahy."

4

Friday was a waste. Allison had tried to talk substance. She'd even pitched her proposal for "zero tolerance" of teenage drinking and driving—*any* amount of alcohol in a teenage driver's blood should be illegal, since it's illegal for teenagers to drink in the first place. But all anyone wanted to hear about was her sleeping habits.

Her mind really had been elsewhere since the morning limo ride, when the accusatory tone of her own campaign manager got her to thinking that perhaps her husband, too, had doubts. His uncharacteristic failure to return her phone call at lunch hadn't exactly allayed her fears. She canceled her final Friday-evening appearance to make sure she was home in her own bed tonight, with Peter at her side.

At 10:55 P.M. the private Carrier jet finally landed at Washington National Airport. From the terminal she rode home alone in the back of her limousine. Her usual escorts rode in front, two of the four FBI agents who had guarded the attorney general even before she'd announced her candidacy and became an even more appealing target in need of Secret Service protection.

The trappings of Washington power and history illuminated the night sky along the expressway. The crowning Jefferson Memorial. The towering

Washington Memorial. The Capitol dome in the distance. The ride brought back memories of her first family trip to Washington, forty years ago, when she'd slugged her ten-year-old brother for telling her only boys could become president. Viewed through the cracked windshield of the family station wagon or the dark tinted windows of the attorney general's limousine, the impressive stone monuments had a way of inspiring dreams and dignifying politics.

What an illusion, she thought.

She switched on the small television mounted into the console. The screen blinked on, bathing her in flickering light. It was just past eleven-thirty. Out of morbid curiosity, she wanted to see what the talk show hosts were saying about her tonight. Jay Leno was just beginning his *Tonight Show* monologue. He was standing before a cheering crowd, wearing his usual dark suit and devilish grin.

"But in all fairness to Attorney General Leahy," cracked Leno, "she has been hit with some really tough questions. Just today, a reporter asked her point blank if she ever talks dirty to her husband while having sex. Ms. Leahy candidly responded, 'Only if I answer the telephone.' Now that's a classy lady, folks. She is simply not going to take this sex controversy lying down!"

Leno grinned, the crowd roared. The band banged out a heavy-guitar version of Roy Orbison's "Pretty Woman," an old song now best remembered as the theme from Julia Roberts's movie about a street-walking prostitute.

Allison switched off the television as the limo stopped at the curb outside her nineteenth-century Federal-style townhouse at 3321 Dent Place. It was a simple abode rich with nostalgia: Freshman Senator Jack Kennedy and his wife, Jackie, had made it their first Washington home nearly fifty years ago. It wasn't Allison's first choice and wasn't even listed for sale at the time. But Peter figured that if they were going to own real estate in the capital, they might as well get a piece of Camelot.

The car door opened, and her FBI escort stepped to the side. She gathered her purse and briefcase and stepped onto the sidewalk, wrapped in her navy blue trench coat. Her escort walked her past the twelve-foot-high iron-picket gate to the front door. The porch light cast an eerie yellow glow in the darkness. Her breath steamed slightly in the chilly night air as she dug for her house key. It lay buried at the bottom, naturally.

"Good night, Roberto," she said with a polite smile.

He responded with a simple nod, then turned away without saying a word. Allison watched from her front porch as he headed down the old brick sidewalk, back to the limo. He had always been the strong and silent type, but he seemed even more silent tonight. Perhaps he, too, thought less of her now.

Or maybe you're just paranoid.

She opened the front door, stepped into the marble-floored foyer, and deactivated the alarm.

"Peter?" she called. The downstairs was completely dark. Allison dropped her briefcase and hung her coat on the rack, then flipped on the hall light and started upstairs. Her heels clicked on the old oak steps. As she reached the top she could hear the television playing in the bedroom. Her stomach knotted. She hoped Peter wasn't watching the *Tonight Show.*

The bedroom door was half open. With a gentle push, it opened the rest of the way. A Tiffany lamp on the dresser softly illuminated a room filled with French antiques, most of them purchased straight from the Louvre des Antiquaires in Paris. A Baccarat chandelier hung from the fourteen-foot coffered mahogany ceiling. The décor was more her taste than Peter's, though she'd have been the first to admit that it wasn't her government salary that made it affordable. Early in their relationship, Peter had seemed to derive a sense of purpose from buying her expensive things, replacing her memories, bankrolling the complete makeover that passed for life after Emily.

From the doorway, she first noticed the beam of light from the walk-in closet, and then the suitcase lying atop the four-poster bed. She took the remote control from the nightstand and switched off the television.

"Peter?"

"In here." His muffled voice came from deep inside the closet.

She tentatively crossed the room, glancing at the half-packed suitcase. The shirts were folded. Socks and underwear were neatly arranged. It didn't look as if he was *un*packing. Her eyes clouded with concern. "What are you doing?"

He emerged from the closet carrying three business suits on hangers in one hand, a pair of dress shoes in the other. He shrugged, as if her question were stupid. "Packing."

She suddenly felt as if she had grossly underestimated Peter's reaction to the debate. Her voice shook. "What for?"

He dropped the business suits on the bed.

"There's only eleven days until the election. If I was ever going to hit the campaign trail at your side, I'd say now was the time."

Her eyes brightened as she came to him, hugged him with relief, and said softly, "Thank you. Thank *God*. You scared the hell out of me. I thought you were leaving me."

He stepped back, looking her in the eye. "Were you scared I was leaving, Allison? Or scared I was leaving *before* the election?"

His words hit like ice water. Deep down, she knew it was *both*. But that didn't mean she loved him any less. "My feelings for you have nothing to do with politics."

He smiled, then led her to the bed and sat her down beside him, squeezing her hand as he spoke. "I've been doing a lot of thinking in the last twenty-four hours. I feel like this adultery scandal is at least partly my fault."

"Your fault?"

"Yeah. The fact is, people are bound to have questions about our marriage if they don't see me with you. Look at the way Lincoln Howe's wife has been on the road campaigning for him. Just because I'm not the typical First *Lady* doesn't mean I should make myself invisible."

"You haven't made yourself invisible. I just haven't done enough to include you."

"You do want me involved, don't you?"

"Yes, I do. But I've made it so complicated, at least in my own mind. You know what a total wreck I was after Emily disappeared. In one night I went from a career woman who thought she could raise a child on her own to—well, I don't even want to think about it. You're the one who helped me want to go on living. You made me get out of bed every morning, get on my feet, get a life. I needed you like I've never needed anyone. But no one can go on needing someone like that forever. At least not if you want some self-respect."

"Sounds like you almost resent me."

"Not at all, darling. I still need you, but in different ways. I think part of me just wanted to say, Hey, I'm back. I can do this. I can do it *on my own*."

"Come on, Allison. You're running for president of the United States, not president of the Elvis Forever Fan Club. No one will fault you for enlisting a little help from your husband."

She smiled thinly, then turned serious. "Once you jump in, you'll be fair game."

"Like I'm not already? Hell, half the world thinks I have to stand in line to have sex with my wife."

Allison lowered her eyes.

He brushed her cheek. "Hey, I'm sorry. I only said that to show how ridiculous these rumors are, not to hurt your feelings. I know the reason you dodged that question last night was to protect our privacy. That took courage. It means a lot to me that you're willing to take the political knocks to protect what's important to us. I have never doubted you, and this media circus isn't about to make me start."

Allison leaned closer and gave him a hug. He was right. She *was* trying to protect their privacy. But that didn't completely ease her conscience. The fact was, there were things the public didn't need to know. Strange things the media might misconstrue. Not things she had done, but things that had happened to her. Secrets she hadn't told anyone—including Peter.

"Peter, I—" She paused, struggling with what she was about to tell him.

"What?"

She put her arms around him, resting her chin on his shoulder. It was a tactical move, a way of embracing him without looking him in the eye. "I love you," she said with her eyes wide open.

She stared over his shoulder and kissed the back of his neck, leaving it at that—for now.

At midnight Lincoln Howe was in his pajamas, staring out the window from the twentieth floor of the Houston Hyatt. Two days ago Texas was Leahy territory. Not anymore.

He pulled back the swag drapes for a panoramic view. A half moon hung low in the night sky. A sea of lights from a deserted downtown and sprawling suburbia blanketed the landscape. He took a deep breath, as if he had the power to draw fresh air from some faraway Texas plain.

"Lincoln, come to bed," his sleepy wife grumbled.

Natalie Howe was the general's wife of forty-one years, the youngest and prettiest daughter of a Southern Baptist preacher. As a homemaker she'd virtually raised their three children alone while their father served his country in Korea and Vietnam. At sixty-three, she retained much of the beauty that had attracted the young enlisted man she'd married in her hometown of Birmingham, Alabama. Dark, almond eyes and smooth, healthy skin were the trademarks of her Ethiopian ancestry. Her shiny black hair was usually worn up or straight back to frame the beauty of her face. She never left the house without her makeup, and she weighed only five pounds more than on the day they were married.

Lincoln rubbed his hands together. "I'm too excited to sleep." He glanced over his shoulder at his wife. She was lying on her back beneath the covers in the twin bed farthest from him. He stepped from the window and sat at the edge of her bed.

"This is the turning point, Natalie. Leahy has finally made the fatal blunder. It's like we've retaken Paris. Now it's on to Berlin."

"A lot can happen in eleven days."

"True," he said confidently. "But something tells me it will only get better."

Natalie propped herself up on an elbow. Her eyes narrowed with disapproval. "Must you gloat so much?"

"I have every right to gloat."

"It bothers me the way you're acting. It's as if you're more excited about her losing than your winning."

"You can't feel sorry for the enemy, Natalie. The minute you do, they'll stick a bayonet in your belly."

"Maybe. But I honestly don't think what she did is all that horrible."

He winced with disbelief. "What she did was downright cowardly. There is nothing the American people hate more than a politician who won't answer a question."

Her eyes became lasers. She had yet to say anything about the debate, but his bravado and self-righteousness were suddenly more than she could stand. "I can certainly think of one thing worse than a woman who won't answer any questions about marital fidelity."

"What's that, honey?"

She rolled away, speaking into the pillow. "A man who lies about it."

He froze, not sure what to say. It wasn't like the debate, where he could simply look into the camera and deny it. They'd passed that point long ago, before the apologies.

He laid a hand on her shoulder, but she didn't respond. He rose from her bed and switched off the lamp, saying nothing.

5

Allison managed a couple of hours sleep after making love to Peter, but at 3:00 A.M. she was wide awake. By six o'clock, the first glow of morning light was seeping in around the edge of the balloon draperies, casting a yellow-white frame around the dark bedroom windows. Allison was staring wide-eyed at the ceiling as Peter lay sleeping at her side.

The latest *ABC News/Washington Post* poll actually had her trailing Lincoln Howe, but that was only in the back of her mind. She was still struggling over her conversation with Peter. She was happy about the way he'd come through for her, agreeing to campaign at her side. Her joy, however, was overshadowed by a nagging concern over her inability to tell him the whole story behind her decision not to answer the adultery question. Maybe what made it so difficult to talk about it now was that the whole thing had started so long ago, and she couldn't explain why she hadn't told him everything from the beginning. For the tenth time tonight, her mind took her back to that evening in August, almost two months ago—analyzing it, dissecting it, and wondering what made it so difficult to tell her husband about a chance reunion with Mitch O'Brien in Miami Beach . . .

Humid breezes rolled off the warm Atlantic, rustling through palm trees at Hotel Fountainbleu. A boardwalk, rolling dunes covered with sea oats, and a wide stretch of open beach separated the ocean from the poolside café. Still, the soothing sounds of gentle waves lapping the shore could be heard in the darkness. Allison sat across from Mitch at a round Cinzano table, sipping a night-cap of Cointreau, straight up.

Allison had just delivered the keynote address at the annual meeting of the National Association of Attorneys General, a large gathering of attorneys general and their staffs from all fifty states. It was a good chance to talk tough on crime as her presidential campaign was turning toward the big autumn push. Mitch surprised her in the lobby as she was heading for the elevator. They hadn't spoken in eight years. After Emily's abduction, she'd broken things off with Mitch completely. He left Chicago and moved to Miami. She'd never felt any animosity toward him, however, and his offer to buy her a drink and catch up on lost time seemed harmless enough, preferable in any event to yet another hotel dinner with her aide.

"So," asked Mitch, "how are things among the National Association of Aspiring Governors?"

Allison smiled. "That's National Association of Attorneys General. And do you *really* want to know?"

"No." He was smiling with his eyes. Mitch had warm, engaging eyes, an asset that this skilled criminal defense lawyer had used to his advantage on many a woman juror. What Allison remembered most about him were his eyes. That, and the irreverent sense of humor that used to make her laugh as she hadn't laughed in years, since the disappearance of her daughter.

"I feel like we've been talking about me all night," she said. "What's new with you?"

"The usual crazy South Florida stuff that makes me glad I left Chicago. I've been offered a criminal case in Key West that I might actually take."

"You're kidding? I thought you'd given up practicing law for good."

"I said I *might* take it. Just for grins. One of my sailing buddies got into a little trouble at the annual Ernest Hemingway look-alike contest."

"Hemingway used to live in Key West, didn't he?"

"Right. This year, they had the usual parade of gray-bearded macho men in bulky turtleneck sweaters—like the Hemingway postage stamp. Then the last contestant walks out looking every bit as much like the real Ernest Hemingway, but with an added touch: He's sucking on the business end of a double-barrel shotgun."

"That's what you Miamians love about Key West. The rest of the world gets to snicker at your bizarre crimes and say, 'Only in Miami.' But every now and then you can look south and say, 'Only in Key West.'"

"Well, it seems the other Hemingway contestants didn't see the humor. They grabbed the shotgun, threw the guy in the trunk of an old convertible, and were zipping north on U.S. 1 at ninety miles an hour when a state trooper stopped them. Imagine the look on this trooper's face when he pulls over a flaming red Cadillac packed full of Hemingways hauling ass up the highway. It's not clear what their intentions were, but the trooper claims he heard the driver shouting, 'Death in the afternoon!' Mister big mouth now wants me to come out of early retirement and represent him. They charged him with kidnapping. Can you believe they're prosecuting?" He laughed, then finished his sparkling water.

Allison forced a smile, but she didn't laugh.

He looked up from his empty glass, alarmed by the somber expression on her face. "Something wrong?" he asked.

"I don't know. I guess I suddenly felt funny about you and me sitting here laughing about a kidnapping."

Their eyes joined. A stillness fell over their table, as if the sounds of the sea in the background were suddenly more audible. Allison looked away.

Mitch turned very serious. "You blamed me for Emily, didn't you?"

Her mouth opened, but she said nothing for a moment. The question seemed out of the blue—but then again, it didn't. "I don't think blame is the right word, Mitch. I did *associate* it with you. Maybe that's not fair, but I can't get it out of my mind that I was on the phone with you when it happened."

He glanced at the swimming pool, then back at Allison. "Do you think we would have gotten back together? I mean, if that had never happened."

"No."

He fell back in his chair. "Whoa. Didn't even have to think about that one, did you."

She sighed. "Mitch, none of this matters. I'm married now. I have a wonderful husband."

"Yeah, and after seven years he still works in New York and visits you on weekends."

"How do you know that?"

"You're a public figure, Allison."

She shifted uncomfortably. "What else do you know?"

"I know he spent over a million dollars of his own money trying to help you find Emily. I'm truly sorry you never found her."

"Thank you."

He leaned forward, cupping his empty glass with both hands. "I'm also sorry that you rewarded his generosity by promising to marry him."

Allison looked him straight in the eye. Her mouth was suddenly dry.

Mitch didn't blink. His stare only tightened.

"I really think I should go now." She rose quickly, digging in her purse for a ten-dollar bill. She dropped it on the table.

He frowned at the money. "You won't even let me buy you a drink?"

"Good-bye, Mitch." She turned and started away. Her FBI escort rose from his discreet post by the door, ready to take her to her room.

"Allison," Mitch called.

She stopped, then turned around reluctantly. It was the eyes. He snared her again with those eyes.

"It's definitely not your fault," he said, speaking softly enough so that no one could overhear. "But somebody still loves you."

She blinked hard, barely comprehending. She turned away nervously and headed for the hotel.

The alarm clock sounded on the nightstand, rousing her from her memories. Her heart skipped a beat as she lunged for the snooze button.

Peter stirred and rubbed his eyes, then rolled toward her. He had the beaming face of a kid cutting school. "Good morning," he said, looking up from his pillow.

Allison wiped a bead of sweat from her upper lip. "Yes," she said with a troubled smile. "It's going to be a very good morning."

6

Early Monday morning, David Wilcox entered the White House through the tunnel that connected a subbasement in the East Wing to the basement of the Treasury Building. It was an alternative entrance for recognizable visitors who didn't want their arrival noted by the press. Wilcox had insisted on using it, fearing that a highly visible, personal visit with the president might be seen as an act of desperation by the Leahy campaign.

Two Secret Service agents led the underground journey. One flanked Wilcox. The other watched Eric Helmers, the popular governor of Georgia whom Allison had selected as her vice presidential running mate. Helmers brought balance to the ticket in more ways than one. Aside from being a handsome and well-spoken southern man, he was a decorated Vietnam War veteran who had lost half of his left foot to a land mine. His lifelong work on behalf of the physically challenged had earned him national acclaim, and his well-publicized participation in the Boston Marathon each year was a genuine inspiration to everyone. Wilcox and the Secret Service agents were struggling to keep pace with him, short of breath and sweating at the brow by the time they emerged from the White House basement.

The meeting was scheduled for seven-thirty in

the Oval Office. As usual, President Sires was late. Wilcox and Helmers sat in silence in the first-floor lobby of the West Wing, sipping White House coffee beneath a framed antique map of Colorado, the president's home state. At eight-fifteen the president's executive secretary led them to the Oval Office. Barbara Killian, the stoic chief of staff, greeted them at the door.

"Gentlemen," she said ominously.

The president stood at the center of the room, dressed in a madras shirt and khaki slacks, crouched over a little white ball in a somewhat awkward putting stance. A long, thin strip of synthetic putting green stretched across the presidential seal woven into the oval office carpet. A half-dozen golf balls surrounded the plastic cup at the other end of the greenery, each engraved with the slogan "Fore More Years."

He took a smooth stroke, sending the ball eighteen feet straight into the cup. "Yesssss!"

"Good shot, Mr. President," said the chief of staff.

He flashed a boyish grin. "They don't call me Lucky Chucky for nothing." He laid his putter aside and greeted his guests, directing them to the armchairs facing his desk. No introductions were necessary.

"Thank you for taking the time to meet with us, Mr. President," said Wilcox.

The president returned to his leather chair, flashing his trademark smile. "Hey, we lame ducks have all the time in the world."

Then why the hell did you keep us waiting for forty-five minutes? thought Wilcox. "Not to be disrespectful, sir, but with just eight days to the election, time is running out for Allison Leahy. She is going to lose this election if she doesn't get her head out of the sand and flat out deny that she has ever cheated on her husband. I've told her that. Eric has told her that. The polls are telling her that."

"Shoot, David. You can't put that much stock in polls. If I actually believed my public approval rating was as high as the pollsters say it is, I'd be out there dating again."

Wilcox grimaced.

"That was a joke," said the president.

The chief of staff chuckled dutifully. Wilcox forced a smile, then turned serious. "Someone needs to talk to her, sir. You're still her boss. It should come from you."

The president leaned back in his chair, framed by the American flags behind him. "Allison is a woman of strong principles. That's why I named her attorney general. It's not my place to tell her what to say on matters relating to her own personal integrity."

"Sir, I wouldn't ask you to do this if it weren't crunch time."

President Sires folded his hands atop the desk. The smile was gone. He was suddenly presidential. "Let's be frank. The whole world knows that Allison Leahy wasn't my first choice for the Democratic nomination. To this day, I believe there was no stronger successor to the Sires administration than my own vice president."

Wilcox bristled. "So you're saying you *want* Allison to lose?"

"Of course not. Personal feelings aside, I realize that a lot of senators, congressmen, governors, and everyone else on down the line could get hurt bad by a presidential candidate with no coattails. So I support Allison. But I'm not going to micromanage her campaign."

"This is not micromanagement. This is the difference between winning and losing."

The chief of staff checked her watch, catching the president's eye.

He rose from behind his desk, taking the cue. "Just one more thing before we break, gentlemen. Although I didn't support Allison for the nomination, I respect her position on this issue. I have no doubt in my mind that she could truthfully deny she's ever cheated on her husband. But if she answers that question, she's setting a precedent that will haunt every woman who ever runs for president in the future. Now, I won't stand here and pretend that an unfaithful husband has never been elected president of the United States. But as a matter of political reality, I'm not sure voters would be so forgiving of an unfaithful *wife* who seeks this office. I'm not saying that's fair. It's just a fact. And I can say one thing about Allison Leahy: She knows the facts."

He shook hands, first with Wilcox, then Helmers. The pumping motion seemed to reengage the friendly smile, as if it were one reflex. "Thanks for stoppin' by, boys. Y'all come fly fishin' with me after January twentieth, ya hear?"

"Thank you, sir," they said in unison. Wilcox wanted to push it, but the good ol' boy accent and hollow invitations were a sure sign that presidential business was over. The chief of staff saw them to the door. Wilcox gave her a smile that was, at best, polite, then exited the Oval Office with Governor Helmers at his side. They took the longer route back to the lobby, past the president's study. Wilcox eyed the adjacent office, small but coveted.

For White House staff, a windowless closet near the president was preferable to an entire floor in the old Executive Office Building across the street. This one, thought Wilcox, might someday be his.

"What now?" asked Helmers. He had a pained expression, the look of man who'd already lost his bid for vice president.

"Plan B," said Wilcox.

"What's Plan B?"

They stopped at the foot of the stairs before reaching the lobby and their Secret Service escorts. Wilcox spoke quietly so no one could overhear. "General Howe may be a whiz at conventional warfare. Let's see how he fares at nuclear politics."

By 9:00 A.M., Buck LaBelle was on his sixth cup of coffee. The waitress brought him three fried eggs and five slices of bacon, which he devoured in three-and-a-half minutes. He'd have to do without his usual mound of cheese grits. He was, after all, in Cincinnati.

LaBelle spent the better part of the breakfast hour trying to persuade the president and vice president of the National Fraternal Order of Police that, as the debates had made clear, the nation's largest law enforcement organization had thrown the weight of its 300,000 members behind the wrong candidate. By 10:30 they'd heard enough. LaBelle returned to his hotel room and phoned General Howe.

"They won't pull the endorsement," said LaBelle.

"Son of a bitch!" his voice erupted over the line. "We've been hearing the same damn thing all weekend from everyone—teachers, labor, police. This character horseshit you cooked up just isn't going to carry me through the election. Especially now that Leahy has her loving husband campaigning at her side."

"Be patient. We're spinning some new commercials."

"That's not enough. Bottom line, Buck, is that we've milked this adultery cow for all it's worth. It eroded Leahy's soft support, and it pulled us even in the polls. But we need to jab her in the eye with a sharper stick if we want to snare some of her core supporters."

LaBelle sighed. "If we just stick to the game plan—"

"I need a *battle* plan. No more games. Now, I'm on stage in ninety seconds, so let's talk this afternoon. But I'm telling you up front: One thing I learned after forty years in the army is that keeping the wrong man on the job gets other men killed. You understand me, Buck?"

LaBelle bristled. No one had *ever* threatened to fire him. "Sounds like you're looking for something drastic."

"Drastic, yes. Desperate, no. You understand the difference?"

"Yes, sir."

"Good. We'll talk later." The line clicked.

LaBelle wondered if the general's cryptic distinction between "drastic" and "desperate" was his subtle way of drawing some ethical line that his staff shouldn't cross. Not likely. In fact, he was certain they were on the same Machiavellian wavelength—and that whatever plan he devised would be judged only in hindsight.

If it worked, it was drastic; if it failed, it was desperate.

7

From her hotel suite in Los Angeles, Allison watched as much of the Monday evening news as she could while getting cleaned up and dressed for the evening schedule. She was combing through tangled, wet hair when an in-depth report on ABC caught her attention. A smart-looking female reporter was standing before a huge colored map, pointing out eight key states that used to be Allison's but were now "undecided."

"Without question," said the correspondent, "Ms. Leahy's recent public appearances with her husband at her side have been effective damage-control measures. Yet insiders say that morale is at an all-time low among the rank and file in the Leahy campaign. Many are angry that Ms. Leahy ducked the adultery question in the first place. Others are incensed that this election may be determined by what they view as a bogus character issue.

"The bright spot for the Democrats is that even some of General Howe's supporters are quietly beginning to wonder if the debates will have a lasting impact. With less than eight days remaining until voters head for the polls, the experts seem to agree on just one thing: The first presidential election of the twenty-first century could well be the closest in American history."

Allison switched off the set. Interesting, she thought. The minute a politician acts on principle the immediate assumption is that she has something to hide. Then again, there was something inherently suspect about a politician acting on principle.

She combed through the last of the knots, then stopped and shot herself an assessing look in the mirror. *Who are you kidding?*

Sure, her refusal to answer was based in part on principle. She vividly recalled her reaction to the late Senator John Tower's confession of adultery on national television in 1988— how embarrassing it was for everyone, how little it contributed to meaningful political discourse. But no decision—even one based on principle—was made in a vacuum. The simple fact was, there were recent ambiguities she'd really rather not explain.

Her eyes shifted toward the king-sized bed, where tonight's evening gown lay beside her handbag. She'd worn it once before, just two months ago. Wearing it again would probably keep her from repeating as one of *People* magazine's annual "Best Dressed"—oh, horror of horrors. But Peter liked it and had picked it out specially, so to hell with the fashion police. Of all the dresses in her closet, however, his fancy for this one was terribly ironic. The last time she'd worn it was just a week after her poolside reunion in Miami Beach with Mitch O'Brien. She and Peter were at a gala in Washington—where Mitch had made a surprise reappearance.

Her gaze lingered, until the hundreds of tiny beads and sequins on the gown began to blur and move about, the way the stars began to swirl if you lay on your back in a field of grass and stared into outer space. The tiny points of light distorted her vision, yet they sharpened her mind's eye in hypnotic fashion. She felt oddly detached, trance-like, as her memory drifted back to that crowded ballroom at the Capitol Hilton, where things with Mitch really started to get strange . . .

"Excuse me," said the eighty-six-year-old senator from South Carolina. In one false step, he'd crushed Allison's foot and spilled champagne down her dress.

Allison dabbed the stain with a cocktail napkin. "That's okay, Senator. But usually I don't bathe in champagne until after the party." She tantalized him with a wink. The old bigot was her biggest detractor on the Hill, though his ringing endorsement of Lincoln Howe had been somewhat neutralized after a reporter overheard him tell his aide he'd vote for the Little Rascals' Buckwheat before putting a woman in the White House.

He apologized nervously, then forged through the crowd.

Beyond being the world's most prestigious black-tie gathering of influential Italians and Italian Americans, the annual gala for the National Italian American Federation was one of those see-and-be-seen events for Washington heavyweights, Italian and non-Italian alike. Since Allison had become attorney general, it was the one annual event that Peter actually looked forward to. This year, as usual, Allison found herself mingling alone in the political circles while Peter went off with his Sinatra-esque rat pack, working his way through the other three thousand guests who wanted to rub elbows with the likes of Nicolas Cage and John Travolta.

"Damn it," she muttered as the cold champagne

soaked through to her skin. She checked for the nearest exit to the rest rooms, then suddenly did a double take.

Mitch was standing alone by the bar when Allison spotted him, staring right at her, cocktail in hand. He was as handsome as ever in classic black tie, but she immediately recognized the glazed look in his eyes. Allison answered his smile with a cold stare. With a subtle jerk of her head she directed him to the double doors leading to an isolated hallway near the kitchen. Mitch took the hint and started for the exit. Allison waited a few moments, then excused herself from her circle of conversation. A Secret Service agent met her at the door.

"That won't be necessary," she said politely. She clutched her evening bag, indicating that she was carrying her panic button. "I'll beep you if I need you."

He nodded, allowing her to pass through the doors alone.

The west hallways leading to the Grand Ballroom were part of a secured area, so they were virtually deserted. Mitch was waiting around the corner in a dimly lit alcove. He leaned against the wall, smirking in the glow of a crystal wall sconce.

"What are you doing here?" Her tone was harsh, but she kept her voice low.

He slapped his forehead in an exaggerated, comedic fashion. "Jeez, I forgot. My last name doesn't end in a vowel. It begins with one. Ah, no problem," he said, grabbing his crotch and laying on the accent, "I can tawk Italian."

"You're drunk."

He shrugged, dismissing it. "I'm Irish."

"You're obnoxious. You were always obnoxious when you drank. How many times did I have to tell you that?"

His smile faded. "About as many times as I had to ask you when we were getting married. Why didn't you just pick a date, Allison? Any date. Why mess with a guy's mind and tell him you'll marry him if you won't say when?"

She blinked with disbelief. "That was eight years ago."

"What about last week?"

"What about it?"

"Doesn't what I said to you mean anything?"

"You think I'm supposed to melt or something, just because out of the blue you tell me you still love me? Get over it, Mitch. And knock off the self-pity."

"Fuck you, Allison. Is that what you think? That I've spent the last eight years drowning my sorrows over you? Well, I got news for you, baby. Any married woman who's willing to meet an old lover at a Miami Beach hotel is hardly worth the liver damage."

She glared. Never mind that it was *he* who had tracked *her* down at the hotel. She knew, however, that arguing was pointless. This was the ugly side of Mitch that had made it impossible for her to marry him. Still, she wasn't totally sure if it was just the liquor talking, or if he was deliberately trying to make last week at the Hotel Fountainbleu sound like something it wasn't.

"I don't know what trouble you're trying to start. But nothing happened between us last week, and nothing ever will. Got it? So don't follow me again—*ever.* Now get out of here before I call security."

He challenged her with a stare, but Allison

didn't blink. Finally he staggered away mad, like the bad old days when Allison used to banish him to the sofa to sleep it off.

Her gaze fixed on the back of his head until he disappeared around the corner. Part of her wanted to run after him and strangle him. But another part wanted to grab him and shake him and tell him to stop wasting his life.

Suddenly, she heard heels clicking on the marble floor. *Was he coming back?*

She listened more intently. It couldn't be Mitch. It was the lonely sound of someone walking in the opposite direction, away from her, down a side corridor. *Security?* she wondered.

She peered around the corner. The footsteps stopped. She ducked back into the alcove and listened again. The clicking resumed, but it was muffled this time, as if someone were walking more carefully, sneaking away.

It wasn't like security to skulk like a stalker.

Quietly, she walked halfway down the long corridor, then stopped and listened. All was still.

A door slammed, echoing through the marble hallway.

She hurried ahead, made a quick turn at the bank of telephones, and found a metal fire door. She pulled the handle. Locked. She peered through the small window at eye level. Up or down, she saw endless flights of concrete steps with metal railings. She put her ear to the door. Silence. She opened her evening bag—the panic button would summon a team of FBI and Secret Service agents to her side in an instant. But what would she tell them? That she was having a spat with her ex-fiancé? She closed the bag. Better to leave this one alone.

"Is everything all right, Ms. Leahy?"

It was Secret Service. "Yes," she said, her heart in her throat. "I was just looking for the ladies' room."

"This way," he said, offering to lead her.

She walked at his side, a half step behind him. After several steps, she noticed his shoes. They were the rubber-soled type. They didn't make a sound. No clicking of the heels, like before. It definitely wasn't security she'd heard earlier.

Her hands shook as she tucked her evening bag beneath her arm. She walked with her head up, keeping her composure. But fear was gripping her by the throat as one thought consumed her: *Had someone overheard everything?* . . .

"Allison, aren't you ready yet?"

"Huh?" she said, shaken from her memories by the sound of Peter's voice. He was standing in the doorway that divided their suite—dressed and ready to go. She was still seated at the vanity mirror in her robe and wet hair.

"The helicopter leaves in fifteen minutes." He leaned forward and kissed the top of her head. "Don't make me leave without you."

She smiled awkwardly. "I'll be ready in ten."

He returned the smile and headed for the door.

"Peter?" she said, stopping him in his tracks. Her expression was serious. "Do you really think I did the right thing at the debate?"

"Absolutely, darling." He raised an eyebrow, sensing her anguish. "I hope you're not second-guessing yourself."

She sighed, wishing she had just told him everything two months ago. She knew his temper, however, and telling him that an ex-fiancé was still in love with her seemed utterly pointless at the time. And what would he think if she told him now, well after the fact, on the heels of her public refusal to confirm or deny that she'd ever had an affair? Would *anyone* believe that nothing had happened?

"No second thoughts," she said with a forced but appreciative smile. "I'm still convinced that silence was the right response."

He nodded in agreement, then left the room.

She checked her reflection in the mirror, still shaky from the memory of Mitch at the gala. Maybe she was paranoid, but she had a horrible gut feeling that she was being set up—that someone wanted her to deny she'd ever cheated on Peter, only to hit her with a tape recording and a mystery witness who would totally distort her encounter with Mitch. She'd be worse than an adulteress. She'd be an adulteress *and* a liar, another presidential hopeful sinking on the charter boat *Monkey Business.* With that, she was indeed convinced that silence was the correct response.

More convinced than ever, she told the troubled face staring back at her in the mirror.

8

Bright autumn colors lit up the tree-lined streets of Nashville, Tennessee, on Tuesday, Halloween morning. One good rainfall and it would all be gone, but a solid week of chilly nights and sunny days had set the leaves ablaze.

The sun was shining brightly as twelve-year-old Kristen boarded the transport van at Wharton Middle School. It was the same routine each morning, Monday through Friday. Kristen attended homeroom at Wharton until nine o'clock, then rode the van to Martin Luther King, Jr., High School, a magnet school on the other side of picturesque Fisk University. Kristen was a gifted sixth grader who studied English literature at a tenth-grade level. Schoolwork was easy; looking older was the hard part. Her heart-shaped face was just beginning to show angles of maturity, and the results were promising—too promising, as far as her protective mother was concerned. Makeup was forbidden until she turned thirteen, but Kristen still managed a little mascara to accentuate her huge dark eyes, her best feature. She knew, too, that her long legs would someday be an asset, but for now the gangly pre-teenager was happy just to get by without tripping over them.

"Hi, Reggie." She was her usual cheery self as she bounded into the front passenger seat. The middle school was having a contest, so she was dressed in her Halloween costume. A red, white, and blue sweat suit with the TEAM USA logo and a big snack food insignia that marked it as the official sweat suit of the 2000 Olympics.

Sixty-year-old Reggie tipped his driving cap. "Mornin', Miss Kristen."

"Will you please *stop* calling me 'Miss Kristen.' It's so aristocratic."

His eyes widened. "Now that's a high-falutin' word if I ever did hear one. They teachin' you real good over at the high school, ain't they, Miss Kristen?"

"I guess."

The van merged into traffic on the busy Dr. D. B. Todd Boulevard. The street bordered Fisk University, which lay roughly midway between Wharton Middle School and Martin Luther King High School. Reggie turned onto the campus at Meharry Street, then parked in front of Jubilee Hall, a six-story dormitory built in the nineteenth century in Victorian Gothic style.

The campus detour was part of their agreed-upon routine. From the very first day, Kristen had hated arriving at the high school in a van marked WHARTON MIDDLE SCHOOL. She thought she could make a much more fitting entrance if Reggie simply dropped her off at the university and let her walk the remaining three blocks to the high school. She had been forced to bat her eyes and turn on the charm, but after two weeks she'd finally sold Reggie on the arrangement. The only condition was that he be allowed to trail behind in the van, keeping an eye on her from a safe but inconspicuous distance.

"See you tomorrow, Reggie." She eagerly

opened the passenger door, jumped down with her book bag, and started across the college campus. She passed the old library with its big broken clock, an imposing building of brick and stone that now housed administration. To her left were the towering Fisk Memorial Chapel, the quaint Harris Music Building with Italianate detail, and a modern three-story library with a long concrete colonnade. The two-block walk across campus inspired her with dreams of becoming the youngest student ever at the nation's oldest black college.

As she exited beneath the iron campus gate, she noticed the Wharton Middle School van trailing slowly, no more than fifty feet behind her. She crossed Jackson Street and started down Seventeenth Avenue. The van was creeping along, now less than fifty feet behind her.

She stopped and grimaced. With her hands on hips she glared back at the van, as if to say, "Reggie, you're following too close."

She turned and headed for the high school, strolling down a cracked old sidewalk that had been rearranged by the twisted roots of hundred-year-old oaks. A bench at the corner was the perfect place to stop and undo the awful pigtails her mother had weaved for her. The left one unfurled quickly. She was tugging on the other when she noticed the Wharton Middle School van drawing closer.

"Darn it, Reggie," she muttered. She shook her hair out, styling it the cool way she liked it, then picked up her book bag and started toward the corner.

The van was just twenty feet behind her.

Kristen ignored him, refusing to look back. Her eyes were fixed straight ahead until she stopped at the corner to check traffic. Not a car in sight. The van rolled through the intersection, right past her. It stopped on the other side of the street, as if positioned to lead her straight to the high school.

She was mad now. *What the heck is Reggie up to?*

She crossed the street and stopped even with the van. The colored leaves from the canopy overhead reflected off the windshield, making it difficult for her to see inside. But she could make out Reggie's familiar old driving cap. From the sidewalk, she glared and shouted, "Reggie, we had a deal!"

The engine was running, but the van stayed put.

With angry steps she approached the van and yanked the passenger door open.

She started, then smiled. He was wearing a rubberized Lincoln Howe mask, the most popular mask for Halloween 2000. "Very cute, Reggie. Happy Halloween to you, too."

The driver grabbed her wrist.

"Reggie, come on—"

She froze in mid-sentence. The hand was white. It wasn't Reggie.

The grip tightened—the powerful grip of a man much younger than Reggie. A quick yank nearly ripped her arm from its socket. In a split second she was off her feet, flying through the open door. She landed upside down on the passenger seat. Another man grabbed her legs, threw a sack over her head, and pulled her to the rear of the van.

"Go!" he shouted.

The door slammed, the locks clicked. Kristen tried to kick and punch, but her wrists and ankles were bound with plastic cuffs. The heavy sack muted her screams. Her thigh burned with the jab of a needle, like the vaccinations at school.

The driver pulled off his mask and drove away slowly—just like Reggie Miles, the most careful old driver at Wharton Middle School.

A sharp bell rang through the high school halls. Lockers slammed. Cigarette smoke poured from the boys' and girls' bathrooms. A fight beneath the stairwell finally broke up, leaving one kid crying. A steady stream of latecomers trickled into Mrs. Roberta Hood's tenth-grade English class, though a few students just seemed to come and go as they pleased, unwilling to commit to in or out. The raucous Halloween spirit had invaded Martin Luther King, Jr., High School.

Mrs. Hood was middle-aged, but she looked much older. Her hair was completely gray, and her glasses were so thick they distorted her eyeballs. She'd taught high school English for over twenty years, searching for the next Ralph Ellison or Maya Angelou. She was quite certain her protégé wasn't among the delinquents in the back flicking lighted matches into a waste can.

"Boys, stop it!"

The class laughed as she stomped out the flames. She brushed the ashes from her elaborate costume—authentic black and leopard-spotted robes of African tribal royalty—then returned to her desk and checked the seating chart. Some of the students were too cool for costumes, but many came dressed. Werewolves and vampires were especially popular. She noted the usual no-shows—and one who was not so usual. Her favorite student was missing. She scanned the room to see if she'd taken a different seat, or if she'd just missed her in her costume. She didn't see her. She rose from her desk and checked the hallway. Not there, either.

A look of concern came over her face. She felt particularly protective of Kristen, given her age and her family's stature. Kristen had missed class only once before. That time, the assistant principal had called from the middle school to say she wasn't coming.

Mrs. Hood cleared her throat and called for attention. "Class, quiet, please."

A mob by the window was fighting to have their palms read by a girl who'd come as a gypsy. The rest of the students kept talking. Even in a magnet high school, it took only a few bad kids to disrupt the entire class, especially on Halloween.

"*Claaaaaass!*"

Her shriek was louder than even she thought possible. The room was startled into silence. As she paused to catch her breath, the concern in her eyes turned to fear.

"Please," she said breathlessly. "Has anyone seen Kristen Howe?"

Reggie Miles reached into his pants pocket.

His head was throbbing from the blow he'd received, but it had rendered him unconscious for only a moment. He'd pretended to be out for much longer than he was. Though blindfolded, he'd heard enough to realize they'd gotten Kristen, too.

Reggie hadn't heard a peep from her since the abduction. He'd overheard the men talking about some kind of injection they'd given her—something to make her sleep. He could still hear them talking, presumably in the front seat. That meant he and Kristen had to be in the back. Engine vibrations told him they were moving, as did the gentle rocking of the vehicle that came with maneuvering through traffic. He was counting the turns—left, right, right again—trying to figure where they were headed. He was losing track, though with all the stops and starts he was sure they had yet to reach the expressway.

His hand moved a centimeter at a time, deeper and deeper into his pocket. The plastic cuffs pinched his wrists, but after twenty minutes he'd worked his hands into the right position. Finally, he reached his key chain. He cupped the entire ring in his palm, so it wouldn't jingle. He slipped it from his pocket, then slid his hands back into the restrained position, behind his back. Reggie's fingers weren't as nimble as they used to be, but fifty years of whittling had made him pretty facile with a jackknife. He opened the blade.

Slowly he started to cut through the plastic ties that bound his wrists.

9

The Wharton Middle School van pulled into a narrow alley behind an old redbrick warehouse. It bounced over a pile of rusty pipes and a series of muddy potholes, slowing as it reached the garage at the end of the alley. The corrugated metal door rattled as it recoiled on noisy spring hinges. It opened just enough to allow the van to pass, then quickly rolled down. The van stopped inside, beside a white Buick Riviera with New York license plates.

Fluorescent lights blinked on from the rafters overhead, illuminating the garage. Oil stains dotted the cracked cement floors like huge amoebas. Beneath the dusty canvas tarpaulins lay mounds of useless machine parts.

Two men jumped out of the van, both wearing leather gloves and black leather jackets. The driver was Tony Delgado, a heavyset Italian with a Brooklyn accent. His younger brother Johnny was smiling widely.

"Perfecta-mundo!" Johnny crowed. He and his brother slapped each other on the back.

A third man emerged from behind the Buick. He was tall and clean-shaven, easily more handsome than the others. He was younger, too, in his early twenties, closer in age to Johnny than the older Delgado. Tony, the ringleader, had purposely kept his accomplices from meeting each other before the kidnapping, to prevent leaks. He quickly made the introductions.

"Johnny, this is Repo."

They shook hands. "Repo what?"

"Just Repo."

Johnny scoffed. "What, like Cher or Madonna?"

He looked confused. "No. Like Repo."

Tony rolled his eyes. "I don't give a rat's ass if it's like Lassie. Let's get the little princess out of the van and into the car. You got the trunk ready, Repo? She's not gonna suffocate in there, right?"

"Have a look for yourself," said Repo.

Tony glanced at his brother. "Johnny, empty out the van."

Repo led Tony to the car and popped the trunk. Johnny went to the van and opened the rear emergency door.

The cargo lay exactly where he'd put it. The old man on the left, the girl on the right. Their bodies stretched from front to back beneath the bench-style seats that normally seated schoolchildren. The old man's gag and blindfold were still in place. A black hood covered the girl's head to make extra sure she didn't see any of her kidnappers, just in case the injection of secobarbital sodium wore off prematurely.

Reggie lay on his left side with his back to the wall, concealing his hands behind his back, trying to act as if he were still unconscious.

Johnny grabbed the old man by the ankles, like a butcher handling a side of beef. With one foot on the bumper for leverage, he yanked his cargo, sliding him back. The bony old legs dangled over the back.

Suddenly, the limp torso sprang to life, lunging

forward, leading with a jackknife. The blade stuck in Johnny's shoulder.

"*Son of a bitch!*"

Reggie surged forward with all his strength, ripping off his blindfold, swinging his fists, kicking and twisting as they wrestled to the ground.

The younger man was quickly on top, staring right into the old man's eyes as he pulled out a pistol and jammed it under his chin.

Tony grabbed him before he could pull the trigger. "Johnny, stop!"

Johnny was breathing heavy, seething with anger. Tony took the gun, but he kept it pointed right at Reggie's head.

Reggie lay flat on his back, his chest heaving, eyes wide with panic.

Johnny rose and dabbed the blood on his nice leather jacket, checking the wound. "The old bastard stabbed me." He kicked him in the kidneys. "And he ruined my fucking jacket!" He kicked him again.

Reggie groaned through the gag in his mouth.

Tony checked his brother's shoulder. "Just a flesh wound. But damned if it wasn't just six inches from your heart." He sneered at Reggie, as if it were too close for comfort. "You coulda fucking killed my little brother." He kicked him even harder than Johnny had.

Another muffled cry. The body coiled with pain.

Johnny grimaced—not for the old man, but for himself. The stab wound was starting to throb. His face reddened with anger. He slammed his fist against the door of the van, then kicked the old man in the groin and stomach.

"You black piece of shit!" He kicked him again

and again, in quick succession. He was yelling at him, pausing between each syllable to kick him in the ribs and kidneys, alternating left and right foot. "Don't you ever fuck with me again."

His brother added a final kick to the head.

Reggie went limp.

Twenty feet away, Repo was in the trunk of the Buick, drilling more air holes between the trunk and passenger compartment. When the electric drill stopped whining, he heard laughter coming from over by the van. He crawled out of the trunk to investigate, then froze at the sight of the old man sprawled on the floor with the Delgado brothers standing over him.

"What the hell you guys doing?"

Johnny pressed a bloody rag to his shoulder. "Teaching the old nigger a lesson."

Repo took a closer look at the twisted heap on the ground. Blood had oozed from the mouth and ears. Repo's eyes widened with concern as he knelt and checked the pulse—first the wrist, then the jugular. He looked up in disbelief. "He's dead."

Johnny shifted uncomfortably. "All we did was kick him."

Repo glanced at Johnny's boots. Blood covered the steel toe. "You morons killed him."

"He tried to kill *me*. Shit happens."

Repo grabbed him by the collar, pinning him against the van. "Nobody was supposed to get killed!"

Tony split them apart. "Hey, hey, hey! He's dead. It's over."

"The hell it's over," said Repo. "Now we're all up for murder. All because this stupid jag off—"

"Hey, enough!" said Tony. He grabbed Repo by the shoulders, looking him straight in the eye.

"You gonna stand here and shit your pants? Or you gonna act like a man? This is no big deal. We just gotta dump the body, that's all."

"I ain't dumping the body. It's Johnny's body. He can dump it."

"Just leave it here," said Johnny. "We're leaving the van here anyway."

Tony shook his head. "The van is one thing. We can wipe it clean. But dead bodies leave too much evidence. After that fight, the old man could easily have enough of your skin under his fingernails for some geek with a microscope to identify your DNA. He's probably got some of your blood on him, too."

Johnny grimaced, concerned. "That means we can't leave the van here, either. We can't leave nothin' that shows we were here. They might find a little drop of my blood on the floor."

Tony glared at his brother. "Damn it, Johnny. You fucked up already."

"*Me?* You helped."

"Shut up!" said Repo. "Here's the deal. We need to get the girl out of Nashville—now. I say Johnny takes the van and dumps the body. Me and Tony take the girl. We all meet up later."

"I can't drive the van around Nashville," said Johnny. "I'll get caught for sure."

Repo checked his watch. "Kristen's class just started five minutes ago. The van isn't due back at the middle school for another fifteen. It'll be at least that long before the school confirms she isn't sick or skipping class, or that the van isn't just stuck in traffic. I figure Johnny's got at least that long to dump the van, before the cops put out an APB."

The Delgados exchanged glances, then Tony

nodded. "You gotta do it, Johnny. We'll meet up in Maryland. You know the address, right? Forty-six Commonwealth Boulevard."

Johnny scoffed. "How the hell do you expect me to get there? School bus?"

"I don't care how," said Tony. "Just make sure you're not being followed. If you fly, make a connection. If you drive, change cars at least once."

"What about my shoulder?"

"It's a scratch," said Tony. "Just don't go around wearing that jacket with the knife hole in it. Take the old man's coat."

"I ain't wearing no nigger's clothes."

Repo shoved him in the shoulder. Johnny shrieked in pain.

"Who the hell are you," snapped Repo, "Calvin Klein? Enough with the fucking wardrobe already. Just shut up and dump the body."

He rubbed his sore shoulder, glaring at Repo. "Where am I supposed to dump it?"

"You should have thought of that before you kicked his teeth in."

Tony grumbled. "Just dump it somewhere that will throw the cops off our trail. And do it soon. Like Repo says, you got only about fifteen minutes before word gets out she's missing and the cops start searching for the van. Now, let's move it."

Repo and Johnny exchanged glares, then looked away. The Delgados loaded the body into the van. Repo gently carried Kristen from the van to the car, placing her comfortably in the trunk. He was glad she hadn't heard any of it, as she was still unconscious from the injection. The garage door opened. Johnny drove the van out, followed by Tony in the Buick. Repo jumped in the passenger side, beside Tony.

Steering down the alley, Tony lit up a cigarette and handed it to Repo. He lit another for himself. "You know we had to kill that guy. He saw Johnny's face. Mine, too."

Repo took a drag from the cigarette, held it, then exhaled a huge cloud of smoke. "You should have given him a shot, knocked him out good, like the girl."

"That's risky with old people. If he was on some kind of medication, a shot could have killed him."

Repo shook his head, nervously puffing his cigarette. "I don't like this, man. Wasn't nobody supposed to get killed."

Tony turned deadly serious. "Deal with it, partner. The rules just changed."

10

Allison spent Tuesday in Indianapolis. At 3:35 P.M. she received an emergency telephone call from James O'Doud, director of the FBI. He was calling from headquarters in Washington. She took the call in the privacy of her hotel room.

"We got a Code One abduction out of Tennessee," said O'Doud. "Sometime after nine-thirty this morning, central time. Twelve-year-old girl. Her identity isn't public yet. But I thought you should know right away, since there's bound to be all kinds of fallout."

"Who is she?"

His voice took on an ominous tone. "Kristen Howe. Lincoln Howe's granddaughter."

Allison closed her eyes in anguish. After the abduction of her own daughter eight years ago, she'd managed to pick herself up off the floor and reenter the real world by helping other families who'd suffered the same horrific fate. Not even as attorney general, however, did the abduction of any child ever boil down to statistics. Every single one was personal, hitting close to home. That she knew Lincoln Howe only made it tougher.

"Is she still alive?"

"We don't know. A school van was taking her from middle school to the high school for some special classes. A Fisk University student found her book bag two blocks from campus. No one's seen her, the driver, or the van since this morning."

"Any ransom demand, anything?"

"Nothing yet."

A million thoughts raced through her head, including a flood of political ramifications. "Obviously I want the FBI all over this immediately. This is way too big to defer to local law enforcement. How clear is our jurisdiction?"

"Nothing concrete yet to suggest they've crossed state lines. And the locals know the law. More than once they've reminded us that the girl has to be missing for twenty-four hours before we can presume interstate transport and officially take over the investigation."

"When does twenty-four hours kick in?"

"By our calculations, just after ten A.M. tomorrow, eastern time. But as a practical matter, all that means is that we'll hold off any official announcement of the FBI's involvement until mid-morning. We're already in up to our eyeballs."

"Good. Who are your point people?"

"I've asked the Nashville supervisory senior resident agent and Memphis special agent in charge to pull together his brightest—agents who really know the area. But I really don't expect this to stay in Nashville, or even Tennessee. I'm appointing an inspector to oversee the entire investigation, wherever it goes."

"You mean for administrative matters? Like the Oklahoma City bombing?"

"More than that. He'll be right in the field, hands on. Kind of like the case agent, but with more authority. It's a little out of the ordinary, but this isn't your run-of-the-mill kidnapping."

"I'll say. Who do you have in mind?"

"I've already sent Harley Abrams down from Quantico. He spent twenty years in the field, mostly in Atlanta. He's still a field agent at heart. Now he's the best damn profiler we've got in CASKU."

Allison nodded, as if to approve the selection. As attorney general, she had come to respect Abrams's work with the FBI's Child Abduction and Serial Killer Unit—CASKU, for short. "What's been done so far?"

"Plenty. We're checking every channel we have for connections to terrorism, so I have Hostage Rescue on alert. Secret Service is stepping up protection for the candidates and their families. I've always thought Secret Service should protect a candidate's grandchildren, but obviously the boys over at Treasury don't like to expand their protection until someone gets nabbed. Locally, I've brought in backup from Memphis to supplement Nashville. Apart from that, it's pretty much standard procedure, albeit on a grander scale than usual."

"I want details, James. Don't feed me that standard procedure baloney."

"Okay, details. We've deployed a team to the victim's residence to gather personal articles—hairbrush, diary, anything with the child's fingerprints, footprints, or teeth impressions. We took the bedsheets and some clothing, too, for the scent dogs. Technical agents are setting up trap-and-trace for incoming calls, and we're installing a dedicated hot line for tips. I'm told we have a good current photo that our media coordinator is disseminating, and the NCIC Missing Person File has been fully loaded. Updates are being broadcast on all police communication channels as well as the NLETS telecommunication network. We're compiling a list of known sex offenders in the region and constructing a possible profile of the abductor. Abrams is personally coordinating with the local command center, and he's already got them on line with the NCMEC case-management system."

"Where's the local command center? Not at Kristen's home, I hope."

"They set up on the Fisk campus, midway between the point of last sighting and the child's ultimate point of destination. It's right in the heart of our perimeter patrol, which is well underway. We're checking the entire area around the college campus, middle school, and high school for witnesses, possible clues." He paused, then added, "We're also working with the local search and rescue detail. They're dragging the river."

Her pain deepened at the thought. "You think—"

"Don't know. We got a possible lead on a van in the Cumberland River."

Allison looked at her watch. "I can be in Nashville in two hours."

"There's really no need. We can keep you posted."

"I know. But I want to be more hands-on, especially at the beginning."

He paused, then cleared his throat. "Allison, I'm not sure how to say this, other than to just come right out and say it. But I sincerely hope you will give very careful thought to the role you intend to play in this investigation."

She bristled at his tone, though it wouldn't be the first time O'Doud had started a turf war. A

Republican president had appointed him director in 1992, and even though his term was limited by law to ten years, he fancied himself another J. Edgar Hoover—accountable to no one, especially a Democratic attorney general.

"The role I intend to play," she said firmly, "is that of attorney general. Last time I checked, that makes me the nation's chief law enforcement officer."

"I accept that. But you're also a candidate. And the kidnap victim is the granddaughter of your opponent. My advice is that you simply step aside and defer to those who are above politics."

"Meaning someone like *you*?" she asked incredulously.

"Yes, frankly."

Allison gripped the phone. "My life has been ruined once by a child abductor. I'm not going to let it happen again. When you figure out where politics fits into that equation, you let me know. I'll be in Nashville in two hours," she said coolly, then hung up the phone.

Part 2

11

At 5:30 P.M. an FBI field agent met Allison at Nashville International Airport and drove her straight to the soggy banks of the Cumberland River. Night had fallen, and powerful floodlights suspended overhead from cranes created intermittent bright spots on the river and its banks. The glow of downtown Nashville added a hazy blanket of illumination near the Jefferson Street bridge. Low-flying helicopters swept the area with searchlights, while marine patrol cruised up and down the river. Swarms of law enforcement officers paced through patches of gravel and weeds along the river, their crisscrossing paths lighted by flashlights. Several agents gathered by a muddy four-wheel-drive vehicle on the embankment beneath the bridge. They wore the familiar dark blue windbreakers with bright yellow lettering that read, FBI.

Allison stepped carefully down the steep embankment accompanied by a Secret Service agent. She hadn't had time to change clothes since leaving her rally in Indianapolis, which left her in a business suit with skirt and dress shoes. The arctic chill of the brisk north wind was way beyond the thermal capabilities of her panty hose. She was starting to shiver when she noticed an agent on the bank barking out orders to an exhausted search and rescue team leader.

"I know it's dark, damn it. But there's virtually zero visibility in this water even in daylight, and if there's a body out there, this current is moving it another mile away with every half hour we lose. Just keep running nice and safe shore-based parallel patterns until we get the trapping devices in place. Use the underwater radios, and keep the divers on a short tether. And for crying out loud, move the number one team *down*stream from Jefferson Street. We're not looking for spawning salmon."

A huge man wearing a big orange flotation device lowered his head and turned back toward the muddy river. The swishing sounds of cold, moving river water muffled his cursing. The supervisor breathed a heavy sigh. In the chilly air, he looked as if he were literally blowing off steam.

"You must be Harley Abrams," said Allison. She was standing at the end of a footpath that wound through the weeds and down the embankment. She could tell from his confused expression that he hadn't recognized her voice, but with the aid of a flashlight he quickly placed her.

"You must be freezing," he said, glancing discreetly at her legs. "Here, have some coffee."

She smiled and took the hot paper cup. "Thank you."

They'd never actually met before, though Allison had seen his instructional videotapes. Meeting him in person suddenly brought back the eight-year-old memories of how, overnight, she'd gone from collecting *Bambi* and *Snow White* videos to Harley Abrams's FBI lectures on child abduction.

Abrams was actually more handsome in person than on tape, thought Allison. He had "the look," other agents said, the kind of classic, handsome features that would have served him well in the old days of J. Edgar Hoover. He was an ex-Marine with an impressive stature that commanded immediate respect. At forty-six he was still eleven years away from the bureau's mandatory retirement age, but he had a youthful energy that seemed part of him for life, making a second career inevitable.

"What do you have so far?" asked Allison.

"We found the school van. A homeless guy living under the Jefferson Street bridge saw it roll down the embankment just north of his cardboard living room. The river current took it downstream, where it sank in this eddy. No victims inside, but we're taking it slow to maximize evidence recovery. I've got search and rescue combing a full square-mile area. No sign of any bodies yet."

"You think they had an accident?"

"There's no skid marks off the road, so I don't think so. My guess is they just changed vehicles and ditched the van."

"They could have just parked it on the street somewhere. Why go to all the trouble of running it into the river?"

"If they hadn't, then we wouldn't have wasted half a day poking around in the mud, would we? They're probably clear across Kentucky by now."

Allison nodded, then turned very serious. "I guess I don't need to tell you that we need this one solved in record time."

"We'll do our best. But if it weren't bad enough that we've got every nut in America running around in Halloween costume, the Nashville playing field definitely favors the abductor. The river winds like a snake, and at least a dozen bridges would make convenient drop points for anyone trying to unload a body. The two major lakes nearby—

Old Hickory and Percy Priest—are so big it's conceivable they'd never give up their dead. You've got twelve states within a two-hundred-fifty-mile radius, with three major interstates running out of the city in six different directions for a convenient getaway. And the international airport can take you just about anywhere—over a hundred different cities. It's like Atlanta in the early eighties, when we were trying to find the black child murderer."

"That was before my time," she said.

"That's why the FBI has the CASKU and people like me in it. I'm not saying this to be disrespectful, but the riverbank is no place for the attorney general."

"Director O'Doud has already made that clear. But let's just say I have a special interest in this case."

A sudden flash of light startled her. A photographer emerged from beneath the bridge. His red hair was shoulder length, but he was bald on top. Allison thought of Bozo with a perm gone limp.

Abrams scowled. "Hey, buddy. Didn't you see the police tape? No press allowed."

"I'm not the press." He squinted into his camera, focusing. "If I could just get a couple more, Ms. Leahy. Just so Mr. Wilcox has a few good shots to choose from."

Abrams asked, "Who the hell is Mr. Wilcox?"

A combined rush of anger and embarrassment swept over Allison. "He's my campaign strategist."

Abrams bristled with disbelief. "Is that what you're here for? A campaign photo op?"

"Not at all. I promise you, this is not what it looks like."

"Politics never is," he said dryly. "If you'll

excuse me, Ms. Leahy, I have work to do." He turned and walked away.

Allison cringed. The last thing she needed was to lose credibility with the point man on the investigation. She was about to pursue him, but enough had been said in the presence of a photographer. She stepped closer to the river, out of earshot from the photographer and her own Secret Service protection, then pulled her portable phone from her jacket. She dialed David Wilcox.

"Allison, where are you?" he asked.

"You know damn well where I am. I'm at the river—where you sent that photographer to take pictures of me on the front line of the investigation."

"I didn't send any photographer."

"Don't get cute, David."

"I'm not being cute. I'll check with my aides. Maybe they sent him. When you think about it, it's not a bad idea."

"It's a terrible idea."

"Come on, Allison. Haven't you seen the polls? In just four hours, the sympathy factor has blown us off the map. The only way to neutralize this disaster is to do exactly what you're doing. Roll up your sleeves and get right into it. Just leave the spin to me."

She shook with anger. "You don't spin when a twelve-year-old girl's life is at stake."

"Bullshit. You think General Howe isn't spinning this? The man has sent eighteen-year-old boys marching straight into machine gun nests, all in the name of a higher cause. He's a big-picture guy, Allison. Every war has casualties."

"Have you lost your mind? We're talking about his granddaughter."

"We're talking about the presidency of the United States! *That's* what we're talking about!" He sighed heavily, as if suddenly embarrassed by the shrillness in his voice. "Just work with me, will you, please? I'll get to the bottom of this photographer situation. But keep an open mind on it. I'll call you later."

The line clicked.

As she tucked the phone in her coat pocket, she was disturbed by his desperate tone. She'd never known David to be a liar, at least not to her. The way he'd immediately latched onto the idea of a photo shoot, however, made it difficult to believe he had nothing to do with hiring the photographer. Then again, it wouldn't have been like David to hire someone stupid enough to start snapping photos right in front of Harley Abrams and the rest of the FBI.

Maybe, she thought, the photographer could bring matters into focus.

She turned and looked back to the grassy patch on the embankment where he'd been standing. He was gone. She looked down the riverbank, then toward the bridge. No sign of him. Anywhere.

An FBI agent passed by.

"Have you seen a photographer?" she asked. "Short guy. Long red hair. Bald on top."

He shook his head. "Sorry, Ms. Leahy. You want us to look for him?"

"No, that's not necessary."

She turned toward the river, mulling over her thoughts. *Who the heck was that weird-looking guy? And just what did he intend to do with the pictures he'd taken?*

12

The disappearance and likely abduction of Kristen Howe was the lead story on the Tuesday evening national news. The FBI had reportedly ruled out nothing at this point, including the possibility that she'd been abducted by her own bus driver, who, along with the middle school van, was also still missing.

Lincoln Howe watched the evening network news from the backseat of his limousine while en route from the Nashville International Airport. After reporting what little information that had actually been confirmed, the broadcast segued into "news analysis," which amounted to nothing more than wild speculation about the possible political ramifications of the abduction. Lincoln watched intently as a stoic young female correspondent reported from outside the Wharton Middle School in Nashville.

"While no one has claimed responsibility," she reported, "the public perception so far seems to be that the most likely culprits are political extremists who want to keep Lincoln Howe from becoming president. That perception, combined with a nationwide outpouring of sympathy for the Howe family, has already propelled General Howe anywhere from five to seven points ahead of Attorney General Leahy in the latest polls, with the election just one week from today."

Howe switched off the television. Never had he reacted so flatly to news of his own political momentum.

The limo slowed as it reached a redbrick house with a mansard roof. At least a dozen media vans were parked across the street, each with a different logo—EYEWITNESS NEWS, ACTION NEWS, and others. Wires and cables crisscrossed the normally quiet street. Television reporters primped and reviewed their notes in preparation for live broadcasts on the late news. Cameramen toting heavy equipment on their shoulders paced the sidewalk, searching for the best view of the house.

Lincoln peered out of the limo. The name HOWE on the mailbox brought a lump to his throat. Tonight marked his first visit to his daughter's home.

Lincoln had seen very little of Tanya Howe since she'd dropped out of college thirteen years ago to give birth to Kristen. She had since earned a bachelor's degree at night school, and she now taught art history at the community college. Most of what Lincoln knew about her adult life had come through his wife. Despite the differences between father and daughter, Natalie had remained close to her. She had been at Tanya's side since noon today, with the first reports of Kristen's disappearance.

The media encircled the limousine in the driveway. Three Secret Service agents pushed the mob back to the street. General Howe emerged without ceremony and headed up the walkway to the front door. His wife Natalie answered. She was incredibly calm with a stiff expression, but Lincoln knew she was just trying to be strong in front of their daughter. She led him straight to the dining room, where Tanya was seated at the table. Two FBI agents sat across from her, one taking notes as she spoke. The conversation stopped as General Howe and his wife appeared in the doorway.

Tanya was blessed with her mother's looks and her father's brain. Her sparkling eyes normally lit up the room. Tonight, Lincoln noted, they were puffy and red. Her hand clenched a wadded tissue.

She glanced at the FBI. "Excuse me a moment, please."

They gathered their notes and disappeared into the kitchen. Natalie followed. Lincoln laid his trench coat aside and closed the pocket door between the kitchen and dining room, giving them privacy. He waited for his daughter to rise, feeling the urge to embrace her, despite their past differences. She didn't move. He took the chair at the far end of the table, away from Tanya.

She stared at him, saying nothing in the dim glow of a brass chandelier. Her face was expressionless, her troubled eyes impassive. Finally she spoke.

"I wondered if you'd come."

"Of course I would come. You're my daughter."

"And Kristen? What is she?" Her eyes narrowed. "Is it still that hard for you to say she's your granddaughter?"

"Let's not get into that, okay?"

"Why not?"

"Because I'm here for you. Right now, that's all that matters."

"Did you wave to the cameras on your way in?"

"That's not why I came."

"Exactly why did you come, then? To tell me

this is God's way of punishing me for having a child out of wedlock? Or to tell me if I had listened to you and had an abortion in the first place I never would have gotten myself into this mess?"

He winced and shook his head. "How can you say those things?"

"Look me in the eye and tell me you haven't thought those things."

He blinked, then look away. "I can't change the past. I know I haven't been much of a grandfather."

"You don't even know Kristen. All she's ever been to you is an illegitimate political liability."

"That isn't true, Tanya. But even if you think those things, we have to put our differences aside now. I know this is the worst thing that could ever happen to a parent, and I understand your anger. Maybe you even blame me for putting our family in the public spotlight."

"I blame you for putting us at risk. You knew that something like this could happen. But you ran anyway."

He paused, then spoke in his most sincere tone. "I want you to know I'll do everything in my power to bring Kristen back."

"Oh, really?" she said with doubt in her eyes. "What if the kidnappers are genocidal racists who will do anything to keep a black man from being elected president? What if they threaten to kill Kristen unless you withdraw from the race and let your white opponent or your white VP walk into the White House? Would you do *that*?"

He struggled. "We can't just give in to terrorism. I know you don't want me to do that."

"Yes." Her voice shook. "I *do* want you to do that. I want my daughter back—period. So don't you dare come into my house and tell me you'll do whatever it takes to get her back if you don't mean it."

"I will do whatever it takes. Within reason."

"Within reason? What's more important than the life of an innocent twelve-year-old child?"

"It's not that simple."

"It is that simple." Her glare tightened. "Mother may have forgiven you for the way you've lived your life, but I haven't. You've always made the wrong choices. You chose the military over your wife and children. And you'll choose the presidency over the life of your own granddaughter. Family first—so long as it doesn't get in the way of your ambition. It's your nature, Lincoln Howe. It's just your *nature*."

He tried to speak, but emotion had hold of his throat. "I—"

She rose from her chair, cutting him off with a wave of her hand. "Please, just leave." She crossed the room and handed him his coat.

He rose slowly, then stopped before the pocket door, his shoulders slumped. His eyes met hers. "Tanya, I'm truly sorry."

Her lips quivered. "Tell it to Kristen," she said, then showed him the door.

Allison took a room at the airport Marriott. She wasn't sure if she was spending the night in Nashville, but she needed a place to change clothes and shower off the smell of the river. While unpacking, she realized Peter was waiting for her at a previously arranged fund-raiser in Kansas City. Surely by now he realized he was going stag. She phoned him anyway and told him all she knew, which wasn't much more than he'd already heard on the evening newscasts.

"I can't believe this happened," she said as she grabbed a diet soda from the mini-bar.

He scoffed. "The only thing I can't believe is that stuff like this doesn't happen more often. The world is crazy. You should know that better than anyone. Maybe in your own mind you've tried to downplay the dangers of campaigning, so that you're not checking over your shoulder for some lunatic every time you take a step. But if you truly can't believe this happened, you've brainwashed yourself too thoroughly."

"I didn't mean I *literally* can't believe it. I just meant it's horrible when something like this happens. I know you worry about me, Peter. But I'm not stupid."

"Allison, I love you. And you're without a doubt the smartest woman I've ever met. But every now and then, I honestly do worry that your view of politics is a little too romantic for your own good."

She kicked off her shoes and plopped on the bed. "Peter, I ran my first election in Chicago—a city where my grandmother voted for six years after she was dead. I'm well aware that politics is no romance."

"Your roots are solid, that's for sure." He lowered his voice, turning more sincere. "It's the more recent experiences that I'm worried about. I hinted at this over a year ago, when you were first talking about running. But you just didn't seem to want to hear it."

She sat up against the headboard. "Hear what?"

"In hindsight," he said with some difficulty, "don't you think the loss of your daughter made your introduction to Washington a little . . . misleading?"

"What does Emily have to do with this?"

He paused, well aware of the delicate nature of the subject matter. "That was the greatest tragedy of your life, no doubt. But at the same time, it was your greatest unspoken political advantage."

"I never used Emily for political advantage."

"Of course not. But the fact is, no one could attack a woman who had lost a child. Not your opponents, not the press. Even when you were nominated for attorney general, you were insulated from the usual character assassination that goes on in Senate confirmation hearings. The city embraced you—*exulted* in you—from the day you stepped foot into the Justice Building. You're a wonderful person and extremely talented. I'm not dismissing that. But at least part of the reason they loved you so much is because, deep down, they felt sorry for you and wanted to see you rebound. It's human nature."

"As much as I'd like to, I can't change my past."

"And now, Lincoln Howe can't change his. So don't be surprised if voters feel the same sympathy toward him. More important, don't be surprised if he milks it."

"Funny. That's what David Wilcox thinks, too."

"You disagree?"

She gazed into the mirror above the bureau, thinking of the way her opponent had run with the adultery accusations. "After the debates," her voice tightened, "I guess nothing would surprise me."

Photographers peered through the windows as the general's stretch limo pulled away from the house. He was oblivious to the swarming media, alone in the backseat and deep in his thoughts.

What his daughter had said wasn't far from the truth. He had indeed made choices. The jungles of Vietnam over the birth of his son. A tour in Korea over Tanya's school plays and piano recitals.

And now this.

They rode in expressway traffic for several minutes, then he glanced out the window. They were crossing the river. A chill hit his spine. He knew at that very moment divers were feeling their way through inky black river water, groping for anything that resembled a body.

A sudden nausea swelled from within. He leaned forward and tapped on the privacy partition that separated him from the driver and Secret Service agent in the front seat. The partition slid open.

"I want to make a stop," he said.

The driver caught his eye in the rearview mirror. "But, sir, your plane."

"I don't care. Exit here."

General Howe directed them past the downtown area, toward Fisk University and the surrounding neighborhood from which Kristen had been abducted. He drew several deep breaths as they passed Martin Luther King, Jr., High School, the destination she'd never reached. Wooden barricades and yellow police tape blocked access to Seventeenth Avenue, her usual route.

"Stop here," said Howe.

The limo stopped in the intersection, perpendicular to the temporarily closed Seventeenth Avenue. The lighting was poor, but with some effort the general could still see all the way down the street, clear to Fisk University. The FBI and other law enforcement officers were slowly walking the area, searching for evidence. Flashlights dotted the neighborhood like flittering fireflies. Scent dogs from K-9 patrol zigzagged down both sides of the street. The steady whump of helicopters beat overhead, scanning the fields with infrared sensors, picking up body heat in the darkness. To the general, it seemed about as futile as the "urine sniffers" used in Vietnam, high-tech sensors that detected concentrations of excrement so that American bombers could pinpoint the enemy—or obliterate hapless groups of wandering peasants and smelly herds of water buffalo.

Anxiety set in as he watched from the back of his limo, the image of twelve-year-old Kristen burning in his mind. *Who would do such a thing?* he wondered. To be sure, a man didn't reach his stature without making enemies. Some of his decisions had ended promising military careers. Many of his orders had gotten soldiers killed. Too, he couldn't rule out the lunatic who simply didn't like the way he looked.

An FBI agent tapped on the windshield. The driver opened the window.

"You can't park here," said the agent.

The driver was about to protest, but Howe intervened. "It's okay," he told his driver. "Let's be on our way."

A traffic cop rerouted them to a side street. They rode in silence for several short blocks, until they reached Fisk University.

"Stop here," said Howe.

The driver stopped beside Fisk Memorial Chapel. Howe peered out the window. The old brick building was impressive in the moonlight, with a tall center bell tower and Gothic stone windows.

"I want to get out."

The Secret Service agent did a double take. "Here?"

Howe nodded. "I want to say a prayer," he said with a lump in his throat. "For my granddaughter."

The agent sighed, but he couldn't argue. He spoke into his hand-held radio. "This is Bravo-one. Short stop at Fisk campus. Must leave the vehicle." After a brief pause, a clipped confirmation crackled over the radio. He glanced back at the general. "Let's go."

The agent led him up the steps to the double doors beneath the arched Romanesque entrance. He pulled on one door. Locked. He tried the other. Also locked.

"Sorry, sir. But it is late."

His heart sank with disappointment. He turned slowly and walked back to the car. A sadness washed over him that bordered on despair. Being turned away by his daughter was bad enough. *But had God shut His doors?*

They walked side by side down the chapel's front steps, until the agent stopped short. His expression turned very serious as he adjusted the ear piece on his radio.

The general watched with concern. "What is it?"

The agent paused, then looked him in the eye. "Divers found a body in the river, sir. No positive ID yet. They're pulling it out now."

His mouth went dry. "Where?"

"South of the Jefferson Street Bridge."

He looked away, suddenly in a daze. "Let's go there."

The agent helped him into the backseat, then walked around to the front of the car.

As the engine started, the general's hands began

to tremble. A tightness gripped his chest. He suddenly needed air. He'd felt this way only once before in his life, some thirty years ago, after getting word that his best friend had stepped on a powerful land mine off the Ho Chi Minh Trail. He reached forward and closed the partition between the back and front seat, so the driver and the agent wouldn't be able to see him. Then his chin hit his chest as he fought back the tears.

They flowed slowly at first, then like never before. In a matter of moments he was sobbing cathartically, releasing emotions that had been swelling for years.

A hundred yards away, from the front seat of a Ford Taurus parked at the dark end of the grassy campus quadrangle, a photographer focused his telephoto lens. The infrared camera cut through the darkness, zeroing in on the general's face as if it were daylight. Howe looked haggard and beaten, much older than his years. Tears were plainly visible.

The shutter clicked. A perfect shot.

The limousine pulled away from the chapel.

The old Ford raced in the opposite direction, picking up speed with each passing second.

13

The Nashville skyline was alight across the river, stretching from the traditional old State Capitol dome to the modern BellSouth Tower that resembled an ice palace. Police had roped off a stretch of the Cumberland River's east bank, north of the Victory Memorial Bridge that fed into downtown and south of the Jefferson Street Bridge—the exact area Harley Abrams had ordered divers to search.

Allison had been alerted immediately to the discovery of a body. She arrived in an FBI sedan at 10:20 P.M., just as divers were pulling the body from the moving water.

In less than five hours, the temperature had dropped even further to a brisk twenty degrees. Lights from emergency vehicles bathed the law enforcement crowd in orange and yellow swirls. Swarms of helicopters—some media, some law enforcement—buzzed overhead. Divers struggled to maintain their footing as they climbed out of the river. Search and rescue team members stood ankle-deep in cold mud, guiding the polypropylene line that reeled in the catch.

Allison was thirty feet from the river when the body bag broke the surface. Water gushed from the bag's mesh openings. It looked large for a little girl, though she knew bodies could bloat after a day in the river.

"It's the bus driver," said Abrams.

Allison started. He had seemingly come out of nowhere.

"Any sign of Kristen?" she asked.

"No."

She felt relief and sadness at the very same time. "I want a top-notch forensic pathologist doing the autopsy. The locals can watch."

He gave her a funny look, as if she were stating the obvious. "I've already called Walter Reed Hospital."

"What kind of shape is the body in?"

"Water's pretty cold, so there's not much decomposition. But he's pretty banged up."

"Rivers can do that."

"Yeah," he scoffed. "So can thugs. I'll be curious to see what our pathologist thinks."

In the distance, Allison noticed a black limousine racing down a street that ran parallel to the river. It rocked to a quick halt in the parking lot above them, twenty yards away. The door flew open. Out stepped Lincoln Howe. His movement was erratic, almost spastic. An FBI agent approached him. Allison could see them talking. The general leaned against the car, apparently relieved. Allison presumed he'd just been informed that the body wasn't Kristen's.

"Excuse me a moment," she said to Abrams. She started up the embankment, toward the limousine. It was a steep climb, and she was slightly winded when she reached the top.

The general was still talking to the FBI agent, but he stopped in mid-sentence when he saw Allison.

"Lincoln," she said in a sympathetic tone. "Can I talk to you for a minute, please?"

He seemed surprised to see her. "Sure," he

said. He thanked the FBI agent, then opened his car door, inviting her in with a jerk of the head. "It's warmer in here."

He held the door as she slid into the backseat, then he slid in beside her and closed the door. He signaled with his eyes, and the driver and Secret Service escort emptied the front seat to give them privacy.

Allison swallowed hard, finding it difficult to speak. "I just wanted to say how very sorry I am that this horrible thing had to happen."

"Thank you."

"How is your daughter holding up?"

"About the way you'd expect."

Allison blinked. She knew the feeling too well. "I know you're probably hearing from hundreds of well-meaning friends who tell you that if there's anything they can do, just ask. Well, I'm obviously one of the few people who is actually in position to do something helpful. I won't let you down. I've ordered the Department of Justice to call upon its every resource to launch the largest manhunt in American history. We'll find Kristen. We'll bring her kidnappers to justice."

"You sound like tomorrow's press release."

His tone surprised her. "I know we've had our differences. But this comes from the heart."

"Thank you for sharing that. But let me be very frank with you. I heard about the little campaign photo session you held out here today."

She flinched. Word traveled fast. Harley Abrams must have said something to his superiors. "That was a complete misunderstanding."

"Call it whatever you like. I simply won't stand for anyone using my granddaughter's abduction for political gain."

"And I would never politicize a matter like this. You have my word on that."

"That's not enough."

"I don't know what more I can give you."

His eyes narrowed. "Then let me spell it out for you. I want you completely out of the investigation. Just step aside and let the FBI do its job. Director O'Doud is more than capable. He doesn't need you looking over his shoulder for your own political purposes."

Her mouth opened, but words came slowly. "This affects all of us, Lincoln. If it hadn't been your granddaughter, it could have been my husband. Or maybe some fanatic with a high-powered rifle plans to take out me or you. Just because I'm a candidate doesn't mean the country has to be without an attorney general. I won't just step aside."

"Fine," he said with a steely glare. "Then prepare to be pushed."

Their eyes locked in a tense stare. Allison broke it off, then opened the door. "Good night, Lincoln." She stepped out, then glanced back. "And in case you're wondering, I always push back."

The door closed with an emphatic thud.

At 1:00 A.M. Wednesday Buck LaBelle was still on the telephone in his Opry Land Hotel suite. Since his promotion to national campaign director, he'd been living on three hours of sleep each night. A stained coffee cup and a bottle of bourbon rested on the table. Cigar ash dotted the front of his shirt. The television was on, but the sound was muted. He'd spent the last forty-five minutes screening the new campaign commercials for the final push to election day. A Madison Avenue media consultant was on the other end of the line. Buck was pacing furiously, fired up with anger as he shouted into the phone.

"I don't want to see one more cotton-pickin' commercial showing Lincoln Howe shaking hands with a black man. That demographic is already in our hip pocket." He paused, still pacing as he listened with the phone pressed to his ear. "I don't care if it does send a new message. Messages are lost on these people anyway. Hell, half the black men in America think Lincoln Howe was named after a fucking town car. I want a new ad by five o'clock, and I want it geared toward white women. You got it? That's our target group. White women!"

He slammed down the phone, then belted back the last of his bourbon. A knock at the door brought a groan from his belly. *What now?* he thought.

He checked the peephole. His lips curled into a smile as he opened the door.

In walked a man dressed in torn Levi's, a flannel shirt, and an insulated hunting vest. His dark red hair was shoulder length. He took off his Atlanta Braves baseball cap, exposing his shiny crown of baldness.

"Pay dirt," the man said with a devious grin. He pitched a manila envelope on the desk.

LaBelle eagerly opened the envelope and inspected the large glossy photographs. He shuffled through the entire stack, sucking on his cigar more intently as he moved from one to the next. They'd obviously been shot in quick succession, all of the same subject: Lincoln Howe, sobbing in the backseat of his limousine.

LaBelle grimaced as he looked up from the stack. "I can't use a single one of these."

The photographer leaned against the wall, stunned. "It's what you wanted. Lincoln Howe in a sensitive moment."

"Sensitive, yeah. Something that will make a hard-nosed old army general more appealing to female voters. Maybe a shot of him consoling his distraught daughter. Maybe even the general himself getting a little choked up and misty eyed. You didn't bring me sensitive. You brought me a grown man blubbering like a baby in the face of personal crisis. How on God's green earth do you expect me to get a marshmallow elected president?"

"You should have been more explicit."

"Damn it, Red. Five years ago did I have to tell you to bring me a picture of Congressman Butler bopping his secretary? No. All I had to say was get him in a compromising position. That's all I've ever had to say. You knew the drill. Except now, on the most important job I've ever given you, you suddenly go stupid on me."

He shook his head. "Look, I did my job. It wasn't easy tailing Lincoln Howe with all the extra Secret Service protection around him. And at least the first part of the assignment went off without a hitch. I made Leahy look like a political whore down by the river. I'm sure the FBI thinks she hired me herself to do a photo shoot of the attorney general on the crime scene. I was damn lucky to get out of there before Leahy caught on. I earned my five grand. A deal is a deal."

LaBelle glared. He felt like telling him to take a flying leap, but he didn't want to risk trouble from a malcontent with the election so close. He laid his briefcase on the desk, unlocking it with the combination. He removed a thick envelope and handed it over. "Fifty one-hundred dollar bills," he said, chomping on his cigar.

Red peeked inside, then stuffed the envelope inside his vest. "Pleasure doing business with you. You can keep the photos."

"Screw the photos. I want the negatives."

He smirked coyly. "Well, now, that wasn't exactly part of our deal. I never sell my negatives. That'll cost you extra."

LaBelle grumbled as he opened his briefcase. "You bastard. How much?"

"Fifty grand."

The cigar nearly fell from his mouth. "For negatives I can't even use?"

"Maybe *you* can't use them," he said with a shrug. "But now that I've taken a closer look at them, I can think of somebody who might be able to use a photograph of a presidential candidate looking . . . how did you put it? Like a blubbering baby in the face of personal crisis?"

LaBelle clenched his fists. The veins in his thick neck were about to burst. "You son of a bitch. This is extortion. I'm not forking over fifty grand."

"Fine," he said as he started for the door. "I'm sure somebody will."

He was fuming, then blurted, "All right, all right."

Red stopped at the door. "That's more like it."

"I don't keep that kind of money just lying around a hotel room. Give me till noon tomorrow."

"Nine A.M. Not a minute later."

LaBelle made a face, but he didn't argue. He unlocked the door. "I don't appreciate being treated this way by people I trust."

"Hey, I still love you, Buck." He winked on his way out. "But you know what they say about love and war, right?"

"All's fair," he said, losing the smile as he closed the door. *And there are casualties in both.*

14

Since leaving Nashville, Repo and Tony Delgado had taken turns driving virtually nonstop. They cruised well below the posted speed limits, taking no chances on being pulled over by highway patrol. By 2:00 A.M. Wednesday they were fifty miles outside Richmond, Virginia, heading north.

"You think she's awake yet?" asked Repo.

Tony didn't respond. He was slumped in the passenger seat, eyes shut.

The glow of the dashboard illuminated Repo's worried face. He switched on the radio, trying to wake his partner.

Tony stirred. "What the hell?"

"Sorry," he said, switching off the volume. "I was just thinking, you know. That injection you gave the girl. How long is she out for?"

"Twenty-four hours, at least. Don't worry about her."

"I—" He stopped, reluctant to speak his mind. "I just thought, you know, somebody should kind of be there when she wakes up. Maybe explain what's happening. She's only twelve. It's gotta be pretty scary to wake up with a bag over your head, not knowing where the hell you're at or where you're going."

Tony snorted, then shot him a funny look. "What are you, a mommy?"

"No. I just don't see no need to scar the kid for life, that's all."

Tony straightened up in his seat, giving his partner an assessing look. "You're making me real nervous, the way you're talking. I picked you for this job because I thought you had guts."

"I got guts, sure. Just we agreed wasn't nobody supposed to get killed."

"Are you still fucking obsessing about that old man?"

"It's murder, Tony. You guys killed him."

Tony paused, then turned very serious. "Do you have any idea how many people I've killed in my lifetime?"

"All I know is you killed that guy for nothing."

"It wasn't for *nothing*. We had to do it. Those are the rules. We all gotta be willing to do whatever it takes to get the job done."

Repo stared into the oncoming headlights, thinking. "Maybe. But an old man is one thing. I don't see any reason why we gotta make it any worse for the kid than absolutely necessary. She's just a girl."

Tony grabbed him by the wrist, seizing his attention. "She's not a girl. She's a bargaining chip. Don't ever forget it."

Repo's eyes darted, meeting Tony's glare.

He released his grip, then looked away.

Repo's attention turned back to the road. He said nothing, steering down the expressway in uneasy silence.

Red Weber stumbled up the stairway at the Thrifty Inn, an old motor lodge that offered rooms by the week, day, or hour, and that provided clean towels and sheets only with a cash deposit. After leaving

Buck LaBelle, he'd stopped at a bar to celebrate his renegotiated deal. He closed down the Tennessee Tavern at 2:00 A.M., but it took him another forty-five minutes to find his way back to his hotel. He knew he'd have a tequila hangover in the morning. But he'd also be $50,000 richer.

That'll buy a shitload of aspirin.

The old wooden stairs creaked beneath his feet. The banisters had been ripped from the stairwell, so he took one step at a time—slowly, balancing himself with flailing arms, like a novice on a tightrope. He stopped at the top of the stairs, smiling with a silly sense of accomplishment. With both hands he dug the room key from his front pocket, then aimed it at the keyhole, one hand steadying the other as he poked unsuccessfully around the lock. Frustrated, he gave up and tried the knob. The door opened.

He could have sworn he'd locked it, but he just laughed as he stepped inside.

He fumbled with the lamp but managed only to knock it off the dresser. He laughed at the mess he'd made, then went rigid. His stomach heaved. The last shot of tequila was doing an about-face. He ran for the bathroom, tripping in the darkness.

Just as he reached the threshold, the bathroom door slammed in his face, knocking him back onto the floor. He staggered to his feet. The door suddenly flew open. He saw his reflection standing in the doorway—or maybe it was a shadow. He squinted to focus.

"What the hell?"

The shadow lunged toward him. A blow to the head stunned him, and Red went down with a thud. His chin was on the carpet as the boots raced by his eyes. He tried to yell, but he'd bitten his tongue and couldn't speak. He heard the door fly open, then the sound of footsteps in the hallway, like somebody running.

Dizzy and groggy, he lifted himself from the floor. He limped to the door and peered down the hall. Nothing. He grimaced with pain, then froze.

The negatives, he thought—and he was suddenly sober.

He flipped on the light and ran to the closet. He grabbed his camera bag and zipped it open. The camera was gone.

"Shit!"

He checked the film pack. No film. No negatives. He checked every zip pocket, every side pouch, searching frantically. It was all gone, even the film he hadn't used yet.

Red fell to his knees, feeling a $50,000 pit in the bottom of his stomach. "Son of a bitch," he groaned.

At 5:00 A.M. the telephone rang in David Wilcox's hotel room. He was already awake, sipping coffee, reworking a press release he hoped to be able to persuade Allison to issue later in the day.

"Hello," he answered.

"Mission accomplished," said the voice on the line.

"You found him?" asked Wilcox.

"Wasn't too difficult. Aren't that many photographers running around Nashville who look like Bozo the clown. Red Weber's his name. Staying at some dive called the Thrifty Inn."

"Anybody see you?"

"Nah. He caught me by surprise before I left, but I blew by him so fast he couldn't have seen a thing."

"What about the pictures?"

"I got the camera and the film. He had probably half a dozen shots of Ms. Leahy down by the river. Her and that FBI guy, Abrams."

Wilcox sneered. "Sneaky bastards. Hiring their own damn photographer to make Allison look like a publicity hound. Burn the damn pictures."

"Okay. But I don't think you want me burning everything. It's kind of a godsend, but I came across some shots of General Howe that may actually be worth keeping."

"Is that so?" he said with a thin smile. "Tell me about them."

15

On Wednesday morning, the press room at the United States Department of Justice was filled to capacity. Eager reporters sat shoulder to shoulder in crowded rows of folding chairs. A simple blue backdrop displayed two round seals, one of the Department of Justice, the other of the Federal Bureau of Investigation. The American flag was draped on a pole.

At precisely 10:30 A.M., Allison entered from a side door, leading a somber entourage of men in dark suits to the rostrum. James O'Doud, FBI director, was directly behind her. Six other FBI and Justice Department officials filed in behind them. Cameras clicked and reporters jostled for position as she stepped up to the podium.

"Good morning," she said. "As you all know by know, Kristen Howe, the twelve-year-old granddaughter of General Lincoln Howe, is missing. At nine o'clock central time yesterday morning, Kristen left Wharton Middle School in Nashville, Tennessee. She and the driver, Reggie Miles, were the only persons aboard the school jitney. Somewhere in transit the bus was apparently hijacked. As yet, we don't know how or by whom.

"Last night, divers recovered the school van in the Cumberland River, near downtown Nashville. Later last night, we recovered the body of Reggie

Miles, the driver. His official cause of death has yet to be determined. Kristen Howe is still unaccounted for.

"Let me say first that we condemn these cowardly acts. The Department of Justice has called upon its every resource to launch the largest manhunt in American history. Director O'Doud has assembled a team of the FBI's most talented agents, and they are working literally around the clock. We will find Kristen Howe. We will bring these criminals to justice. I, personally, am devoting my full attention to these matters as attorney general. My presidential campaigning has been suspended."

She paused and surveyed the crowd. "I will briefly take questions."

Reporters leaped from their seats. Allison singled one out.

"Ms. Leahy," he said, "the American people will elect their next president in just six days. The photographs of General Howe that surfaced this morning make it clear that this personal tragedy has hit him very hard. Do you agree with those who say that the long-term psychological effects of the abduction may leave General Howe in no condition to serve as president of the United States? And do you think his reaction says anything at all about his ability to lead the nation in times of crisis?"

She gripped the podium, responding without hesitation. "I don't intend to politicize this tragedy in any way. My heart goes out to General Howe and his family. As I've stated, the safe return of Kristen Howe is now the number-one priority of the United States Department of Justice."

She pointed to another reporter in the second row.

He rose. "Ms. Leahy, will the Justice Department seek the death penalty for the murder of Reggie Miles?"

She paused. With a hostage still in the kidnapper's hands, she knew it just wasn't smart to say anything publicly about the death penalty.

"It's premature to talk about that. The medical examiner has not even ruled Mr. Miles's death a homicide yet. Even if it is homicide, it would not be a federal crime unless it can be shown that his murder was part of an interstate kidnapping. So, in response to your specific question, the answer is no, we have not yet made any decisions concerning the death penalty."

O'Doud stepped forward. "Let me add one quick thought here."

Allison glanced over her shoulder, containing her surprise. O'Doud did not retreat. He stood beside the podium as he spoke.

"Although the current administration has yet to execute a single federal prisoner for any federal crime, the FBI will treat this case as if capital punishment were a real option. By that, I simply mean that we will lawfully endeavor to gain all evidence that is relevant to an informed determination of whether the death penalty fits this particular crime. We fully expect that the prosecutorial arm of the next administration will evaluate that evidence and see to it that the appropriate punishment is imposed."

He glanced at Allison, then returned to his place beside the American flag. Reporters pressed forward, arms waving, shouting a flurry of follow-up questions. Allison quickly determined it was time to shut things down.

"Thank you," she said. "That's all for now."

Eager reporters continued to hurl questions,

but they went unanswered. Allison and her DOJ representatives exited first, followed by O'Doud and his assistants. When they reached the hall, she pulled the director into a vacant office and closed the door, nearly slamming it shut.

"What the hell was that all about?" she demanded.

O'Doud shrugged, feigning ignorance. "Just doing my job."

She moved closer, using her height advantage in heels. "It's not your job to talk about the death penalty. Prosecutors will make that decision. Not the FBI."

"I wasn't making any decisions. I was just telling it like it is."

"You were campaigning against me and my record on the death penalty, that's what you were doing. This was supposed to be an apolitical press conference."

He stepped back, guffawing. "Apolitical, my foot. Thirty minutes before you appear on national television, the press somehow gets its hands on some mysterious photos that make the general look like a sniveling wimp. What do you call that? Coincidence?"

"Are you suggesting *I* released those photographs?"

"Are you denying it?"

Her face reddened. "Yes, I deny it."

"Fine. But unless you'd enjoy having to deny these kinds of accusations to the American public, I suggest you take the advice I gave you from the start. Stay out of the investigation."

"Am I hearing things," she scoffed, "or did one incredibly pompous ass just threaten to smear my name in the media?"

"I'm not threatening anything. I simply won't allow this investigation to be directed by an attorney general who may be more interested in winning an election than solving a crime."

"You won't *allow* it?" she said incredulously. "You work for me, O'Doud."

He made a face. "A mere technicality, given the circumstances. Somehow, I don't think the director of the FBI is in any real danger of being fired by the president just twenty-four hours after the nation's biggest kidnapping since the Lindbergh baby. Somehow, I don't think you want to be skewered as the attorney general who is more interested in protecting her own turf than saving the life of a twelve-year-old girl."

"You're the most amoral human being I've ever met."

"You're the politician, not me. It's you who has the conflict of interest."

"Who the hell gave *you* the authority to decide whether I have a conflict of interest?"

His expression turned cold, but smug. "The next president of the United States. That's who."

She watched in silence as he left the room, numbed by his words. Alone.

16

Repo switched off the television set and rubbed his tired eyes. The drive from Nashville to Baltimore had been exhausting, but he and Tony Delgado were both too full of caffeine to sleep.

The living room went dark without the light from the television. Old heavy drapes blocked out the morning sun. The green sculptured carpet reminded Repo of his grandmother's house, only this place was even smaller. The tiny Formica kitchen with harvest gold appliances was in full view from the combined living and dining rooms. The vintage sixties bathroom was at the end of the hall. On the right was the master bedroom, where Tony and his brother Johnny would sleep. Kristen was in the other bedroom. Repo got the couch.

The toilet flushed, the bathroom door opened, and Tony came back in the living room.

Repo switched on the table lamp, then sank back into the couch, glaring. "They're seeking the death penalty."

"What?"

"I just heard the press conference. The head of the FBI just said they're gonna seek the death penalty for the murder of Reggie Miles."

"They gotta catch us first."

Repo shook his head, exasperated. "I've been thinking about this since Nashville, and I'm telling you straight up. Your brother is trouble."

A sarcastic smile came to Tony's face. "And I think you're a pussy. So that makes us the perfect triangle. Nobody trusts nobody."

"I'm not kidding around."

Tony's smile faded. "What do you want me to do, Repo?" He turned in anger, grabbing the phone. "You want me to call Elliot Ness right now and turn Johnny in?" His voice rose as he slammed down the phone and grabbed his gun. "You want me to blow Johnny's brains out when he gets here? *You* wanna blow his brains out? Is that what you want? Tell me. Because I'm sick of your whining."

Repo stared him down. "I took this job because *you* were heading it up. You're the one with the brains. Not Johnny. If you just rubber-stamp every stupid mistake your brother makes, this ship is going down. I just want you to have the balls to keep your own brother in line. That's all."

"Don't tell me how to handle Johnny. If he makes a mistake, I'll deal with him the way I'd deal with you. But killing Reggie Miles was no mistake. In fact, Johnny did us a favor."

"A *favor*? Thanks to him, now we got the death penalty hanging over our heads."

"Which is perfect. Now it's an all-or-nothing game, and we're free to do whatever it takes to pull off the job. No matter what else we do, they can only execute us once. So if we need to kill a cop, we're free to kill a cop. If some hero gets in our way, we're free to kill him, too. We're free—absolutely free—to do whatever we want. Which means that if we have to kill Kristen Howe . . ."

Repo's expression fell.

He smiled thinly. "Say it, Repo. I want to hear you say it. If we have to kill Kristen Howe . . ."

Repo blinked hard, then looked away.

Tony laughed and headed for the kitchen. "Free at last, free at last! Thank God Almighty, we're free, at last!"

Allison went home for lunch, not so much to eat as to talk to Peter. She couldn't remember the last time she and her husband had eaten together alone in their own dining room, but after the morning press conference and the exchange with O'Doud, she simply needed to get out of the Justice Building and clear her head. It seemed everyone around her had a political stake in her next move.

She dropped her coat on the sofa and fixed on the news-at-noon broadcast blaring from the television in the kitchen. She recognized her voice, but it was old footage—almost a year old. As attorney general she had downplayed her own personal tragedy, lest she be typecast as an irrational zealot with no respect for the rights of the accused. She knew, however, that the media would dig up the past once she launched her presidential campaign. Upon announcing her candidacy last December, therefore, Allison had granted just one "tell-all" prime-time interview to talk about Emily's abduction and her own eight-year ordeal. The strategy was to get it out of the way early and move forward with the real campaign issues. With Kristen Howe's abduction, the media had resurrected that old interview, replaying one sound bite in particular.

"One thing remains as true today as it was then," Allison said in the taped interview. "The first twenty-four hours are crucial in any case involving the abduction of a child by a nonfamily member."

The reporter was back on the television screen

live, standing outside the FBI headquarters. "This afternoon, as the investigation into Kristen Howe's disappearance moves into its second day, the attorney general's words of one year ago weigh heavy in the minds and hearts of all Americans. We can only hope for a happier ending than there was for Allison and Emily Leahy."

The anchor replied in a solemn voice, "Absolutely."

Allison cringed. *Absolutely*—the TV journalists' all-purpose idiotic response, suitable for any occasion. Hotter than blazes out there today, eh, Ted? Traffic's a mess this morning, isn't it, Jamie? Sure hope we're first on the scene when they pull that girl's dead body out of the woods, huh, boys? Absolutely, absolutely, absolutely.

Nice to know they care.

"Hi, sweetheart." It was Peter, emerging from the dining room. He had blocked out a week of work in New York to campaign with his wife, but with Allison's sudden diversion he was sort of on vacation, in the most absurd sense of the word.

Allison gave him a quick kiss, then switched off the television. She followed him to the dining room table and sat at the place setting across from him. She was deep in thought, shaking off that television reporter's last crack about a "happier ending" and trying to focus on the morning's disastrous press conference.

Peter sipped his iced tea, studying the stressed-out look on his wife's face. "Well," he said, "Wally is at football practice, and Beaver has to stay after school for letting a toad loose in Mrs. Mergatroid's science class."

Allison shook herself free from alpha-land. "Huh?" she said, not really listening.

Peter's eyes warmed. "Why don't you tell me what's rattling around in your head?"

She sighed, then held her thought as their multilingual housekeeper served them boneless chicken breasts baked in what she called a lovely "moose turd" sauce, which Allison was relieved to discover was actually a mustard sauce. When the housekeeper left, she spent the next twenty minutes telling Peter all that had happened, never once lifting a fork.

Peter pushed his half-empty plate aside, then said, "Are you really that surprised by any of this? The stakes don't get any higher, and you're dealing with Washington egos. You have to expect some political maneuvering."

"It's more than just maneuvering. I feel like the whole kidnapping is being . . . manipulated."

The word hung in the air. "In what way?" he asked.

"In every way. First a cameraman ambushes me at the river trying to make me look like a publicity hound. Then the press runs photos of Lincoln Howe that make him look like a wimp. This morning the FBI director tells me point-blank that Howe has ordered him to cut me out of the investigation. It seems like nobody gives a damn about getting Kristen Howe back alive. All that matters is the spin."

"If that's the way it is, maybe you're better off being out of the investigation."

She shook her head. "Don't you see it, Peter? By cutting me out, they're pushing me into a no-win position. If Kristen is found, Howe's campaign will vilify me as the missing attorney general who wouldn't lift a finger to help save her opponent's own granddaughter. But, God forbid, if something goes wrong, you can bet I'll get all the blame. I'm the attorney general. The ultimate responsibility for Kristen's life is mine."

Peter poured another iced tea from the pitcher. "Sounds to me like you're suggesting that the kidnapping isn't just being politically manipulated. Sounds like you think it was politically motivated."

"Meaning?"

"Meaning that everything that has happened in the past twenty-four hours isn't just a bunch of political strategists reacting to a terrible tragedy. Maybe the terrible tragedy was part of the strategy in the first place."

Allison looked him in the eye. "I would hate to attribute those kinds of motives to anyone."

"It doesn't seem beyond the realm of possibility. Some die-hard supporter of General Howe snags his granddaughter in the demented hope that the sympathy factor will help push him over the top."

She swallowed hard. "Or a die-hard Leahy supporter who figures the kidnapping will send the Howe campaign into utter chaos, will take the public's eye off the bogus infidelity issue that nearly ruined me at the debate, and will allow me to flood the media with tough-on-crime speeches for a solid week before the election."

"I hadn't thought about it being someone on your side."

"I have. How much ink have the media spilled on adultery since Kristen's abduction? Not a drop. Overnight, it went from becoming the deciding factor in the election to a complete nonissue."

"Well," he said, arching an eyebrow. "Which side is the bad guy on? Howe's? Or yours?"

Allison sighed, then looked out the window. "Honest to God, Peter. I don't have a clue."

17

Room service at the Opry Land Hotel offered lunch as early as eleven, but Lincoln Howe was still too angry to eat. The photographs of him sobbing in the back of his limo had captured a side of himself that he didn't think existed. Ed Muskie must be smiling, he thought. From now on, when the world spoke of weepy presidential candidates, they'd mean Lincoln Howe in 2000, not the late senator in the 1972 Democratic primaries.

Howe loathed public displays of emotion. Even when he was leaving for extended tours of duty with the army overseas, he had never let his wife see him off at the airport. They said their goodbyes at home, in private. No tears in public places. No hugs and kisses in front of the troops.

The thought of his teary face plastered on every newspaper in the country was enough to make him fall on his proverbial military sword. He needed someone to blame, and his anger was only fueled by his campaign director's courageous confession that it was he who had hired the man who'd snapped the pictures.

Howe was pacing across LaBelle's hotel suite, saying nothing, digesting everything he'd just heard. Blind with anger, he nearly tripped over an electrical cord that snaked across the oriental carpet. Since the abduction, the suite had been wired like a satellite campaign headquarters with computers and extra fax machines, but not even the phone dared to ring as he formulated a response.

"Of all the stupid-assed ideas," the general boomed, pacing more furiously and waving his arms as he spoke. "Where the hell do you come off hiring someone to take my photograph without me knowing it?"

LaBelle cowered in the armchair, staring blankly at the floor. "I wanted candid shots, so naturally I couldn't tell you about it in advance. But I would never have actually used them without your approval."

"You could at least have hired someone you could trust."

"I thought I could trust him."

Howe faced him squarely, sharpening his tone. "Does that mean you believe this Red Weber character? Did somebody really break into his hotel room and steal his negatives, or did he just double-cross you and sell them to somebody else?"

"I don't know. Seems to me that if he had wanted to double-cross me he would have waited until after I paid him the fifty grand. Then he'd sell an extra set of photos to somebody else."

Howe nodded, agreeing with the logic. He was pacing again. "So, suppose there was a break-in. And suppose we can even raise the inference that Leahy's campaign was behind it. Where does that take us?"

LaBelle scratched his head, thinking. "It's a two-edged sword, I think. We can't really make much of it in the press. Sure, a break-in orchestrated by Leahy's supporters makes them look bad. But once the cops or the media start to probe, it's bound to come out that we hired Weber to photograph you.

That makes us look even worse than them."

"Damn it, Buck! I thought you were fucking smarter than this." He was more furious than ever, the veins bulging in his neck. "Don't you see what kind of a bind this puts me in? I've been taking the high road with everybody. With the FBI, the press, even Allison Leahy. I'm on the record saying over and over again that I will not tolerate any manipulation of this kidnapping for political gain. How the hell is it going to look if it comes out that you hired a photographer to snag some candid Kodak moments of me mourning the loss of my granddaughter?"

"Sir, I—"

"Shut up, soldier!"

They exchanged glances, saying nothing about the general's lapse into "soldier" talk.

His hands tightened into huge, angry fists. "I swear, Buck, if the election weren't so close, I'd fire your ass. No, by God, I'd take you out and shoot you. This is a time bomb we're sitting on. What's to keep this low-life Weber from running to the press and telling them what you hired him to do? Tabloids would pay big money for a story like this."

LaBelle sat in silence, as if the question were rhetorical. "I can think of one thing that might keep him quiet," he said finally. "Pay Weber his fifty thousand dollars."

The general froze in his tracks, stunned, like a man punched in the chest. "Hush money?"

"That's such a negative term. But, yeah. I guess you'd call it hush money."

The general made a face. "Are you serious?"

"Do you want Weber to keep quiet? Or do you want to go back to being five points *behind* Allison Leahy?"

Howe turned away, riddled with anguish, speaking aloud but to himself. "Son of a bitch," he muttered. "I can't believe this." He leaned on the windowsill and stared out at the parking lot. A mother and young daughter were walking to their car, reminding him of his own offspring. An urge arose to fire LaBelle on the spot, but he knew of few things more dangerous than a disgruntled ex-campaign insider. The bastard would probably catch the next plane to New York and auction off his tell-all memoirs to the big publishing houses.

"Even if we pay," he said with his back to LaBelle, "there's no guarantee it won't leak."

"True. I suppose there's only one sure thing. But you don't look like a break-legs kind of guy, general. At least not in a civilian setting."

Howe blinked hard, not sure what to do—then a faint image in the glass gave him pause. It was LaBelle, sitting behind him, watching him, unaware that the general could see his reflection on the window. He detected a certain gleam in his eye, a smirk on his lips, as if relishing the fact that the general was even considering the payment of hush money.

This was the nightmare General Howe had feared, the reason he'd refused to run for office in 1996, the reason he'd so reluctantly sought the nomination in 2000. A surge of anger swelled within—anger at himself for having entered this despicable arena called politics. He drew a deep breath and quelled the rage within, recognizing that, under the circumstances, there really was nothing else to do.

"All right," said the candidate. "Pay the man his damn money."

* * *

Johnny Delgado heard a noise.

He was half asleep, lying in bed. He checked the digital alarm clock: 12:20 P.M.

He'd driven straight through from Nashville after dumping the body, arriving in Philadelphia around 4:00 A.M. Wednesday. His brother had told him to take a circuitous route, to avoid being followed, so he figured he'd catch some sleep at his old girlfriend's apartment in Philly, then press on to Maryland.

He sat up in bed, listening, wearing only boxer shorts. His shirt and pants lay on the floor beside the bed, next to Honey's red nightgown. The blackout shades were shut tight, but a punishing beam of afternoon sunlight slashed through a missing panel, hitting Johnny squarely in the eyes.

"Did you hear something?" he asked.

Diane Combs—"Honey"—lay sprawled on her stomach on the other side of the bed. Last night's heated reunion had been an unexpected but welcome loss of sleep. She rolled on her side and smiled. "Hear what?"

He didn't return the smile. "I thought I heard voices out by the car."

"Could be my neighbors."

"Check the window, will ya, babe? See if it's somebody you know."

"What's all the paranoia?"

"Just check it," he said firmly.

Her eyes darted nervously. She didn't like his tone. "All right," she said, rising from the bed. She wrapped her naked body in the sheet, then stepped to the window and peeped through the blinds. She glanced back at Johnny. "It's the cops."

"Shit!" He jumped out of bed and frantically pulled on his trousers. "What are they doing?"

"Looks like they're running some kind of check on your car."

"Oh, *shit*!"

Her brow furrowed with concern. "What the hell's going on?"

"It's stolen."

She stepped away from the window. "You bastard. I don't hear from you for a month, then you show up in the middle of the night in a stolen car?"

He tucked his shirt, then zipped his fly. "This ain't about stolen cars."

"Then what's going on?"

"It's big." He sat on the bed and pulled on his boots. "Very big."

Her lips went dry. "Tell me. I want to know what you—"

He pulled a pistol from his bag, stopping her in mid-sentence. "Just shut your mouth and be still." He stepped quickly to the window, peering out carefully with his back to the wall.

Honey started to shake.

"Is there a back way out of this rat hole?"

She nodded nervously. "Yeah. The kitchen. But you'll need a key to get out."

"Where is it?"

"My purse."

"Get it."

Still wrapped in the bedsheet, she tripped as she crossed the room, then grabbed her purse and removed the key from the ring. Her hand shook as she gave it to him.

"Johnny, are you in some kind of trouble?"

"Not yet."

"Why'd you steal the car?"

"Just shut up!" He pointed the gun right at her.

"Johnny. Come on. You don't have to point that thing at me."

He winced, agonizing. "I can't believe I gotta do this."

"Do what?" Her voice was shaking.

"I stole the car in Nashville. They'll know I was in Nashville yesterday."

Her face went ashen. She'd watched last night's news. "Are you saying you had something to do with the kidnapping of that little girl?"

He glanced out the window. The cop was writing down the license tag number. Johnny bit his lip and muttered, "I can't fucking believe I gotta do this."

Honey moved nervously to the edge of the bed. "Just go, right now. Out the back door. I won't say you were here. I'll tell them I don't know who parked the car there. I woke up, and there it was."

He grimaced and shook his head. "This is way too important for them to be stonewalled by some small-time ex-hooker." He reached into his bag and affixed a silencer to his pistol.

She rose, taking three steps back. "Johnny," her voice shook, "please. If you don't think I can keep quiet, just take me with you. We can take my car. Gag me and throw me in the trunk, if you want. Just—God, *please*—don't shoot me."

He paused to consider, but the Reggie Miles disaster made taking another hostage unthinkable. "No can do, Honey."

Her plea turned shrill as she fell to her knees, crying. "Johnny, I swear. I won't say anything. Not to anyone. Ever."

He closed one eye and aimed at her forehead. "I know you won't," he said, then squeezed the trigger.

18

Harley Abrams arrived in Philadelphia just before 3:00 P.M. It had been his idea to put a nationwide trace on every vehicle that had been rented or stolen in Nashville in the past week. With virtually every law enforcement agency on alert, it had taken less than twenty-four hours to locate them. Only one trace, however, had led to the doorstep of a murder victim. Harley figured this one was worth a trip.

A young female agent from the Philadelphia field office met him at the airport in a four-door Mercury, a typical "Bucar," the Bureau's appellation for its vehicles. Harley sat in the passenger seat, deep in thought, jotting down notes on a yellow pad as they headed down the expressway. As they exited near downtown, he looked up, pen in hand.

"I don't want any snags with any evidence pulled from this apartment," he said. "You see any problems with the search warrant the Philadelphia police obtained?"

She shrugged, keeping her eyes on the road. "Our assistant U.S. attorney doesn't think so. The patrolman ran a check on the license tag, confirmed it was reported stolen in Nashville just two hours after Kristen Howe was abducted. Police checked with the landlord, found the parking space was assigned to Diane Combs in apartment two-oh-one. They knocked on the door, nobody answered. They called her work, found out she didn't show up this morning. Didn't call in sick, nothing. I think it all adds up to probable cause. Obviously the magistrate thinks so, too, or he wouldn't have issued the warrant."

Harley nodded, satisfied.

They turned at the main entrance to Chestnut Apartments, a sprawling collection of beige, low-rent, two-story units with red shingle roofs. A fence surrounded the complex, but it had no security gate. This afternoon, however, a patrolman was posted at the entrance. Harley rolled down his window and flashed his credentials.

"I'm looking for Detective Wyatt," he said.

The patrolman pointed the way, then radioed ahead to let the crime scene investigation team know Abrams was coming.

Gawkers had gathered in the parking lot, and a police officer split the crowd, allowing the FBI car to pass. They parked at the yellow police tape, near a van marked MEDICAL EXAMINER. Three squad cars and two unmarked cars formed a semicircle around the stolen 1997 Chevy Camaro with Tennessee license tags. Forensic experts were checking for fingerprints and gathering fibers from the seats and carpet. Two men from the medical examiner's office were wheeling a gurney through the open door to apartment 201.

Harley stepped down from the Bucar and buttoned his jacket, thinking it felt more like January than November. A tall black man wearing a frumpy brown trench coat and a five o'clock shadow approached.

"Detective Wyatt," he said, introducing himself. "Homicide."

"Harley Abrams, FBI. I'm the inspector overseeing the Howe kidnapping case."

"I know who you are. What can I do for you?"

"I'm simply trying to coordinate our efforts. I recognize homicide is your jurisdiction, but this crime scene could yield some important evidence in our kidnapping case."

Wyatt made a face. "You think the people who pulled off the kidnapping of Lincoln Howe's granddaughter were actually stupid enough to steal a getaway car in Nashville and drive it all the way to Philly?"

"When you're dealing with crimes this big, you often see a bravado that makes these guys think no matter what they do, they won't get caught. Six years ago, we caught the World Trade Center bombers because they went back to the rental agency to claim the deposit on the truck they'd used to blow up the building. Stealing a getaway car doesn't seem half that stupid."

The detective nodded in apparent agreement.

"Tell me about the victim," said Abrams.

"Diane Combs. Worked as a grocery store cashier most of the time, but dabbled in prostitution when she needed drugs. Been in and out of rehab eleven times in six years. If you ask me, she doesn't seem much like the big-time kidnapper type."

"You mind if I look inside the apartment?"

"Be my guest."

Harley followed the cracked sidewalk to the open front door. A forensic evidence squad was scouring the living room carpet and furniture. Harley stepped by them without a word, turned down the hall, and headed straight for the bedroom. He stopped in the doorway.

Diane Combs's body lay on the floor, still wrapped in a bedsheet, outlined in chalk. Her open eyes were beginning to flatten from loss of fluid. A trail of blood had oozed from the hole in her forehead, covering one eye, ending in a dark crimson stain on the carpet. Harley noticed that the blood had not yet completely dried. He knelt beside the body, laying the back of his hand against her cheek. It was still warm. Her head moved when he touched it, indicating that rigor mortis had yet to tighten her neck muscles. Probably dead less than three hours, he figured. The killer couldn't be too far away.

Harley rose. "Any sign of struggle or break-in?"

"None," said Wyatt.

Harley stepped toward the bed and pressed down on the mattress. Soft, he noticed. It retained his handprint. He knelt down so that his eyes were at eye level with the mattress.

"You can still see indentions on both sides of the bed," he said. "Looks to me like there were two people sleeping here last night." He rose and glanced at the victim, then at Wyatt. "We know who one of them is. Find out who the other one is, and you'll solve your homicide. And we may solve my kidnapping."

"What's your theory?" asked Wyatt.

"Until now, we've favored the notion that this was a well-planned kidnapping by sophisticated criminals. But maybe it was a spur-of-the-moment fling by some small-time loser who smoked a joint, stole a car, got giddy with excitement, and decided he could actually be somebody if he did something important like kidnapping General Howe's granddaughter. Maybe Ms. Combs is an old girlfriend. He stops here for the night and brings Kristen inside, thinking it would impress the lady. Instead, she freaks out, says she wants no part of it. He freaks at her reaction, kills her. I'm just speculating at this point. But I want to bring an evidence team in to help you. Fortunately, Kristen's mother had the foresight to use a DNA swab kit, so all we need is a single hair to confirm whether Kristen was here or not. I also want to make sure we gather every shred of evidence that will identify whoever it was who put the bullet in Ms. Combs's head."

"Sounds like this could be the break you've been looking for," said Wyatt.

"Let's hope so," said Abrams. "In this business, there's no time for dead ends."

By Wednesday afternoon, Natalie Howe knew her way around her daughter's kitchen. She was making tea for Tanya and the three Nashville FBI agents who were monitoring the house when the doorbell rang. Tanya rose from her chair in front of the television, but one of the agents stopped her.

"Let me check it," he said.

Tanya turned back to the television. She'd been glued to CNN, which had replaced election coverage with frequent updates on the kidnapping.

The agent peered through the peephole. A white van with the familiar blue and red FedEx logo was parked at the curb. The deliverywoman was standing on the porch.

"Just a minute," the agent said through the door. He pulled out his cellular phone and called FedEx to verify the delivery. It checked out. He opened the door.

"I have a letter-pak for Lincoln or Natalie Howe."

"We'll take it," said the agent. He signed for it and closed the door.

Another agent stepped forward with a handheld metal detector and passed it over the flat letter-pak. Nothing. He looked at Mrs. Howe and said, "We can run it over to the field office and have it X-rayed for you, even have dogs sniff it for explosives or poisons."

"How long will that take?" she asked.

"Couple of hours. I strongly advise it."

"But what if this has something to do with Kristen? We may not have a couple of hours." Her eyes begged for someone to tell her what to do.

Tanya stepped forward. "I'll open it."

"No!" said Natalie. "It was addressed to me and Lincoln. If something's going to happen, let it happen to us. I'll open it."

Natalie took the envelope, then retreated alone to the dining room and sat at the head of the table. She drew a deep breath and ripped it open. She paused, as if expecting a mushroom cloud or burst of cyanide gas, but nothing came. She removed a single sheet of paper. Her eyes darted nervously as she read the typewritten message: ONE MILLION DOLLARS. HUNDRED-DOLLAR BILLS. BY FRIDAY. INSTRUCTIONS TO FOLLOW.

She swallowed the lump in her throat, then flipped the message over. Taped to the backside was Kristen Howe's identification card from Wharton Middle School.

She shivered, realizing the demand was no hoax.

Across the bottom, someone had scrawled a handwritten message—almost as if it were written as a postscript. "If the cops see this, Kristen dies."

Her hand shook uncontrollably.

The FBI agent stepped forward. "What is it, Mrs. Howe?"

She pressed the message to her bosom, shielding it from all eyes but her own. "I can't tell you," she said in a quaking voice. "Not until I speak to Lincoln."

19

Harley Abrams was whisked by helicopter from Philadelphia to Washington for an emergency meeting at FBI headquarters. At 4:35 P.M. he reached Director O'Doud's office suite, an impressive ensemble of offices and conference rooms known as "mahogany row" because of the richly paneled walls. The rest of the building sported stark charcoal doors and beige walls unrelieved by artwork, making the director's suite something of an oasis in a building ridiculed for its architecturally appalling exterior walls of pockmarked concrete. Entry into the suite was tightly restricted, requiring advance clearance by the security programs manager. Harley's lapel bore the necessary photo ID with blue background that allowed him to reach the director's receptionist, who then let him inside. Two Secret Service agents waited outside the suite, somewhat out of their jurisdiction at the FBI headquarters, but at this stage of the game they accompanied Lincoln Howe everywhere.

O'Doud was seated behind his antique mahogany desk. Lincoln Howe occupied the armchair facing him. Harley noticed that Howe was wearing a photo ID with a gold background, indicating the highest level of security clearance, a level usually reserved for FBI assistant directors and above.

An unusual if not irregular courtesy, thought Harley, considering the general was still only a civilian, albeit a candidate for the presidency.

Harley greeted both men respectfully. In an ordinary kidnapping, a supervisory special agent from the CASKU would no more report directly to the FBI director than to the Prince of Wales, but nothing about this case was ordinary.

Director O'Doud handed him a faxed copy of the ransom demand. Harley examined it, taking a seat on the striped couch by the window.

Howe said, "My wife received it in Nashville this afternoon. It was sent Federal Express to my daughter's home, but it was addressed to Natalie and me."

Harley looked up. "It wouldn't have made much sense to address it to your daughter. Even the kidnappers must know it would be easier for you than your daughter to raise a million dollars."

O'Doud said, "Another interesting thing. It came from Knoxville, not Nashville."

"I had assumed they'd left Nashville. This confirms they headed east, which lends credence to our theory that the murder in Philadelphia is related."

Howe asked, "But why would they send a package that can pinpoint their location? Why not just make a quick phone call?"

"They probably were afraid a phone call could be traced, or their voices could be identified, or maybe you'd want to talk to Kristen and they'd have to risk bringing her to a pay phone—lots of reasons. So they just dropped this in the overnight box on their way to wherever they were going. By the time it reached your daughter's house in

Nashville I'm sure they were long gone from Knoxville."

O'Doud asked, "How does the ransom demand affect your thinking, Harley? Does it change anything?"

"It's definitely a breakthrough. Any time you have a ransom demand the case gets much easier to solve, since the kidnappers have to contact the family. But as far as the investigation goes, I don't think we should drop everything and say we're looking for financially motivated kidnappers."

"Why not?" Howe asked with a grimace.

"Because I believe the other profiles we've worked out at CASKU are still viable. A financial motive is certainly plausible. But we could still be dealing with a glory-seeking psychopath who targeted a high-profile victim like Kristen Howe just for the thrill and notoriety of it. Look again at the ransom message," he said, reading from the photocopy: "A million dollars by Friday, instructions to follow. It's almost as if ransom were an afterthought. The kidnapper hasn't even figured out how to get the money yet. At this stage, we simply can't rule out other possibilities, including the theory that this is the rare and maybe even unprecedented case where the real purpose of the kidnapping is to throw a political election."

Howe recoiled, as if uncomfortable with any discussion of political ramifications. "But the ransom demand *has* to blow that theory, doesn't it? I mean, even though Ms. Leahy has obviously tried to exploit the kidnapping for her own political gain, the ransom demand confirms that the kidnappers' motivations are financial, not political."

Harley said, "I would disagree on two levels. One, if the kidnappers *are* politically motivated, a bogus ransom demand would certainly be a clever way to throw the FBI off the trail. And two, I wouldn't say that Ms. Leahy's supporters are the only ones who have exploited the kidnapping for political gain."

The general swelled with indignation. "Are you suggesting *I'm* playing politics?"

Harley met his stare, wondering if now was the time to question both the candidate and the director about the politically transparent capital punishment speech that O'Doud had delivered at this morning's press conference. He decided not. "I would never suggest that, General. Not without more evidence." He glanced at the faxed ransom note. "What I'd really like is to see the original of this."

"It's being flown here as we speak," said O'Doud. "It will have to be analyzed, which is in part the reason for this meeting."

General Howe interrupted, taking control. "I'm sure you noticed the handwritten message on the back—the warning that if we tell the police about the ransom demand, they'll kill the hostage. So far, the only person my wife and I have told about it is our daughter, some close friends who might help us raise the money, and of course Director O'Doud. The director has naturally brought some higher-ranking officials into the loop. The assistant director of the criminal division, the CASKU chief, some very select members of the Hostage Rescue Team, and as of now, you. Obviously you'll need to tell more—laboratory agents who analyze the message and the packaging, a handwriting expert who will analyze the handwritten portion of the message, and so on. As for this support level, I'm counting on you to identify the smallest group possible that needs to know about this. And then I want you to hand-pick those people who can be absolutely trusted to keep this confidential. We have to assume that the kidnappers will act on their threat. We cannot afford a break in security."

"It's always hard to guarantee no leaks, but I will certainly put together a list of those agents I would trust. Just to come at this from another direction, is there anyone you absolutely *don't* want on the access list?"

The general and Director O'Doud exchanged glances. "Only one person I can think of," said Howe, his eyes narrowing. "Allison Leahy."

Rush-hour traffic was streaming down Pennsylvania Avenue, a grand and in many ways metaphorical divide between the Justice Building and FBI headquarters between Ninth and Tenth streets. Allison crossed at the crosswalk with her Secret Service bodyguards at her side.

After lunch with Peter, Allison had reached the conclusion that she needed a one-on-one, face-to-face meeting with the point man on the investigation. His unexpected return to Washington presented the perfect opportunity. She thought about summoning him to her own office, but since it was literally a matter of crossing the street, she preferred meeting him on his own turf—sort of a polite ambush.

Allison entered the relatively modern J. Edgar Hoover Building through the employee entrance on Pennsylvania Avenue. An escort directed her to an interior office near the lab, the visiting agent's office that Harley Abrams used when away from his home base in Quantico. She found the stark surroundings about as aesthetically pleasing as the old

CASKU offices in the underground facilities back at the academy. Beige walls with no artwork. A potted plant in the corner that had seen better days. Abrams was busy behind the basic government-issue metal desk with wood veneer top.

"I need five minutes of your time," she announced, standing in the doorway.

Abrams looked up from his desk, surprised. He rose, then offered the only chair with a wave of his hand. "Please, come in."

Allison entered alone and closed the door, leaving her escort in the hall. Abrams discreetly slid the list he was preparing—the list of those who would be privy to the ransom demand—into the top desk drawer.

"Afraid I might see something?" she asked.

He smiled awkwardly as he closed the drawer. "Oh, this? Just, uh—personal."

"Yeah, I've been catching up with all my letter writing in the past twenty-four hours, too."

"*Touché,*" he said, his smile fading.

"Look, I recognize you're in a tough spot. You work for an FBI director who, even though he technically reports to me, has determined that the attorney general should be excluded from this investigation."

He raised his hands. "Please, if this is a power struggle, I really wish you would have this conversation with Director O'Doud."

"This is not about power. It's about a twelve-year-old girl. Tragically, that fact has been lost in all the political maneuvering over the past thirty-six hours."

"Which is exactly the reason Director O'Doud thinks you should stand aside and let the FBI do its job."

She nodded wearily, as if tired of the party line. Part of her wanted to stand up and scream, *The FBI works for* me, *damn it!* But Abrams was the right man for the job, and she needed his respect, not his resignation. She dug in her purse and removed a small cassette player. "I'd like you to hear something. It'll just take a minute."

She laid the cassette player on the desk and hit the PLAY button.

Abrams stared at the machine, never making eye contact. A cooing sound came from the small speaker. Gurgling, broken sounds. It lasted about fifteen seconds before Allison hit the STOP button.

As it ended, their eyes met.

Her lip quivered as she struggled with her emotions. "That was my four-month-old daughter, Emily. She was abducted from my house eight years ago."

He nodded with some difficulty. "I'd heard about that."

"This is the tape her abductor put in her crib. It played over the baby monitor, so I wouldn't know she was gone. Until it was too late."

"I don't know what to say," he said. "What happened to you in the past is terrible. But your conflict of interest stems not from your past, but from your present status as a presidential candidate."

Her tone sharpened. "My *alleged* conflict of interest stems from the assumption that I would use Kristen Howe's abduction to my own political advantage. After hearing that tape, do you honestly believe I would ever exploit the abduction of *any* child for any purpose?"

His expression answered for him. "What are you asking me to do?"

"I'm asking you to look at reality, not the

rhetoric. When Emily was abducted eight years ago, people told me exactly what Lincoln Howe and Director O'Doud are telling me now. 'Step aside,' they said. 'You can't be objective. Leave it to the experts.' Like an idiot, I listened to them. It hurt like hell, but for the good of the investigation I stood on the sidelines and let them do their jobs. And you know what?"

Abrams shook his head slightly.

"They never found my daughter," she said in a hushed voice. "They never came *close* to finding my daughter. No leads, no motive, no suspects. Vanished."

"I'm sorry."

"Thank you. But I didn't come for sympathy. I came to state my case. I would no more divulge the details of this investigation than would Tanya Howe. As the attorney general I feel a moral responsibility to make sure everything that can possibly be done *is* being done to save Kristen Howe. And as a woman I bring something of value to the process. Experience. Personal experience."

She rose, then stopped and looked him in the eye. "There's one other thing you should know, Inspector."

"What's that?"

"It's killing me to be made into a bystander all over again." She turned and opened the door, never looking back as she headed for the elevator.

At six-thirty Wednesday evening Harley Abrams was at a table by himself in the FBI cafeteria, gobbling down a tuna fish sandwich as he revised his written profile of the kidnappers in light of the day's events. A television set in the corner was tuned to the evening news, but Harley was only half listening.

"Good evening," said the evening news anchorman. His shoulders squared to the camera, filling television screens across America with his handsome face. "In a late-breaking story, ABC News has obtained confirmation through an exclusive source that Kristen Howe's kidnappers have presented a ransom demand of one million dollars."

Harley coughed, nearly choking on his sandwich.

"Details are scarce," said the anchorman. "But the one-page, typewritten note is the first communication from the kidnappers since the twelve-year-old granddaughter of presidential hopeful Lincoln Howe disappeared yesterday morning on her way to school. With more on the story from Washington is—"

Harley's cellular phone rang, but his focus was on the television until he heard Director O'Doud's voice on the line.

"Have you seen tonight's lead story?" snapped O'Doud.

"Yes, sir."

"You told Leahy, didn't you."

Harley grimaced. "No, sir."

"I know you two met this afternoon."

"I met with her, yes. But I didn't tell her anything."

"It had to be Leahy, or someone in her camp. They must have cut a deal—give up the exclusive today for some favorable press coverage tomorrow. I'll bet my right arm that by tomorrow morning we'll see some hogwash story showing Allison Leahy on top of every phase of the investigation."

"Sir, I didn't breathe a word of it to anyone. Unless—"

"Unless what?"

"I suppose she could have seen something on my desk. But I don't think so."

"Well, if it wasn't Leahy, then who in the hell was it?"

"Probably the same people who have been playing politics with the kidnapping all along."

"And who would that be?"

"I'll say this much," said Harley. "The list of suspects is narrowing."

20

At 8:30 P.M. Lincoln Howe arrived at the studio, dressed in a dark suit befitting a funeral. Secret Service agents flanked his sides. The general showed no expression as he marched down the hall to the backstage area. He stood to the side, surveying a set that normally served a local talk show in Arlington, Virginia. The interviewer's desk had been moved to the center of the room, with a large projector screen behind it. Two men were carrying a couch off stage. A tangled mess of wires and cables lay around the perimeter. Hundreds of floodlights dangled from the ceiling. Five cameras were in position.

Buck LaBelle approached. "Just about ready, General," said the campaign manager.

Howe nodded. "What about coverage?"

"From the technical standpoint it's like the debates. CNN will serve as the pool organization, and anybody who wants to pick up the broadcast can subscribe. All the major networks are covering it, and some international. You could have a hundred million viewers."

Howe glanced at the Secret Service agent, who seemed to have overheard. "I'm not concerned about the number of viewers, Buck. I want broad coverage so the kidnappers will see it."

"Yes, sir."

"Two minutes!" shouted the program director. "Two minutes to silence."

"You'd better take your place," said LaBelle.

The general walked across the set, then seated himself behind the desk. A makeup artist powdered his face, then quickly disappeared. Howe sat pensively, orienting himself to the camera, lights, and TelePrompTer.

"Fifteen seconds," shouted the director.

He licked his lips, calming his nerves.

"On the air!"

The general paused two seconds, then spoke directly into camera 1.

"Good evening, my fellow Americans. As you all know, the Howe family has suffered a terrible tragedy. Kristen Howe, my daughter's only child, was abducted yesterday morning. This afternoon, my wife and I received a ransom demand of one million dollars.

"What the media did not report to you, however, is this: The kidnappers threatened to kill their hostage if the ransom demand was made public."

Howe turned in his chair. Camera 3 moved in for a closer shot.

"I don't know how the ransom demand became public. It certainly wasn't leaked by the Howe family. I trust it wasn't leaked by law enforcement. I'm told that the FBI is currently investigating whether it was leaked by someone in the attorney general's office. We will simply have to wait and see. For the moment, however, I have just three things to say.

"First, to my opponent, Allison Leahy. If the ransom demand was leaked by you or your supporters for political gain, this is the most despicable act ever committed in the history of American politics.

"Second, to the cowards who have put a price on the head of an innocent child: I don't have a million dollars, and I wouldn't give it to you if I had it. Unlike my opponent and her millionaire husband, my wife and I subsist on a modest military pension.

"Third, to the American people . . ."

The general rose, then walked to a projection screen at the back of the set. It lit up as he reached it, revealing a wall of photographs, floor to ceiling, each an individual photo of a child. The camera panned the photographs, then returned to General Howe.

"Every one of the young children you see on this wall is missing, the victim of a child abductor. It happens every hour of every day, in every community in the country. In 1990 the Justice Department estimated that as many as 4,600 children were being abducted by nonfamily members each year. Three hundred children were either detained for a long period of time or murdered. Ten years later, the problem is only worse. Much worse."

He walked to another screen. It too lit up—more photographs, men of all ages.

"Each of the men on this board is a known child abductor. More to the point, each of these men is currently roaming the streets of America, preying on young children. We know who they are and what they've done. Law enforcement simply does not have the resources to find them and bring them to justice."

He faced the camera.

"Ladies and gentlemen, I devoted my life to

protecting the national security of this country. Nothing threatens our national security more than a direct attack against our children. Politicians talk about the war against crime. I know what it means to be at war. Believe me. We are *not* at war. But we should be.

"Although the military has shrunk in size over the past ten years, the United States of America now has the most skilled and highly trained army ever assembled on the face of the earth. We should put it to use.

"Tonight, I'm calling upon President Sires, in the final weeks of his service as commander in chief, to sign an executive order that will authorize and direct the use of military personnel to assist in the search for and apprehension of child abductors. If I am elected president, I promise you I will sign such an executive order. In the interest of full disclosure, I also promise that there will be no more important assignment than the apprehension of those responsible for the abduction of Kristen Howe.

"Thank you. May God bless America. And its children."

Tanya Howe sat motionless before the television set in her living room. Her breathing quickened as the rage swelled within. Her eyes nearly burned a path across the carpet as she turned and glared at her mother.

"He just murdered my daughter." Her voice combined anger and disbelief.

Natalie blinked uneasily, struggling to answer. "Your father is a very smart man, Tanya. He knows what he's doing."

•

"No, *I* know what he's doing." She glanced at the FBI agent monitoring the phone. "I want you out of here," she told him.

Her mother rose. "Tanya, please. Don't overreact."

She shook with rage. "The kidnappers have threatened to kill Kristen if the cops are involved. And so what do we do? We have the FBI sitting in my living room and my self-centered excuse for a father declaring war on national television. I'm not overreacting. I'm taking control. Somebody has to."

Natalie took her hand. "I wish you would just wait."

"Wait until she's dead?" she shouted, shaking free. "No, Mom. I'm not waiting."

She grabbed the agent's coat and threw it at him, then ran to the door and flung it open. "Get out of my house! Take your guns, your radios, your tanks, your bazookas, and whatever the hell else it is that you and General Howe think it will take to wage war and get my daughter killed. Get out!"

Cold air rushed through the open door, sending a chill through the room. The agent looked at Natalie. "We have to abide by the wishes of Kristen's mother," he said, then glanced at Tanya. "We'll check back in the morning to make sure your decision is final."

She slammed the door shut as he crossed the threshold. She stood frozen for a moment, alone in the foyer. Her eyes locked on a pair of small, muddy sneakers behind the door—Kristen's shoes, laying right where she always left them, despite her mother's nagging.

Tanya picked one up and clutched it. Her shoulders began to heave. She slumped against the door as the tears began to flow.

* * *

Allison had watched the general's broadcast from her townhouse in Georgetown. She was on the telephone immediately, checking with David Wilcox and others to see if anyone in her camp knew about the ransom demand. If the leak had come from within the Leahy campaign, she wanted to deal with it immediately. She left it to her aide to arrange a morning meeting at campaign headquarters, then she retired to her library to prepare a response to the general's broadcast.

Just after 10:00 P.M. the doorbell rang. Her maid answered in the company of a Secret Service agent. Allison was on her way to the kitchen for a coffee refill when she saw Harley Abrams standing in the foyer. She stopped in the hall.

"Come in," she said.

Harley handed his coat to the maid, then followed Allison into the library.

"Would you like some coffee?"

"No, thank you."

They sat facing each other in matching leather armchairs. Harley scanned the room, seeming to admire its carved mahogany paneling and marble fireplace. *Or maybe he'd gone off the deep end and was checking for hidden microphones.*

She crossed her legs and stirred her coffee. "I've been feeling somewhat torn about our meeting in your office today. The last thing I wanted you to think was that I played Emily's audiocassette for sympathy. That was sacred to me, like showing you my soul. But I was getting pushed out unfairly. I knew the only way to earn your trust was to show you in dramatic fashion that I've walked in Tanya Howe's shoes."

"It was powerful, I'll say that."

"Is that what brings you here tonight? Or is this part of the investigation General Howe referenced in his speech?"

"Investigation?"

"Yes. He said there was an investigation underway to determine whether someone from my staff had leaked confidential details about the investigation—specifically, the ransom demand."

"I suppose you could consider this visit part of that, yes."

Her brow furrowed. "Could you be a little more vague, please?"

He paused, then said, "Between you and me, I think the allegation is totally bogus."

"Oh," she said with a thin smile. "Now we're getting somewhere." Her smile faded. "I guess the tape did make a convert out of you."

"Partly. That, and the simple fact that there was just no way you could have leaked it. You didn't know about the demand. And I didn't tell you."

"You think General Howe leaked it?"

"Do you?"

She sipped her coffee, thinking before she spoke. "I've been thinking about it, trying to figure out what he might have been trying to accomplish. It's true he's not a rich man. I'm sure he doesn't have a million dollars laying around the house. Maybe he thought that leaking the kidnappers' demand would stimulate private donations and help raise the money. Then he blamed the leak on me so the kidnappers wouldn't hold it against the Howe family and take it out on Kristen."

"That's certainly giving him the benefit of the doubt," said Abrams. "But a few things make me wonder whether his motives are all that pure."

Her interest piqued. "What?"

"The first thing is just the whole TV stunt. His declaration of war. It's the kind of macho move you might see in an action-adventure movie, but not in real life. I have to question whether a man who believed his granddaughter's life was on the line would really react that way."

"He is a military man. It may be the only way he knows how to respond."

"True," said Harley. "But his attack on you is also curious. The kidnappers told Tanya not to go to the FBI. Then Howe accuses *you* of leaking the ransom demand to the press. He's basically admitting to the kidnappers that either he or his daughter relayed the demand to the FBI in the first place, against their orders."

"I can't fault him there. That's an inference the kidnappers would make just as soon as the ransom demand became public."

"Possibly. But if he were really concerned about saving his granddaughter, he would have used his airtime to assure the kidnappers that he and his daughter followed their instructions to the letter. He could have said that no one called in the FBI, and that some slimy reporter must have bugged Tanya's apartment and overheard her talking to her mother about the ransom demand. Instead, he essentially admitted he called in the FBI, just so he could take another political shot at you. That troubles me, especially when you consider the more subtle points of his presentation."

"Like what?"

"Most important, the way he talks about his grandchild."

"How do you mean?"

"I noticed it before, but it really came out in

tonight's broadcast. He never refers to Kristen as 'my grandchild.' He rarely even mentions her name. He refers to her as 'this innocent child' or 'this little girl' or 'that poor child.' It's a very subtle thing, but I picked up on this about ten years ago when I moved over to CASKU, one of my first cases. A three-month-old baby disappeared. We interviewed the father. He would talk about how happy he and his wife were when they brought '*our* baby' home—how much they loved little Amy. Then, as the interview progressed, he'd talk about how for three months '*the* baby' just wouldn't stop crying, or '*the* baby' was getting to be a strain on the marriage. You see what I'm getting at? No more 'Amy.' No more '*our* baby.' He was distancing himself. Turned out the father killed '*the* baby.'"

The thought chilled her. "But how could that be in this case? What about the photographs taken the night of the abduction—the ones of Lincoln Howe crying his eyes out in the back of his limo?"

Abrams was deadpan. "There are two kinds of tears. Tears of sorrow. And tears of regret."

Their eyes locked.

"Are you saying that Lincoln Howe arranged for the kidnapping of his own granddaughter?"

"I don't think I'm going that far. Not yet. But think of the possibilities. Some underling stages the kidnapping to push his candidate over the top. Lincoln Howe finds out about it, but he does nothing to stop it. Before he knows it, Reggie Miles is dead and everything's out of control. In a matter of hours he's in deeper than Richard Nixon and his Watergate cover-up."

Allison leaned back, shaking her head in disbelief. "I can't imagine someone like Lincoln Howe actually doing something like that. We've had our differences, but he's a man of integrity."

"He's a man of ambition," said Harley. "Immense ambition."

Allison turned her stare to the logs crackling in the fireplace. Finally she looked back at Harley. "Is this what you came to talk to me about? The possible incrimination of my political adversary?"

"At this point I'm exploring every angle. Including a possible connection between the abduction of Kristen Howe and the abduction of your daughter eight years ago."

Allison knew the danger of false hopes, but the fact that someone other than herself was even considering a possible link to Emily was the best news she'd heard in eight years. "What makes you think there's a connection?"

"Nothing, as yet. But one thing I'd like to examine more closely are the threats you may have received in the past eighteen months or so. See if anything stands out. Particularly anything that might tell us whether the person who took your daughter eight years ago has resurfaced."

Allison thought for a moment, then shook her head. "I can't think of anything. The attorney general gets the usual spate of weird calls and threatening letters from crackpots around the country, all of which the FBI investigated."

"I'll get someone to pull the files, maybe probe a little deeper. I'd like to construct a profile of the person who abducted your daughter, and then compare it to the profile I've constructed of Kristen Howe's kidnapper. To do that, I'll need to flesh out some details that you've probably suppressed in the healing process. I know it's late, and I hate to stir up anything painful. But can we talk?"

She took a deep breath, then smiled sadly. "I'd

better put on another pot of coffee." She started for the kitchen, then stopped and glanced back. Her expression was troubled, a mixture of suspicion and curiosity. "There must be *something* that makes you suspect a connection between Emily's abduction and this kidnapping. Tell me. What is it?"

Harley grimaced, though it didn't seem as though he was holding anything back. Maybe he was just having trouble articulating it. "I think it's just a feeling I have," he said. "Not a goofy groundless thing, like people who think they can pick the winning numbers in the lotto. It's an instinct based on experience."

"And what is your experience telling you?"

"Emily's abduction was very unusual. You don't see many cases where a total stranger actually breaks into a house and snatches an infant right out of her own crib. Emily's abductor took a big risk, and he went to an awful lot of trouble, with the tape recording of her voice and all that. A scheme that elaborate tells me that whoever took her wasn't just after a baby. What they really wanted was to hurt *you*."

Allison shuddered. "How does kidnapping Kristen Howe fit into that scheme?"

"That's the leap of logic, but maybe it's not that big of one. On the surface, it's tempting to look at the way the general has shot up in the polls after Kristen's abduction and infer that her kidnappers are trying to help Lincoln Howe win the election. But maybe that's not their real motivation at all. Maybe they don't really care if Lincoln Howe wins. What they really want is for Allison Leahy to lose. Again, they want to hurt *you*."

She froze, thinking. "But why?"

•

"The more you can tell me, the sooner we'll figure that out." He glanced at her empty cup. "Some more coffee's probably an excellent idea."

"I'm actually immune to the stuff," she said, then shot him a look that drained him. "It's been a long eight years, Harley. Every night's a very long night."

21

The titanium-coated knife hurled through the air, sticking into the plasterboard wall with a quick thud.

Tony Delgado crossed the living room to inspect the damage. Concentric circles drawn in black Magic Marker covered the living room wall, forming the rings of a makeshift dartboard. Inch-long puncture marks dotted the target, most within a few inches of the bull's-eye.

"Good shot," Tony told his younger brother. He yanked the knife from the wall.

Repo sat erect on the couch, stewing in his thoughts.

Tony sucked down the last of his Budweiser, then checked the refrigerator. The twelve-pack his brother had brought with him from Philadelphia was gone. "Repo!" he shouted. "Your turn for a beer run."

"I'm not even drinking."

Tony gave him a friendly pat on the shoulder. "Hey, you didn't kill Reggie Miles, either. But we're all in this together."

The Delgado brothers shared a laugh.

Repo rose from the couch, grumbling. "You two are a couple of real jokesters."

"Just lighten up," said Tony.

Repo turned. "That's your answer to everything. I just gotta roll with it every time you two dickheads change the plan. Well, that isn't the deal I cut. Nobody was supposed to get killed, and there wasn't supposed to be a ransom. All we were supposed to do is hold the girl until after the election."

"That's right. That's what we were supposed to do."

"Then why'd the guy on the news say there was a ransom demand?"

"Because I leaked it to them, that's why. It's just strategy. Kidnapper says don't leak it to the cops, then the kidnapper leaks it to the press. Gets everybody on the other side all fucked up, everybody pointing fingers at each other."

"So the ransom demand isn't for real? It's just a ploy?"

Tony stepped forward, tapping the flat side of the blade against his palm. "You ask too damn many questions, Repo."

"I got as much on the line here as anybody. Is it too much to ask who the hell hired us? Who's in control?"

Tony smiled thinly. "That's two very different questions. Who hired us? That's none of your concern. Who's in control?" He turned and flung the knife at the wall, sticking a bull's-eye. "So long as we got the girl, *I'm* in control."

At 2:00 A.M. Repo lay restless on the couch, staring at shadows on the ceiling in the dark living room, thinking of Kristen Howe alone in the basement. He knew she was terrified. He'd seen it in her eyes. He was the only human being who had looked into those eyes since the abduction. Tony and Johnny had no interest in caring for a twelve-year-old girl, so Repo had volunteered. Every three or four hours he'd don his ski mask to walk her to the bathroom or bring her a sandwich and a glass of water. Tony had ordered him to keep her blindfolded at all times, but Repo figured it would be less scary for her if every few hours she could see that she wasn't buried alive in a coffin or tied to a stake in some imaginary snake pit.

The furnace kicked on, giving Repo a start. Tonight was colder than last, and the drafty old house seemed incapable of warming to a comfortable room temperature. He covered his exposed toes with the blanket, then thought again of the girl. The basement was colder than the rest of the house, and he wasn't sure if the heating vents were open down there. She could be freezing. He slid off the couch, pulled on his trousers, then grabbed his ski mask and headed for the stairway.

He paused halfway down the hall. Loud snoring poured from the master bedroom, where Tony and his brother lay sleeping off a case of beer. He peeked into their room. Sprawled across the bed in their underwear, they seemed more unconscious than asleep. But for the snoring, they almost looked dead—not a wholly unappealing prospect, thought Repo. Quietly he stepped back into the hall and closed the bedroom door.

He stepped slowly toward the door that led to the basement steps, so as not to make a sound. Before opening it, he pulled on his ski mask. He glanced over his shoulder, making sure the Delgados hadn't heard him, then froze. His reflection showed in the bathroom mirror at the end of the hall.

He looked frightening as hell.

He gripped the doorknob as he thought things over. He couldn't let her see his face, but he didn't have to look like a terrorist, either. He pulled off the mask, then grabbed a small hand towel from the bathroom sink and tied it around the lower half of his face. He checked himself in the mirror. He looked like those bank robbers in the old movie westerns. Effective, but not terribly scary. Perfect.

He grabbed the flashlight that was hanging on the wall, then opened the door. He started down the narrow staircase, closing the door behind him.

The wood steps creaked with each step. The light fixture in the stairway was broken, so the narrow beam of the flashlight showed the way. He paused halfway down the steps, taken by the familiar smell. It reminded him of his old house in Philadelphia as a kid, where he'd spent countless hours in a virtual hole in the ground playing Ping Pong and bumper pool. Funny, the way basements all seemed to smell alike.

He stopped at the base of the steps, shining the flashlight ahead of him. Cracked linoleum covered the cold cement floor. It had buckled along the baseboards, where groundwater had seeped in. Mildew stained the corners. Warped sheets of old wood paneling covered the walls, as if some previous owner had made a half-hearted attempt to give the basement a finished look. The small ground-level window, high over the sink, had been boarded from the outside.

Repo fumbled for the lamp on the bar. He switched it on and cut off the flashlight.

In the dim ball of light he saw Kristen lying beneath an old army blanket, her body stretched across the thin mattress of a convertible sofa. Metal cuffs secured one hand to the frame at the top, near the sofa back. Her ankle was cuffed at the opposite end. A black blindfold covered her eyes, and a wide strip of silver duct tape covered her mouth.

Her body tensed with the sudden awareness of someone else in the room.

Repo approached slowly, so as not to startle her, then sat in the chair beside the bed. He leaned forward and whispered, "I'm going to take off your blindfold now."

She didn't move.

He reached behind her head and untied the blindfold. With a gentle tug, it slid out from beneath the pillow. Her long lashes fluttered. Even the dim glow of light from across the basement seemed to bother her unadjusted pupils. Repo watched as she struggled to bring her big brown eyes into focus. Like a sleeping angel, he thought, waking to a nightmare. Finally their eyes met.

She looked confused at first, as if expecting to see the ski mask. She still looked frightened, but less so than before.

"I'm not gonna hurt you," he said in a hushed voice. "And if you just let me help you, ain't nobody else gonna hurt you either."

It was after 3:00 A.M. before Allison finally bid Harley Abrams good night. She headed upstairs, quickly got ready for bed, and quietly crawled beneath the covers beside Peter. He was sound asleep.

She lay on her back, her head sinking into the soft pillow. Her body was exhausted, but her mind was still at work. Just keeping her eyes shut required concentration. They opened instinctively, and as her pupils dilated familiar objects began to take shape in the darkness.

She glanced at Peter. His profile was barely visible, and she wasn't completely sure if she was actually seeing or remembering it. She was good at recalling little details about people—the shape of the eyes, the curve of the cheek. It was an acquired skill, something she'd worked on ever since Emily had disappeared. Memory has a way of improving when it's all you have.

Memory, however, was a two-edged sword. The four-hour conversation with Harley Abrams about Emily had stirred up the bad old days, the sleepless nights. She laid the extra pillow across her eyes, enveloping herself in fluffy goose down. In minutes, the feeling approached sensory deprivation. Hearing nothing. Seeing nothing. Her only connection to the night was the air she breathed. She could feel her eyeballs moving beneath the weight of the pillow. She saw nothing, but the emptiness before her was turning white. As her mind drifted into sleep, the whiteness took shape. A white building. A white door. White columns. The White House . . .

Allison closed the heavy front door at the north portico and stepped into the formal front entrance hall. The State Floor was like she'd never seen it before. Dark and quiet. She flipped the wall switch, lighting the brass chandelier above the grand staircase. She walked to the base of the stairs and called out tentatively, "Hello?"

Her voice echoed. There was no reply. She felt a chill down her spine, a sudden realization. She was home. This was her home. And she was all alone.

She started up the stairs to the executive mansion, the upstairs living quarters. Halfway up she heard a noise. She stopped to listen, then climbed quickly to the top of the staircase.

A long hallway stretched to either side, east and west. Crystal wall sconces provided just enough illumination for her to see all the way to the end of each hallway, right and left. She wasn't sure which way to turn—until she head the noise again, clearer this time.

"Mommy." It was the voice of a young girl, calling from the east bedroom.

Instinctively Allison rushed to the door. She tried the knob, but it wouldn't turn. She pounded with both fists. "Emily!" she shouted. "I'm here! I'm here!"

She shoved with her shoulder, but the door wouldn't budge. Frantically, her eyes searched the hall for a chair or something to help break down the door. Then she froze. At the other end of the long hallway stood a dark-haired girl wearing a pleated pink dress. Allison could barely see her face in the dim lighting, but she could hear the voice as if she were standing right beside her.

"My name's not Emily," she said. "It's Kristen."

Allison sprinted the length of the hall, but the girl disappeared into the bedroom and slammed the door. Again, the knob wouldn't turn.

"Kristen, open the door!" She pounded on the door in frustration, then stopped suddenly, intuitively, as she felt an eerie presence. She turned. At the opposite end of the hall stood a little blond girl wearing the same pink dress. The face was not quite discernible. The voice, however, was plainly heard.

"My name's not Kristen. It's Emily."

"Emily!" She peeled down the hall, past the

center stairwell. She was just a few steps away when the girl ducked back into the room and slammed the door. Allison dove for the knob. This time, it turned. She flung the door open, then stopped cold.

Her heart skipped a beat. It wasn't a bedroom. It wasn't even a room.

She took a deep breath, absorbing the strange surroundings. Thick red velvet curtains shrouded the dark entrance. Four empty chairs faced a brass railing, with more darkness beyond. Allison stepped closer to the rail, then back, frightened. Beyond the rail was a theater full of patrons facing a lighted stage. The audience laughed at one of the actor's lines.

Her mouth went dry. She was standing on a balcony.

A shuffling noise emerged from behind the curtain. She felt the urge to run, but destiny wouldn't allow it. She turned quickly, coming face-to-face with an angry man who resembled no one she knew, yet she had the strange sensation that she knew him well. Her lips were about to utter his name as he aimed his pistol at point-blank range. The thundering crack echoed throughout, robbing Allison of her voice, her sight, and all sense of time. She was falling backward, tumbling over the rail, moving in slow motion. The world seemed to ooze as the cries of a grieving woman filled the old Ford Theater, a haunting replay of the unforgettable words of Mary Todd Lincoln.

"They've killed the president! They've killed—"

"Allison?"

Allison shot up in bed at the sound of Peter's voice. She was soaked in sweat, completely out of breath.

"Are you okay?" asked Peter as he switched on the lamp.

She blinked hard, adjusting to the light. Her heart was racing. She squeezed Peter's hand. "What a horrible dream," she said, her voice quivering. "I think I'm driving myself nuts."

"It's all right. I'm here for you."

"Honest to God, Peter. If they don't find Emily soon, I don't know what I'll do."

"Kristen," he corrected her.

"Huh?"

"You said, 'If they don't find Emily.' You mean Kristen."

Her eyes turned misty. "Of course," she said as Peter held her tight. "I meant Kristen."

22

Harley Abrams caught a few winks of sleep on the airplane, arriving in Nashville at nine o'clock Thursday morning. Tanya Howe's decision to boot the FBI from her home was understandable under the circumstances, and Harley certainly had known other distressed parents who had buckled to a kidnapper's demands to shut out law enforcement. Since the first ransom demand had gone directly to Tanya's home, however, her refusal even to allow the FBI to continue monitoring her telephone could seriously impede the investigation.

Harley arrived at Tanya's house in an unmarked Bucar with a female agent. They carried none of the trappings of the FBI—just a bag of groceries and a casserole dish. He apologized to his colleague for what might appear to be sexist duty, but it was important to demonstrate to Tanya that the FBI could easily come and go from her house in inconspicuous fashion, playing the part of concerned friends or neighbors who would console a grieving mother by relieving her of simple tasks like shopping and cooking which, in a time of crisis, are no longer so simple.

Harley rang the bell and waited.

"Go away, Mr. Abrams." It was Tanya's voice from behind the closed door.

Harley leaned forward. "Tanya, if anybody is watching, it's going to look a lot worse if you turn us away than if you simply let us in. Just greet us as if we were friends, not the FBI."

Thirty seconds passed. The chain rattled and the door opened. In role, Tanya embraced the female agent the way she'd greet a loyal friend, then invited them in and closed the door. Her polite expression faded immediately.

"I told you I don't want the FBI coming to my house anymore."

"I heard," said Harley. "May we sit down and talk, please? If you still feel the same after you've heard the FBI's side of it, I promise we'll respect your wishes."

Tanya looked skeptical, but she took their coats and invited them into the dining room.

Harley and his assistant sat on one side of the table, with Tanya on the other. He took one look at her stern expression and knew he needed an icebreaker—something to cool her contempt. He forced a yawn.

"Excuse me. Didn't get much sleep last night. I was up late talking to the attorney general."

"Is that so?" she scoffed. "Have her spin doctors figured out how she's going to top my father's declaration of war?"

"I wouldn't know about that. But I do want you to know that the FBI had nothing to do with your father's speech last night. That was completely his doing."

"Is that what Ms. Leahy told you to come here and say?"

"She doesn't even know I'm here. As a matter of fact, she and I spent most of the night talking about the abduction of her own four-month-old daughter, eight years ago. They never found her. Never caught the guys, either."

Tanya blinked away some of her rage.

Harley softened his voice, sensing an opening. "I'm working on a theory. Just a theory. No evidence yet. Just trying to see if whoever abducted Ms. Leahy's daughter might also have abducted Kristen. Of course, that will be a very difficult theory for the FBI to pursue if Kristen's mother isn't talking to us."

Her eyes narrowed. "Don't mess with my mind. Just ask what you want to know."

"Fair enough. One of the things that troubled me about Ms. Leahy's case is the manner in which her baby was taken. The abductor broke into the house while she was home, took the baby right out the window. That's a very unusual taking. Most abductions are in public places—the park, department stores. Often the child is tricked or lured away. A stranger posing as an authority figure, a man who offers a boy twenty dollars if he'll help him find his lost dog. Something like that."

"Is that what you think happened to Kristen?"

Abrams shrugged. "Don't know. We have no witnesses. We do know they took the van and that Reggie Miles was killed. He didn't drown. Autopsy showed severe head trauma. That's consistent with a forcible taking. And if both Kristen and Ms. Leahy's daughter were taken by force, that would lend some credence to our theory that there's a common thread."

"I can't see Kristen falling for some ruse," said Tanya.

"Did you warn her about strangers, the tricks they might play?"

"Of course. These days, what mother wouldn't?

But some things you can't teach. Kristen had good instincts. She's a very smart girl."

"Abductors can be clever. Lots of smart kids get abducted."

She shook her head, then smiled sadly. "Let me tell you what Kristen was like. When she was four years old she came home from her first day of Bible study and told me she'd learned all about Adam and Eve. It was so cute the way she told it. They lived in a beautiful garden and had everything they wanted, but God told them not to eat from this one apple tree. Then one day a big snake in the apple tree told Eve to eat the apple. So she did. And so did Adam. That made God angry, so he told Adam and Eve to go find their own garden.

"'Now, Kristen,' I asked, 'what's the moral of that story?' She thought for a few seconds, then looked up at me with this smart expression. 'Mommy,' she said, '*never* talk to snakes.'"

Harley smiled with his eyes.

Tanya's face brightened at the memory, then her eyes clouded. "I can assure you of one thing: Kristen *never* talked to snakes. The only way those monsters could have gotten my Kristen is the same way they got Ms. Leahy's daughter. By force."

"Thank you. That's extremely helpful."

She looked away, then rose and handed both agents their coats. "I think you should go now."

Harley and his assistant rose and followed, slowing as they reached the foyer. "I wish you would reconsider and let me bring back my agents. We need to build some trust here."

"Mr. Abrams, I'm a black woman born and raised in the South. The first time I'd ever heard of the FBI it involved illegal wiretaps the government had put on the phones of black civil rights leaders. The FBI has a long way to go before it can walk into my living room and expect me to trust it." She opened the door, showing him the way.

Harley let his assistant go first, then stopped in the doorway. "I can't defend everything the FBI did in the bad old days under J. Edgar Hoover. But I can tell you this much. The kidnappers are definitely going to contact you. As Kristen might say, you are going to talk to snakes. And when you do, you're going to wish the FBI was right there with you." He flashed his most sobering look, then turned and headed for his car.

After a fitful night, Allison ended up oversleeping for her 9:00 A.M. campaign strategy meeting. It was the first chance for high-level strategists to convene in one place since Tuesday's abduction. She was twenty minutes late by the time she reached the Leahy/Helmers national campaign headquarters on South Capitol Street.

It tickled her to see that the big "Leahy for President" banner was still blaring its message to the stodgy Washington law firm directly across the street, the one that had rejected her résumé a quarter of a century ago. Thirty minutes with the hiring partner—a blue-blooded Yale man—had made it abundantly clear that she wasn't about to get the job. Not only was she a woman, but she was from a state school that wasn't even *geographically* close to the Ivy League. His obligatory offer to take her to lunch had come across like a consolation prize for the small-town girl. Allison declined, then put on her best Ellie Mae Clampet accent and said, "What I'd really like, mister, is to go for a ride on the underground train." The moron had actually given her a buck with directions to the nearest Metro station. She'd spent the rest of the day in the Hall of Presidents at the National Portrait Gallery, dreaming.

Allison left her Secret Service agent at the doorstep and rushed inside.

"Morning, Ms. Leahy," said the young woman at the photocopy machine. "They're waiting in the war room."

"Thank you," she said with a polite smile, then rushed down the hall to the main conference room. She stopped just as she reached the closed door, overhearing some choice words from her strategist, David Wilcox.

"I don't give a shit how Allison feels about this," said Wilcox.

Allison kept her place outside the door, just listening.

"The fact is," he carried on, "Kristen Howe's abduction is going to decide the election. First the sympathy factor vaulted Howe into the lead. Then those wonderful weepy photos of the general gave us a boost. Now his declaration of war against criminals has put him back in the lead. It's not a question of whether we politicize the abduction. It's *how* we do it."

"I'm not so sure," came the response.

Allison recognized the genteel southern accent of her vice presidential running mate, Governor Helmers.

"After that speech last night," said Helmers, "I honestly think that poor girl's a goner. I'm still on the campaign trail, and Allison should be, too. The pledge she made at her press conference to stop campaigning and focus on the abduction is all wrong. She needs to stay as far away as possible from the investigation. Let the stink fall all over Howe and the FBI when they pull that girl's body out of the Potomac."

"We can't just stand back and wait for that to happen," said another man, her media consultant. "What if the girl lives?"

Gee, thought Allison, still standing in the hall. *What a shame that would be.*

"No way she'll live," said another. "I bet she's dead already."

"Okay," Wilcox replied. "Let's assume worst-case scenario. She's dead, but we don't find out about it until after the election. Then what?"

"What do you mean, *then* what?" replied Governor Helmers. "It's too late. The election's over."

Wilcox said, "That's my point. We need to be proactive here."

"What do you have in mind?"

There was a pause. Allison leaned closer to the door, straining to hear the response. Finally she heard Wilcox's voice again.

"We should talk about the attorney general's daughter. Play up the courageous way Allison endured the abduction of her own child. The way she turned her own personal suffering into a nationwide crusade to increase public awareness of the dangers children face. The legislation she fought for. All of the work she did with the National Center for Missing and Exploited Children and the Coalition for America's Children before she became attorney general."

Helmers said, "She won't be thrilled about doing that."

"It's the only way," said Wilcox.

"Let me put it another way. She *won't* do that."

Wilcox said, "Okay, forget that angle. The truth

is, merely reciting her distinguished résumé isn't going to cut it anyway. The only way to neutralize Howe's momentum is to personalize the loss of Allison's daughter for the American public."

"What do you mean, personalize it?"

"Resurrect it. Let the people know what Allison went through."

"Forget it, David."

"I'm talking subtle things. I don't know," he said lightheartedly. "Maybe they can pull her daughter's old picture out of archives and start running it on milk cartons again."

Helmers chuckled. "Oh, *that's* real subtle. While we're at it, why don't we trot out a new campaign slogan? Allison Leahy—the scarlet letter president. Don't think adultery. Think abduction."

Laughter filled the room. Allison pushed the conference door open and stood in the doorway. The laughter ended.

"That's a pretty catchy slogan," she said, glaring at Helmers. Her gaze turned to Wilcox. "But I think I prefer the milk cartons."

The men stewed in their silence. Finally, Wilcox spoke up. "Allison, we, uh—"

"Don't even try to explain, David. Just carry on without me. And get used to it. Because win or lose, that's where you'll be after this election—without me." She turned and hurried down the hall.

Wilcox ran after her. "Allison, we need to talk."

She wheeled and faced him. Her face flushed with anger. "From the very beginning, I laid down one inviolable rule in this campaign. No one was going to make a campaign prop out of my daughter. Did I not say that?"

"Allison—"

"Did I not say that?" she pressed.

"Yes. You said it. But—"

"But you just don't care. Imagine what it's like to actually see your own daughter's picture on a milk carton, or to see her picture on the TV screen at the post office, along with a hundred other kids who've been missing for years and who will probably never be found. Imagine going to the mall or grocery store and checking every baby carriage out of the corner of your eye, thinking maybe it's her. And then imagine—just *imagine*—your own campaign strategist coming up with the brilliant idea of trotting out her memory for political exploitation."

"I wasn't serious."

"You *were* serious. Don't make it worse by lying to me. Please, just stay out of my sight for a while." She turned and charged out the door.

A blast of frigid air from the latest cold front greeted her on the sidewalk, along with her Secret Service escorts. She didn't slow down until she was sliding into her limousine. The car door slammed, and she watched from the backseat as the limo pulled away. Wilcox gave chase along the sidewalk. She couldn't hear his voice, but his pained expression filled the window. His breath steamed in the cold air as he tapped frantically on the glass and mouthed the words, "Allison, *please!*"

"Step on it," she told the driver.

The limo burst into traffic, leaving Wilcox at the curb, shivering in his shirtsleeves.

23

Kristen Howe is not afraid.

Flat on her back in a chilly basement on a too-soft mattress, she kept thinking that same thought over and over again. With eyes shut, the words fixed in her brain like a mantra, just like when she was five years old and afraid to sleep with the light off. Most of the time, the voice in her head sounded like her own. But when the demons ran wild, when her racing heart pushed her to the brink of panic, she would hear her mother's calming voice.

Kristen Howe is not afraid. It's only her imagination.

This time, however, she knew she wasn't imagining. If it was all just in her mind, then how come she couldn't talk? She had tried to speak aloud—to step out of her mind and actually tell herself she was not afraid—but the tape on her mouth was definitely for real. The metal cuffs digging into her wrist and ankle were real, too. The pain in her bulging bladder was real. The footsteps and strange voices she'd overhead were all too real.

Yet, at times, none of it seemed real.

She remembered walking toward the high school, taking her usual route from the college campus. She remembered the van following too close and stopping at the curb. The passenger door opened. The driver's face was hidden beneath the rubberized Lincoln Howe Halloween mask. A man who definitely wasn't Reggie grabbed her by the arm. The rest, however, was a total blur. Flying through the air and tumbling to the floor. A thick blanket of blackness over her eyes. A stabbing pain in her thigh like the jabbing of a needle. And finally, a weird, weightless sensation that numbed her body, the way she felt when she'd had her tonsils removed.

The next thing she knew she was waking up, her hands and feet bound, her mouth taped shut. At first, the blindfold made it impossible to discern whether she was really awake. When she closed her eyes, she saw nothing. Eyes open, nothing still. It was yesterday, or maybe the day before, when the blindfold came off for the first time. The sudden burst of brightness had overpowered her eyes, and when she finally focused she saw a man in a ski mask. She nearly screamed, but the gag prevented it.

By the fourth or fifth time it was becoming a routine, something to mark the passage of time, a ritual that reminded her she was still alive. The man would come and remove the cuffs. He'd lead her up a flight of stairs to the bathroom and remove the gag and blindfold, then leave her alone with soap and a washcloth, a toothbrush. Then he'd give her something to eat. It became a little less scary each time, but his ski mask definitely gave her the creeps. Even so, his voice wasn't mean or anything. He was actually gentle and attentive to her needs, always asking if she was hungry or warm enough. After a few visits, she knew his voice well. When the men talked upstairs, she could distinguish his voice. So far, she'd been able to pick out three different voices. She couldn't hear everything they said, especially when the furnace was running. But she'd heard enough to know that he was the only one looking out for her, making sure she was clean, fed, and comfortable. She'd even heard him threaten one of the other men, telling him no one was going to hurt the girl. Repo was his name. One of the men had called him Repo.

"Kristen," she heard him say. "It's morning."

It was that Repo guy, and his voice made her shudder. She cringed as he gently removed her blindfold. Kristen opened her eyes slowly, then blinked at the ceiling. The dim light from the lamp on the dresser cast a nebulous glow across the basement. The shutter on the little window above the sink made it impossible to tell whether it was night or day. She had no idea if it was actually morning. She would just have to take his word for it.

Last night had been weird. He had talked for several minutes, exactly how long she didn't know. The edge to his voice had made her nervous. He hadn't said anything bad. But even if he weren't a kidnapper, she would be inherently suspicious of any stranger who so desperately wanted her to believe she was safe with him.

Her eyes fixed on a crack in the ceiling. Standing before the lamp, the man cast a shadow across the bed, darkening her torso. She didn't dare look at him, couldn't find the courage to turn her head in his direction again. Last night, when he'd removed the blindfold, she'd caught a glimpse of him without the ski mask, and she didn't want to see more. But as the silence lingered, she felt compelled to look, the way the young eyes of curiosity eventually peer out from the beneath the covers late at night.

Kristen Howe is not afraid, she thought, repeating her mantra. Then she turned her head a smidgen to the left.

She caught her breath, containing her fright. She'd seen the same thing last night, but it still startled her. The ski mask was gone. He was wearing a towel or something over his face, letting her see the top half of his face. She looked away and closed her eyes tightly.

Her hands shook as she wrestled with confusion. He was changing the routine, acting more friendly—like he wanted her to talk. She never talked to strangers, *never* talked to snakes. And she knew that "strangers" weren't just the perverts who hung around playgrounds with slimy drool dripping from their chin. "Say no, walk away, and tell an adult"—that was the rule her mother had drilled into her head. It was a good rule to live by before you'd been abducted. But what's a kid supposed to do *after* it happens?

"I'm going to take the gag off now," he said quietly.

Oh, God, she thought. Another switch from the routine. Did he expect her to say something? *Do* something? Her body stiffened as he tugged at the tape, freeing her mouth. She struggled to repeat her mantra and remind herself she wasn't afraid. But she was too scared to remember the simple words, let alone believe them. She could scream, but that seemed pointless. The only people who would hear were the other kidnappers, the mean ones. At least this Repo *seemed* nice.

Her heart fluttered. Screaming was a bad idea.

He might panic and hurt her. Maybe he'd stay calm so long as she stayed calm—or at least if she acted calm. Acting—yes! That was the key. People always said she could sell snowshoes in Jamaica if she put her mind to it. By turning on the charm, she'd even managed to talk Reggie Miles into letting her walk to the high school.

Reggie? she thought. *What happened to Reggie?* Sweet Reggie. The grandfather she'd never had. The simple but wise old man who'd said Kristen was twelve going on twenty-one and destined to be a heartbreaker who could talk her way out of anything.

Maybe that was true. Maybe she could talk her way out of this mess, too, charming the snake into letting her go home. To do that, she'd have to talk to him. She'd even have to be nice to him. She might even have to flatter him.

No way! She was too afraid to pull it off, too afraid to speak. She was lost for the moment, paralyzed with fear. Her mantra, she thought—*say your mantra.* But the words wouldn't come. Finally she heard it—a message from within.

Kristen Howe, don't be afraid, said the voice in her head.

Her spine tingled. It sounded different this time, nothing like her own voice or that of her mother. It was a deeper voice—peaceful and soothing, one that flowed like a friend's embrace from a faraway place, a safer place, a place beyond. It was only in her mind, but it warmed her entire body and calmed her fears, giving her the courage to do exactly what she needed to do.

She heard the voice of Reggie Miles.

"Time for breakfast," said Repo.

A lump filled her throat. Did she dare speak?

Listen to the voice, she told herself. *Listen to Reggie.* Her mouth struggled to form the words—any words, the first thing that came to mind. "Could—could I maybe have some cereal today?" she asked quietly.

"Sure, what kind do you want?"

"Froot Loops." She cringed inside. She didn't even like Froot Loops, but it was all she could think of.

"I'll get some for you."

A noise rattled above, startling her. A door creaked upstairs, maybe the bathroom or another bedroom. One of the other men was definitely awake.

Repo said, "I gotta go now. No matter what happens, you can't tell the other guys we talked. Okay?"

She nodded timidly, then held her breath as he gently replaced the gag and blindfold. As his heels clicked on the wood stairs, she counted his steps. The door opened, then closed. He was gone.

That wasn't so bad, she thought. She'd taken the first step, started a dialogue. Maybe this Repo really was her ticket out of here. Maybe he wasn't just pretending to be nice. After all, she'd overheard the men talking upstairs, through the old floorboards. She'd even heard Repo stand up to the others, telling them he wouldn't let them touch her.

Panic suddenly gripped her. She realized her mistake.

Kristen Howe is not afraid, she told herself, shivering at the thought of what the other snakes might do when Repo went out to buy her stupid Froot Loops.

* * *

The limousine stopped at the traffic light near Pennsylvania Quarter. Allison sat alone with her thoughts as she glanced at the mix of condominiums, retail outlets, and restaurants that had rejuvenated a three-block stretch of Pennsylvania Avenue between the White House and the Capitol, the district's most famous parade route. Her stomach was still in knots from the outburst at her campaign headquarters. She still wasn't sure if she had simply sounded off or if she'd actually just fired her campaign strategist with less than five days remaining to the election.

The outburst, of course, was a cumulative thing, which had begun with the photographs. Maybe it was true that Wilcox had had nothing to do with that bozo-looking character snapping pictures of Allison down by the river in Nashville. But she was less convinced that the Lincoln Howe photos had leaked to the press with absolutely no help from Wilcox.

She shook her head, clearing her thoughts. One thing, however, wouldn't shake from her mind: the bad joke her running mate had made about Allison, "the scarlet letter president." Life had become such a whirlwind since Kristen's abduction, she'd almost forgotten that her precipitous slide in the polls had begun with the bogus adultery charges. The more she thought about it, the more it seemed the two incidents—the adultery accusation and the abduction—were too proximate to be unrelated. And Governor Helmers's joke had actually sparked a theory on *how* they might relate.

She picked up her phone and rang Harley Abrams on his cellular phone.

"Harley, there's something I have to show you. Can you meet me at Justice?"

"I won't be back from Nashville for another couple of hours or so. What is it?"

"It's—I can't describe it. You have to see it."

"Fax it to me."

"You have to see the original, and I don't want copies floating around anyway. It's too confidential."

"I've been known to handle a few confidences in my career," he scoffed.

"This isn't entirely business. It has to do with me, personally."

There was a pause on the line. "Can it wait until I get back?"

"Yes," she said, reeling in her excitement. "Barely."

24

The office suite of the attorney general was on the fifth floor of the Justice Building, overlooking busy Pennsylvania Avenue. Unlike many of her predecessors, Allison had resisted the urge to turn her small private office into a self-congratulatory shrine. No plaques, commendations, or laminated personal correspondence from the president covered her walnut-paneled walls. A colorful impressionist landscape brightened one wall. Over the fireplace hung a portrait of former Attorney General Robert Kennedy walking on a New England beach. The furniture was early American, some period, some tasteful reproductions. Legal and literary volumes filled the bookshelves behind her desk. Perched above the door was a framed needlepoint inscription that her proud mother had stitched. It quoted the stone-chiseled motto outside the Justice Building, with an added parenthetical: "'Justice is the great interest of man on earth,'" it read, "(and of at least one woman)." An eight-by-ten photograph of her husband graced her leather-top desk. On the credenza, next to the telephone, rested a small framed portrait of a younger Allison Leahy holding her infant daughter.

The intercom buzzed. "Mr. Abrams is here," announced her secretary.

"Send him in, please."

The door opened. Allison welcomed him, offering a seat on the couch. She took the chair facing the window, then laid an expandable file on the coffee table.

"This is what I wanted you to see," she said.

Harley reached for the file, but Allison withdrew.

"A little background first," she said. "Confidential background, I would add. What I'm going to tell you, I haven't even told my husband. I feel since you and I talked last night that we have an understanding. A bond of trust. I hope I'm not wrong."

Harley looked her in the eye. "You're not wrong."

She flashed a thin smile of relief, then spent the next ten minutes telling him about Mitch O'Brien, the awkward reunion at the Fountainbleu Hotel in Miami Beach last August, and the disastrous follow-up a week later in Washington at the gala—including Mitch's drunken blowup and her fear that someone may have overheard.

"About two weeks after that," she continued, "I received this in the mail." She removed a large manila envelope from the file. "You can see it was addressed to my home, marked personal and confidential. Since there was no return address, I brought it to the Justice Building the next morning to have it X-rayed. It checked out, so I opened it. And this is what I found."

Her hand shook—just as it had the first time, more than a month ago—as she removed an enlarged black-and-white photograph. She laid it on the table.

"That's me, obviously."

He leaned forward for a closer look. The photo

had been defaced. In bright red strokes, the letter A had been scrawled across Allison's forehead.

"Obviously the artwork was the handiwork of whoever mailed me the photograph. As is the message on the back." Allison flipped it over, revealing a handwritten message in the same red scrawl.

It read, *Doesn't stand for attorney general, bitch*.

Harley looked up. "What did you do with this when you got it?"

"I just kept it."

"Why didn't you give it to the FBI?"

"Like I said, I get plenty of these threats. The last thing I wanted was a scandal that would have the FBI beating on my ex-fiancé's door. I was pretty convinced it came from Mitch, who I saw as harmless. I just let it go."

"So why dig it up now?"

"Because now I'm not so sure it's harmless."

Harley leaned back. "What's your thinking?"

"I'm sure you're aware that my recent political troubles didn't start with Kristen's abduction. They started with phony accusations of adultery after the last debate."

"Yeah, so?"

"I figured that if this scarlet letter photograph related to anything, it might relate to the recent adultery scandal—which all started less than a month after I got this photograph. But then just this morning I overheard my running mate make this bad joke. A slogan, actually, that went something like this: Allison Leahy, the scarlet letter president—don't think adultery, think abduction."

Harley glanced again at the photograph. "So you're thinking that when your secret admirer scribbled on the back of this photo that the A doesn't stand for attorney general, he didn't mean it stood for adultery."

"It stood for abduction," said Allison. "Maybe it was a warning or a foreshadowing of things to come."

"Seems a stretch."

"It does in the abstract. But think of it in the context of your theory that the same person who abducted my Emily also abducted Kristen Howe. Then it's not such a stretch. It's a bridge between the two."

He stroked his chin, apparently warming to the idea. "Let me take everything over to headquarters for analysis. I also think we should track down Mitch O'Brien, find out once and for all if he sent it. Is he still in Miami?"

"As far as I know."

"I'll send out a couple of Miami field agents."

"Let me at least try to reach him by phone before you call out the troops. The history is kind of complicated here."

"I'd prefer to catch him cold. He is a lawyer, after all. Give a lawyer time to think about it, and they'll never talk to law enforcement. But catch them cold, and they're often as stupid as the rest of us. We don't have time to dance with this guy. Time is of the essence."

"Yeah," she scoffed, thinking of the presidential election less than five days away. "You're telling me."

"By the way," said Harley. "I'll do my best to keep the history between you and O'Brien under wraps, but sometimes these things have a way of leaking. I just mention that, since you said you haven't even told your husband about your . . .

your recent interaction. He probably wouldn't appreciate hearing thirdhand that your drunken ex-fiancé was virtually stalking you, professing his undying love for you one day and then cursing you out the next, maybe even sending you threatening mail. He could even think there's more to it than that."

"I realize that," she said with a sinking sense of dread. "I guess maybe it's time Peter heard the truth. From me."

General Howe entered the White House through the east side residence gate so as not to be seen by the press corps hovering in front of the West Wing, near the Oval Office. The president's personal assistant led him to the Map Room, though he knew the way.

The last time Lincoln Howe had visited the inner sanctums of White House power, President Sires was midway through a tumultuous first term, urging the general to withdraw his resignation as deputy secretary of defense. Sires had assured him that the existing secretary was on his way out, and that the top job at the Pentagon would be his within six months. Howe had yet to declare himself a member of any political party. Although presidents sometimes did look outside their own party to fill their cabinet, Howe had chosen not to remain part of a Democratic administration once he'd resolved in his own heart that he was a Republican with presidential aspirations of his own.

Howe sat in the armchair near the fireplace. Over the mantel hung a small map of Europe with red circles and blue markers. The plaque beside it said it was the last situation map of the Allied and

Axis armies that Franklin Roosevelt saw before his death, just weeks before the Nazi surrender. The general thought it fitting that nearly all great presidents had served in times of war or were themselves war heroes. Washington. Lincoln. Both Roosevelts. He was of the same great tradition. Sires, he knew, was not.

"I saw your speech last night," said President Sires. He was wearing a dark suit and striped tie, his power look. He lowered himself into the matching silk armchair, half-facing Howe, half-facing the fireplace. "Very high drama."

Howe showed no reaction. "It wasn't intended to be dramatic. You just never know how you're going to react in these situations. Until it happens to you."

"Still, it surprised me. I'd always heard that Lincoln Howe is the kind of general who had learned from his experience in Vietnam. Never declare war without a clear set of objectives. Never fight a war you can never win."

"I think my objectives are clear. It's time this country protected its children."

"I'm not talking about your declaration of war against child abductors. I'm talking about your declaration of war against this administration."

Howe bristled. "I'm not sure I follow you, sir."

"Lincoln, I've worked hard over the past eight years to become the education president. I'm proud of my record. As a lame duck president, my record is all I have. Education is my legacy."

"With all due respect, the use of military forces to combat child abduction has nothing to do with education."

"No. But the challenge you issued last night to this administration is a direct attack on my legacy.

You put me on the spot on national television and asked me to sign an executive order that directs the military to round up child abductors. I'm sure plenty of people at home are thinking, yes, let's do it. They forget about the Nazi concentration camps. They forget what our own country did to Japanese Americans during the Second World War. They suddenly need to be reminded that using the military against civilians has a rather catastrophic track record in the course of world history. Your rhetoric puts me in a no-win situation. If I sign this order, the final and most memorable act of my presidency will in the long run leave me branded as the reactionary fool who pandered to hysteria and tried to turn the United States into a fascist military state. You know I'm not going to do that. But by the same token, I don't want to be remembered in the short term as the bleeding-heart liberal who was soft on child abductors."

"I'm sorry you see it that way."

"No you're not," he said sharply. "No one who has devoted his life to defending this country's freedoms could be sincere about a plan to turn the military against its own citizens."

"You think I was bluffing?"

"I know you were. Using the military this way is probably illegal, but let's put that aside. There are two ways we can handle this. One is for you to go back on television and bad-mouth me for refusing to call out the military in aid of your granddaughter and other defenseless children."

"That has definite appeal."

"And it has definite consequences. I would naturally be forced to respond in kind."

"Not to be crass," said Howe, "but just how do

you intend to hit a man whose granddaughter has just been abducted?"

"This is highly confidential, but my sources tell me that the FBI is actually considering the possibility that the abduction of Kristen Howe was planned and executed by your supporters. Possibly even with your blessing."

"That's bullshit," Howe said in an icy, clipped tone.

"It's not bullshit if it's leaked from the White House."

"Mr. President, you *know* that's not the truth."

He smiled wryly. "The truth? That's such an elusive concept. I had a strategist once who had an interesting definition of it. The truth, he said, is that which cannot be proved false."

The general stiffened.

President Sires leaned back in his chair. "Just four more days till the election, General. You think in four days you can prove that neither you nor your supporters had anything to do with an abduction that may single-handedly propel you into the White House?"

He glared. "What are you proposing?"

"Personally, I like alternative number two: You and I simply agree to say nothing more about this. I make no further comment on your granddaughter's abduction. And you say nothing more about me signing an executive order to call up the military."

"Surely the press won't just let it die."

"And our response will be firm but reasonable: In the interest of Kristen's safe return, I will not comment on the investigation strategy at this time. You think you can say that, Lincoln? Or do you want to see just how leaky that White House plumbing can be?"

"Is your legacy really that important to you?" he asked in disbelief.

"Is becoming the next president really that important to *you*?"

Howe grimaced, then rose from his chair and looked out the window. Finally, he drew a deep breath as he turned and faced the president, looking him straight in the eye.

"In the interest of Kristen's safe return," he said in the voice of an obedient soldier, "I will not comment on the investigation strategy at this time."

Repo was out of breath as he raced in from the cold. The kitchen door slammed behind him. He leaned against it, clutching the plastic bag of groceries. He hadn't wanted to leave Kristen alone with Tony and Johnny any longer than necessary, so he'd sprinted down and back from the convenience store at the corner. He checked the clock on the stove. The entire trip took only fourteen minutes.

Three times longer than it took those goons to kill Reggie Miles.

A wave of concern washed over him. He dropped the bag of groceries on the kitchen counter and pulled off his jacket, hat, and gloves.

"What did you get?" asked Tony as he entered the room.

Repo pushed the bag beyond Tony's reach. "Just a few things."

"Let me see." He grabbed the bag and looked inside, then made a face. "Froot Loops? Hey Johnny, look at this. Repo went out and bought us some Froot Loops."

Johnny strutted around the corner, smirking. He was wearing jeans and a muscleman's T-shirt. "Froot Loops? Hell, I'm a Lucky Charms man, myself."

Repo said, "It's for the kid, asshole."

"For the *kid*? You ran out in the freezing damn cold to buy cereal for the kid? What, you trying to get your cock sucked or something?"

"Don't even joke about that."

"What, you afraid Tony and me might get there first?"

Repo grabbed him and pushed him against the refrigerator. "I said *don't*!"

"Hey!" shouted Tony, breaking them apart.

Johnny stepped back and shook it off. Repo was seething as he backed away slowly.

Tony tossed the cereal box on the counter. He looked at Johnny, then glared at Repo. "You went down to see her last night. I heard you going down the stairs."

"What about it?"

"And now you're out buying her favorite cereal."

"She's gotta eat."

Tony laid his hand on Repo's shoulder. His voice had a paternal yet threatening tone, like the Godfather. "You disappoint me, Repo. I always told everybody that Repo was the kid to watch. Young but dependable. Lots of promise. I brought you in on this job because I thought of you like Johnny, my own brother—like family. We're like a little family, the three of us. Except that Johnny and me, we're the only ones in this family who committed murder. That means we got more at stake than you do. And now you're getting chummy with the girl. That makes me very nervous. It makes me wonder, you know, if maybe Repo is going to sell the rest of the family down the river."

"I'm not going to sell anybody out."

Tony shook his head. "You've lost our trust."

Repo shifted nervously. "What are you saying?"

"You gotta earn it back."

"How?"

Tony's expression changed. The jaw tightened. The eyes became dark, menacing slits. "As soon as we get the money, the girl dies. And you'll be the one who kills her."

25

Downtown Washington seemed awash in shades of gray. Overcast skies were a perfect match for the old limestone buildings and marble monuments. Trees stood leafless in Lafayette Square, the impeccably landscaped park north of the White House, directly across Pennsylvania Avenue. As the black limousine pulled from the White House driveway, Lincoln Howe glanced at the circle of protesters in the square. Their signs and slogans decried American exploitation of child labor in foreign countries. He thought of the way President Sires had just obsessed over his legacy, then thought of his own televised speech last night against child abduction. Suddenly it clicked. He had yet to be elected, but he'd already settled on a legacy of his own: Lincoln Howe, the children's president.

The thought pleased him.

"How did the meeting go?" asked LaBelle. He was seated in the rear, across from the general.

"Just fine." The clipped tone made it clear he didn't want to talk about it.

The limo stopped to allow the protesters to cross Pennsylvania Avenue. General Howe's gaze turned toward Lafayette Square, fixing on the huge bronze of Andrew Jackson on horseback in the center. "The Battle of New Orleans," he muttered in a hollow voice.

"Excuse me?" said LaBelle.

"One of General Jackson's most famous military victories." He shot a look of disapproval. "Don't you know anything about the war of eighteen-twelve?"

"Only the year in which it was fought, sir." He checked his watch, mindful of the general's tight schedule.

"Buck?" he said pointedly. "Did you know that black soldiers fought in the Battle of New Orleans?"

He paused, sensing a purpose for the digression. "No, sir. I didn't."

"General Andrew Jackson himself promised to give a tract of land to every black man who would join his army of irregulars and fight the British. They signed up in droves. They fought bravely. Many of them died." His eyes narrowed. "Do you know what they got for their sacrifice?"

"Land, is what I thought you said."

"They got *nothing*. Those courageous black soldiers got nothing but lies and empty promises—straight from the lips of a distinguished general in the United States Army who went on to become one of this nation's most respected presidents." He shook his head, steaming yet again over his meeting with the self-proclaimed education president. "Legacies," he scoffed. "They're all such bullshit anyway."

For once, LaBelle could think of nothing to say.

The telephone rang. It was General Howe's personal line, limited to a handful of callers. He swallowed the bitterness in his throat, then answered on the second piercing ring.

"Sweetheart, it's me," his wife said.

The general glanced up. LaBelle busied himself in his papers, pretending not to listen. Howe spoke softly into the phone. "Where are you, Nat?"

"Still in Nashville. Tanya and I have been talking. She's very upset."

"Can't the doctor prescribe something?"

The line crackled with her sigh of frustration. "That's not the issue."

"I'm sorry. Tell me."

"Well," she struggled, "it seems Tanya wants to pay the ransom." She paused, then added, "And I do, too."

He went rigid, gripping the phone. "Let me get something straight. Does Tanya have a million dollars?"

"Of course not."

"Check our bank book. Do we have a million dollars?"

"No. But you can get it. Surely if you call in some favors we can raise the money."

"No. Absolutely not."

"But, Lincoln. Please."

"Nat, I went on national television last night telling the kidnappers I would never pay their ransom, even if I had the money. I can't back off that position less than twenty-four hours later."

"Is that all you're concerned about? Looking tough to voters?" Her voice was shaking.

"This has nothing to do with votes. It's simple negotiation strategy. We have to be firm. I told them no dealing, and I meant it. Trust me on this."

"I'm scared. We're both scared. I have this horrible feeling that they'll really kill Kristen if we don't pay the money." Her voice trailed off. She was sobbing into the phone.

He swallowed hard, toughening his voice. "Natalie, get hold of yourself. I said no. Don't fight me on this."

She sniffled, then drew a deep breath. "I'm sorry. What do you want me to tell Tanya?"

"Tell Tanya—" He paused, unable to find words.

"That you're doing it for Kristen?" she suggested.

"Yes," he said flatly. "Tell her that."

Allison had been so busy she'd actually forgotten to eat lunch. One of her first official acts as attorney general had been to shut down the private dining room with its personal staff that filled the north end of her office suite, reasoning that the Justice Building had a perfectly fine cafeteria right in the basement. She called down for soup and a salad, and at three o'clock her secretary plopped it on her desk with a can of Diet Pepsi. The phone rang just as she popped open the soda, causing her to start and spill it all over. A garden salad with raspberry-cola vinaigrette dressing was strangely tempting, but she pushed it aside, figuring she had about enough caffeine coursing through her veins anyway.

Her secretary popped back into the office. "It's Harley Abrams on line three."

Allison snatched up the phone. "What did you find out?"

"I just heard from our Miami field office. They can't find O'Brien."

"What do you mean they can't find him? They're the FBI."

"They checked his condo. Nobody home. They went down to the marina. Apparently he has a boat rental place there."

"Right. Mitch used to be a criminal defense lawyer in Chicago, but he burned out and took time off a few years ago to sail all over the world, all by himself. When he came back, he just quit practicing, moved to Miami, and started renting out sailboats."

"Well, he hasn't rented one in over two weeks. It's a little difficult to nail down specifics with a guy who lives alone and works for himself, but the last time anybody saw him was a few days before Halloween."

"Maybe he's on another sailing trip."

"Maybe. But the timing is somewhat suspicious."

"What are you suggesting?"

"I don't know. But there's one thing I'd like you to do. I know there's at least one huge difference between the abduction of your daughter and this kidnapping—namely, you never got a ransom demand. But this O'Brien thing has me intrigued. I could have somebody else do this, but you know more than anyone about your daughter, and we're running out of time."

"I can do it. What?"

"I'd like you to get your hands on the files, the newspaper articles, everything you have on Emily's abduction. And I want you to look—look real hard—for parallels with this case."

"What kinds of things am I looking for?"

"I'll make a checklist and fax it over."

"Okay. I'm getting pressured to start campaigning again, but I can certainly put it off for this. I mean, if you really think—oh, forget it."

"If I think what?"

Her heart swelled, but she was almost afraid to ask. "Harley, let's just assume there is a connection. We both know the statistics on child abduction—how the passage of time affects recovery. But put the dismal data aside and just listen to your gut. After all these years, do you think there's a chance we could still find Emily?"

He paused, choosing his words carefully. "Let's go one step at a time here, okay?"

She nodded wearily, glancing at an old photograph of her and Emily on the credenza. "Right. Just one step at a time."

Tanya and her mother sat in silence in the family room. The drapes were drawn, and the television was off. A lamp on the end table provided the only lighting. The mantel clock ticked above the redbrick fireplace. Tanya stared nervously down at her hands. A neighbor's dog barked across the street, making her jump.

Her mother looked on with concern. "Sweetheart, why don't you try to get some sleep?"

She looked up, eyes glassy. She just shook her head.

The telephone rang, giving them both a jolt. Tanya rose and grabbed the phone on the end table.

"Hello," she answered.

"General Howe broke the rules." The voice was deep and garbled, altered by some kind of mechanical device, like the anonymous informants who appeared as silhouettes on television news shows.

Her eyes widened. "Who is this?"

"I'm national chairman of the Save Kristen Coalition. I'm calling for contributions."

"Is this a crank?"

"Would a crank know that Kristen's school ID was on the back of the ransom demand?"

Tanya shivered at the realization—it was *him*. On impulse, she hit the record button on her answering machine, taping the call. "Please"—her voice shook—"don't hurt my daughter. You can have whatever you want. Just let her go."

"I told you what I want. A million dollars. By tomorrow morning. And no cops."

"I want to give it to you. Really I do."

"That's not what your father said on TV last night."

She winced, silently cursing her father. "Don't listen to him. Just deal with me, all right? I'll get you your money, and I'll keep the cops out of it. I promise. Just don't hurt Kristen."

"What do you mean, you'll get the money? Do you have it or don't you?"

"I don't have it, but I can get it. I just need a little time."

"You've got until tomorrow morning."

"I need more time."

"Bullshit. No stalling."

The harshness came through, even with the distortion. Her hand was suddenly trembling. "I'm not stalling. A million dollars is a lot of money."

"I said tomorrow morning."

"I—I don't know." She could hardly speak. "Okay. Tomorrow morning. I'll have it."

"You're lying."

She swallowed hard. "What?"

"You can't raise the money by tomorrow morning. Not without your old man's help."

"No, I can do it. Really. I can." She waited, but there was no reply. A surge of desperation erupted inside her. "Didn't you hear me?" Her voice cracked. "I said I'll do it. I will. God, yes, I *will*!"

"I don't believe you can." The reply was so calm it chilled her. "And you know what, Tanya? I don't trust you, your father, or anyone in your whole damn family. So why don't you stingy black bastards just keep your million dollars. Truth is, the world is going to be a whole lot better place with one less Howe in it."

"No, wait!"

The line clicked, and she heard only the dial tone.

26

Lincoln Howe summoned the key decision makers for a campaign strategy meeting that afternoon. Howe and his campaign director, Buck LaBelle, shared a limo to Washington National Airport. Some were flying in and others would be flying out, so the airport was a logical meeting spot. The refurbished 727 jet was at the gate when they arrived, its clean white fuselage emblazoned with the bright red and blue campaign message: HOWE-ENDICOTT 2000.

Dwight Endicott was the first person Howe saw as he boarded the airplane. The vice presidential candidate had just flown in from Cleveland after two full days of campaigning in the key state of Ohio. Endicott had never served in the military, but he had the broad shoulders, imposing stature, and no-nonsense expression of an ex-Marine. He'd made his mark as the high-profile head of the Drug Enforcement Agency. A best-selling book and several years on the profitable lecture circuit had helped spin his anti-drug message into a larger theme of renewed morality. His campaign trademark was the flash of the V sign, like Churchill or FDR—only Endicott's V stood not for *victory* but *values*. He was the right-wing component of the Republican ticket, an appeasement to the fundamentalists and pro-life advocates who were concerned, if not alarmed, by General Howe's moderate positions on social issues.

"Did you have a good trip?" Howe asked his running mate.

"Ohio's in the bag," Endicott said with a smile.

The candidates moved to the working area of the airplane, a small room just forward of the galley. Bolted-down couches, leather chairs, and a Formica worktable replaced the usual rows of airline seats. Howe and Endicott sat on the couch with their backs to the portal windows. Buck LaBelle sat across the table with John Eaton, a brilliant but sometimes absent-minded pollster who could work miracles with a notebook computer, provided he hadn't inadvertently left it behind in the airport men's room. Seated beside him was Evan Fitzgerald, the media consultant Endicott had insisted be in charge of developing and testing all television ads. Howe respected Fitzgerald's work, even though he was one of those self-important Ivy League snobs whom Howe hated, the kind of guy who would never come right out and tell you he was a Harvard man, but who somehow managed to weave into every conversation a sentence that began with "When I lived in Cambridge . . ."

The plane wasn't scheduled to leave Washington for an hour, and it would be at least thirty minutes before the crew, the campaign staffers, and the traveling media would board. For the moment, the brain trust had the desired privacy. Howe took the opening few minutes telling them about his Oval Office meeting with President Sires.

"The bottom line," he concluded, "is that the president doesn't want me to say another word about calling out the troops to fight child abductors. If I don't put a lid on it, we'll have to contend with a nasty White House leak to the effect that the FBI's investigation is now focusing on someone from my own campaign staff who orchestrated Kristen's abduction to swing the election."

"I say let them leak it." It was Eaton, the pollster, speaking with the open computer in his lap. "My numbers show that people just won't buy it. Men, women, black, white, old, young. It doesn't matter. Ninety percent of the American public believes that your speech last night was made purely out of love for your granddaughter. The mere suggestion that you or anyone around you is behind the kidnapping will be Leahy's political death knell."

LaBelle chomped on his unlit cigar. "I agree with Eaton, but let's take it a step further. First rule of politics: If you've got bad news, out it yourself. Let's not wait for the White House to leak it. Let's do it ourselves, up front. Call a press conference and tell the American people that it's come to our attention that the FBI is focusing on Howe's campaign, and that it's politically motivated propaganda orchestrated by the attorney general's office."

"Wait a minute," said Endicott. The vice presidential candidate extended his arms like a preacher on his pulpit, reeling in everyone. "First of all, do we know for a fact that it *isn't* one of our supporters who's behind the kidnapping?"

An uncomfortable silence shrouded the group. Endicott waited, but no one spoke. "Second of all," he continued, "who said Attorney General Leahy is behind the FBI's investigation of our campaign? Do we know that to be true?"

The silence thickened. The men exchanged glances, saying nothing. Finally Howe spoke.

"It's true," he said, harking back to his conversation with the president, "because it can't be proven false."

LaBelle smiled wryly. "Well, General, I see you've transitioned very well from the rules of war to the rules of politics."

"This *is* war," he said somberly.

Allison reached her home in Georgetown within twenty minutes of her phone call with Harley Abrams, having left the Federal Triangle just before rush hour. With Peter's help, she pulled down more than a dozen dust-covered boxes from the attic.

She flipped through several boxes at random, and chills went down her spine. Inside were yellowed newspaper clippings, a copy of the police report, cards and letters from friends and strangers alike, videotapes of television coverage, flyers and posters offering rewards, and reams of other materials—some relevant, some not so relevant to Emily's abduction. The boxes made it all seem so organized, deceptively so. Much of it was a blur to her, not because of the passage of time, but because at the time it all happened her senses were numb. She knew that she'd attended the Crime Stopper meetings, that she'd personally thanked the hundreds of volunteers who searched the neighborhood. Yet she had little memory of it. The notes of phone calls were definitely hers. She logged every phone call. Reporters who wanted the personal touch to their stories. Well-meaning strangers and their false sightings. The false confessors—sickos who just wanted attention, and the genuinely depraved who had hurt someone else's child and cleansed themselves by confessing to crimes they hadn't committed. There was even a business card from the psychic she'd turned to in utter desperation, an old gypsy woman who held Emily's blanket and picked Allison's wallet, sending her on fruitless and frantic searches in places as far away as Canada.

Allison stepped back from the table, overwhelmed by the memories. In hindsight, it all seemed like a huge hole in her life. The size of the hole was measured in boxes, each bearing a printed date on the outside, starting with March 1992. Allison had never really focused on it before, but at first she'd filled a box a week, then a box a month, then a box a year. The last one had almost nothing in it, as if the boxes themselves were a sign of a lost trail and fading hope.

The boxes were stacked on the dining room table, end to end, in a mound that nearly reached the chandelier. Allison shuddered as she returned to the first box for a more careful review. At worst, it was like opening a grave, but she hated that thought. At best, it was opening old wounds.

"What exactly prompted all this?" asked Peter.

He was standing in the doorway between the dining and living rooms, wiping the attic dust from his trousers. Allison looked up from her seat at the head of the dining room table, peering over the box.

"It's kind of a long story." Her voice strained with dread at the thought of having to tell him about Mitch O'Brien.

"Maybe I can help," he said as he pulled up a chair beside her. "I was there for you then. Why shut me out now?"

"I'm not shutting you out, Peter. Believe it or

not, it's even more complicated now than it was eight years ago."

"It can't be that complicated. Just tell me."

She hesitated, then resigned herself and faced him. "Harley Abrams thinks there's a possible connection between this kidnapping and Emily's abduction."

"Why?"

"Lots of reasons. But I think he's suddenly very suspicious of my ex-fiancé, Mitch O'Brien."

Peter winced. "O'Brien? What does he have to do with this?"

"I don't know. But to be honest, in the back of my mind I've sometimes wondered about Mitch. Was it purely coincidence that I happened to be talking on the phone with him when someone sneaked into my house and stole Emily from right under my nose? Or was Mitch purposely distracting me?"

His eyes widened, as if surprised by the accusation. "But what does that have to do with Kristen Howe's kidnapping?"

"Nothing. But we just found out today that Mitch is missing. Has been missing since some time before the kidnapping."

"You think he's in hiding?"

"I don't know. But there's more. He'd been acting strange a few months before the kidnapping. Before he disappeared."

"How do you know that?"

"I saw him a couple of months ago. A couple of times, actually."

Peter went rigid, then swallowed with trepidation. "What are you telling me?"

The phone rang. Allison paused, as if waiting for Peter to say it was okay to answer. He didn't flinch.

"I'm sorry," she said. "That could be Abrams. I really should get it." She grabbed the phone.

"Hello," she answered.

"Howe won't pay."

Allison bristled. It was a garbled, mechanically disguised voice. "Who is this?"

"Kristen's guardian angel."

Her pulse quickened. "What do you want?"

"I want my money. But like I said, Lincoln Howe won't pay."

"That's his decision."

"Maybe. But what about you?"

"What about me?"

"You saw the general's speech last night. Howe says you're rich, you and your husband. You want to let the girl die and watch your hopes of becoming president die right along with her? Or you want to save the day, hotshot?"

The words caught in her throat. "You're getting in way over your head. This is a very dangerous game."

"It's just simple economics. Supply and demand. I supply the girl. Now here's my demand. A million bucks, cash. By Monday. Pay it, or the girl dies. Be by the phone at eight A.M. We'll talk."

The line clicked.

Allison lowered the phone, momentarily stunned. This was a turn she hadn't seen coming. She turned to face Peter, but his chair was empty.

"Peter?" she called out.

The front door slammed. She ran to the foyer and peered out the window. He was already in his Jaguar. She blinked with confusion, then realized that the telephone interruption must have left him with the wrong idea about her and Mitch O'Brien. When she said she'd seen Mitch a couple of times,

Peter must have thought she'd *seen* him. She flung open the door and ran outside.

"Peter!" she shouted, but it was too late. The car squealed away. Peter was gone.

She felt an impulse to give chase, but there was something even more pressing. She hurried back inside and picked up the telephone, then punched out the number.

"Harley," she said, completely out of breath. "They just called. It's a whole new ball game."

Part 3

27

The quick response surprised even Allison. Ninety seconds after she hit the emergency call button, the first team of FBI agents were at her front door. Secret Service was right behind. Within minutes, the entire block surrounding her townhouse was secured, and checkpoints were posted on every street corner leading in or out of Georgetown. Agents patrolled the neighborhood, searching for any suspicious activity or abandoned vehicles. Police recorded all license tags, which would be run through the National Crime Information Center. Trained dogs sniffed bushes and trash receptacles on the sidewalks and alleys for possible explosive devices.

Inside, Allison's home was becoming a fortress. Agents stood guard at the front and back doors. Forensic teams searched for any signs of an attempted break-in. Harley Abrams arrived with a team of crack technical agents who were eager to take her house high-tech. He was standing in her kitchen, leaning against her refrigerator with a pencil tucked behind his ear, reviewing a checklist on his clipboard.

"Security still needs to come up a notch," he said.

Allison was polite, but firm. "I don't want the FBI moving into my living room."

"There's a townhouse for rent across the street. We're leasing it to set up a satellite command center. A team will be on call twenty-four hours a day. They'll patrol the street on foot, blending right into the neighborhood. Even the homeless guy at the bus stop will actually be one of our agents. If anything happens here, the response time will be virtually instantaneous."

"That's good enough."

"We'll also install additional security cameras, which will feed back to the command center. Our techies are putting up at least eight more to cover every angle of the outside of your townhouse. They'll be hidden in the lamppost, bushes, cars parked on the street. That kind of thing. No one will even notice them. It's your call as to whether you want indoor surveillance."

"Sorry, but I stopped posing naked in front of cameras years ago."

Harley cracked a smile but remained professional. "I would at least recommend phone surveillance."

"I need a private line. Not that I don't trust you, but, well, I don't trust anybody."

"We can install a manual activation switch. Just answer the phone as you normally would. If it's something you want us to hear, just hit the star key and punch eight. An agent will be on the line to record and trace the call."

"That's acceptable."

Harley glanced at the telephone, which was resting on the counter that separated the kitchen from the family room. One of the technical agents was unscrewing the casing, busily rewiring it. "It would have been nice to have the phone monitor in place before this afternoon's call. Although I'm not sure how he got your home number anyway."

"It leaks out. I've always had to change it every few weeks. People hound the attorney general on all kinds of issues—abortion, gun control, capital punishment. You wouldn't believe the number of organizations that pass out my address and phone number to their members."

He nodded, not surprised.

She asked, "Any information yet on the source of the call?"

"He used a cellular phone, and with today's roaming capabilities it could have been placed from Honolulu, for all we know. The phone is a clone—some number he stole from a real estate agent in New York. The phone company picked that up immediately. Their computers are designed to recognize a call on a cloned phone and disconnect it immediately, which protects their legitimate customers from having their numbers pirated. Our kidnappers have obviously figured out a way to override the system. My guess is that every call we get will be on a different clone, each with its own unique frequency and a different roaming pattern."

"So we're not dealing with total dummies."

"At least not technological dummies. We're installing the software to trace any future calls from cellular phones, but naturally it's a little more difficult to pinpoint an exact location when you're trying to measure signal strength and intersecting radio frequencies. I'm sure that's why they're using cellular."

Allison looked away, thinking.

"What's wrong?" asked Harley.

"All this talk about intersecting radio frequencies just got me to thinking about how Emily was abducted. Baby monitors like the one I had operate on radio frequencies. We figured somebody must have eavesdropped on the baby monitor from outside the house to tape-record her noises. That's how they made the tape they left in her crib."

"Allison, just because somebody knows how to clone a cellular phone with an ESN detector they bought at some spy shop doesn't mean he's the same guy who camped outside your house listening to your baby monitor. When I said we're not dealing with technological dummies, I didn't mean to imply there are only five or six people on the planet who know how to do this. Hell, there are probably five or six people sitting at DuPont Circle doing it right now."

"I know," she said, shaking off the thought. "What else do we need to cover?"

"I faxed your notes back to Quantico for our profilers to analyze. Is there anything else you remember about the phone call? Anything you might have left out?"

She shook her head. "I did exactly what you said. As soon as I got off the phone with you, I wrote down everything I could remember, word for word."

"We're obviously treating this call as the real thing. But I didn't read anything in your notes that would confirm one way or the other if this was legitimate, or if it was just some nut pulling a prank. You're the only one who heard his voice, so I need you to listen to something. Just to give us a voice confirmation."

"You have the kidnapper's voice on tape?"

"Yes. They called Tanya Howe this afternoon, before you got your call."

"I know *that.* What I didn't know is that you

had it on tape. I thought she kicked the FBI out of her house."

"She taped it herself. I guess she didn't know it was a felony to tape-record a conversation without a court order or the other person's consent. The manufacturers of these phones always print legal warnings in the instruction manuals, but nobody ever reads them. I trust she won't be prosecuted."

"I think the state attorney in Nashville might see his way around this one. We'll definitely have a problem with an illegal recording if this case goes to trial, but I'll worry about that later."

Harley pulled a cassette tape from his pocket. "Do you have a cassette player?"

"In the family room." She led him from the kitchen to the adjacent entertainment center, near the big screen television.

Harley switched on the amplifier, dropped the tape into the cassette player, and then hit the PLAY button. The speakers hissed. He adjusted the volume to minimize the distortion. Allison leaned forward, listening intently. It began with Tanya's voice, in the middle of the conversation, where she had started taping.

"Please, don't hurt my daughter. You can have whatever you want. Just let her go."

The words pierced Allison's heart. The angst, the desperation in her voice. She closed her eyes and braced herself for the mechanical-sounding response.

"I told you what I want. A million dollars. By tomorrow morning. And no cops."

Her eyes opened, but the room was suddenly spinning. It was any parent's worst nightmare—or was it? All those nights she rushed to the phone hoping for a call about Emily. Nothing ever came, just a few false sightings and some cruel cranks. She'd never talked to anyone who'd actually seen Emily, who knew exactly where she was and had the power to return her. She felt sick to her stomach, selfishly sick, listening to another poor woman agonize over her lost child, yet thinking all the while that Tanya was the lucky one, that she would cut off her arm just for the chance to get Emily back for the mere payment of money.

"Allison?" asked Harley. "Is it the same voice?"

The tape had finished. Allison was ashen. "It's the same voice," she said. "Same disguise, I should say."

Harley sighed, looking her in the eye. "Then you were right. We really do have a new ball game."

Allison looked past him as he spoke. Her attention had shifted to the front door. Peter was standing in the foyer, next to an FBI agent. He seemed flustered. She excused herself from Harley, then met her husband alone in the living room, away from the commotion.

"What the heck is going on?" he asked her.

Allison wasn't sure where to begin. "That phone call I took right before you left. It was Kristen Howe's kidnappers. They want us—you and me—to pay the ransom."

His mouth opened, but words didn't come.

She said, "It blew me away, too. But before we deal with that, I think you got the wrong idea about me and Mitch. When I said I had seen Mitch, that's all I meant. There was nothing romantic between us. There's never been anything romantic with anyone. Not since I met you."

He gave her a funny look.

"That didn't come out right. I mean, there hasn't been anything romantic with *anyone else* since I met you."

He lowered his eyes, then sighed. "I'm sorry I ran out before you could explain."

"It's okay. But maybe now you know why I didn't tell you Mitch had contacted me, even though there was nothing to it."

"I know," he said with a sheepish smile. "It's that curse of being married to a beautiful woman. It can make you crazy jealous."

She kissed him, but she knew he wasn't just being sweet. Peter was not exactly a looker, and having such a beautiful wife sometimes played to that insecurity.

Two FBI agents whisked past them on their way to the kitchen. Peter grimaced, as if overwhelmed by the sudden intrusion of law enforcement. He looked back at Allison, seemingly annoyed. "What a way to live. FBI, Secret Service all over the place." He peered through the window, grimacing at the technical agents wiring the outdoor surveillance cameras. "Guess I better get used to it, huh?"

"Peter, let's be fair. Even before I got back into politics, you had your own corporate security. Some of those guys were just as intrusive."

"I know. But I trusted them."

"I can't change what I am, Peter. And this is not forever."

He nodded, as if to concede. Then he refocused. "What did you tell the kidnappers about the ransom?"

"I didn't really tell them anything."

"How much do they want?"

"A million dollars. By Monday."

His eyebrows rose. "That's a big pot of money."

"I know. But if we don't pay it, they'll kill Kristen."

"And you'll lose the election."

"That's really secondary."

"Is it?" he said, raising a doubt.

"Yes," she said firmly. "It is."

He gave her an assessing look. "Do you want to pay the money?"

"I think you and I need to decide that together."

"I'm asking you. Do you want to pay the money?"

She snagged her lip with her teeth, thinking. "If it were Emily's life on the line, could we come up with a million dollars by Monday?"

"Absolutely."

She looked away, then back at him. "Then the answer is yes. If that's what it's going to take to get Kristen back safely, we should pay it."

"If that's what you want to do."

"That's what I want," she said with conviction.

"I'll take care of it. Don't worry about the money. You do whatever it is you have to do."

She embraced him tightly, her eyes welling with emotion. "Thank you, Peter."

He held her for a moment, then asked, "What are you going to do now?"

She stepped out of his embrace and looked him in the eye. "I think it's time I had a talk with Tanya Howe."

28

The jet engines purred at thirty thousand feet as Allison released her seat belt and reclined in the leather chair. She had stopped flying on the Justice Department's Sabre Liner Jet almost a year ago, ever since she'd announced her candidacy, out of fear that someone would accuse her of misappropriating federal property for her own political purposes. This morning, however, with Harley Abrams at her side, she made an exception.

Allison sipped her coffee from a paper cup, thinking about what she might say to Tanya Howe. She glanced at the clouds drifting outside her window, well beneath the aircraft. White and fluffy, with a perfect blue sky above. It looked like the ceiling in Emily's nursery, the way Allison had hand-painted it before she was born. Her baby would always wake to a bright blue sky, another perfect and happy day. Or so she'd planned.

"Can I ask you a personal question?" asked Harley. He was in the seat next to her. A mess of papers covered the tray table in his lap.

Allison stirred from her thoughts. "Only if I can reserve the right not to answer."

"Deal." He shifted in his seat so he could look at her as he spoke. "Actually, my question is marginally relevant to the investigation. I was thinking about your case last night—Emily's abduction. I conjured up this image of a career-minded, unmarried thirty-nine-year-old state attorney. I couldn't help but wonder, why did she adopt a baby?"

She glanced out the window again, admiring the clouds. Then she looked back and said, "I wish I could tell you I was moved by some noble and selfless agenda, like nurturing a crack baby or rescuing a battered child from abuse. But the truth is, I adopted a baby because I wanted one."

"But how did you come around to actually going through with the adoption?"

"I was engaged to Mitch when I decided to adopt. We talked about it, and I told him I would never have children of my own. Polycystic kidney disease runs in my family, which we didn't know until my brother was diagnosed after he was married. His son got it and died from it. There's no preventive treatment, and it's usually fatal if it develops during childhood, so I wasn't going to take the risk of passing it on to my own child. I also knew it could take a long time to adopt a newborn. So I got on a list before we even set a wedding date."

"And you still adopted, even after you broke off the engagement."

"By the time I ended it with Mitch, I was psychologically ready to have a baby. I was thirty-nine years old. I had already gone through the hassle and expense of preparing for adoption, and I was excited about becoming a mother. So I figured, Why not just go through with it? My mother raised me and my brother without a father. I could do it, too."

"Makes sense," he said, scratching his chin like Sigmund Freud himself. His eyes returned to the notes in his lap.

"My turn," she said, drawing him back.

"Your turn for what?"

"You think this is a court-ordered deposition or something? You're the only guy who gets to ask questions?"

He smirked. "What do you want to know?"

"Something I've just been curious about. It's interesting the way you see me as someone too wrapped up in a career to have children. What about you? A guy who makes a career out of chasing child abductors, with no family of his own. Is this the kind of work that makes you never want to have kids? Or did it just kind of work out that way?"

"Some of the profilers back at Quantico get that way. They see too much. But that wasn't what stopped me." His eyes drifted off to the middle distance. "I was married once. Long time ago. We tried to have children. It just didn't happen."

"Sorry."

"Thanks. That's about all you can say. It always rubbed me the wrong way when friends tried to comfort us by rattling off statistics. After my wife's first miscarriage, they would say things like, 'Did you know that sixty percent of women experience a miscarriage in their lifetime?' Great. I figured these must be the same people who walk up to grieving widows at funerals and say, 'Sorry about your husband, Mrs. Jones, but did you know that a hundred percent of the people on this planet eventually drop dead?' Like that's supposed to make you feel better."

Allison nodded. He had a point. "So you never thought about adoption?"

"We did, but the marriage didn't work out. I was twenty, she was nineteen when we got married. Her heart wandered while I was up to my waist in Vietnamese rice paddies, and I guess I never really got over that. I've been divorced—jeez, forever. More than twenty years now."

"You never found anyone else?"

"My, this *is* getting personal."

She blushed. "Sorry, you don't have to answer that."

"No, I guess I don't mind." He paused, smiling thinly. "I always thought someday I would meet someone. In fact, I was positively sure of it. When my dad got cancer a few years ago, I got depressed thinking that when I eventually did have kids, their grandfather would be gone and they'd never get to know him. So I interviewed him on videotape, for his future grandchildren. I asked him all about the family, his whole life story. Eighty years of memories."

"That's a great idea."

"It was, even though my old man was kind of cranky about the whole filming process. The most interesting part was at the end. We were a little punchy and were getting philosophical, talking about who was the greatest leader of all time, things like that. Off the wall, I asked him one final question: What do you think is the greatest threat to civilized society today? He paused for the longest time. Just dead silence as the videotape kept running. Finally he looks straight into the camera and says, 'Videotape.'"

Allison laughed lightly, then smiled with her eyes. "I think I would have liked your father."

Harley returned the smile, then turned a little serious. "I'm actually a lot like him."

Silence filled the space between them. They locked eyes a little longer than they might have, but it wasn't uncomfortable. Far from it.

Allison slowly turned her head, returning to the clouds.

The plane landed at Nashville International late Friday evening. As previously arranged, Allison rode in an FBI Bucar to Nashville's upscale Brentwood area. Harley Abrams and two other agents traveled with her in the same unmarked vehicle, but there was no motorcade or police escort that would alert the media to the attorney general's arrival.

Tanya Howe drove alone to Brentwood in her own car. Harley had personally called to tell her about the demand Allison had received from the kidnappers. She agreed to a meeting, but they both agreed it should be secret, away from the house. No one could say how the kidnappers would react if they knew Tanya was meeting with the attorney general. No one knew what kind of speculation the media might generate about a face-to-face meeting between Allison and Tanya Howe. The media was camped outside Tanya's home for the long haul, so there was no sure way to bring Allison inside without the world knowing about it. Tanya's principal concern, however, wasn't the rest of the world. It was her parents. She feared how they—particularly her father—might react to her meeting with the other candidate. She told her mother she was going to see a friend, just to get out of the house.

Allison's Bucar crushed a layer of twigs and fallen leaves as it rolled up the long uphill driveway to Sofia Johnson's home. Nestled behind a stand of trees that had dropped their leaves was a small, two-story Tudor-style house with a stone fireplace and a wood shingle roof. A waft of gray smoke curled from the chimney. The smell of burning oak filled the chilly night air. A porch light glowed in the darkness, and the garage door was open. The driver pulled the Bucar inside and cut off the engine.

The door closed automatically. After quick introductions, Sofia whisked them into the house, through a door that connected the garage to the kitchen.

Five minutes later, a white Chrysler pulled up the driveway. Tanya hadn't succeeded in losing every media tail, but it didn't matter. Sofia Johnson truly was a friend of hers, and no one but Tanya knew that the attorney general was waiting inside.

She parked in the driveway. Sofia greeted her at the front door. Harley introduced the two other agents, then Sofia led her upstairs to a small sitting room. The agents waited downstairs.

"I really appreciate this," Tanya said to her friend as they headed up the narrow staircase.

"No problem," said Sofia. "It's not like I'm harboring the enemy. I wasn't going to vote for your father anyway."

Tanya cracked a faint smile, appreciating a little levity. They embraced on the upstairs landing, then Tanya headed down the hall, alone.

Allison drummed her fingers nervously on the armchair, waiting. Finally the door opened. She rose to greet the younger woman.

"I'm Allison," she said, extending her hand.

"No kidding," said Tanya.

Allison recoiled. "Sorry. I wasn't trying to insult your intelligence by stating the obvious. Just wanted to get us on a first-name basis, as opposed to Ms. Leahy or something really obnoxious, like Madam Attorney General. May I call you Tanya?"

"Sure." She took a seat in the rocking chair by the bookshelf. Allison returned to the plaid upholstered armchair facing the window. The drapes were drawn, shutting out any enterprising photographers who might be curious about Tanya's sudden visit to a friend.

Allison studied her pained expression. The eyes were hollow. The worry lines on her face seemed carved in wax. Allison suddenly felt guilty about her earlier reaction to the tape recording of Tanya's conversation with the kidnappers. True, Tanya had a better shot at getting her daughter back than Allison did. But to think of Tanya as the lucky one was a senseless comparison, like saying the dying were luckier than the dead because the dead had shown them the way.

Allison began, "I don't want you to think of me as the attorney general. Don't look at me as a presidential candidate. I'm not here for either of those reasons."

"I know. Mr. Abrams explained everything. I'm just thankful there's still hope. When the kidnapper hung up on me this afternoon, I thought they were through negotiating. I never dreamed they'd call you. I guess they believed my father when he said he'd never pay."

"He was pretty convincing."

"That's because he meant it. You know the reputation my father had at the Pentagon, the hardliner on terrorism. No negotiations. Period."

"Reputation is one thing. You'd think he might budge when his own granddaughter was at stake."

"You'd think," she said vaguely.

Allison sensed Tanya was about to say more.

She waited, but Tanya fell silent. Allison said, "If you want us to pay the kidnappers, my husband and I will come up with the money. A million dollars."

"What's the catch?"

"No catch, really. The only thing I would ask is that you allow two FBI agents back into your home, for your own protection. And that you allow the FBI to monitor your phones. I know the kidnappers told you no FBI. But kidnappers always say that. Unless they're total idiots, they'll execute their plan on the assumption that you *did* call the FBI. I'm not asking you to do anything I wouldn't do myself, if I were in your shoes."

"That's all I have to do? I don't have to endorse you for president or anything?"

Allison smiled faintly. "No. We won't publicize it. No one ever has to know that we supplied the money. Not even your parents."

"Especially not my parents."

"That's fine. It's your call. I'm not doing this for publicity or political advantage."

Tanya narrowed her eyes suspiciously. "Then why are you doing it?"

"To save Kristen. And . . ."

"And what?"

Allison sighed. "It's important to me that we find Kristen. Don't discount my feelings about that. But I'll be perfectly honest with you. There may be more to this kidnapping than you or your father understand."

"What do you mean?"

"We're looking for a possible connection between Kristen's kidnapping and the abduction of my daughter eight years ago."

"So you're paying the million dollars in the

hope that it will lead to evidence that might lead you to Emily?"

"In a way, I guess that's true. But it's not conditioned on that. We're paying the money, period. If it brings Kristen back, that alone will be worth it."

"Look, I appreciate your generosity. But I don't want anyone who gets involved in this to have any personal agenda. My only objective is getting Kristen back safe."

"I agree with you. It's not a question of putting one person's daughter ahead of the other's. You have to look at it as an opportunity for us to help each other. If the kidnappings are connected, it only makes sense to be thinking about both of them. A pretty good argument can be made that Kristen was kidnapped for the same reason Emily was abducted eight years ago—to hurt *me*. Mr. Abrams doesn't think my baby was abducted by someone who wanted a child of their own or who wanted to sell her for profit. There are much easier ways of getting an infant than breaking into someone's house—like stealing a newborn from a hospital, for instance. And if you look at Kristen's kidnapping, it's tempting to say that somebody is trying to make your father win the election. But it's just as easy to say that somebody is trying to make me *lose*. The fact that the kidnappers have now demanded ransom from *me* would only seem to bolster the possibility of a connection."

Tanya had that look on her face again—as if she was struggling to say something. But she remained silent.

Allison picked up on it this time. "You look troubled, Tanya. Is there something about this connection theory that doesn't sit well with you?"

She looked away, breathing a heavy sigh. "It's

just your whole theory about the motivation for Kristen's kidnapping—that it's designed to hurt you, as opposed to helping my father."

"You don't see it that way?" asked Allison.

She closed her eyes, as if suddenly in sharp pain. "I don't know."

Allison leaned forward, softening her voice. "Tanya, what is it?"

Her moist eyes glistened. "I'll leave it to you to figure out motives. But you should know all the facts."

"Is there something more you'd like to tell me?"

She nodded. "It's about Kristen's father."

Allison sunk in her chair, listening. "Go on, please."

"You see, Kristen was born while I was in college. I wasn't married. But I was definitely in love. Mark was his name. Mark Buckley."

"He was Kristen's father?"

She bit her lip, nodding. "When I got pregnant, Mark said he'd marry me. I thought about it, and I talked to my parents. My mother was supportive. But my father went ballistic. Even though he says he's against abortion while he's out campaigning, he practically threw me in the car to take me to the clinic."

"I take it he didn't like Mark."

"He didn't even know Mark. Never met him."

"Then what was the problem?"

"Mark was white."

The room suddenly seemed colder. Allison didn't move. "That was a problem for General Howe?" she asked incredulously.

"I know," she scoffed. "Seems hard to believe, doesn't it? General Howe, Mister opportunity himself. Can't handle the fact that his granddaughter is half white. Never sent her a Christmas present. Never a birthday card. To him, she didn't exist. *I* no longer existed."

Allison sighed, collecting herself. "I don't know what to say. Thank you for telling me. I suppose it could change our thinking."

"It sure colored mine. When I see my father shoot up in the polls, coming from behind to blaze into the White House, it's hard not to think there's a plan behind it. When I saw him on television, I could have strangled him. Such brazen exploitation. It's a dangerous combination—a military man in the political arena. I hate to say it, but if you take the old military mindset to its ugliest extreme, Kristen is just one more expendable casualty in the march to victory. And the fact that her father was white makes her all the more expendable, at least in the general's eyes."

Allison's throat went dry. Part of her couldn't believe what she was hearing, the other part didn't want to believe. Until now, she'd been on a road that was leading somewhere, possibly to Emily. A political scheme to elect Lincoln Howe was another route entirely.

"Tell me something," said Allison. "Have you been in touch with Mark at all? Since the kidnapping, I mean?"

Tanya lowered her head. "Mark's dead."

"I'm sorry. When did he die?"

"Before Kristen was born. Before we could get married. Car accident."

Allison froze, thinking.

Tanya stiffened. "The last couple of days, I've asked myself over and over again whether I'm being unfair to my father. Part of me just doesn't want to think that he could actually allow something to happen to Kristen to get himself elected president. But whenever I have those doubts, I ask myself the same thing I've been asking myself for the past twelve years."

"What's that?" asked Allison.

"Whether Mark's accident was really an accident."

Allison looked her straight in the eye, trying to stay focused. "I don't think we'll find the answer to that before Monday."

"Monday?" she asked, somewhat surprised. "You mean you'll still pay the ransom?"

"Yes, I'll still pay," she said as she touched Tanya's hand. *And I'll still hope*, she thought, though Emily's hand seemed farther away than ever.

29

Late Friday evening, Repo was stretched out on the couch, channel-surfing with the remote control. He fixed on a black-and-white rerun of the *Dick Van Dyke Show*, but he couldn't hear it. The Delgados were belting down tequila in the kitchen as the same old Pearl Jam compact disc blasted on the boom box for the fourth time around.

Repo had been stewing in his thoughts, trying to figure out why the Delgados were in such a party mood. He'd watched the evening news to see if General Howe had possibly changed his mind about not paying the million dollar ransom. As far as the media were reporting, however, nothing had changed since the general had appeared on television Wednesday night. Still, he had the distinct feeling his partners weren't telling him something.

The rock music grew louder. Repo glanced over his shoulder. Johnny was slamming down another shot, wincing from the bite of tequila and lemon.

Repo looked away, fretting. The girl had to be petrified with fear. She'd been shaky at dinner tonight, hardly eating anything. With the music blasting in the kitchen, it had to sound like a freak show to anyone stuck in the basement. No way she was asleep, not with this noise.

He shot another glance toward the kitchen. The

Delgados were practically falling over each other, laughing. Repo rose from the couch and started down the hall. He moved quickly but quietly, hoping to get past them without incident. They were too wrapped up in the music and drinking to notice.

Repo opened the door to the basement, then scampered down the steps. He didn't need the flashlight, since he'd left the lamp burning from his last visit. He'd heard somewhere that burning light bulbs emitted heat, and he figured that every little bit would help in the cold basement.

Kristen stirred on the mattress as he approached.

"It's okay," he said. "It's me."

She relaxed slightly—but only slightly. The silver duct tape no longer covered her mouth, as Repo had permanently removed it. He'd left her ankle free, too, so she could at least roll over. She was cuffed only at the wrist, and the blindfold was still in place—just so Tony wouldn't think he'd gone *too* soft on her.

He sat on the chair beside her. "You didn't eat much for dinner. I thought I'd check to see if you're hungry."

She shook her head, saying nothing.

He softened his tone, trying to put her at ease. "Maybe the menu's the problem. Guess when you asked for Froot Loops you didn't figure on having them three times a day."

No response—not even a twitch. She'd clammed up again, even more than at dinner. He leaned forward, speaking in a calm, reassuring voice. "Listen, something is going to happen soon."

She lay motionless, then swallowed hard. Her voice was shaking. "They don't want to let me go, do they?"

He bristled, not sure what to say. "Don't worry about them."

"Why do—" she stammered. "Why do you want to help me?"

"I don't know. You're just a kid."

"You like kids?"

"Not all of them. But you kind of remind me of someone."

"Whitney Houston?" she said faintly.

He smiled to himself. The kid had a sense of humor—pretty amazing, under the circumstances. "Actually, you're a lot like my sister. She was eleven."

"*Was?* What happened to her?"

The door flew open at the top of the stairs. A burst of light and loud music invaded the basement. A voice boomed, "Repo, get your ass up here!"

He cringed. It was Tony—obviously drunk, since he'd used Repo's name. He drew a deep breath as he rose from the chair. "Real soon," he said, speaking to himself as much as to Kristen. "Something's gonna happen real soon."

He started up the stairs, taking his time. Tony looked down impatiently from the top step. "Hurry it up, already."

His speech was slurred, noted Repo. As he reached the landing at the top of the stairs, Tony angrily slammed the basement door behind him. He had a wild look in his eyes, one that suggested to Repo that the Delgados had been doing more than just shots of tequila.

Tony jerked his head, pointing toward the kitchen. Repo started down the hall. Tony followed. The kitchen floor was sticky with lemon juice. Spilled salt and lemon rinds covered the countertop. An empty bottle of tequila lay in a sink full of ice cubes. Johnny was dancing clumsily to the music, digging his hand into the box of Froot Loops. *A bad case of the munchies,* thought Repo.

Johnny shoved another fistful of cereal into his mouth, then tossed the empty box on the counter. A stupid grin covered his face as he grabbed the big kitchen knife they'd used to slice up the lemons. "Hey, Tony," he slurred. "What am I?"

He swung the big knife over his head in a sweeping arc. Repo flinched, but Johnny whisked by him and stabbed the box of Froot Loops, sticking the blade right through the colorful cover drawing of Toucan Sam, pinning the box to the counter. He narrowed his eyes, speaking in a mock-scary voice. "I'm a *cereal* killer."

The Delgados burst into laughter.

Repo scowled. "Is this what you assholes dragged me up here for? Another live episode of *Beavis and Butt-head*?"

Tony wheezed, still laughing. Then he turned serious. "We brought you up because Johnny says you don't have the balls to follow my orders."

Repo looked at Tony, then at his brother. "What are you talking about?"

Johnny said, "Killing the girl. I don't think you're gonna do it."

"We'll find out on Monday, won't we?" said Repo.

"Maybe," said Tony. "But I think you could use a little incentive." He glanced at his brother. "Get the girl, Johnny."

Repo grabbed his arm, stopping him. He could smell the tequila oozing from his pores. "You guys are drunk. Don't mess around."

"Take your fucking hands off me." Johnny shook himself free, then hurried toward the basement. Repo started after him, but Tony grabbed him.

"Just wait here."

Repo resisted at first, then stopped. He turned down the volume on the CD player so he could hear what was going on in the basement. He heard Johnny shuffling down the stairs, and then a muffled curse. The drunken jerk had tripped and fallen on the last step. Then all was quiet. In a minute, Johnny was on his way up. This time, two sets of feet clattered on the stairs.

Kristen emerged first, blindfolded, her hands bound behind her back. Johnny had her by the arm, steering her through the hall. He handed her off to Tony, then continued to the far side of the kitchen by the sink. Tony stood in the doorway, right behind Kristen. Repo was at his side. The three of them were facing Johnny, though Kristen was blindfolded.

"Take it off," said Johnny.

Repo winced, confused. "She'll see your face."

"*Duh*," he said, mocking Repo. "Take it off."

"Don't do it, Tony. He's drunk, man. This is stupid."

"Take it off!" Johnny shouted.

From behind, Tony held Kristen's face in his hands, so she couldn't turn her head. She could look in one direction only—straight at Johnny. Tony untied the blindfold. Slowly it slid from her face.

Kristen blinked rapidly as her eyes adjusted to the light.

"Don't turn your head," Tony told her. "Just look straight ahead."

She stared across the kitchen. Johnny Delgado was in plain view, looking straight at her. He stepped closer, smirking, sticking his face right before hers. He was nearly nose to nose, less than a foot away. "Take a good look, you bratty little bitch. Take a real good look."

"Kristen, don't look!" shouted Repo.

"*Way* too late," Johnny said smugly. Tony put the blindfold back on her.

"You assholes," said Repo. "She's seen your face."

"That's right," said Tony. "She seen it. And you know what that meant for Reggie Miles."

Kristen cringed, not sure if this was a cruel game or a genuine power struggle.

Repo shook with anger. "You didn't have to do this."

Tony tightened the blindfold. "It's the point of no return, Repo. Now you know that if you don't do your job, Johnny has to do it for you."

"Yeah," Johnny scoffed. "And if I'm the one who does her, you *know* she won't die a virgin."

Repo lunged forward, shoving Johnny across the room. Johnny slammed into the counter. The two men froze, breathing heavily, staring at each other. Repo glanced at the knife protruding from the counter—the big kitchen knife Johnny had stuck through the cereal box.

Johnny smiled, challenging him. "Go for it, Repo. You want a piece of me? Now's your chance."

A tense silence filled the room. Repo was poised to lunge for the knife. Johnny braced his foot against the cabinet behind him, like a sprinter in the blocks. Tony slowly edged the girl out of the kitchen, into the hallway. His face beamed with anticipation, like a boxing fanatic with ringside seats. Finally he broke the silence.

"Stick him, Johnny!"

Johnny shot across the room and grabbed the knife by the handle. Repo leaped forward and hit him broadside. They smashed against the kitchen cabinets, then tumbled to the floor. The long knife glistened in the light as they rolled across the floor, struggling for the weapon.

"Stick him!" Tony shouted.

Johnny rolled on top, pinning Repo on his back. He clenched the knife in his right hand, but Repo had his wrist. With a quick jerk he shook his hand free and brought the knife down, full force, aiming for Repo's throat. On impulse, Repo kicked against the oven door, launching Johnny up and forward. The blade stuck in the linoleum floor, nearly scalping Repo. Repo kicked again, harder, sending Johnny headlong into the refrigerator. The blow stunned him. The knife fell to the floor. Repo scooped it up and pointed it at him.

"Johnny!" his brother shouted.

"Just stop!" cried Repo.

Johnny lunged straight toward him. Repo fell backward to the floor, and Johnny crashed down on him with his full weight, swinging his arms wildly. They landed with a thud, with Repo on his back and Johnny on top. Johnny groaned, then went limp. Repo lay motionless, stunned at the warm and wet sensation on his hands and stomach. Johnny still didn't move. Repo pushed him off and rolled him on his back. His arms flailed like a rag doll. His shirt was torn and soaked in crimson. The knife was buried up to the handle in his chest, between the ribs.

Tony rushed forward, leaving Kristen in the hall. "Johnny! Oh, shit!"

Repo sprung from the floor and flew across the

kitchen. In a blur he slammed Tony against the cabinet, then grabbed the electric toaster and slammed it on his head. Tony fell at his brother's side, half conscious. Repo sprinted to the hall and grabbed Kristen.

"Let's go!"

He tore off her blindfold so she could run with him, then took her by the arm and rushed out the door. In seconds he was galloping down the front steps, digging in his pocket for the car keys with one hand and pulling Kristen with the other. He threw open the door and shoved her in the backseat.

"Stay down!" he shouted. She dove for the floor, face down.

He jumped in the driver's seat and fired up the ignition. He saw Tony stumbling down the porch as he slammed the transmission into reverse. The car squealed out of the driveway, fishtailed on a patch of ice, then peeled off into the night.

He checked the rearview mirror as he sped away. Tony was running back inside the house. Repo figured he had a gun, but he was probably afraid to fire a shot and attract the neighbors' attention.

Repo struggled to catch his breath, panting so hard he was fogging the windshield. He blasted on the heater to warm things up. Thankfully, the traffic lights were cooperating. Just one more green light and they'd make the expressway. He sighed with relief as they cruised up the entrance ramp. Then he heard Kristen sob, and panic struck him.

His hands and shirt were covered with blood. He had General Howe's granddaughter facedown in the backseat.

And worst of all—what frightened him to the core—was knowing he'd just killed the nephew of Vincent Gambrelli.

"I'm a dead man," he uttered as the car merged onto the expressway.

30

Allison arrived home at midnight, just in time for a telephone conference that would map out the final weekend of the Leahy-Helmers campaign. She pitched her business suit into her bag for the cleaners, threw on a bathrobe, and took the call on the couch downstairs, so as not to wake Peter. Helmers and his chief adviser were patched in from their hotel in California. The media consultants connected from New York. David Wilcox and his lead pollster originated the call from a campaign headquarters that, at this stage of the game, was busy around the clock. Allison and Wilcox had yet to make peace since their blowup earlier that week, but with the election looming, everyone seemed to understand that, like it or not, they were stuck with one another for a few more days.

The meeting followed the usual agenda, beginning with the latest polls. The race was dead even in the popular vote, but Howe was beginning to pull ahead in the decisive electoral college. Two hundred and seventy votes were needed to win. Howe had a lock on a hundred and eight. Leahy could count only seventy as firm—down from over a hundred just two weeks ago. They could write off both Ohio and Pennsylvania, despite last week's advertising blitz. Florida and California were the big undecided states.

"We need Allison in Florida," said Wilcox. "Howe is invading the whole damn state."

Allison rubbed a throbbing temple. Now that she'd actually spoken to the kidnappers, the campaign in some ways was little more than a distraction. But she didn't dare reveal that she and Peter were preparing to pay Kristen Howe's ransom. "What about Eric?" she asked.

Helmers cleared his throat. His voice was raw from a week of nonstop stumping. "I think it's best if I stay on the West Coast. We need both Florida *and* California to win the election. Howe needs only one or the other, and he's clearly focusing on Florida. Allison should go head-to-head with him down there, and I'll do my best to pull in California."

Allison asked, "What about the pledge I made to devote my full attention to finding Kristen Howe? I told the American people at my press conference that I was suspending all personal appearances."

"And you *did* suspend them," said Wilcox. "You did your job as attorney general to make sure the investigation is properly focused, but now it's time to resume normal campaign activities. You're running for president. Not sainthood."

She bristled at his tone. She was about to put him in his place when Helmers spoke up again. "Allison, think of all the people who believe in you. Thousands of workers who have been out there killing themselves day after day, many of them since New Hampshire. Some haven't been paid in a month, but they keep showing up for work. It's all for nothing if you don't get back out there. Please, I can't do this by myself."

Helmers's voice had actually cracked. His plea seemed to catch everyone off guard, including

Allison. An eerie silence lingered as she mulled things over, like the deceptively calm passing of the eye of the hurricane.

"Don't cheat your destiny," added Wilcox, breaking the silence. "It's no accident you've come this far. Things happen for a reason."

Allison paused, confused by his cryptic remark. She shook it off, responding more to Helmers than to Wilcox. "All right, gentlemen. I'll do Florida."

A cheery sense of relief buzzed over the phone lines. They were quickly saying good-bye, as if the candidate might change her mind if the meeting continued. She snagged Wilcox before he could sign off. "David, stay on the line."

The others disconnected, leaving only Allison and her strategist on the line.

"What is it, boss?" His tone was light, like in the old days, when things were good between them.

"I was confused by that comment you made about my destiny. How it's no accident that I've come this far. How things happen for a reason. What exactly were you talking about?"

"Nothing specific."

"You must have had something in mind."

He chuckled, but it seemed like a nervous chuckle. "Not really."

"David, if you don't tell me what the hell you meant, I'm not going to Florida."

"Relax, okay? There's no big mystery here. It's just something you told me a long time ago, in one of our more serious discussions. You called it the Leahy creed—the way your mother used to say that everything happens for a reason. That's all I meant."

She gripped the phone, thinking. She did have a

vague recollection of a relatively deep conversation with David over Dewars on the rocks in O'Hare International Airport. "All right. Forget it."

"What did you think I meant?"

"David, I said forget it."

"Fine. I'll fax you a Florida schedule."

"I can't wait," she said, then hung up the phone.

Bright Florida sunshine glistened off the black sheen of limousines as Lincoln Howe's motorcade entered the University of Miami campus. With the third largest state's twenty-five electoral college votes still up for grabs, the general had two South Florida stops planned for Saturday morning, then afternoon rallies in Orlando and in Jacksonville.

Two vans and the limos stopped beside the Palm Court of the McLamore Plaza, a central campus meeting spot. A circular fountain shot thin spires of water straight into the air. They bubbled at the apex, spilling foam like huge roman candles. Forty-foot palm trees offered spotty shade, leaving most onlookers in need of hats and sunscreen. More than five thousand people had showed up, even more than expected. The crowd was spread across the campus lawn, facing a stage near the plaza, cheering and squinting into the morning sun as the general stepped down from the limo. A brass band cranked up the campaign theme song, "I'm a Yankee Doodle Dandy." The crowd surged forward, but the Secret Service kept them at bay.

"We love you, Lincoln!" a beaming woman shouted over the music. He smiled and touched a few outstretched hands as he moved quickly toward the stage. He paused for the cameras as they passed the press corps, then continued on his way to the backstage area. Buck LaBelle was waiting for him in an out-of-the-way alcove. He pulled the candidate away from the Secret Service escorts for a last-minute pep talk.

"Good turnout," said the general.

"Good media coverage, too," said LaBelle. The crowd was clapping to the music, keeping time. LaBelle seemed energized by it. "I think this is the place to drop the bomb."

"I thought we agreed that was tomorrow."

"It may be too late by then. I feel it. Now's the time."

"Fine by me. The sooner we get this out of the way, the better."

LaBelle turned serious, shifting into his teaching mode. "Your tone of voice is very important, General. The first part is matter-of-fact: 'It has come to my attention that the FBI is investigating the possibility that the kidnapping was orchestrated by one of my own supporters, designed to elicit sympathy and further my campaign.' Second part, get angry and indignant: 'So far, the only thing political about this kidnapping is the investigation, itself—which is headed by my opponent, the attorney general.'"

Howe winced. "I don't like the second part."

"The second part is the key."

"Leahy has walked on eggshells trying not to say anything that might politicize the investigation. I'll look like a bully if I start making bald accusations."

"It's like we talked about at the airport, General. Sooner or later the press is going to hear that the investigation may be turning against your own campaign. You can't let Leahy or the White House be the ones to leak it to them. We have to steal their thunder. If they reveal it, you can bet your ass the American people will be suspicious of us. But if we do it ourselves, and if we do it *my* way, they'll get angry—not at us, but at *them*. Trust me."

"I can't just get all huffy and say the investigation is being politically manipulated. Let's face it, Harley Abrams doesn't come across as a man who's politically motivated. We need a hook. Something that will lend credence to our claim that Leahy is manipulating things to her advantage."

The marching band reached its big finish. The crowd clapped to the music, then erupted in one enthusiastic cheer. Howe and his campaign manager were deep in thought, oblivious to the noise.

"I've got an idea," said LaBelle, his face alight. "We'll tell them about the campaign spending controversy."

"*What* spending controversy?"

"You haven't heard?" he said, making a face. "It's unconscionable. Leahy and her band of unscrupulous political hacks have demanded that the Howe family take down all of the Find Kristen billboards we've put up across the country. They want us to stop running the TV commercials advertising the tips hot line. According to those cynics, it's just a backhanded way of promoting the Howe name—and therefore the Lincoln Howe candidacy. They claim it's illegal campaign spending."

"They're actually saying that?" he asked incredulously.

"Well, admittedly it's just a rumor at this point. But a reliable one."

"Why didn't I hear about this before? When the hell did it start?"

"When?" LaBelle said as his mouth curled into a smirk. "Right now. *You're* starting it."

Howe was dumbfounded. From center stage, the speaker's voice suddenly boomed over the loudspeaker. "And now, ladies and gentlemen, it is my great pleasure to present to you a true American hero, a man who will bring honesty and integrity back to Washington—the next president of the United States of America—General Lincoln Howe!"

The marching band cranked up again. A swarm of red, white, and blue helium balloons raced for the sky. Five thousand people jumped to their feet, cheering wildly.

Howe locked eyes with his campaign manager for a tense, expectant moment, the wheels turning in his head. Finally he drew a deep breath, then gave a quick and solemn nod of agreement. LaBelle smiled thinly, patting him on the back with encouragement.

"Go get 'em, General."

Howe put on his campaign smile and hurried up to the stage, waving with both hands to throngs of adoring fans.

31

Kristen Howe woke to a dimly lit room. She lay on her back, staring up at a grimy airduct stain on an old popcorn ceiling. The stiff pillow crackled beneath her ears as she slowly turned her head to scan her surroundings. The double bed beside hers was empty but messed, as if someone had slept there. Atop the bureau rested a color television set that was tuned to CNN, though the sound was muted. Heavy drapes covered the window, while airborne dust motes floated in the narrow rays of sunlight streaming in at the edges. A diagram was posted on the back of the chain-locked door, showing where to exit in case of fire.

Kristen had been awake when they'd stopped late last night at the Motel 6, a typical two-story building with separate outside entrances for each room. Before going inside to register, that Repo guy had laid her low in the back of the car and handcuffed her to the seat frame. She didn't dare scream for help, since she couldn't be sure how far away he really was. They'd parked in the back, away from the highway, directly in front of their ground-level room. He'd led her inside without cuffs or a blindfold. She never looked at him, however, and she closed her eyes and pretended to fall asleep the moment he laid her in the bed. She didn't want to see his face—not after what happened earlier, after she'd looked at that other guy named Johnny.

She heard a toilet flush, and the bathroom door opened. Repo was back. She shut her eyes so tightly that her eyelids quivered.

"You don't have to close your eyes," he said.

She gulped, afraid to speak. "I didn't see your face. I promise. I didn't. I didn't look last night, either."

"I'm not going to blindfold you, Kristen. So just open your eyes."

She made a face, closing them even more tightly.

He smiled halfheartedly. It was kind of cute, the way she thought she could erase her memory by squeezing her eyes shut. He gently sat on the edge of the bed. "Kristen, I know you saw my face last night."

"No, I *didn't*. I didn't see anything." Her eyes were still shut.

He sighed, shaking his head. "Okay, you didn't. But it doesn't matter if you see my face now."

"You're going to kill me. Just like you killed Reggie."

"No," he said, agonizing. "I promise I'm not going to kill you."

"Reggie's dead. I know he's dead."

He paused, not sure how much to tell her. "Yes. Reggie is dead."

Her body stiffened.

"But I didn't kill him," he said. "Johnny killed him. That guy who got killed last night."

"Why did you kill your friend?"

Repo looked away, then back. "Look, we're both in deep shit, so I want to be honest with you. But you have to open your eyes. I can't lead you around like a Seeing Eye dog."

She opened her eyes. Her line of sight aimed at his torso at first, then slowly drifted toward his face.

"There," he said, "that wasn't so hard. Was it?"

She shook her head, avoiding his eyes. He shifted on the bed, facing her more directly. "Kristen, I'm involved with some very bad people. People who will do whatever they get paid to do. If a guy gets fired and wants to burn his old boss's house down, they'll do it. If some lady wants her ex-husband beat up, no problem. And if somebody wants to kidnap a twelve-year-old girl, they'll do that, too."

"What if somebody wants to kill that girl?"

"They'll do it. But I won't. That's why I killed Johnny. We had a disagreement, I guess you'd call it, as to whether we should let you go."

"Then why don't you just let me go now?"

"Because you wouldn't be safe. I know that sounds crazy, but if I just drove you back to Nashville and gave you back to your mom, they'd find you. These people would find you."

"The police will protect me."

"They *won't.* They say they will, but they won't."

"How do you know?"

"I *know*, damn it!" He drew a deep breath, rubbing his face. "I'm sorry. I didn't mean to yell. It's just, when I tell you I know, you gotta believe me. I have experience in these kinds of things." His expression soured, as if he were suddenly looking inside himself. "Six years ago, I went to court and testified against a guy who was selling drugs in our neighborhood. Not just the jerk down on the corner. The big guy who was supplying everybody. The cops said they'd protect me if I went to court. Said I had nothing to worry about. So I did it. And the minute the trial was over, the cops disappeared. They didn't do shit for protection."

"What happened?"

He looked away, sinking deeper into the past. His voice was flat and distant. "I came home from work one night, and I just found them. Laying there on the kitchen floor, blood everywhere. My mother and my sister. They killed them both."

"This is that sister you mentioned before? The one I remind you of?"

"Yeah. But don't worry. You're not gonna get shot. Not if I can help it."

She paused, studying his face. He suddenly seemed more human to her. "Why do you work for such bad people?"

"It's not really a choice you make. It's just survival. I was eighteen years old when all this happened. I figured the creeps who killed my mom and my sister would probably come and kill me next. The cops were no help. So, you know, in my neighborhood if you wanted real protection, you went to work for—" he stopped, deciding not to use names. "Well, you went to work for the man who could protect you. So that's what I did. It's been six years and nobody's touched me. Nobody dares."

"So, this man you went to work for—he's the one who's going to come looking for me?"

"You and me both. I killed his nephew. And for some reason, his nephew wanted me to kill you."

Her eyes welled with tears. "Why would they want me dead?"

"I don't know. It has nothing to do with you or anything you did, though. It's just that somebody, somewhere, decided it was necessary. Maybe it was Johnny. Maybe it was his brother—the other guy who was in the house with us. Maybe it was their uncle. Or maybe it was the person who hired us in the first place. Whoever that is."

Silence fell between them. Kristen broke eye contact. She was looking right past him. "It's my grandfather," she said.

"What?"

She nodded toward the television. The picture was on, but the sound was off. "My grandfather is on the news."

Repo shook off the confusion. For a second, he'd thought she was confirming that Lincoln Howe had hired him. He turned toward the set and switched on the volume.

Howe was standing at a podium with flags and balloons behind him. The candidate had a solemn look on his face as he spoke into the microphone. "It has come to my attention that the FBI is investigating the possibility that the kidnapping of Kristen Howe was orchestrated by one of my own supporters as a political ploy to elicit sympathy from voters. So far," he said in an indignant tone, "the only thing political about this kidnapping is the investigation itself—which is being manipulated by my opponent."

The image on the screen quickly shifted back to the CNN anchorwoman. "General Howe made the remarks earlier this morning at rally on the University of Miami campus in Coral Gables, Florida. Neither the FBI nor the Justice Department has confirmed or denied that the investigation is, in fact, focusing on a Howe supporter. In a written statement, Attorney General Leahy has stated only that it would be improper to comment on an ongoing investigation."

Repo hit the MUTE button, then looked at Kristen. Her expression was pained and incredulous. She asked, "The FBI thinks my grandfather hired you to kidnap me?"

He shifted uncomfortably. "I guess maybe they do. Honestly, I don't know who hired us. But the thought has crossed my mind, you know, that maybe your grandfather or one of his supporters was behind it. You wouldn't know anything about this, since you haven't seen any of the news. But people feel sorry for your grandfather since you were kidnapped. So sorry that it might even get him elected."

"But—*no*, it can't be him!"

"Maybe it's not him. I hope it's not. But we just have to be extra careful for a while until the FBI sorts this out. This is why I can't just turn you loose. For your own good, I mean. We just have to stay out of sight, at least until the election is over. Do you understand what I'm saying?"

She nodded, staring at the television in disbelief. She sniffled and wiped her nose. "I understand," she said as her worried eyes met his. "I can't go home."

32

The Florida campaign schedule had Allison set to leave Washington at noon, with a symbolic first stop in St. Petersburg that was calculated to impress Florida's huge block of senior citizens. She'd visited St. Pete only once before, years ago on vacation. A shriveled ninety-two-year-old man with a metal detector had helped her look for an earring she'd lost on the famous white sandy beach. In a matter of minutes, eight of his retired friends had joined the hunt, combing the beach like minesweepers, three of them veterans of the *First* World War. "Land of the newly wed and nearly dead," she'd heard a young honeymooner at the bar call it. That wasn't exactly true, but it seemed so.

Before heading to the airport, Allison decided to go into her office for an hour of secluded thought. Whenever she really wanted to get away from the world's distractions, she did her best thinking in the tiny loft between the sixth and fifth floors of the Justice Building.

The loft was sparsely furnished with a recliner chair, a small bureau and mirror, a window air conditioner, and a daybed that allowed the attorney general to sleep over in times of crisis. It was accessible from a hidden staircase just off a small sitting room in the attorney general's office suite.

It was also near a private elevator that ran all the way to the basement. President Kennedy had made use of the elevator when his brother Robert was attorney general. He and Marilyn Monroe could steal away to the attorney general's loft, entering through the basement without being noticed.

Allison thought with bitter irony that in this very room the happily married president had romped naked with the world's most famous sex symbol. Americans could apparently overlook that in a man, but a trumped-up adultery scandal had been enough to send Allison into a political death spiral.

She started in her chair, emerging from her thoughts. All this cogitation on adultery had her thinking of Mitch O'Brien and the scarlet letter photograph, and it suddenly occurred to her that she'd heard nothing more about either of them from Harley Abrams. She assumed he was still in Nashville, so she picked up the phone and dialed his mobile number.

"Harley, it's me. A loose end just jumped out at me. Any progress on finding Mitch O'Brien, my ex-fiancé?"

Harley was just getting into his car, parked outside the Nashville field office. "Nothing concrete. In fact, it's just getting stranger. He appears to have left Miami, but wherever he went, he's leaving no trails. There's been no activity on his credit cards or cellular phone for over two weeks."

"I want to get to the bottom of this. If there's any kind of connection between the adultery accusations and Kristen's kidnapping, he's our best lead. And I still think he might be able to tell us something about Emily's abduction."

Harley sighed—it was almost a groan. "Allison, I can understand your hoping for a connection between Kristen and Emily. But after last night's conversation with Tanya Howe, I truly believe that our best theory is that someone kidnapped Kristen to help Lincoln Howe get elected. And if that's the case, it doesn't seem likely that there's any connection at all to what happened to you eight years ago. That may be hard for you to accept, but you can't let wishful thinking steer you off course."

"I'm not sailing off course. I'm just fishing with a bigger net. We can't write off Mitch as a possible suspect just because Lincoln Howe turns out to be a racist who doesn't love his granddaughter. We have no physical evidence whatsoever to incriminate Lincoln Howe or his supporters. All we have is motive. And you want to talk motive, then I say you have to look at Mitch O'Brien. For all we know, Mitch has been on a mission to destroy me ever since I broke off our engagement eight years ago. He took it very hard when I broke off the engagement, and he was frankly a little paranoid when I started dating Peter. He was the guy who kept me talking on the phone while someone was sneaking into my house to steal Emily. Coincidence? Maybe. But isn't it also possible that he was intentionally distracting me? You yourself said that Emily's taking was unusual—that whoever did it didn't just want a baby. They wanted to hurt me."

"And eight years later he's still mad as hell?" His question was laden with doubt.

"Yes. I saw him, I *know* he's still mad. He was sweet the first time, when he had a drink at the hotel. But when he showed up at that gala in

Washington he was downright scary. Maybe he put a bug in the Republicans' ear, implying that something sordid had happened between us that night in Miami, implying that I'd been unfaithful to Peter just to get back at me. When the fallout from the adultery controversy didn't completely knock me out of the race, maybe he got desperate and hired somebody to abduct Howe's granddaughter. Mitch *was* a criminal defense lawyer back in Chicago. He met some pretty unsavory characters."

Harley started his car and turned on the heat. "It's plausible, I guess. But why would a guy hire somebody to take your baby, virtually disappear from your life, then reappear eight years later only to destroy you all over again?"

"It could have been smoldering inside him all along. Only when he saw me on television every day running for president did it trigger something inside him. Like that guy who killed John Lennon. What's his name?"

"Mark David Chapman."

"Right, Chapman. He was just a regular guy when Lennon went into relative obscurity. But as soon as his idol starts to make a big comeback, Chapman snaps and shoots him in the back."

"Chapman had psychological problems that we can't assume about Mitch. All we know for sure about your ex-fiancé is that he got drunk and cursed you out at a black-tie event."

"What about the photograph—the scarlet letter message?"

"We don't know that he sent it."

"Who *else* could it be?"

"The lab is analyzing it. Maybe they can tell us. I should be getting a report soon."

"What are the forensic experts telling you?"

He scoffed with sarcasm. "Unfortunately, I've been playing in a golf tournament all week. I haven't had time to talk to them."

"Get them on the phone. This is important. I want to talk to them now."

"Allison—"

"Just get them on the phone. I don't have time to wait around for a typed and bound report in triplicate."

"Hold on," he said with a sigh. Allison drummed her fingers, waiting. After thirty seconds, the line clicked for the conference call.

"Allison Leahy," said Harley, "I have Dr. Gus Eversol on the line, from our lab at headquarters."

"Good morning, Doctor."

"Good morning," he replied. "Abrams tells me you would like a preliminary report."

"Yes. A preliminary report. I suppose that's an appropriate label. Or as my dear old mentor used to say, tell me what the hell you've figured out so far."

Eversol stuttered, then spoke in the stilted voice of a scientist. "I have two preliminary findings at this time. The first shall come as no surprise to you. The active ingredient in the red substance used to create the message on the photograph is octyl methoxycinnamate. It also includes lesser quantities of petrolatum, polybutene, microcrystalline wax, castor oil, lanolin, and propylene carbonate. But, as I say, that comes as no surprise."

Allison said, "Are you trying to say it's lipstick, as we suspected all along?"

"Uh, yes. Lipstick."

"What kind?"

"That's something I haven't narrowed down as

yet. They're all very similar, so pinpointing an exact brand is not as easy as you might think. In any event, you may find it more interesting to know that, in addition to the traditional ingredients of lipstick, I have isolated one definite foreign substance."

"What kind of foreign substance?" asked Harley.

"Human saliva."

Allison winced with disbelief. "Doctor, are you saying that somebody scrawled that message on the photograph with a tube of *used* lipstick?"

"Precisely," he replied.

The line went silent. Finally Allison spoke. "Can you tell anything as yet about the person who may have used this particular lipstick?"

"Not really. In an hour or so I should have a blood type, and I should know whether the person is a secretor or a nonsecretor. The genetic testing will take a little longer, but I will positively determine the sex. In the meantime, if you wanted to play the odds, I suppose you might go ahead and assume it's a woman."

Allison said, "I'd like to identify her, if possible. Do you have enough saliva to do DNA testing?"

"Certainly. Just bring me a sample to compare it with. Blood, hair. Whatever you can get from your suspect."

"That's very helpful," said Allison. "Thank you, Doctor. We'll be in touch. Harley, stay on the line." She waited for Eversol's line to click, then continued. "Harley, do you have any female suspects?"

"Not really."

"What about that woman who was shot in her apartment in Philadelphia?"

"Yeah, Diane Combs, but that's a long shot. My

original theory was that the stolen Camaro with the Tennessee tags found outside her apartment had been used to transport Kristen, but we scoured the entire vehicle and didn't find a single hair or fiber from Kristen. Whoever stole it doesn't have a criminal record, either, since none of the fingerprints in the car or in the apartment turned up a match. I guess what I'm saying is that we're making a double inference here. We're assuming the photo is connected to the kidnapping, and we're assuming that Combs was connected to the kidnappers."

She kneaded her brow, thinking. "What can it hurt? Call the morgue and get a tissue sample."

"Will do. But I'd still like to broaden the search. Maybe pursue some other suspects simultaneously."

"I thought you said you didn't have any other female suspects."

"True. But we could just proceed by process of elimination."

"Meaning what?"

"Meaning that we assume everything is connected, like you say. Or let's at least assume that the scarlet letter photo you received last month is connected to Kristen's abduction. We start by eliminating the women with a direct connection to Emily, to the photo, or to Kristen."

"Harley, I didn't send the damn photo to *myself.*"

"Okay, that eliminates one mother. There's still another."

Allison shook her head. "No way Tanya Howe's dirty. I'd bet my life on that."

"I agree. I guess I was thinking more along the lines of a grandmother than a mother."

Allison sank in her chair. “You mean Natalie Howe?”

The line crackled with Harley’s sigh, as if he were thinking very hard before he spoke. “Stranger things have happened.”

“Not in my lifetime,” she scoffed.

“I’m right here in Nashville. Are you saying you don’t want me to check it out?”

She bit her lip, weighing it. “I’m saying you’d better be discreet.”

33

Harley had slept only four hours since arriving in Nashville last night, having risen well before the Saturday morning sun. At 8:00 A.M. he'd held a case briefing for the Metro Nashville Police, Davidson County Sheriff's Department and various other local law enforcement agencies involved in the multi-jurisdictional task force. He'd spent another hour with his key people at the local command center—the lead room manager, the hot-line operators and investigators, and their local supervisors. The system was apparently working well. Each agency was using uniform lead sheets and hot-line intake forms, uniform summary reports and tracking forms, uniform statement forms and consent forms. Follow-up appeared to be good as well. All information was properly collected, entered into the computer database, analyzed, and compared. As far as Harley could tell, there was just one problem. No Kristen.

The unexpected phone call from Allison hadn't really changed his plans, though it was mid-afternoon before he was able to set aside a block of time to visit Tanya Howe's residence in Enchanted Hills. The most positive thing to come out of last night's meeting, in Harley's view, was that Allison had secured Tanya's agreement to allow the FBI back inside to monitor her phones. The technical agents had arrived early Saturday and should have been fully operational by now. Harley was stopping by not so much to check on their work—those guys knew what they were doing—but to let Tanya know that she had the ear of someone in the FBI with authority. And to take a closer look at Natalie Howe—discreetly.

Natalie greeted him at the door, pleasant and presentable. Some mothers and even grandmothers neglected their appearance in times like these. Not Natalie Howe. Hair looked good, makeup was in place.

She wore lipstick, too. Red.

"Come in, please," she said.

Harley nodded appreciatively as she took his coat and led him down the hall to the family room.

"Can I get you anything, Mr. Abrams? Coffee? Tea?"

How about a hair sample? he thought. "Nothing, thank you."

The technical agents had transformed the family room into a small-scale nerve center. The ivory leather couch had been pushed into the corner. In its place was a rectangular worktable loaded with state-of-the-art track and trace equipment. A thick power supply cable snaked across the carpet, feeding to a tower computer terminal under the table and a backup desk terminal. Two relatively young agents were busy behind the worktable. They talked their techie lingo while adjusting the color monitor and double-checking the phone line connection.

Tanya was seated on a bar stool at the kitchen counter. She was deep in conversation with an agent Harley had called up from the Atlanta office, Pat Collins, a black woman about Tanya's age who had worked as a family counselor before joining the FBI.

"Is everything okay here?" Harley interrupted.

Tanya looked up. Her eyes were dark, vacuous pools, as if life itself had been slowly seeping away since the moment she'd lost her precious reason for living. "*Nothing* is okay."

Harley merely blinked. Over the years, grieving parents had snapped at him, screamed at him, even punched him. Never did he take it personally.

Agent Collins said, "We've covered everything at least once, some of it twice. I was just giving Tanya some tips on how to control her emotions on the line. When the call comes, she'll be ready."

The phone rang. Harley and his colleague exchanged glances, as if it were almost too weird. The technical agents jumped into action, throwing on headphones, adjusting their tracking and recording devices.

"It's cellular," one of them said urgently. "A clone. It bypassed the central office computer cut-off—just like the call to the AG's house."

A second ring pierced the tension.

Harley nodded to Tanya, confirming this was probably the real thing. "Remember to stretch. We need time to pinpoint the call."

A third ring. Tanya breathed deeply, standing beside the phone, unable to sit down. She looked at her mother for support, then answered on the fourth ring. "Hello."

"Tanya Howe?"

The distorted message came across deep and mechanical, just like yesterday's call. But it somehow sounded different—like a different person. Tanya shuddered, confused and creeped out by the voice. "Yes, it's me."

On the other end of the line, Repo adjusted the bulky extension on the mouthpiece. He was behind the steering wheel in a parked car, speaking through a voice-altering device. "I'm calling to tell you your daughter is safe."

"Where is she?"

"Stay calm. I'm keeping her with me until after the election. Someone wants her dead. I'm not going to let that happen."

"Let me talk to her—*please*."

Repo ripped off the voice-altering equipment and tossed it on the dashboard, then shot a stern look at Kristen. "You have twenty seconds. No more."

She nodded, then eagerly snatched the phone. Repo leaned across the console and kept a close ear, listening in.

"Mom?"

"Kristen!" Her heart swelled with joy and pain. She was pacing, suddenly oblivious to everyone else in the room.

"I'm okay, Mom."

"Oh, sweetheart, thank God. Are you hurt?"

"No."

"It's so cold outside. Are you warm enough?"

"Fine, yeah."

"Are they feeding you?"

"Yes. Froot Loops and stuff."

"Do you know where you are? You don't have to tell me where. Just, do you know?"

Repo shot Kristen a look, shaking his head.

"I can't answer that, Mom. But everything's okay. Really. Please, don't worry."

Repo pointed at his watch, signaling the time.

"Mom, I have to hang up now."

"No!" She struggled not to lose it, but her

thoughts scattered. Tears began to flow. Through misty eyes she watched the agents busy at their computers.

Blinking coordinates dotted the bright blue screen. She knew vaguely that they were tracking radio signals from cellular transmission towers, calculating angles and points of intersection, but the flashy high-tech gadgets only added to her confusion. Abrams shot her an urgent look, as if a few more seconds would do it.

"Kristen, I love you," her voice cracked.

"Mom, please don't cry."

Repo grimaced, feeling for her mother. He checked his watch again. Forty seconds. *Way too long.* "Say good-bye," he whispered frantically.

"I love you, too, Mom. I'll be home soon. I promise."

The line disconnected. Abrams looked at Tanya, then at the agents, bursting with anticipation. The computer screen blinked as two yellow dots intersected. It blinked again, superimposing a grid map over the coordinates. Data scrolled in a separate window, rolling like a slot machine. It stopped suddenly and flashed a range of possible addresses.

The techies leaped from their chairs, shouting in unison, "Got it!"

"Where?" asked Harley.

"Right here! Nashville."

Harley snatched the phone and dialed headquarters.

34

"I knew it, I knew it, I *knew* it!" Repo pounded the steering wheel as he spoke, his breath steaming inside the chilly parked car. Steady traffic cruised by in both directions on the wide city street, though no one could see in through the tinted windows.

"I knew I shouldn't have put you on the line. You talked so long even Barney Fife could have traced that call."

Kristen sank in the passenger seat, near tears, but she acted tough. "So sorry," she snapped. "But my mom was crying. I couldn't just hang up on her."

He took a deep breath, then spoke in a softer but urgent tone. "It's okay, forget it. It's not your fault."

"I want to go home."

"You will. Just a few more days."

"I want to go *now*."

"You can't. We gotta go—like *now*."

"*You* go. I just want to go home."

He grimaced, frustrated, then pushed the power lock button to unlock her door. "You want to go? Go. You'll be dead before the election, I guarantee it. It's like I said, the cops can't protect you. They'll tell you with a straight face they can, but they can't. I got a dead family to prove it. My mother had her throat slashed. My sister was shot six times, twice in the head. You want to end up like them, then go. Be my guest."

She grabbed the door handle, thinking.

"Just remember one thing," he said. "I may be no saint, but yesterday was the first time I've ever killed anybody. I did it to save you. Your own grandfather won't even cough up a ransom."

Her grip on the handle tightened. "You really think he's involved, don't you?"

"Whoever it is, *you* are far less important than the White House."

She swallowed hard. Part of her said run, the other said stay. For the first time, she looked Repo squarely in the eye. It unnerved her at first, but he had familiar-looking eyes. Eyes she could trust. Eyes like Reggie Miles.

She took a deep breath, then released the handle. "We'd better get out of here."

He started the engine. A quick check in the rearview mirror showed a police car round the corner just a block behind them.

"Where are we going?" she asked.

"Definitely not far. In five minutes they'll have this city surrounded, probably set up roadblocks. We just need a place to hide out for a while." He shifted into gear and merged into a wide, busy boulevard. "Duck down, Kristen."

"Why? Nobody can see in through these windows."

"Just get down."

She slowly slid from her seat to the floor. Repo reached over the seat, popped open the glove compartment, and grabbed an extra ammunition clip. Kristen looked up nervously as he tucked it into the inside pocket of his leather jacket, next to the black pistol handle.

He watched his speedometer, staying just below the limit. His heart pounded as he rechecked the rearview mirror. The squad car was gaining steadily, though it was traveling too slowly to be in pursuit. No siren, no emergency flashers. *No need to panic.*

Not yet.

He slowed the car as they neared the intersection, praying the red light would change. It flashed green. He accelerated through a six-lane cross street. The squad car pulled even in the left lane. Repo reached for his gun.

"Don't!" Kristen shrieked.

He let his hand slide past the pistol and into his lap. The squad car was passing, pulling away. Repo sighed. "Looks like we may have lucked out."

He glanced in the mirror. Three cars back was a white sedan, possibly an unmarked police car. "Then again, maybe not."

In fifteen minutes, Harley was cruising in a Jayhawk helicopter above the old neighborhoods near Vanderbilt University. The orange setting sun hovered before him, its sharp glare cut by the tinted Plexiglas bubble. Below, a tangle of commercial and residential streets fed into increasingly residential areas as the chopper sped away from downtown Nashville. The rolling landscape had a bemusing schizophrenia, a contrast of wintry bare trees and lush green lawns that had been raked of fallen leaves.

Harley's conference call with his unit chief and both the special agent in charge and the assistant special agent in charge of the Critical Incident Response Group had taken only minutes. Kristen's hometown of Nashville was one of a handful of cities in which a squad from the FBI's elite Hostage Rescue Team was on ready-alert. The decision to deploy them was quick and unanimous.

From his copilot seat in the cockpit, Harley glanced over his shoulder at five specially trained HRT members in the compartment behind him. All were dressed in full SWAT regalia with Kevlar helmets and flak jackets. Four were armed with fully automated M-16 rifles. The fifth, a sniper, touted a 308 sniper rifle. Harley's gaze drifted back toward the setting sun, which was now little more than a half circle on the horizon. He spoke into the microphone attached to his flight helmet.

"Not much daylight left," said Harley.

"We have night vision," came the team leader's reply.

Harley drew a deep breath. He knew the FBI was prepared, but he was more concerned about what a panicked kidnapper might do in the darkness when the bullets started flying.

He turned off the intercom on his headset and switched to cellular capability. He'd already told Allison about the successful tracing, and she'd insisted on being kept apprised of further developments. He connected his phone and dialed her emergency number.

"Allison, it's Harley. We've got a possible positive ID on a suspect."

She was backstage at a rally. She pressed the phone to one ear and plugged the other with a finger, blocking out a long-winded introduction by a Florida congressman on stage. "Already? How?"

"We narrowed the trace on the cellular phone to less than a square mile. Our voice analyst identified the disguised voice as that of a white male, so we issued a be-on-the-lookout broadcast on police radio for any white male traveling in the area with a young black female."

"And you got a hit?"

"A Davidson County deputy sheriff responded. Says he saw a white male with a black female in a sedan headed west out of downtown Nashville. He gave silent chase for about six miles to a private residence."

"Whose residence?"

"Not clear yet. It's leased. We can't reach the landlord, so we're not sure who the tenants are. I'm headed there now."

The helicopter dipped to the right in its initial descent. The open green space of Centennial Park came into view. Harley noticed the makeshift heliport and staging area near the imposing Parthenon, a to-scale remake of the ancient Greek ruin.

"We're landing," said Harley. "I have to hang up and clear the airwaves."

"Call me when you get down. Make whatever contact as a negotiator that's appropriate, but I want to be fully briefed before any paramilitary offensive is launched."

"Roger," he said, then switched off the phone.

The helicopter hovered over the park. Gusts from its whirling blade stripped nearby trees of the last vestiges of autumn color. The final fifty feet were slow and straight down, until the runners settled in the grass less than thirty yards from the stone Parthenon. Five HRT squad members quickly unbuckled their seat straps, pushed open the door, and jumped to the ground. Harley sprinted with them to the unmarked van waiting in the parking lot. He took the front passenger seat. An agent was behind the wheel with the motor running.

"Let's go!" Harley shouted.

The van shot from the lot, speeding down West End Avenue until they passed beneath the interstate. After a few quick turns through quiet side streets, they came to an abrupt stop in a parking lot atop the hill. A recreational vehicle was parked at one end. A large antenna protruded from the roof. Loaded with high-tech equipment, the RV would serve as the FBI's on-site command center. Three other vans loaded with FBI SWAT from the field offices were unloading simultaneously. Another van marked DAVIDSON COUNTY SHERIFF squealed into the parking lot, nearly flattening Harley. A SWAT team jumped out, led by the county sheriff. He had the neck of an Olympic wrestler and the mustache of a walrus, an imposing man in a Paul Bunyan sort of way—neither fat nor muscular, just large.

Harley hurried toward him. "Evening, Sheriff. I'm Harley Abrams, FBI."

The sheriff shook his hand firmly—too firmly, as if showing off his strength. "Thanks for coming, boys. Good to have the backup."

Wonderful, thought Harley. *A turf war.* "We're not here as backup, Sheriff. This is what we do."

"It's what we do, too. Got a SWAT team of our own."

"Doesn't everybody? Pretty soon the Neighborhood Crime Watch is gonna get one."

His eyes narrowed, shooting daggers at the FBI. "We know what we're doing, and we have every reason to be here. It was *my* deputy who spotted the suspect."

Harley nodded, shifting to a more conciliatory

tone. "That's true. And that was good work. I'd like to talk to him. How positive is he on the ID?"

"Not a hundred percent, but it looks very good. He spotted the vehicle well within the area you described in the broadcast. Never once lost sight of it."

"Any chance the suspect knew he was being followed?"

The sheriff made a face. "We're talking about one of my most experienced deputies here. Never turned on his lights or siren, nothing to cause alarm. Pretty heads-up on his part. We still have the element of surprise."

Harley sighed, as if wary of surprises. "Sheriff, you and your men can be of greatest assistance by helping us seal off the neighborhood at both ends of the street. I'll position our snipers on rooftops across the street and behind the house. If anybody is going into the house, it will be my squad from the Hostage Rescue Team. But first, we're bringing in floodlights and a loudspeaker. We'll give a verbal warning, try to start a dialogue. I want to do everything possible to reach a peaceful solution."

The sheriff shook his head, grumbling as he placed his hands on his hips. "Well, damn it. That means we lose the element of surprise."

"I'd rather lose that than lose the girl. Let's be a little patient. And in the meantime, let's be damn sure nobody gets trigger happy. Got it?"

The sheriff shot him a cold glare, not so much as blinking. "Got it," he muttered.

35

Kristen sat on the bare hardwood floor with her knees up and her back against the wall. Repo sat on the floor in the corner, near the window with no drapes. The empty living room was dark, but there was nothing to see anyway. No pictures on the walls. No rugs or furniture. They'd tried to turn on a light, but the power had been cut off. The house was growing colder as night settled in.

Kristen drew her knees closer to her chest, trying to get warmer. "How did you know this house would be empty?" Her voice echoed in the empty room.

Repo shifted his eyes from the window. "The sign out front."

"Oh, you mean the one that says, 'This house is empty'?"

"No, smarty-pants. Back in high school, whenever me and my buddies wanted a place to party, we used to drive around looking for the houses with the 'for sale' signs out front. If you see one that says 'price reduced,' nine times out of ten it means the owners are desperate to sell because they've already moved out. Empty house. Party time."

She nodded, thinking how her mother would kill her if she broke into somebody's house. Her toes were getting cold. She scrunched them in her shoes, finding warmth in the friction.

"By the way," she said. "Thanks for letting me call my mom. I'm sorry I caused so much trouble."

"Not a problem." Repo kept staring out the window.

"I was kind of wondering, you know, why you're so careless."

"What do you mean?"

She shrugged. "Well, you let me see your face. You let me call home and talk too long. You don't even wear a goofy wig or a hat for disguise. I have friends who are more careful when they cut class."

"You watch too many detective shows."

"Do I? Or have you, like, just become totally fatalistic about this whole thing?"

He winced, confused. "Totally *what*?"

"Fatalistic. Do you think your fate is sealed? No matter what you do—hide your face, wear a disguise—you can't change the outcome."

He smiled weakly. "Fatalistic, huh? That's a fancy word. Where I grew up, we used to just say your ass is grass."

"Okay, then. Do you think your ass is grass?"

"Definitely."

"And who's the lawn mower?"

"You don't really want to know."

"You don't really want to tell me."

He shook his head, smirking. "For a kid, you're not too dumb."

"And you're not too smart," she said in deep, affected voice. "I like that in a man."

He shot a funny look. "Huh?"

"Just kidding. That was my Kathleen Turner imitation. Didn't you see *Body Heat*?"

"Uh, no."

"It's, like, my mom's favorite movie. We have it on tape. You really should rent it."

"For sure," he scoffed. "Maybe we can all go see it sometime."

They sat in silence. Kristen glanced out the window. It was completely dark now, inside and out, but her eyes had adjusted. "I'm kind of hungry."

"I'd make you a sandwich, but the meat's all gone."

"Yuck. I hate bologna anyway. Got any more Froot Loops?"

"I bet Kathleen Turner doesn't eat Froot Loops."

"I bet she doesn't eat bologna, either."

They both smiled this time. A noise rumbled outside the house, loud enough to be in the yard. Kristen stirred. "What was that?"

He raised a hand, hushing her. He listened, but all was still. "Wait here." Staying low, he cautiously approached the window, kneeling on one knee as he peered out over the sill.

A silent projectile hit the window, shattering it, raining glass upon them. Kristen screamed. Repo dove toward her, wrapping himself around her like a protective shield and covering her mouth.

"Quiet!" he whispered. They waited. All was still. He released her from his arms.

"What's happening?" Her voice was hushed but racing with panic.

"Somebody's shooting at us. With silencers." He pulled his gun from his jacket and quickly slid on his knees to the other window. Slowly he raised his head above the sill. It was brighter outside the house than in, which enabled him to see clear across the lawn. He looked toward the driveway but saw nothing. The sidewalk was clear. He rose higher in his crouch, still on his knees. He kept his head behind the wall as he strained to see the front porch.

The glass shattered, again in silence. Repo was knocked to the floor, landing on his shoulder with a heavy thud.

Kristen screamed as she cowered in the corner. Repo scrambled toward her. His left arm protruded like a broken wing. He slammed against the wall beside her, groaning with pain.

Tears streamed down Kristen's face. "Why are they shooting?"

Repo stretched his shoulder, fighting the pain. "Doorbell must be broken."

His humor landed flat. Then she saw the blood. "You're shot!"

He bit his lip. The pain was excruciating. "Hollow point ammunition," he said, speaking more to himself. "These bastards mean business."

Kristen curled into a tight little ball, quivering as she spoke. "They're going to kill us. We gotta get out of here!"

"Stay down," he said. He struggled to his knees, then maneuvered back toward the window. He gripped his pistol tightly. "I have twenty-one bullets in here. I'm going to fire them off, almost like a machine gun. As soon as I start shooting, you crawl as fast as you can on your hands and knees for the back door. No matter what happens, just keep on going and don't look back."

She looked up. Her face was frozen with fear.

"You hear me?" he said. "Just keep on going."

She took quick and shallow breaths, on the verge of hyperventilation. "Okay," she nodded.

Repo nodded back. "On three," he said. "One. Two. Three."

He hurled a leather bag through the window

to shatter the remaining glass, then jumped to his feet and started firing like a gunslinger. The shots cracked in quick succession from his semi-automatic pistol. Kristen sprinted on hands and knees toward the kitchen, glancing back only once to see Repo tumbling back and his gun flying in the air. He hit the floor hard and grabbed his bloody hand.

"Repo!"

He rolled toward her, grimacing in pain. "Just go!"

His right hand was a shattered mess. He grabbed the gun with his left hand and cleared away a hunk of his own flesh and bone from the trigger hole. He jumped back to the window, firing again in rapid succession. As the shots rang out, Kristen got up from her knees and sprinted for the back door, too frightened to look back.

Another precision shot hit Repo in the left hand. He cried out as the gun flew from his hand and skidded on the floor. It landed in the middle of the room. Repo looked toward the kitchen. The back door was open and there was no sign of Kristen. He checked his bloody hands. They were useless, both of them. He kicked his leg out like a hook, trying to curl the gun toward him. Another shot from nowhere hit him in the foot. He recoiled as two more quick shots hit the gun in quick succession, sending it skidding across the room, well out of his reach. Repo shuddered. The shooter was a pro.

He rolled to the corner, leaving a thick trail of hot blood. The pain from each of his four hits was coalescing into a full-body numbness. He lay flat on his back, helplessly staring at the ceiling.

He heard footsteps pounding on the wood floor, but he lacked the strength or the will to turn his head and look. Suddenly the marksman was standing over him, a black silhouette in the darkness. His deep voice echoed in the empty room.

"Did you really think you could run away, Repo—that I would never find you?"

Struggling, Repo raised his head an inch from the floor. He could barely see, but he knew the voice.

He lowered his head and closed his eyes, bracing for the worst.

Harley Abrams gave a hand signal from the field across the street. With a flip of the switch, a battery of fifteen-hundred-watt floods lit up the yard and the front of the house. Patchy fog sparkled in refracted light, giving the scene a mystical shroud.

The porch light switched on, but there was no other sign of motion from within the house.

Snipers readied themselves in trees and on rooftops surrounding the house. SWAT members lay in the grassy ditch across the street and in the back, behind the hedge. Harley picked up the microphone and switched on the loudspeaker.

"This is the FBI," he said, his voicing blaring at the brightly lit house. "You are surrounded. Come out with your hands up."

Trigger fingers twitched in the edgy silence. Generators hummed with power for the lights, the only sound in the neighborhood. Fog swirled up from the ground in slow motion, making the wait seem even longer.

Harley reached for the microphone, then stopped. The front door opened. Harley announced, "Keep your hands above your head."

A man came out first. He stepped tentatively onto the porch, nervously thrusting his arms in the air. A woman followed with a young girl at her side.

The SWAT team raced across the lawn, pointing their automated rifles. "Down, down, everybody down!" they ordered. The petrified family fell to their knees, then flat on their stomachs in the dew-covered grass. The SWAT leader put a gun to the man's head and another grabbed the girl. Five others burst through the front door and into the house. Another team raced in the back. Harley ran to the suspect in the lawn. Up close, it was plain to see the man wasn't white.

"Where's the white guy?" the SWAT leader demanded.

The man was shaking. "There ain't no white guy."

"Where is he?!"

Another man in SWAT gear rushed from the house, bounding down the front steps. "House is clear. No suspect."

Harley glanced at the young girl. She was African American and probably twelve or thirteen. But she definitely wasn't Kristen Howe. He took a closer look at the man in the grass. He, too, was African American, but his skin was lighter than his wife's and daughter's. The deputy sheriff had obviously mistaken him for white.

"It's not them. We've got the wrong place."

The man lifted his face from the lawn and looked up angrily. "Damn straight you got the wrong house. I'm gonna sue your Nazi asses."

Harley looked away, running a hand through his hair with exasperation. "Just what I need," he said, groaning.

36

Vincent Gambrelli stood directly over Repo, watching him wallow in pain. "Hurts, doesn't it?" he said flatly. "It's the price you pay for killing my favorite nephew."

Repo was still on his back, his blood pooling around him. "Johnny Delgado was a moron."

"Oh, really? That's quite an indictment from a guy who's stupid enough to let the girl call her mother. Did it not occur to you that I might be monitoring a cellular phone that I fucking cloned myself?"

Repo grimaced, saying nothing.

"I guess not," said Gambrelli. "But what can I expect from a guy who leads me right to his door? Those auto security tracking chips are really so easy to follow. You should have at least ditched the car, dumb shit."

"The cops," he coughed. "They traced the call. They'll be here any minute."

"Not a chance. That phone was preprogrammed to make the FBI think the call came from Nashville. So don't expect the cavalry to come charging through the door to save your sorry ass."

Tony Delgado suddenly emerged in the doorway, wheezing, as if he'd been running. His belly protruded from his tight-fitting black pants and sweater, and he had a pistol in his hand. "She ain't here. I checked everywhere."

Gambrelli calmly reloaded his gun. "Looks like we have a little situation here, Repo. Not to state the obvious, but there are just two possibilities. This can be bad for you. Or it can be awful. It's your choice. So tell me. Where's the girl?"

Repo breathed hard, reeling from his wounds.

Gambrelli pointed the gun at his good knee. "Three seconds, Repo."

His lips bubbled with blood and saliva. "She went to spit," his voice faded, "on Johnny's grave."

Gambrelli snarled as he pulled the trigger, shattering Repo's knee. His body jackknifed, energized for a moment with sheer pain. Then he sprawled across the floor, almost limp, barely clinging to life.

Gambrelli said, "With all those noisy gunshots you fired, I can't wait around here all night. But the short time you have left can be made to feel like hours. I promise."

"You'll never find her," he said in a weak, raspy voice. "I sent her back to her mother."

Gambrelli scoffed. "We both know that's total bullshit. I was listening to the phone call, remember? You said you were keeping her until after the election." His smirk faded. Slowly he stepped on Repo's bloody hand, crushing the shattered bones beneath his heel.

Repo winced, trying not to give him the satisfaction of a scream.

Suddenly a loud clatter emerged from outside the apartment, like trash cans overturning in the alley—like someone trying to make a run for it.

Gambrelli looked up, flashing a knowing smile. Tony ran to the kitchen and peered out the window. "It's the kid!"

Repo cringed—not for himself, but for Kristen.

Gambrelli wiped his bloody shoe on Repo's shirt, using him like a doormat. "I pity you, Repo. You died a useless man." He fired a bullet into his face.

"Let's go," he said, leading his nephew out the back door.

Kristen ran at full speed through the backyard, past the dilapidated garage that faced the alley. Like Spiderman she scaled the chain-link fence, but her jacket sleeve caught on the jagged post. Momentum carried her over the top, but her arm was snagged. She tumbled into the dark alley on the other side, landing awkwardly on one leg and twisting her knee. She rolled to the ground but bounced up immediately, sprinting and then hobbling another fifteen yards before the pain slowed her to little more than a brisk walk.

She checked over her shoulder. Still no Repo. She'd waited for him by the garage, even though he'd told her not to. *Gotta keep going now.*

Behind her, the chain-link fence shook and rattled. She glanced back again, hoping it was Repo. The sight of *two* men ripped her with panic. Repo was dead, she knew it. They were coming for her.

The alley fed into a side street fifty feet ahead, but with her throbbing leg she knew she'd never make it. She ducked behind some trash cans and buried herself in hiding. She tried to be still, but her body trembled. Her breathing was uncontrollably rapid, like the beat of her racing heart. The darkness frightened her, but it could be her strongest ally. If she could just keep still, they might pass right by her.

She tucked herself into a tight ball and cowered

beneath the trash pile. She pushed aside a stinky bag of coffee grinds to open a narrow line of vision, just enough to let one eye see down the alley, back toward the garage. The men were just twenty yards away, coming toward her. Both were dressed in black. The tall, scary-looking guy she'd never seen before. The other man seemed vaguely familiar.

"Come on out, Kristen," he said. "We're not going to hurt you. We're with the police."

She shuddered—it was the voice of the other kidnapper, Johnny's brother. She'd never seen his face, but she'd never forget the voice—and she knew he was no cop. She burrowed deeper beneath the trash, still watching with one eye as they approached. The scary guy sidestepped a puddle and peered over the fence into the neighbor's yard. Johnny's brother checked the trash cans on the other side of the alley, probing the bulging plastic bags with a metal pipe he'd found in the pile. He turned and was looking right at her—or at least at her hiding spot. He kicked the trash can, then poked at the bags. She had to make a move.

She pushed the trash cans with all her strength, knocking him over. She raced down the alley, swallowing the pain that shot from her knee.

"Get her!" she heard him shout.

She was pumping her arms, running faster than she'd ever run before. She tried to scream, but she could barely even breath. Her eyes fixed on the streetlight that marked the end of the alley. Just a little further and she would reach the side street—freedom—but the footsteps behind her were drawing closer. She reached inside for more speed, but her legs didn't have it. She looked back. The scary guy was after her. With legs so long he was gaining with ease. A side-stitch was tugging at her guts. Her twisted knee buckled, and she fell hard to the pavement.

He was on her in an instant, driving a knee into her back, pinning her to the ground. A big gloved hand covered her mouth. The cold steel gun barrel met the base of her skull. She tried to wriggle free, but it was futile.

"Don't fight it," he said in a hushed voice that chilled her. "No one escapes from *me*."

Part 4

37

Allison received word of the botched arrest almost immediately, in a frank and somber phone call from a beleaguered Harley Abrams. Minutes later, the breaking news was reaching television and radio audiences across the country. It was inevitable that the media would jump all over the story, but a local sheriff who was quick to shift blame to the federal authorities had turned the leak to a flood.

Allison canceled her Saturday-evening campaign rally at the University of Florida homecoming celebration and headed straight for the airport. She had summoned the FBI director, the special agent in charge of the Critical Incident Response Group, and others to a briefing in Washington to figure out what went wrong and what to do next. She would have preferred to reach Washington without addressing the media, but a barrage of hungry reporters was waiting for her at the airport, blocking her way to the gate.

A team of Secret Service agents forged an opening as swarming reporters completely encircled her. Microphones and cameras were thrust in her face. Blinding white lights hit her squarely in the eyes. Shouts came from every direction. The questions ran together, until a bruising, elbow-throwing rookie with a crew cut managed to plant himself beside her and get a microphone in her face.

"Ms. Leahy!" he blurted in a husky voice.

Allison kept walking, but it was impossible to ignore him. The guy was built like a college jock turned sportscaster, wired like a bodybuilder on steroids. It was as if some desperate newsroom editor had decided the only way to get this story was to send its biggest running back barreling over the goal line.

"Will Mr. Abrams be fired?" he shouted, just two feet from her eardrum. "Will he be pulled from the investigation?"

Allison started say "No comment," but then it struck that the last time she refused to answer a question she'd been labeled an adulteress. It wasn't fair to leave Harley twisting in the wind. "I've heard nothing to indicate that Mr. Abrams acted irresponsibly," she replied.

Her response fueled the mob. Smaller but meaner seasoned journalists overtook the neophyte from Muscle Beach. A television reporter came out on top, shouting over the raucous crowd, "Ms. Leahy, do you believe the FBI is acting responsibly when it holds an innocent family at gunpoint in their own front yard?"

Allison stopped and shot him an angry glare. The traveling circus seemed to drop a few decibel levels in anticipation of her statement.

She looked directly into the nearest camera. "Law enforcement acts responsibly when the circumstances suggest that they must act quickly to save an innocent girl's life, when they rely on the best information available to them at the time, and when they employ measures that allow mistakes to be discovered before a single shot is fired and before a single person is injured. That appears to be what happened here. Yes, I believe the FBI acted responsibly." She looked away from the camera and pushed ahead.

The frenzy reignited. A square-jawed correspondent from one of the national networks was right in her face. "We hear reports that the family has threatened to sue."

"That's between them and their lawyers," she said as she breezed past him and approached the gate.

He kept pace. "Is that the reason you're justifying the FBI's actions—because you're afraid of being sued?"

She stopped short again, shooting an even more intense glare. "Never in my life have I let the threat of a civil lawsuit color my independent assessment of government action."

"Does that mean you're *not* afraid of being sued?"

"It means that as attorney general I take full responsibility for what took place today. That you can bank on. Now, if you'll please excuse me, I have a plane to catch."

A disheveled young woman with a broken heel on her shoe and mussy black hair popped from the crowd, looking as if she'd literally crawled to the front at ground level. A Secret Service agent grabbed her, but she shouted her question as he pulled her aside. "What about the pledge you made to the American people, Ms. Leahy? Your promise to suspend your personal campaigning and to make this investigation your primary responsibility?"

"I believe I kept that promise," said Allison.

The mob swallowed the reporter, but the question rang in Allison's ears. "Then why?" she shouted. "Why were you campaigning in Florida when what could have been the biggest break in the case was underway in Nashville?"

Allison continued toward the gate. A wall of security guards kept the press from surging forward. Allison ducked into the long tunnel that led to her plane, still focused on that lone voice in the confusion.

She heard it again. "Why were you in Florida?"

Her entourage whisked Allison on board. The flight attendant closed the door. The jet engines screamed. But that last question echoed in her mind. What *was* she doing in Florida?

She glanced out the oval window and stared at the runway. The answer escaped her.

General Howe was a blue suit in a sea of tuxedos as he left the historic Biltmore Hotel in Coral Gables, Florida. He knew the event was formal, but Buck LaBelle worried about how the average voter might respond to a candidate in such aristocratic attire just two days before the election. Better to be out of place at some swanky hotel, he figured, than to be out of step with the millions of viewers who might see him on television.

Outside the lower lobby entrance, members of the media stood shoulder to shoulder beneath a red canvas canopy with shiny brass poles. They surged forward the instant the door opened, shouting a collective, "There he is!"

The general maintained a serious, nearly somber expression, reminding himself to convey the proper level of concern over the FBI's bungled invasion of the wrong house.

"General Howe," someone asked, "are you angry about the news from Nashville?"

He kept walking as he talked, heading for his car. "Of course I'm angry. The entire nation should be angry."

"Angry at who, sir?"

The car door flew open as Howe stopped at the curb. "It is my understanding that this invasion was approved by Ms. Leahy personally. All along she has insisted on controlling this investigation for her own purposes. The end result is the most ill-conceived plan of attack since the Bay of Pigs invasion. Apparently, her only goal is to bring this tragedy to an explosive conclusion on the eve of the election, which she hopes will whisk her into the White House."

Another reporter jumped in. "We've just received word that she has taken full responsibility for today's events. What do you say to that, sir?"

"I say, it's not enough for the attorney general simply to *say* she takes full responsibility. Those who assume positions of responsibility must answer not with words, but with accountability."

"General, are you calling for Ms. Leahy to resign?"

He paused to choose his words. "If Ms. Leahy will not step aside from this investigation, then I'm calling on the president to order her to do so."

A barrage of questions followed. The general simply waved and nodded as he ducked into the backseat. The door slammed, and the limousine whisked away, headed for the airport.

Allison's flight landed at Washington National Airport just after 10:00 P.M. A limousine was waiting for her, but it wasn't her usual car and driver. President Sires had phoned her in mid-flight and summoned her to an emergency meeting. She made the trip from the airport to Pennsylvania Avenue in record time, thanks to the use of traffic-stopping White House wheels. Secret Service took her directly to the Oval Office, which struck her as odd. Given the hour, she would have expected they'd meet in the residential side of the White House. He obviously wanted his most powerful setting.

President Sires was staring out the window, his back to her as she entered. His weight-of-the-world posture reminded her of that famous photograph of a slump-shouldered John Kennedy staring out the Oval Office window as he pondered the Cuban missile crisis. But the president's Saturday-evening cardigan sweater looked more like Jimmy Carter during his fireside chat.

Allison seated herself in the silk-covered armchair facing his desk. The president still hadn't looked at her, was still looking out the window. Finally he faced her and said, "I want you off the Kristen Howe investigation."

"May I ask why?"

His jaw cocked, as if she'd hit him with a left hook. "Because there's no other option. You did a commendable thing tonight. You went on record taking full responsibility for today's mishap. But Lincoln Howe has a point. It means nothing to take responsibility if you don't also take the consequences."

"Are you firing me as attorney general?"

"Of course not."

"Are you suspending me?"

"All I'm asking is that you step aside from this investigation—voluntarily."

She looked away for a moment, then looked him in the eye. "Respectfully, sir, I won't step aside."

"Allison, it's just one case. It won't kill you to give in."

"And if I don't?"

He moved toward his desk and eased into his chair. His shoulders squared as he laid his folded hands atop the inlaid leather. "Please don't make me force you."

She nodded, biting her tongue. The anger was boiling inside, rising, until a bitterness lodged in her throat. "How do you plan to handle the announcement?"

"With as little fanfare as possible. We'll do a press release, no press conference. I want to get this behind us without making a major protracted news event out of it. The timing is perfect. A simple press release on Saturday night should dilute the impact."

"You mean a press release from the White House or from the Department of Justice?"

"Both. My staff has already prepared them. Would you like to see the one from Justice?"

He offered, but she didn't reach for it. "I'm sure it's just perfect," she said in a voice laden with sarcasm. "I mean, what better way to run the Department of Justice than to have the White House drafting its press releases? It's like I always say, a president doesn't need a pesky attorney general looking over his shoulder anyway. In fact, you don't even need an attorney general. Why don't I just do the honorable thing and go back to my office right now and fall on my sword? Except—aw shoot," she said, grimacing in mock frustration, "I don't have a sword. I know! Let's call Lincoln Howe. I'll bet he can *lend* us one."

"You're making a grave mistake by not taking this seriously."

"I'm taking this very seriously. That's why I'm not stepping aside from the investigation. So unless you plan to suspend me, I should be leaving now. I have a meeting to attend at FBI headquarters." She rose and started for the door, hoping for a clean getaway.

"Allison," he said harshly, stopping her in her tracks.

She turned to catch his eye, saying nothing.

"Skip the meeting," he said. "I've made my decision. You're off the investigation. That's final."

"You're suspending me?"

"Come on," he said, "you leave me no choice. You know I hate to do this to you just two days before the election, but look at the polls. You're losing ground by the hour. Politically you're a lost cause. If I don't take you out of this investigation right now, Lincoln Howe will keep on attacking until your negative ratings spill over into every congressional race in the country. It's bad enough the party is losing the White House. But I'm seriously worried that we're going to lose control of the House and Senate, too."

She looked at him with disbelief, her eyes burning. "Silly me, Mr. President. I was worried about finding a twelve-year-old girl."

Her glare tightened, and the president looked away. She turned and let herself out, never looking back as she walked briskly down the hall, knowing in all likelihood that she'd just paid her last visit ever to the Oval Office.

38

Vincent Gambrelli woke at sunrise, five minutes before the alarm would have sounded. He'd risen the same time every morning for more than thirty years, since his first night as a Green Beret in the jungles in Vietnam. He'd never really needed an alarm clock, and he'd only started setting one in the last few months, as he neared the half-century mark. It was a kind of competition for him, man against machine. The day his body no longer knew it was time to get up was the day he would no longer trust it.

His six-foot frame was covered in his usual sleepwear, dark green sweat pants and a camouflage T-shirt. He dropped to the carpet and lay on his back, knees up, bracing his ankles beneath the bed frame. He breathed audibly, inhaling and exhaling at regular intervals as he ripped off two hundred sit-ups. He rolled onto his chest, facedown with his hands planted firmly in the push-up position. His back was rigid as a steel rod for the first set of fifty. Up on his fingertips for fifty more. Another twenty-five using just his right arm, then twenty-five more using only the left.

He sprung to his feet, pumped with energy. He swung his arms across his body, stimulating the circulation as he crossed the room and entered the bathroom. Stripped of the T-shirt, he checked himself in the mirror. The red glow of the heat lamp gave him an evil cast, which he rather liked. Thick purple veins bulged from his forearms and biceps. His clean-shaven head glistened with tiny beads of sweat. He turned for a look at his profile. Lean. Nothing he didn't need. Not an extra gram of body fat. Not an extraneous hair on his head. Not a hint of compassion in the cold, dark eyes.

He showered and dressed quickly. Hunger pangs gripped his belly, but that would have to wait.

He pulled a duffel bag from the closet, laid it on the floor, and unlocked the zipper. He smoothed out the bedspread and pulled on a pair of thin rubber surgical gloves. Gloves were a must when handling the equipment. No prints.

Carefully, almost lovingly, he reached inside the bag and removed a sleek and lightweight AR-7 rifle, laying it on the bed. The barrel was already broken down for storage inside the stock with the clip, and the serial number just above the clip port had been completely drilled out. Beside it, he laid the three-to-six-powered rifle scope, powerful enough to ensure deadly accuracy up to sixty-five yards. That was far more scope than he'd needed last night. From across the street, Repo had been easy prey.

With a small screwdriver he methodically disassembled the rifle. He ran a wire cleaning brush down the bore, then used a rattail file to alter the barrel, shell chamber, loading ramp, firing pin, and ejector pin—all the parts that created ballistic markings. It seemed like overkill in a way, going to all this trouble to thwart an unlikely attempt by police to match the bullets in Repo's body to the ballistic markings on Gambrelli's weapons. Even if the cops could find Gambrelli—*good luck*—no one was likely to find Repo's body in the smoldering ashes, let alone the bullets. A generous sprinkling of wood alcohol and a single match had taken care of the crime scene. The police would likely surmise that some crack-addicted vagrant in search of shelter had broken into a vacant house and forgotten to open the flue before lighting the fireplace, setting the place ablaze and toasting himself in the process.

Still, it was good practice—if not just an ingrained Gambrelli habit—either to dump the weapons or change the ballistic markings after every kill. With General Howe's granddaughter in the next room, this wasn't the time to be out shopping for a new gun. That left only one choice.

A knock on the door broke his concentration. On impulse, he grabbed his pistol from the duffel bag.

"It's me," came the voice from behind the door. "Tony."

Gambrelli looked up from his disassembled rifle. "Come in."

The door opened. Tony Delgado stood in the doorway. His eyes were slits, still crusted with sleep. "You want me to feed the kid?"

Gambrelli was deadpan. "Did I tell you to feed the kid?"

"No."

"Then don't feed the kid. Don't blow your nose, don't wipe your ass. From now on, don't do anything unless I tell you to do it."

Delgado lowered his head like a chided boy. "You know, nobody feels worse about what happened to Johnny than I do."

Gambrelli shook his head, the disapproving

uncle. "Siddown," he said, pointing to the chair in the corner.

He moved without a sound, slow but obedient.

Gambrelli said, "Johnny was family, but he was a fuckup. Too damn cocky for his own good. Somebody was gonna do him, sooner or later."

Delgado made a face. "That's it? *C'est la vie?*"

"Shut up, Tony. *I'm* talking here."

A lump swelled in the younger man's throat, visible from across the room.

Gambrelli narrowed his eyes. "Let me explain something to you, Tony. Your brother was how old, twenty?"

"Twenty-one."

"When I was his age, I had one concern. Kill the Viet Cong before they killed me. One mistake, you were dead. You can see it in my eyes—I lived because I killed. Take a good look at me, then look at somebody like your little brother. Johnny and every kid born after him is part of an entire generation of whiny little brats who think the whole damn world is a video game. You screw up, you put another quarter in the slot. And Mommy never lets you run out of quarters. That's why boys like Johnny never grow up to be men. Their idea of fighting for their own survival is going on TV talk shows to bitch about having to put on a condom before they fuck their fifteen-year-old girlfriend. Useless. An entire generation. Utterly *useless*."

"Are you saying Johnny deserved to die?"

"I'm saying that with one less Johnny or Repo or Kristen Howe, for that matter, the world is no worse off. It's better off."

"What about me?"

"You're older," Gambrelli said with a shrug. "I

thought maybe you were different. I trusted you with this job, Tony. It was just my bad fucking luck that after twenty years in the business, my biggest job ever comes after I'm married and retired. My old lady's not cool, you know what I'm saying? I can't tell her I'm taking the week off to go kidnap General Howe's granddaughter. But this job was too big to pass up. So I figured, hey, Tony can handle this. He's got guts. Got some brains. I figure I'll be like a general myself, in the background, you know, giving orders. So I cut the deal, I get everything lined up. All you gotta do is stick to the plan. Next thing I know, Johnny's dead on the kitchen floor with a knife in his chest, you're hung over from too much tequila, and the girl's fucking gone—she's flying down the highway with some amateur named Repo, like a twelve-year-old Bonnie and a shit-for-brains Clyde."

"I'm sorry, I—"

"*Shut up*, Tony." He gnawed his lower lip in anger, glaring at his nephew. "I don't like doing it this way, me being directly involved. This is one of those jobs where the triggerman should never know his client, and the client should never know the triggerman. Too much publicity in this case, too much risk of people talking. When people talk, they start pointing fingers. But if the middleman does his job, the client can't finger the triggerman, and the triggerman can't finger the client. Ever. Which makes it real tough for the cops to prove a conspiracy. Thanks to you, asshole, I'm not the middleman anymore. Now there's a direct link between the client and triggerman. *That's* why I'm pissed at you, Tony."

Tony sank in his chair. "I don't know what to say."

"Don't say anything. Just don't screw up. Ever again."

He lowered his head. "I won't."

Gambrelli took a deep breath, cooling his anger. The kid was appropriately contrite, remorseful. If he weren't family, he'd be dead. But like it or not, he *was* family. If Gambrelli had to keep him around, he had to lift his spirits. A partner with no self-confidence was a dangerous liability. He reached across the bed and grabbed a white spiral binder from the nightstand, which he'd been reading last night before going to sleep. "Here," he said as he tossed it to him.

He caught it and checked the title: *Missing and Abducted Children: A Law Enforcement Guide to Case Investigation and Program Management.*

Gambrelli said, "It's published by the National Center for Missing and Exploited Children. The bible for cops who chase child abductors. The bible for men like us who elude them."

"You want me to read this whole thing?"

"I want you to *absorb* it. You have to start thinking like the FBI. That book, right there, it's written by an FBI special agent named Harley Abrams. If you read this, you know exactly how he thinks—very analytical, step-by-step. Last night I was rereading the part where he lays out all the possible motives for child abductions. Sexual savagery, ransom, sale of children for profit, a few others. He comes up with a total of seven most likely motives. At the end, he theorizes that an eighth possible motive is political gain. But this is very interesting. He says that never in the history of the United States has there been a documented case of a child abduction for political purposes. What do you think of that, Tony?"

His eyes widened, like the kid in class who hated to be called on. "I don't know. Guess it means there are easier ways to screw up an election than to kidnap a child."

"Smart boy," he said with approval. "Very smart boy. I suppose the FBI could be thinking that. What else could they be thinking?"

He made a face, thinking. "That there's a first time for everything."

Gambrelli smiled thinly. "Sometimes I think you're too ugly to be my sister's kid. But you just might be smart enough."

He cracked a thin smile.

Gambrelli winked. Mission accomplished. His confidence was building; the boy was back on the team. He pulled a Polaroid camera from his duffel bag, then popped open the film compartment and loaded it. "You just go on and read that book, okay? Study hard. I have to go shoot some pictures."

"Pictures? What kind of pictures?"

Gambrelli looked up. All traces of a smile had fallen from his face. "You'll see. Just one good shot is all I'm after. The kind of shot that drains mothers of emotion. And families of their bank accounts."

39

Allison tugged the bedroom drapes aside no more than an inch, just far enough to peek inconspicuously at the quaint Georgetown street below. The neighborhood was normally peaceful on Sundays at sunrise. From her upstairs window, however, she could see the media camped outside her townhouse. Some were sleeping inside parked cars and vans, staying warm. Others huddled in chatty circles along the old brick sidewalk, their faces indistinguishable in the eerie predawn glow from the decorative old street lamps. Dressed in wool hats and bulky winter jackets, they shifted their weight from one foot to the other in a dancelike ritual, fighting off the morning chill. Heads occasionally rolled back in laughter as they cavorted over steamy paper cups of coffee. She wondered what they jabbered about to pass the time. Football? Basketball? Or maybe the beloved blood sport of Washington, the ultimate spectator thrill—watching yet another presidential hopeful tumble off the high wire and splatter onto Pennsylvania Avenue.

She turned away from the window and crawled back into bed. Peter was sitting up with his back against the headboard, still in his pajamas, devouring the *Washington Post*. It was well before his normal Sunday waking hour, but they'd both been wide awake when the paper landed on the doorstep. The headline said it all: LEAHY SUSPENDED AS ATTORNEY GENERAL.

President Sires had indeed kept his promise and issued the White House press release. His chief of staff was scheduled to appear later in the day on *Meet the Press* to explain the suspension. Allison's running mate, Governor Helmers, was appearing at that very moment on another morning newscast, doing his best at damage control. Late last night, the Leahy/Helmers campaign strategists had agreed that Helmers, not Allison, should do the early morning shows. He could stand up for her without sounding defensive, and he could draw out some of the sting on the less popular early morning shows so that Allison would be better prepared when the sharpshooting TV journalists fired away on the prime-time shows between 9:00 A.M. and noon.

Allison lay listlessly on the bed, her voice filled with dread. "I have to get ready."

Peter looked up from the newspaper. "You sound like you're going to a funeral."

"I am, in a way. President Sires said it last night, and my own pollsters are saying the same thing. Statistically, I'm a lost cause."

He tossed the newspaper aside. "I don't hear any fat lady singing. Helmers and Wilcox and the rest of those guys wouldn't be scrambling the way they are if they thought it was really over."

Allison shook her head. "At this point, everyone is just running on momentum, not enthusiasm. They're not looking for me to pull off a come-from-behind miracle in the next two days. They're just trying to keep my taint from spoiling Helmers's shot at the White House in another four years."

"Does Wilcox or Helmers know anything about how you agreed to pay Kristen Howe's ransom?"

"No."

"What about the president? Did you tell him?"

"No. I couldn't. If any of those guys find out, they'll exploit it. They'll leak it to the press, try to portray me as a hero and swing the election back in my favor."

"What," he scoffed, "you don't want to win?"

"Of course I want to win. But not at any cost. If word hits the street that you and I have agreed to pay the very ransom that General Howe refused to pay, it would be disastrous. Howe could override his daughter and forbid us from paying. The publicity could make the kidnappers back off and kill Kristen. Any number of things could happen, none of them good."

"So—I'm confused. Are we paying the ransom or not?"

"Yes, we are. If they still want it."

"What do you mean by that?"

"The kidnappers are sending out some mixed signals. On Friday they demanded the money, then yesterday someone else called and said that Kristen is safe until the election is over. It sounds like they may be arguing among themselves, but we still have to be prepared to deliver the ransom if they call on Monday morning, like they said they would."

"Do you really think you're going to be able to keep this quiet?"

"We have to. I know it must be hard for you to understand, especially with headlines like today's. But I promised Tanya Howe we'd keep this quiet because that's the only way it will work. Bear that in mind when you're finalizing the money. You might want to use several different banks, keeping each individual transfer and withdrawal small, so that no suspicions are aroused. Just do whatever you can to obscure the fact that we're paying the ransom."

He made a face. "In essence, you want me to promise that I won't try to capitalize on the one thing that could help you pull off the election."

"In a way, yes." She shook her head, almost laughing at the absurdity. "I know it's crazy. A year ago in this very room you begged me not to run for president. You said it would screw up our lives. Now look where we are. How ironic is this?"

"If you could only imagine."

"Please, Peter. I don't want anyone turning this ransom payment into a political football. Especially not you. Do you promise me that?"

He fell quiet, as if his mind were in another place. Then his hand slid across the sheets and he touched her face, his mouth curling into a soft, reassuring smile. "Of course, darling. I promise."

Tanya Howe recognized her father's black limousine in the driveway. She turned away from the window and glared at her mother. "What's *he* doing here?"

Natalie was sitting at the kitchen table, stirring half-and-half into her morning coffee. The shaking spoon clattered as she laid it in the saucer. She spoke in a soft, nearly apologetic tone. "Your father asked if he could come over. I told him it was okay."

"Why on earth would you tell him that?"

"Tanya, people are talking. The press is starting to say mean things. It reflects poorly on your father if he never even stops by the house when his own daughter is suffering."

"So you told him he could stop by for a campaign photo op?"

"Sweetheart, no. I just thought—I hoped—that if the two of you got together in the same room, for whatever reason, maybe something good would come of it."

"Forget it. He's not coming inside."

The doorbell rang. Tanya didn't flinch. Natalie looked anxiously toward the living room, then back at her daughter. "Tanya, please. Do this for me."

An FBI agent stepped into the kitchen. "Ms. Howe, it's your father. Would you like me to let him in?"

Tanya struggled to say no, but she couldn't get past her mother's pained expression. She sighed with frustration. "All right. Fine. He can come in."

"Thank you," said Natalie. She rose from the table and scurried into the living room.

Tanya stared out the kitchen window as she waited, her eyes clouding over as she looked toward the old swing set in the backyard. She recalled how Kristen had needed a push from Mommy when it first went up. Before long, Mommy was dead meat if she even suggested her baby was swinging too high and shouldn't be so daring. Kristen hadn't used it much in the last few years, but Tanya had left it up anyway. Part of her had refused to accept that her daughter was growing up—the same part that refused to believe she wasn't coming home.

"Hello, Tanya," said General Howe. His deep voice snatched her from her memories. He stood alone in the doorway with his trench coat draped over his forearm.

Tanya's face showed no emotion. "Hello."

He took another half-step into the room and closed the pocket door behind him. "Mind if I sit down?" he said as he pulled up a chair at the table.

She voiced no objection. He laid his coat on the chair beside him, then looked her in the eye from across the kitchen table. "Tanya, I think you know why I'm here."

"Yes," she scoffed. "Mom explained."

He nodded, seemingly pleased to be able to dispense with the groundwork. "Good. I know it's a difficult subject for you, but I'd appreciate it if you could just tell me whatever you know about it."

Tanya winced with confusion. "What are you talking about?"

"You know. This whole thing with the accident."

Her face showed even more confusion.

"You did say your mother explained, didn't you?" he asked.

She shook her head slowly, sensing that this meeting had been arranged under false pretenses. Anger was beginning to boil inside—not just at her father, but at her mother, too, for sandbagging her. "Explain *what*?"

He paused to organize his thoughts. "Maybe I'd better back up a little. It's like I told your mother. Sources tell me that the FBI is looking into the car accident that killed Mark Buckley."

She shivered inside. It had been twelve years since she'd even heard her father invoke the name of Kristen's father. "Is that so?"

"I've come here because I think you might know something about all this sudden renewed interest."

"Why would I know anything?"

"I'm not accusing you of anything. I was just wondering, has anybody come by to ask you any questions?"

"Maybe."

"Tanya, this is no time to be coy."

"What did you expect me to be? Submissive? Obedient?"

"Just honest."

"All right. Here's something I can say in all honesty. I'd like to know the truth about Mark's death."

"Tanya, you know the truth. We all know the truth. I hope you're not looking to rewrite history."

"No," she said in a serious voice. "I just think a very important part of this history was never recorded."

He glared sternly across the table, speaking in a level tone. "The boy hit an oak tree going eighty-five miles an hour. He was drunk out of his mind. That's all the history you need."

She sat erect, looking him in the eye, as if to say his tone would not intimidate her. "That night—that night Mark died. He called me. Very short conversation. He sounded drunk. Didn't really even sound himself. All he said was, 'Tanya, I think you should have an abortion.'"

"What did you tell him?"

"I told him no, obviously. But this isn't about what I said. It's about what he said. It was very strange. An abortion was the last thing Mark wanted. He wanted me to have this child."

"You don't know that. What twenty-year-old boy really knows what he wants?"

"He knew. We both knew."

"Okay. So he got drunk and said something he didn't mean."

"That's what I used to think. But to this day, I can't forget the tone in his voice. He didn't sound like he was just saying it for effect, or even like he was saying it to be cruel. He sounded . . . scared."

"Lots of boys get scared when they knock up their girlfriend."

"I wasn't *knocked up*. And it wasn't that kind of scared. It was different. He was scared like I've never heard anybody be scared. Like, scared for his life."

The general swallowed hard.

Tanya leaned forward, boring in with eyes that burned. "I think he knew what was coming."

"That's ridiculous. The boy got drunk. He got in his car. He smashed into a tree. End of story."

"Then why were there no skid marks?"

The general paused, but his voice was firm. "Because he was so cockeyed drunk he passed out at the wheel."

"That's your theory, Father."

"That was the coroner's theory."

"The coroner wasn't there."

He snapped, "Why the hell else wouldn't he hit the brakes?"

"You tell me."

"I can't, Tanya. I don't have a damn clue."

"I think you do."

"Don't you *dare* show me that disrespect."

She pushed on, defiant. "I know Mark didn't really want me to have an abortion."

"Tanya—"

"I think he said it because he was forced."

"Stop."

"He didn't say it because he was drunk. I think he was drunk because he was scared."

"Stop right there."

"I think he was scared because he was threatened."

"Stop it."

"I think there were no skid marks because he killed himself. Because he had no other option."

"Shut up, Tanya!"

"Because *you* gave him no other option."

"Damn you!"

"Because *you* threatened him!"

"So what!" he shouted as he shot from his chair.

Tanya fell back in her chair, shaking and exhausted. A frigid silence filled the room. "So *what*?" she asked incredulously.

The general took several deep breaths, checking his anger, considering his words. He walked away from the table, leaning over the sink as he stared out the window. Finally, he turned back to face her, speaking in a firm, even tone. "I told him to stay away from my daughter. That's *all* I ever said to him. You want to call that a threat, that's your choice. But I don't hold myself responsible for some fool who gets himself drunk, gets behind the wheel, and kills himself."

"But I do," she said with contempt. "I most certainly do."

A combination of anger and disgust swelled within her until she could no longer stand to be in the same room with him. She rose from the table and started for the living room, then stopped suddenly at the closed pocket door, preferring not to have to deal with her mother—the woman who had surreptitiously arranged this meeting in the first place. She turned and took the rear hallway to her bedroom.

A flurry of emotions brought a tear to her eye.

In need of a tissue, she made a quick turn for the back bathroom, which was accessible primarily from the front hallway, but also from a walk-in storage closet in the back of the house. She passed through it. The bathroom door was closed, but she was too consumed in her own thoughts to even think about knocking before entering. She opened it, then froze.

One of the FBI agents was standing at the counter before the vanity mirror. Surprise covered his face, as if he were unaware that a second entrance to the room even existed, or at least that anyone ever used it. The door to the front hallway was closed and locked. His sleeves were rolled up to the elbow, and he was wearing rubber gloves. A pair of tweezers lay on the counter, right beside a hairbrush she recognized as belonging to her mother. His left hand clutched a clear plastic evidence bag. His right was stuffed inside an unzipped cosmetic bag—also her mother's.

He looked up, stunned, unable to speak or even move.

"What the hell do you think you're doing?" she snapped.

He nearly melted in her glare. "I, uh—I'm not sure I'm at liberty to explain."

"Wonderful," she scoffed. "Then let's you and I talk to someone who is."

40

Driving toward Georgetown, Harley Abrams considered a variety of clever and surreptitious ways to reach Allison's townhouse without being noticed by the media. Certainly an early Sunday morning meeting between the lead investigator and the recently suspended attorney general would raise questions. But if he tried to keep it secret and was nonetheless detected, a "secret rendezvous" would make even better headlines. He decided against the furtive approach. Short of a sex change and digging a tunnel, nothing was foolproof anyway.

He parked his car two blocks from Allison's townhouse, the closest spot he could find. He walked briskly down the shady, colder side of the street. Most of the reporters were on the sunny and warmer side, a fair indication that the media weren't *complete* idiots. He was a half block from Allison's doorstop before he was recognized.

"Mr. Abrams!" someone shouted from the across the street.

Harley kept walking, same pace. Media crews jumped into action, dashing into the street like unruly Mardi Gras revelers. In seconds he was surrounded. The first question hit him like hot shrapnel. "Do you agree with Ms. Leahy's suspension?" Others fired queries to the same effect.

Harley never broke stride. Reporters fought with each other for strategic position, trampling plants and statuettes on neighbors' doorsteps. They lumbered down the sidewalk in one cohesive mass, a ravenous species of carnivores unto themselves. Harley stopped at the iron gate outside Allison's townhouse. He rang the bell and waited.

Another reporter shouted, "Is this meeting business or personal?" Others picked up on the same theme, each one trying to outshout the next.

The buzzer rang and the gate unlocked electronically. Harley opened the latch and stepped inside the small, secured courtyard. The mob surged forward. He turned and spoke firmly but civilly. "You're on private property. Please stay behind the gate."

They backed off, cameras rolling. Harley closed the gate and headed for the front door. It opened before he could knock. The housekeeper rushed him inside and quickly shut the door.

"This way," she said. She took his coat and led him to the family room in the back of the house. Allison was dressed sharply in a blue suit, ready for her morning news conference.

Harley did a double take, surprised. "You look—good."

She managed a meager smile. "What were you expecting? Tattered robe, fuzzy slippers, and a fistful of cyanide tablets?"

He blushed with embarrassment. "I don't know what I was expecting, really. Anyway, I did want to tell you I think it's wrong the way they're treating you."

"Worse things have happened to me."

He blinked, knowing how true that was. "I also wanted to thank you."

"Thank me? For what?"

"For the way you stood up for me last night. I saw the statement you gave to the press at the airport. You could easily have pointed the finger at me for the botched arrest. Instead, you took responsibility."

"I just hate to see the media trashing good people. There's a big difference between incompetence and a talented FBI agent who's hamstrung by outsiders who keep manipulating the investigation for their own political benefit."

"Still, what you did took guts."

She smiled faintly. "It took guts for you to come over here, too. I appreciate the gesture. But if you stay here much longer, we'll only be making more problems for each other."

"I suppose that's true. But there is one problem I'd like to solve before I go. How do you and I stay in touch?"

"What do you mean?"

"You know—how do I keep you informed?"

"Harley, I've been suspended."

"All that means is you're no longer my boss. But I'm still in charge of the investigation, and I still haven't ruled out the possibility of a link between Kristen's kidnapping and your daughter's abduction. To that extent alone, I need your input. Layer on top of that the fact that you and your husband have agreed to pay Kristen's ransom and I'd say you're an indispensable player—suspension or no suspension."

"Harley, my suspension is a direct order from the president of the United States. You're jeopardizing your career."

"Not much of a career, is it, if I just stand by and let someone else take the fall for my mistake?

I know there's nothing I can do to make the president reverse the suspension. But there's plenty we can do to make sure this investigation runs the way it should."

"How intriguing, Mr. Abrams. I've never seen your devilish side."

He blushed again. She seemed to have a knack for making him do that. "Twenty-two years with the FBI, I didn't know I had one."

Her smile faded as she turned more serious. "Peter and I were actually talking about this whole situation earlier. Do you think the kidnappers are still after a ransom?"

"Hard to say. Our voice analysts are positive that the man who called yesterday and let Tanya talk to Kristen is definitely not the man who called you and Tanya on Friday. The guy said he would keep Kristen safe until after the election, but with all the media hoopla about yesterday's botched arrest, he might not be feeling so protective."

"What's your best guess as to what's going on?"

"The confusion suggests a pretty volatile situation, which heightens the risk of harm to the child. I see two likely scenarios, both bad. One, Kristen's already dead and we'll never hear from either of those two callers again. Or two, they'll keep her alive at least until tomorrow morning at eight o'clock, when the guy who called on Friday said he would call you for the ransom. We hope it's the second. If they make contact for the ransom, we at least have a shot at catching them before they kill her. If they don't make contact—well, you get the picture."

"It doesn't sound like you think there's much chance they'll let her go, even if we pay."

He sighed, unsure. "Paying the ransom at least

buys a little time, maybe gives us a chance to stall. I'd say the twenty-four-hour period between Monday at eight A.M. and the opening of the polls on Tuesday morning is Kristen's primary danger zone. If they're going to kill her, they'll want to maximize the impact on the election, probably dump her body on the Justice Department steps or some other dramatic setting. If you wanted to narrow the time frame even further, I'd say between eight A.M. and six P.M. Monday, in time for her murder to be the lead story on the evening news on election eve and the headline story in every election-day newspaper in the country."

"So, you're saying that even if we pay, we've got at most thirty-six hours to find her."

"Basically, that's it."

"And if we don't pay?"

"She's dead for sure in twenty-four."

Allison looked away, thinking how little progress she'd made toward finding Emily in more than eight years of effort. "Thirty-six hours," she said softly, her eyes drifting back toward Harley. "God help us."

Allison didn't watch Harley leave. She knew, without watching, that he was walking into a First Amendment frenzy outside her townhouse. Reporters started shouting the minute the front door cracked open. Closing it barely muffled their cries. Allison refilled her coffee cup at the kitchen counter, dreading the thought of venturing outside.

The phone rang, startling her. It was her personal private line, which narrowed the possible callers to a handful—even less than a handful, since Peter was upstairs and Harley was right outside being drawn and quartered by a pack of hungry coyotes. She answered with a mixture of curiosity and concern.

"Hello."

"Ms. Leahy, this is Tanya Howe."

Allison felt relief, then embarrassment—she really should have called Tanya. "I'm glad you called. I was meaning to call you."

"You told me to call if I ever needed anything. Well, I'm in need of some answers."

Allison settled onto the bar stool at the counter. The edge to Tanya's voice was alarming. "You mean about last night?"

"No, I mean this morning. I found an FBI agent in my bathroom plucking a hair sample from my mother's brush, rummaging through her cosmetic bag."

Allison closed her eyes, like a woman with a migraine. *So much for being discreet, Harley*, she thought. "Tanya, please. I can explain."

In minutes, she told her about the scarlet letter photograph, the message scrawled in red lipstick, the traces of saliva found at the lab, the need for a DNA sample to test for a match. She skirted around the ever-elusive Mitch O'Brien, focusing instead on the two female suspects they'd identified so far—one of whom was her mother.

Allison braced herself for a loyal daughter's fury, but Tanya's response was slow in coming. Finally she simply said, "You should have told me what you were doing."

Her tone was surprisingly reasonable, putting Allison somewhat at ease. "I'm sorry," said Allison. "Honestly, I thought the chances of your mother being involved were so remote that I didn't want to alarm you."

"You're right. My mother would never do that.

And even if your DNA test confirms that the lipstick was hers, that doesn't mean my mother was involved."

"DNA tests are very reliable."

"I'm sure they are. But that doesn't rule out the possibility that someone took my mother's lipstick and scrawled the message, without her knowledge. Someone like my father."

Allison paused. Suddenly the chances of a DNA match seemed much greater. "That sounds more plausible to me."

Tanya was silent, as if thinking something over. "Or," she said quietly, "I suppose someone could have scrawled the message *with* her knowledge."

"Is there something in particular that makes you say that?"

"Not a big thing, but big enough. My father came by this morning to see if I knew anything about the FBI looking into the death of Kristen's father. My mom arranged the meeting, which doesn't sound bad in itself. She just did it in a very surreptitious way. She obviously knew that my father wanted to grill me about Mark, but she never even gave me a clue about the purpose of his visit. In fact, she led me to believe it was going to be another attempt at father-daughter reconciliation. I never would have thought she'd mislead me like that, especially while my daughter is kidnapped. I guess my father has more control over her than I thought."

Allison drummed her nails on the countertop, thinking. "Tanya, I don't like to ask you to play spy, but is there any possible way you could get your mother and father together and just watch them? See how they act toward one another, listen to what they say to each other about Kristen's kidnapping?"

"It would be hard. My father is campaigning full blast now."

"He has to sleep somewhere tonight. Maybe he could spend the night with your mother in the spare bedroom. Tell your mother you'd like to have the family pull together as the crisis comes to a head."

"He and I had a pretty big blowup before he left this morning. I don't know that he'll ever come back, even if my mother and I both ask him."

"He'll come back. If nothing else, I'm sure the image of family togetherness is something that appeals to his campaign instincts. To be honest with you, it wouldn't hurt for the kidnappers to at least think that you're pulling together. It might make them think they have an even greater chance of collecting a ransom."

"Is this really necessary?"

"We've reached the point where we have to do everything we possibly can, as quickly as we can. If anywhere in your heart you feel there's even a remote possibility that your father is in any way involved in that scarlet letter photograph I received or in the kidnapping of your daughter, then I'd say it's absolutely necessary for you to get him in a position where you can watch him, at least for a little while. I hate to scare you, Tanya. But Harley and I both think we're running out of time."

"Don't worry about scaring me," she said. "I'm beyond scared."

"I know you are. Just don't let it paralyze you."

She sighed deeply. "I'll take care of it," she said in a shaky voice. "Somehow I'll get the general back here tonight."

41

Kristen wasn't sure she was awake. The last thing she'd heard was that voice in the alley, the scary guy who'd tackled her and said she'd never escape. The last thing she'd felt was that needle in her leg, like when those men had dragged her into the van and injected her with something to make her pass out. This time, however, the sleep seemed even deeper, harder to shake. Maybe this time she was waking before the drugs had worn off. Maybe this time a part of her just didn't want to wake up.

Kristen Howe is not afraid. She thought it, formed the words in her mind, could almost see her mantra etched in big puffy white letters across a bright blue sky. But she didn't believe, couldn't make herself believe it. This time the mantra was nothing more than words. *Less* than words. Just lofty thoughts in the air that faded into smoke and dissolved in the wind.

She felt sticky, smelly, wet. Then a flash hit her eyes, though her eyes were not open. Another white flash, like lightning at midnight that brightens a black room and then leaves you in darkness. She opened her mouth to catch the raindrops on her tongue. But it wasn't raining. And she heard no thunder.

She struggled to open her eyes, but the lids

were too heavy. The harder she tried, the heavier they seemed. Sight was the one sense that completely eluded her. The others, however, were slowly come back to her. Taste, salty. And the smell was familiar. Like meat. Bloody, red meat.

Panic raced through her. *Am I bleeding?*

Couldn't be. No pain, not anywhere on her body. And the blood was cold—icy cold, as if it had been stored in the refrigerator. *That's* what it was! It was like the pig's blood in biology class, when the teacher took it from the refrigerator in the middle school laboratory, and the students put a drop on the glass slide to examine it under the microscope. The same pig's blood she'd tasted on a dare from her girlfriends. The pig's blood she'd smelled when those boys dropped the jar on the floor.

Pig's blood. All over her body.

Another flash, this time even brighter. She was floating. Not just in her mind, but physically floating. Her eyes began to open, the left, then the right. Two narrow slits unaccustomed to light, unable to form images.

Suddenly it was raining. Warm water pelting her body, rinsing the sticky, thick, smelly mess from her body. Steam filled the air, more like a hot shower than any rain she'd ever known. The wet warmth made her sleepier. Her eyes were closing once again, but not without a lucid moment. White everywhere. White tiles above. White curtain at her side. Smooth white porcelain all around her. A dark red stream swirling down the drain at her feet.

Another jab in her leg—that needle again. Then blackness and a quick return to blissful sleep.

* * *

The pain was worse at the end of the day. Allison had been going through the motions since last night's meeting with President Sires, never really absorbing the full impact of her "suspension." Finally it was beginning to hurt. Friends were already expressing their condolences. Foes were smiling and sharpening their knives for the November version of the bloody Ides of March.

The mob of reporters outside her door had dealt the first blow. It was only a few steps from her front door to the curb, but it had seemed like miles. Without Secret Service leading the way, she might never have reached her limousine. The ride to the studio had offered a moment of peace, but it was fireworks again on ABC's political talk show, *This Week in Washington.* One outspoken panelist, in particular, seemed out to get her.

"Why didn't you just stay out of the investigation from the beginning," he'd asked pointedly, "and simply avoid the whole conflict-of-interest controversy?"

"It's interesting you ask that," was her dry reply. "Especially since you're the one who blasted me in last week's editorial for not doing more to save Kristen Howe."

It had been downhill from there. Worse, actually. More like falling off a cliff.

How things change, she thought. Four years ago, her first appearance on a Sunday morning political talk show had been a virtual love fest—Allison Leahy, Washington's new wonder woman. Back then, even the president had seemed taken with her. She recalled their first chat in her new office suite, just a day or so after her Senate confirmation. A photographer had snapped a shot of the two of them in front of the fireplace as they looked up with admiration at the portrait of Robert Kennedy hanging over the mantel. Later, the president had personally signed and inscribed the photograph for her: "Someday a new attorney general will be admiring a portrait of *you*."

Fat chance. She had the sinking feeling that her place in history was now considerably lower, more like the basement of the Justice Building, tucked behind the group portrait of former Nixon Attorney General John Mitchell and his prison-garbed Watergate coconspirators.

At 10:00 P.M. her limousine was finally taking her home from the airport. She'd filled Sunday afternoon with quick appearances in Philadelphia and New Jersey, followed by an in-flight meeting with her strategists to approve some new commercials. Somewhere between it all she did manage to call Harley to tell him about her conversation with Tanya Howe. He loved the idea of luring the general to Tanya's house, though he had a more active notion of daughter-turned-spy than Allison had envisioned. She figured she'd leave it to Harley to work out the details, knowing that Tanya wasn't the kind of woman who could be talked into anything that made her uncomfortable.

"Should I run them over?" asked her FBI driver.

Allison peered ahead through the windshield, shaking off her thoughts. Reporters were still crowding outside her townhouse awaiting her return. She was tempted to say yes.

"That's okay. I'll just phone ahead and ask Peter to dump the pot of boiling oil out of the second-story window."

The agent smiled, then braced himself for the frantic members of the media rushing toward the moving car. Excited faces and probing cameras filled the car windows, but Allison knew the tinted glass made it impossible for anyone to see inside. From her vantage point, they were everywhere—front, back, both sides. Had the limo stopped rolling they would have jumped on the hood. It was a theater of the absurd, the way they hollered and gawked, pressing their noses against the glass, assuming that Allison was inside and listening. She thought of the underwater exhibit at Sea World, where you could sit on the safe side of protective glass and watch sharks and barracudas swim by in the tank.

The limo stopped directly in front of her townhouse. One of her FBI escorts forced his door open, muscled his way around the car, and opened Allison's door for her. With an agent on each arm she made it to the iron gate, bathed in almost constant blinding light from camera flashes. She opened the gate and hurried to the front door. One agent stayed outside, the other followed her in.

"Thank you," she told him. She was out of breath, exhausted from the gauntlet. It was then that she noticed the package tucked under the agent's arm.

He handed it to her. "A mutual friend asked me to give this to you."

She looked at him curiously, taking it. It was wrapped in brown paper, about the size of a shoe box. "What is it?" she said with some trepidation.

"It's okay. I've checked it out." He gave her a thin smile, then said good night and let himself out. The noise cranked up when the front door opened, then leveled off at an audible level of disappointment the moment the crowd realized it was only an FBI agent.

Allison carried the package to the kitchen and laid it on the table. She filled a glass with ice water and drank half of it while staring at the package. It creeped her out a little. A mysterious package from "a mutual friend." But she'd known her escort for almost six months. If he said he'd checked it out, he'd surely checked it out.

She tore away the packaging. It was indeed a shoe box. With care, she removed the lid and tissue paper. She paused.

What in the heck?

A smile came to her face as she removed the pink fuzzy slippers; then she chuckled to herself. The card was on the bottom. She tore open the envelope and read it to herself: COULDN'T FIND A TATTERED ROBE. STRONGLY DISCOURAGE THE CYANIDE TABLETS. HANG IN THERE. HARLEY.

Her heart swelled. For a brief moment, she didn't feel so bad. "Thank you, Harley," she said with a grin.

By 10:30 P.M., the pit in Tanya's stomach had grown to canyon proportions. Allison had been right. All she had to do was ask, and her father would come.

Not only was he coming, but he had made a point of telling everyone all about it at every stop along his Sunday campaign trail. A family pulling together in a time of crisis did indeed mesh perfectly with the general's campaign strategy.

Tanya rose from the couch and switched off the ten o'clock evening news. If she heard one more sappy news report about the general taking time away from his busy campaign schedule to be at his daughter's side, she would surely vomit.

She heard a commotion outside the house. She

knew that sound by now, had come to react to it, the way others might respond to the bark of their dog or the ring of their doorbell. The ever-present media watch was stirring to life, signaling the arrival of a visitor to the Howe household. She stepped to the front window and peered from behind the draperies. It was the black limo brigade.

Tanya flinched at the hand on her shoulder. Her mother withdrew her touch and said, "I'm proud of you, Tanya. It's important for you and your father to come together at a time like this. He's a wonderful man. He can be a real source of strength."

She stared straight ahead, fixing on the candidate waving at the media as he cut across her lawn. She felt a pang of guilt about deceiving her mother, about not telling her the real reason she'd invited him. But she had to put Kristen first.

"Tanya, you're doing the right thing."

She turned and looked her mother in the eye. "Yes. I know I am."

42

The doorbell rang in the middle of her dreams. Tanya shot up in bed and checked the glowing liquid crystal numbers on the clock on her nightstand: 2:20 A.M. Her heart thumped. Her mind raced with thoughts of her daughter. Bad news, she feared. Nothing but bad news came in the middle of the night. So bad that a phone call wouldn't suffice. It had to be delivered to her in person.

She threw on a robe and rushed to the living room. The FBI agent who was serving night watch was already answering the door. He opened it. Tanya didn't know who to expect, but she couldn't hide her surprise. She'd never met him before, but she instantly recognized her father's chief campaign strategist from the news and magazines.

"Mr. LaBelle?" she asked in a tone that sounded like *What are* you *doing here?*

LaBelle stepped into the foyer, speaking to Tanya in his most polite, southern accent. "Sorry to disturb you at this hour, Miss Tanya. But it's very important that I speak to your father."

"He's asleep."

"Not anymore," the general grumbled from the hallway.

LaBelle closed the door, shutting out the cold draft. He glanced at Tanya and the FBI agent. "I'm very sorry to intrude, but would the two of you mind giving the general and me just one moment, please?"

"By all means," Tanya said with sarcasm. She and the agent shuffled out of the room, he to the kitchen and she to her bedroom.

The general stepped into the foyer, speaking softly so as not be overheard. "What's going on?"

"It's important. I didn't want to risk a phone call to your daughter's house. Thought someone might be listening. Come on," he said as he reached for the door. "Let's talk in the car."

Howe bristled. "It's freezing out there, Buck. And there's a ton of media—even more than usual, since I decided to stay here. What are they going to think? It looks conspiratorial, me sneaking out of my daughter's house in my pajamas in the middle of the damn night, two men sitting in the back of the limo talking at two o'clock in the morning. It looks bad enough for you to come here."

"Sir, this is *extremely* important."

The general looked around with a pained expression. The FBI agent was fixing himself a cup of coffee in the kitchen. The media were parked on the street. "Come on," said Howe. "We can talk in the spare bedroom."

The general led the way down the hall, to the opposite side of the house in which Natalie was sleeping. Tanya's room was at the far end of the hall. He stepped quietly through the carpeted hallway, trying not to disturb her. The hinges creaked as he opened the door. Tanya had converted the spare bedroom into a combination guest room and home office. LaBelle took a seat on the Hide-A-Bed sofa. The general closed the door quietly, then sat in the swivel chair in front of the computer.

"Talk to me," he ordered.

LaBelle's face was filled with concern. "They're looking for Mitch O'Brien."

"Who's looking for O'Brien?"

"The FBI. They're down in Miami, snooping around the marina, his house, asking neighbors questions. Nobody seems to know where he is."

The general suddenly had that look on his face—the look of a volcano on the verge of eruption. He drew a deep breath, controlling it. He rose from the chair, as if towering over LaBelle made it easier to question him. "Does the FBI know anything?"

"I don't know. I guess they suspect something."

He began to pace slowly, adjusting his stride to accommodate the small room. "What could they possibly know unless they've talked to him?"

"Hard to say."

"Maybe we should beat them to the punch. You know, release the O'Brien story ourselves, like I did with the rumors that the investigation was focusing on my own campaign."

LaBelle shook his head. "I don't think that rule applies here."

"Why not?"

He sighed. "It would be different if the whole thing didn't unravel at the end. I mean, it would be perfectly all right to say that Leahy's ex-fiancé came to us before the Atlanta debates and said he was living proof that the attorney general had been unfaithful to her husband. The fact that he offered to take a polygraph is even better. It was like Anita Hill taking her polygraph to substantiate her sexual harassment allegations against

Clarence Thomas. Problem is, the polygraph is where our story begins to fall apart."

"We don't have to tell anyone he failed the damn thing. We just say he offered to take a polygraph. Period."

"Too risky. We can't contain it. Once the FBI or the media gets hold of O'Brien, it's bound to come out that the guy failed the polygraph and—worse—that we still painted Leahy as an adulteress after we knew he had failed."

"I still don't understand why that fool offered to take a polygraph examination if he was lying about him and Leahy having sex."

"O'Brien was a hotshot criminal defense lawyer. He's probably seen a hundred lying clients fool polygraph examiners. He probably thought he could, too."

The general stopped pacing. His eyes were aimed at LaBelle, but he was looking right through him. Finally he came back from the place his mind had taken him. "Have you talked to O'Brien?"

"Not since the polygraph."

"Any idea where he is?"

"Not really."

His glare tightened. "There's only one thing to do, Buck."

"What's that, sir?"

"Find him. Before the FBI does."

Natalie lay awake, wishing Lincoln would come back to bed. Tonight hadn't been the reunion she had hoped for. He and Tanya had hardly looked at each other when he'd arrived, let alone spoken. Natalie had hoped he might get through the night just tending to his family, without interruption from the campaign strategists.

She should have known better.

The bedroom door opened. A shaft of light from the hallway cut across the dark room. Lincoln entered quietly and closed the door behind him. Natalie lay still beneath the covers, watching as he carefully crossed the room without switching on a light, listening as he tucked himself back into the twin bed beside hers. She saw him check the clock, then heard a deep sigh of exhaustion.

Her voice pierced the darkness. "You promised no politics in Tanya's house."

"I know. It was an emergency."

She propped herself up on her elbow and looked right at him. "What kind of emergency?"

He rolled over to face her, fluffing the pillow. "Campaign emergency."

"Lincoln, you broke your promise. I want to know why."

"LaBelle thought it was urgent. Turns out it's just more about those adultery rumors that surfaced about Leahy."

"Good heavens. All that adultery stuff doesn't even seem remotely important anymore."

He rolled onto his back and sighed smugly, hands clasped behind his head. "You're right, Nat. In less than two days your Lincoln will be elected president of the United States of America."

He reached across the space dividing their twin beds, groping for her hand. She pulled away, out of his reach. "I meant the kidnapping," she said sharply. "The adultery accusations seem silly compared to what happened to Kristen. Not compared to your election."

He withdrew his hand. "I—uh. Of course that's what you meant. I was just looking for a silver lining, I guess."

She got up from her bed, then quickly put on her robe and slippers for a trip to the bathroom. She stopped at the door, looking back at him in the darkness. "Maybe it's about time you stopped looking for the silver lining and started looking for your granddaughter."

She waited, expecting him to say *something*. The lack of response made the room seem darker. She stepped out and headed down the hall.

Tanya sat motionless on the floor, right beside the vent to the heating duct. The air flow to the master bedroom was on a split duct. Part of it led to her room. The other led to the guest bedroom—the room she'd converted into an office. It had been Kristen's room originally, but her daughter had insisted on moving to the other side of the house after she'd grown wise to the fact that, because of the ducts, her mother could hear everything in there just by putting her ear to the heating vent in the master bedroom. Kristen was a sharp girl. Much sharper than her grandfather.

Tanya glanced at the phone on the nightstand. She was tempted to phone Allison or Harley to help make sense of what she'd heard, but she had to organize her thoughts first.

Find O'Brien—her father's order rang in her head. What did that mean? Find him and talk to him? Find him and silence him? Find him and kill him?

She took a deep breath, shuddering at the thought, struggling to stay focused. First, Mark Buckley. Dead on the highway after a threat from her father. Now Mitch O'Brien. Apparently hiding from the FBI, maybe hiding from her father, too. Or hiding from the men who worked for her father. Maybe the same men who took Kristen.

Her head was pounding with the horrible possibilities. It didn't make total sense to her, but this O'Brien character seemed like a logical fit somewhere into the adultery scandal and scarlet letter photograph Allison had briefly explained to her on the telephone.

In all the confusion whirling in her mind, one thing that stood out was the last warning from Harley Abrams. He had pushed her to spy on her father. It was possible, he'd explained, that if Kristen's taking was politically motivated, the kidnappers might now be content to let the election simply run its course, never following up on their demand for a ransom. That was Kristen's most dangerous scenario. That made it imperative to do more than just sit around and wait. They needed some offense—something to draw the kidnappers out of hiding.

Her eyes drifted to the photograph on her dresser. The two of them, her and Kristen. The last picture of them together.

She wiped away the tears and rose to her feet. Anger filled her veins, but in anger she found strength. She put on her robe and stepped into the hall.

A crack of light shone from beneath the bathroom door at the other end of the house. Her poor mother and her peanut-sized bladder were undoubtedly making one of the four or five trips she seemed to make each night. Tanya hurried down the hall, taking extra care to be quiet as she passed the FBI agent sitting in the kitchen. She stopped at the bathroom door. She heard the turning of a magazine page. Definitely her mother.

She continued down the hall, past Kristen's room. The door was closed; her room had been secured like a crime scene. She stopped at the door beside it, the room her mother and father were using. Quietly she opened the door.

The bedroom was dark, save for the glowing face of the alarm clock on the dresser and the horizontal shafts of moonlight that cut through the miniblinds covering the window. Her father lay on the bed by the window, a hulk of man beneath the heavy blanket. She stepped quietly toward him, stopping near the foot of the bed to look at his face. He was deeply asleep.

She moved closer, then knelt right beside him. He was lying on his side, his cheek on the pillow. She crouched down until they were eye to eye and stared into his face. She could feel him breathing. Finally he seemed to sense her presence. His eyes blinked open.

"Don't move," she said in a cold, harsh whisper.

He froze, as if she'd put a gun to his head. "What is it, Tanya?" he asked with concern.

"I heard your conversation with Buck LaBelle."

His eyes became wider. The whites were huge in the darkness. He said nothing.

She whispered, "I think you would stop at nothing to get elected. I think you would kidnap your own granddaughter to get elected. And if Kristen isn't home before the polls open on Tuesday morning, I'm going on national television to tell the voters what I think."

"Tanya," he gulped, "you're making a horrible mistake."

"Be still. Those are my terms."

The door opened. Natalie stepped a foot inside, then stopped. "Tanya?"

She rose slowly, her expression pleasant. “Dad and I were just talking.”

Natalie came to them and sat on the edge of the bed. “That’s a good thing. You two should talk more.”

Tanya glanced at her mother, then back at her father. “Something tells me we will. It seems we have lots to talk about.”

“Wonderful,” said Natalie. “I knew this was a good idea.”

“It was a great idea, Mom.” She kissed her on the cheek, then crossed the room without a sound, stopping in the doorway. “Good night, Father.”

The general nearly bit his tongue, careful not to say anything in front of his wife. “Good night, Tanya.”

The door creaked open, and then she was gone.

43

The telephone rang at precisely eight o'clock Monday morning. Allison was dressed and standing beside the phone, waiting and hoping for—if not expecting—the call. The shrill ring still startled her. She snatched up the receiver.

"This is Allison."

A shaky, high-pitched voice came on the line. "This is Kristen Howe."

Allison immediately hit the button on the phone that triggered the FBI intercept. "Kristen, where are you?"

A pause, followed by that disguised, mechanical voice—Kristen was gone. "Between a rock and a hard place. Same as you. Do you have the money?"

She checked the clock on the wall. Fourteen seconds. It sounded like another cellular phone, which meant that she needed to stall if the FBI was going to trace it. "Yes, I have it. But I want to talk to Kristen."

"Go to the old Pension Building at ten A.M. Enter on Fifth Street. Go through the atrium, and exit on F Street."

Allison bristled at the tone. The voice was disguised, like before, but it didn't sound like Friday's caller or the caller on Saturday. It sounded altogether different. "Put Kristen back on the line," she said. "Just so I know for sure she's alive."

"Wait on the sidewalk outside the building on F Street. And bring the money."

She grimaced. Whoever he was, the caller was no fool—no wasted words. "You want *me* to deliver the money?"

"Yes, you. Personally. Alone. No FBI."

"I don't think I can get out undetected."

"Sure you can. A suspended attorney general doesn't need an FBI escort."

Smart-ass, she thought. "It's not the FBI I'm worried about. The press is camped outside my door."

"And Kristen Howe has a gun to her head. You think you got problems? Beat the media. Be there. Ten A.M. You're late, she's dead."

She started to say something—anything—to keep him talking, but the line clicked. She checked the clock. Less than forty seconds. "Damn," she muttered, knowing it probably wasn't enough time for a trace on a wireless. She disconnected with her finger and speed-dialed Harley Abrams.

He answered immediately, having heard the entire conversation through the intercept.

"You heard?" asked Allison.

"Yeah," he said. "You really got the money?"

"Not on me. Peter called his banker at home this morning. It's at the bank."

"Can you trust the bank to keep it confidential? A cash withdrawal as big as this isn't exactly an everyday occurrence."

"It's structured to be not so obvious. Peter has been wire-transferring it in small installments over the past couple of days from several banks—some offshore—to nine different accounts held in the names of nine different companies he controls. Nobody but Peter's banker will really know the money is going to us personally. I told Peter this has to be confidential."

"You trust his banker?"

"Peter says he does."

Harley paused. "You don't have to pay it, you know."

"We've already made our decision."

"There's a wrinkle," said Harley.

"What kind of wrinkle?"

"I got a call from Lincoln Howe about twenty minutes ago."

"And?" she asked urgently.

"Seems he's had a change of heart. He told me that if the kidnappers make a ransom demand, he and his wife have decided to pay it."

Allison froze. "Did he say why?"

"Just that some wealthy friends offered him the money, and he changed his mind. He's not making it public. Nothing more than that."

"Why didn't you tell me before?"

"Allison, I'm being as straight as I possibly can. Howe told me not to tell you, and Director O'Doud gave me a direct order to abide by his wishes. If the kidnappers hadn't renewed their demand, there wouldn't have been any need for you to know. I'm telling you now because it affects you directly. You and Peter don't have to pay."

"But I still have to *deliver*. That's what the kidnappers are expecting. If we change the plan, they'll kill Kristen."

Harley groaned. "That's pretty sticky. If Howe is supplying the money, I'm not sure he'll want you delivering it."

"Then Peter and I will supply the money."

"That doesn't solve everything. It's bad enough

that you're the point person on the phone calls. Making you the deliveryperson only compounds the problem."

"What problem?"

"It's like a case one of my mentors had back in the seventies, when Jimmy Carter offered to negotiate with a hostage taker who demanded to talk to the president. It's just not smart to put someone with ultimate power in direct communication with a hostage taker. You can't stall. You can't say you have to check with your superiors before giving into their demands."

"What power do I have, Harley? I'm suspended."

"The kidnappers won't care."

"Look, we're not going to make a unilateral change to the kidnappers' plan and get Kristen Howe killed. Got it?"

"Hey, come on now. I'm on your side."

She took a deep breath. "Sorry. Didn't mean to be harsh. But Howe's sudden reversal on the ransom doesn't sit well with me. Not twenty minutes before a call from the kidnappers."

"Not much we can do before ten o'clock."

"No," she agreed. "But it might be worth five minutes to talk to Tanya Howe."

Allison conferenced in Tanya Howe, who took the call in the privacy of her bedroom. It took only moments for Allison to give her the gist of the kidnapper's demands.

"Did Kristen sound okay?" were Tanya's first words.

Allison paused. She wanted to be straight but not a pessimist. "She sounded scared, but okay. To be honest, there's no way for me to know if Kristen was actually on the line or if it was a recording. I asked to talk to her so I could hear her respond to a question, but he wouldn't put her on."

"So you don't know if she's alive?" said Tanya.

"We have to assume."

"I don't want to *assume*. I need to *know* my baby's all right."

Harley interceded. "We'll know soon, Tanya."

"When?"

Allison said, "They want me to deliver the ransom at ten o'clock."

"And," said Harley, "there's something else you should know. Your father called earlier this morning. He's agreed to pay a ransom."

Tanya paused, seeming to catch her breath. "Don't deliver it."

"Come again?" said Allison.

"You're being set up."

"Set up?" asked Harley. "How?"

Tanya quickly explained her confrontation with her father last night—her demand to publicly accuse him of being involved in the kidnapping if Kristen was not returned safely before Tuesday morning.

"Don't you see?" she continued. "This morning's ransom demand and my father's sudden agreement to pay it were both triggered by my threat last night. The kidnappers are offering to return Kristen before the election only because my father controls them. At the same time, he's agreed to pay the ransom so that it looks like he had nothing to do with her kidnapping or her return. In my mind, this just slam-dunk confirms his involvement."

Harley said, "I understand what you're saying, Tanya. But it doesn't necessarily follow that all of this was triggered by last night's conversation. Remember, the caller on *Friday* said he would call Allison at eight o'clock Monday morning. So, at most, the only thing that was triggered by your argument with your father last night was his decision to pay a ransom—which, by itself, isn't all that incriminating. I mean, if someone threatened to ruin my career and reputation unless Kristen were returned safely before Tuesday morning, I'd probably offer to pay a ransom for her safe return, too."

"Harley has a point," said Allison. "If your father were really behind this, I have to think that the last person he'd want to deliver the ransom would be me. If Kristen is returned safely, I could be hailed as a hero on the eve of the election. I could be right back in the race."

Tanya scoffed. "Don't you people get it? Kristen is *not* going to be returned safely. This is all a setup. You have to think the way my father thinks. Of course he wouldn't create a situation where you might be a hero. He's putting you in a position where things are going to go wrong—*very* wrong—and you alone are going to be responsible."

Allison gripped the phone a little tighter, thinking. "All right, Tanya. Say it is a setup. But consider the possibility that it's a setup going the other way. Not a setup to kill Kristen after I deliver the ransom, but a setup to kill her if I *don't.* General Howe or his crazed supporters are betting I'll do the cowardly thing and refuse to deliver the ransom. When I refuse, they kill your daughter. If that happens, your father knows I couldn't be elected dog catcher, let alone president."

All three fell silent. Finally, Harley said, "Either theory is equally plausible."

"You're a big help, Mr. Abrams."

"Tanya," said Allison, "please listen to me. I kicked myself eight years ago for listening to others instead of myself. But I didn't have anyone who'd been through the same thing I'd been through. I've been through it. I'm *still* going through it. I wouldn't tell you what to do if I didn't feel in my heart it was the right thing to do. Trust my instincts on this."

Tanya said nothing.

Harley asked, "Tanya, what do you want to do?"

Her voice shook, but her decision seemed firm. "Whatever Allison decides. That's what I'll do."

"Thank you," said Allison. "If I only get one vote this week, that's the one I wanted."

"Call me," said Tanya. "Just keep me informed."

"I will," said Allison.

Tanya hung up. Harley stayed on the line. "You're putting yourself in real danger, Allison. We should use a double."

"In two hours you think you're going to round up a female FBI agent who looks enough like me to fool the kidnappers? Come on, Harley, get real."

"I just don't want to see you hurt."

She was about to snap, tell him she could handle herself, but she stopped. He wasn't condescending. Just concerned. "Look, Harley, if this kidnapping really is politically motivated, then delivering the ransom isn't likely to put me at any greater risk than a candidate for the presidency faces every day. If someone had wanted to put General Howe in the White House by killing me outright, they could have done that a long time ago."

"Shit happens, Allison. You could get killed

even if they don't intend to kill you. And you can't rule out the possibility that more is at work here than some lunatic's obsession with winning. Maybe they're simply determined not to let Lincoln Howe be the first man, black or white, to lose the presidency to a woman. To achieve that goal, they might well kill off the opposition. And they might do it by luring her into a botched ransom delivery."

Allison thought for a moment. "Enough about elections. Have you ruled out the possibility that Kristen's kidnapping is related to Emily's abduction?"

He sighed, knowing where this was headed. "No."

"Of course you haven't. You're thinking the same thing I'm thinking. Why else would the kidnapper want *me* to deliver the ransom? There's only one logical answer. It's because this isn't about Kristen. It isn't about Lincoln Howe. Maybe it isn't even really about politics. It's about *me*. And if it's about me, then there's a good chance that it's about Emily."

"So you're delivering the ransom." It was less a question, more reluctant resignation.

"What do you think?"

"I think I'll need clearance from headquarters. Probably the director himself."

"Then get it," she said.

44

At nine o'clock, Allison was slipping on her overcoat, ready to go. She had already left messages for her running mate and campaign strategists, explaining that the number-one woman on the ticket was unable to campaign today, at least until the afternoon. She knew it was lame to leave messages, but she couldn't tell them *why* she was canceling her morning appearances, so she purposely avoided a direct conversation.

Her cellular phone rang in her purse as she reached for the doorknob. She did a double take. It was a number the kidnapper couldn't have gotten. Only a select few had it. She answered tentatively.

It was her campaign strategist. "What's this bullshit about cancellations?" Wilcox blurted.

Her stomach did a flip-flop. Somehow, she knew he'd find her. "I'm sorry, David. I have some personal matters to take care of this morning."

"Personal! The election is *tomorrow*. This is no time to go get your teeth cleaned."

"David, unless you want your *clock* cleaned, I suggest you change your tone."

"We're all getting our clock cleaned. One of my aides just faxed me a summary of an AP story. Listen to this." Papers shuffled as he read from the fax. "'Washington—With every major poll showing General Howe at least five points ahead, an anonymous White House source reports that Attorney General Leahy has privately conceded defeat. Democratic leaders are concerned that any further public appearances by Leahy in swing states might actually hurt Democratic congressional candidates. In what insiders are calling an unprecedented acknowledgment of the accuracy of modern pre-election polling, voters may actually see a presidential candidate assume a low profile on the eve of the election.'"

Allison grimaced. "It's Howe. I know it's him. It's no White House source."

"I don't care if it's the president's golden retriever. The point is, if you cancel any more engagements, you're just substantiating this nonsense. People are going to think you've thrown in the towel."

"I can't help that, David. I'm out of pocket for the rest of the morning. I'll be back this afternoon."

"Allison!"

"Clear the decks until one o'clock. That's the best I can do. I'll call you." She hit the cancel button in the midst of his screaming, then quickly dialed Harley Abrams.

He answered directly. "What is it?"

Her tone was angry, though she didn't really blame Harley. "Did you get approval from your superiors for me to deliver the ransom?"

"Yes, I told you I would."

"Who did you talk to?"

"Director O'Doud, himself."

"Any chance he contacted Lincoln Howe?"

"I suppose so. I don't know. Why?"

"They're frying me. They knew I'd have to cancel my morning campaign appearances to deliver the ransom. Now, a supposed White House source is saying that I'm deliberately making myself scarce so I can't take any congressional candidates down with me."

"Why would the White House say that?"

"It's *not* the White House, Harley. It's Lincoln Howe."

"You think even Lincoln Howe is dirty enough to let you deliver the ransom and then make political hay out of the fact that you're not out there campaigning?"

"Who *else*?"

His pause only confirmed the lack of other suspects. "I'm sorry, Allison. I'm not the one playing politics. I'm just following FBI procedure. I didn't feel I could send you in with the ransom without approval."

"I know, it's not your fault."

"Are you changing your mind about the delivery?"

"No. Of course not."

"Do you want to make it public? I mean, if Lincoln Howe knows you're delivering the ransom, maybe we don't have to keep your role a secret anymore."

"Too risky," she said. "If I go public, the kidnappers might think I'm using the ransom delivery purely as a political stunt. That could get Kristen killed in a heartbeat."

"You're right. But are you sure you want to go through with this?"

"Yes, damn it. I'll see you in fifteen minutes." She switched off the phone and tucked it back into her purse, then braced herself as she opened the front door.

The cacophony hit her as quickly as the cold morning air. Her FBI escort met her on the front steps. He opened the iron gate and pushed the media aside, clearing a short path across the width of the sidewalk. Her limo was at the curb with the motor running. Another agent inside pushed the rear door open. Allison hurried through the narrow opening in the mob and slid into the backseat. A boom microphone clobbered her FBI escort in the head, but no one but the agent even seemed to notice. Without interruption, the steady roar of reporters continued even after the limo door had shut.

"Ms. Leahy!" they shouted. "Is it true you've stopped campaigning?"

Allison ignored it. Her limo pulled away, and the media vans were on her tail before they reached the stop sign at the corner. The driver headed directly for the Federal Triangle at regular speed, the normal route, giving no indication that he was trying to ditch the media. He stopped at the curb on Pennsylvania Avenue. Another mob of reporters was waiting on the Justice Building steps, as if the entire camp had been magically transported from her home to work. They flocked to her car with instinctive determination, like blind puppies stumbling over each other on their way to mother's milk.

The car door opened. The agent led the way across the packed sidewalk. Allison kept a hand on his back as they forged toward the entrance. The heavy brass and glass doors opened, and the media pushed its way inside, right on their heels. Allison and her escorts whisked through the security checkpoint. The federal marshals and metal detectors put the stop on the charging media. Another marshal held the elevator for the attorney general. Allison left her escorts behind and keyed the elevator for her fifth-floor suite. The door closed in what seemed like slow motion, as the building was more than half a century old and so were its elevators. The doors opened on the fifth floor. Harley was waiting in the lobby.

"Jeez," she said. "It was like the Beatles at Shea Stadium out there."

"McCartney played for the Mets?" he kidded.

"Watch it, Abrams. I'm not *that* much older than you."

He smirked as he pulled on his leather jacket, then turned serious. "Ready?"

Allison nodded and led the way to the private elevator—the so-called Marilyn Monroe elevator that led from the attorney general's suite to the basement of the Justice Building. Allison hit the CALL button, and the doors opened. She entered first, then Harley, and the doors closed behind them. The motor hummed as they descended down the shaft. They stood side by side, staring up at the numbered lights over the door.

"You know," said Harley, "I heard JFK and Marilyn Monroe used to take this elevator up to the loft when his brother was attorney general."

She smiled faintly. "Yes, I've heard that."

"I guess if the president and the world's most famous sex symbol could get in and out of this building without anybody noticing, so can we."

"Theoretically, I could still be president." She shot him a mischievous look. "Guess that makes you the sex symbol."

He fought the surge inside, but she had him blushing again. He blinked and looked away.

"By the way," she said. "Thank you for the fuzzy slippers. And the little note."

"Oh, that was nothing. Just thought it would lift your spirits."

"It did." She waited for him to look back, and their eyes met again. "You're a very sweet guy, Harley. Handsome, too. Not your typical FBI, hard-edged ex-Marine. I think you could make a woman very happy."

He shrugged modestly. "Well, maybe."

She raised an eyebrow. "I hope you find one who isn't already married."

The elevator stopped. Harley froze, like a man punched in the chest.

She said, "I'm not being mean. That's just the way it is."

The doors opened, and Allison stepped out. The color drained from Harley's cheeks as the attorney general went straight to her husband and gave him a kiss.

Harley took a deep breath, shaking off the exchange. As he stepped from the elevator, he noted the small metal suitcase at Peter's feet. "Is the money all here?" he asked in his most businesslike tone.

"All here," said Peter, still holding his wife's hand. "You want to count it, Mr. Abrams?"

Harley bristled at the edge to Peter's voice. He'd spat out the words, as if talking to someone he disliked. And he'd almost clutched Allison's hand as he spoke—a possessive thing, very territorial. Maybe he'd seen the slippers and the card, which would explain Allison's put-down in the elevator. Maybe he just didn't like how much time Harley had been spending with his wife, or the way Harley might have looked at her. *Maybe you're just paranoid.* "No," said Harley. "I don't need to count it."

Peter said, "I hear General Howe has finally offered to pay a ransom. Does that mean Allison and I will be reimbursed?"

"Probably," said Harley. "But if all goes well, that won't be an issue. Our primary objective is to save Kristen, but we hope to catch a kidnapper in the process."

"Which means we get our money back."

"Yeah," said Harley. "Not to mention Allison's safe return."

"What the hell is *that* supposed to mean, Mr. Abrams? You think I take my wife's safety for granted? Well, I don't, pal. Not when she's in the hands of some Keystone Kop who invades the wrong house in Nashville."

"Peter, please," said Allison.

"It's okay," said Harley. "I think maybe I deserved that."

Allison touched her husband on the forearm, calming him. "Harley, could you excuse us for a second?"

Harley hesitated. Time was short, but he knew she really wasn't asking permission. "I'll wait by the door. If you don't mind, why don't you step into the bathroom over there and get your husband to help you with the Kevlar vest. I don't want you going into this unprotected."

The other agent handed her the vest. "This is the kind you wear underneath your clothes," he said.

"I know. I've worn one before." She took it, then led Peter to the bathroom and closed the door. She spoke as she undressed.

"Are you with me on this or not, Peter?" she asked as she handed him her blouse.

"Of course. I'm always with you."

"Yes, in *words*." She stuck her arms through the vest, cinched up the Velcro straps on the side, and tucked the flaps into her pants. She looked him in the eye. "You always *say* the right thing. Tell me what you're feeling. Do you think I'm crazy for doing this?"

He looked away, sighing. "Look, we both know that the only chance Allison Leahy has at being elected president is if the American people are convinced that she's done everything possible to save Kristen Howe. That requires nothing short of meeting the kidnappers' demand to deliver the ransom. No, I don't think you're crazy."

She winced. "It's more than politics, Peter."

"I know. Sorry."

She buttoned her blouse over the vest. It was snug, but it fit.

Harley was knocking at the door. "Hate to interrupt," he said. "But we really have to go."

She looked at Peter. "Wish me luck?"

He nodded, then handed her the suitcase full of cash. She touched his hand as she took it, then winked. "I'll be sure to send you a postcard from Switzerland."

That got a smile.

She opened the door and stepped out quickly, breezing by Harley without making eye contact. Harley followed her to the fire exit, which led to the stairs that would take them up to the alley.

Harley handed her a stylish winter hat. "Wear this at all times," he said. "There's a two-way radio in the earpiece. We'll be able to track your steps across town, and we'll be in constant radio contact. It's encrypted, of course, so the frequency can't be intercepted. Just talk in a normal voice, we'll hear you."

She made a face. "How normal can it look for a woman to go around talking to herself?"

"Hey, we're in D.C. Everyone's just a pink slip away from becoming a bag lady."

"Good point."

He handed her a blue overcoat that looked nothing like the one she'd worn into the building—unlike anything she owned, for that matter. A matching scarf around her neck and big dark sunglasses completed the ensemble. "The idea," said Harley, "is to disguise your appearance without making it look like an obvious disguise. We want the kidnappers to recognize you. But anyone who doesn't know you're supposed to be there shouldn't be able to tell it's you."

She put on her outfit, then looked at Peter. "What do you think?"

"I'd walk right by you, stranger."

"Good," said Harley. He checked his watch. Nine-thirty. "Okay. Time to go."

Allison glanced at Peter. His smile was a little nervous, but so was hers. They said good-bye without words.

Harley opened the door. They ducked outside, leaving Peter behind. They walked quickly up the cement steps to the car waiting in the alley. The rear door swung open. Allison jumped in back, followed by Harley. The windows were tinted, making it impossible for anyone to see inside. The sedan rolled slowly down the alley so as not to draw attention. They turned onto Ninth Street and crossed Pennsylvania Avenue. Allison glanced to her left. The media was still swarming outside the main entrance to the building, waiting for her to come out.

She looked away, focusing on her mission.

"We'll drop you off at F Street," said Harley, "just in case the kidnappers are staking out the drop site. You'll walk alone on F Street, four blocks up to Fifth Street. The Pension Building is right there. Be sure to follow the kidnapper's instructions to the letter. We have agents positioned all along the route, inside and outside the building."

"Where will you be?" she asked.

"I'll be in radio contact from headquarters, the Op Center. At least six field agents will have you in their sight at any point in time—dozens, most of the time. You'll never know they're there. The minute anything hits you as strange or risky, bail out. Your only job is to drop the money and get out safely. We'll do the rest."

The car stopped at the traffic light on Ninth and F streets.

"Good luck," said Harley.

She grabbed the suitcase and nodded, then opened the door and stepped out.

A steady stream of cars cruised through the intersection. Pedestrians jammed the sidewalks. Briefcase-toting businesspeople charged along with purpose. Camera-snapping tourists meandered toward the sights. The city noises were a reminder that life as usual went on all around her. She knew the FBI was watching her. Maybe even the kidnappers were watching. The whole world could have been watching, and it wouldn't have changed the sensation.

She felt eerily alone upon taking that first step toward the drop point.

Tanya Howe was putting on her shoes, seated on the edge of her bed, when she saw her mother's reflection in the dressing mirror. She turned, concerned by the troubled expression.

"What's wrong, Mom?"

Natalie stepped into the bedroom and closed the door. "I just came from the grocery store. Buck LaBelle stopped me in the parking lot."

Her concern heightened. She hadn't said a word to her mother about the high-level conversation she'd overheard last night. "What did he want?"

"He told me what you did, Tanya. How you threatened your father last night."

"Is that all he told you? That I made a threat?"

Natalie grimaced, then came and sat beside her on the edge of the bed. "Tanya, I know this ordeal must be agonizing for you. But the notion that you can bring Kristen back by threatening your father is just lunacy."

"How can you say that, Mom?"

"I've been married to your father for forty years. That's how."

Tanya narrowed her eyes. "Did you know he intentionally smeared Allison Leahy's reputation with that phony adultery scandal? He and LaBelle cooked the whole thing up with some guy named Mitch O'Brien."

She blinked nervously.

"Did you know the FBI is looking for O'Brien? Nobody can find him."

Her hands began to shake. "I—I don't need to know about that."

"Did you know he ordered LaBelle to find O'Brien before the FBI did?"

"Tanya, please."

"Did you know he threatened Mark the night he died in that so-called car accident?"

She covered her ears. "Tanya—"

"Did you know that when I was pregnant he *ordered* me to get an abortion?"

She sprung to her feet. "I don't *want* to hear it!"

Tanya froze in the chilling silence, her eyes filled with incredulity. "Damn it, Mom. That's exactly how you've managed to stay married to that monster. Ignoring the other women, the brothels overseas. Blocking out the truth. Denying his deceit."

"Stop it! That's none of your business."

"Just listen to me, please."

"No! You listen to me. Mr. LaBelle is waiting for you. Now you go see him—*right now.*"

She winced, confused. "Waiting to see me? Where?"

"At his hotel."

"You're his messenger now?"

Her voice quaked. "I love you, Tanya. And I love Kristen. But I won't stand by and let you destroy your father's dreams with this whacked-out theory that he's behind Kristen's kidnapping. Now go see Mr. LaBelle. He's waiting at the fitness center on the second floor of the hotel. And bring your bathing suit. He'll meet you in the hot tub."

"Hot tub? What kind of nonsense is that?"

"He wants to make sure you're not wearing a wire, and having you up to your neck in hot water is the only way to guard against that. He thinks you might take something out of context and use it against your father. He simply doesn't trust you. And may God forgive me for saying this, but I don't blame him."

"Forget it. I'm not going anywhere."

Natalie's expression turned very serious. "Yes,

you are. Mr. LaBelle assured me that this will be the most important conversation you'll ever have in your life. And I believe him."

A chill went down her spine. She was suddenly eager to go. "So do I, Mother. Somehow, so do I."

45

Allison stopped at Fifth Street, midway between F and G streets. The mammoth redbrick Pension Building loomed before her.

"I'm here," she said into the microphone, trying not to be too obvious about moving her lips.

Harley's reply buzzed in her ear. "Got you. Go on inside."

She checked her watch. She had ten minutes to get through the building and exit back on F Street. She wasn't sure why the kidnappers wanted her to walk through it, when she could have just as easily walked around it. Maybe they were watching, and they just wanted to make sure she'd go wherever they sent her. Or perhaps they simply had a flair for the poetic, and they were toying with the woman who dreamed of being president. The Pension Building, after all, had been the site of every presidential inaugural ball since Grover Cleveland's election.

Allison climbed the front steps and entered the vast open atrium—one of the city's truly great interiors. The eight central Corinthian columns were the largest in the world, rising to a height of seventy-six feet. The plaster casings were painted to resemble Siena marble, and the entire building had the awe-inspiring feel of the Italian Renaissance. As she passed beneath the arching ceilings, she felt dwarfed by it all—physically, but not emotionally. The grand and timeless surroundings seemed to mock the significance of any single person doing any single deed at any single moment in time. Allison, however, was undaunted.

This was important.

She exited on the side, straight onto F Street. She spotted the fireplug the kidnapper had mentioned on the phone. She stopped at the curb, just a few feet from the plug, suitcase firmly in hand.

Harley's voice was in her ear. "Just stay put. We're watching you."

The pay phone rang nearby at the curb. Several pedestrians passed by, ignoring it. It kept ringing. Allison looked around, unsure of what to do. She checked her watch. Exactly ten o'clock.

"Answer it," said Harley.

She stepped toward the phone and lifted the receiver. "Hello."

A quick response, a gravelly voice: "Cross F Street to Judiciary Square. Wait at the police memorial." The line clicked.

She shook her head with confusion, then spoke to Harley. "Did you hear?"

"Yes. Proceed. We're still watching you."

She glanced up the sidewalk, then in the other direction, seeing nothing conspicuous. *Nice surveillance,* she thought, then hurried across F Street.

Judiciary Square was exactly what the name implied, the district's judicial core, home to both the city and federal courthouses. The police memorial the caller had mentioned had to be the National Law Enforcement Officers Memorial, a three-foot-high wall that bore the name of more than fifteen thousand American police officers who had been killed in the line of duty since 1794. Allison had attended the dedication in 1991. Another poetic flair, she presumed—a not-so-subtle message that if the cops were tailing her, there might be a few more names on the wall.

She stopped at a panel near the center of the wall. Behind her, a pay phone rang.

This time she didn't hesitate to answer. "What now?"

"See the subway station?"

She turned, searching. The tall brown pylon marked METRO was about twenty meters away. "Yes."

"Go down the escalator. Take the red line, Wheaton train, to the Forest Glen station. Get out and wait on the platform."

"Which train?" she said with urgency, sensing he was about to hang up. "They run every few minutes."

"The *next* train," he replied. "It leaves at ten past the hour. Don't miss it. Or Kristen pays."

The line clicked.

She hung up quickly and looked around, wondering which, if any, of the people milling about the square were her FBI escorts.

"Did you hear?" she asked Harley.

"Yes, wait there. I don't want you in the subway."

She started toward the station entrance. "I can't *wait*. The train leaves in three minutes."

She was walking fast, almost jogging, as she reached the escalator that fed into the tunnel. She walked down it, speeding her descent. It was a little unnerving, following a kidnapper's instructions to climb into what was essentially a big hole in the ground. But she didn't stop to think.

Suddenly a crackling filled her ear.

"Harley?" she asked.

Another crackle, but Harley's voice was breaking up. Then a click, as if he were switching radio frequencies.

"Allison, can you hear me?"

"Barely."

"We're losing radio between ground level and the subway station below, and it's only getting worse. Forest Glen is the deepest station in the metro system—twenty-one stories straight down an elevator shaft. There's not even an escalator. I won't be able to talk to you. Turn back."

"I'm not turning back."

"Damn it, Allison, I don't want you seventy meters underground with some lunatic."

"Then send someone with me."

"All right, I'm sending agents to pose as riders."

"Make it quick. I'm boarding the train in ninety seconds."

"Allison—" His voice cut off. The radio was dead.

She stepped off the escalator and hurried toward the machines that sold Farecards. The line was long and slow-moving. She rushed to the old man at the head of the line and handed him a twenty-dollar bill.

"Buy me a card and you can keep the change," she said urgently.

The people behind shot dirty looks and grumbled. The old man snatched the crisp bill and inserted it in the slot. The fare was only a few dollars. Allison left him the change, as promised, and grabbed her Farecard. The train arrived as she dashed through a turnstile that led to the platform. She elbowed through the crowd of commuters and stopped at the blinking granite lights on the edge of the platform, waiting for the doors to open. She checked her watch. Exactly 10:10. This was definitely the train. Her mind raced. She could abort and run the risk that the kidnappers would kill Kristen when she didn't show at the Forest Glen station. Or she could just keep going.

The chimes sounded, signaling that the train's automatic doors were about to close. She swallowed hard and stepped inside, hoping the FBI was somewhere nearby. The doors closed, and the train pulled away from the platform. She glanced out the window. The billboards and signs along the platform became a blur as the train picked up speed, then the view turned to darkness as she entered the black tunnel to the lowest point beneath the city.

She turned and surveyed the crowded car. She wondered if any of the passengers were actually FBI. She wondered if any were actually the kidnapper.

No turning back now, she thought.

Tanya rode to the hotel in the backseat of her mother's car, crouched on the floor, hidden from public view by the tinted bulletproof glass. She couldn't drive her own car without the media following. The only way to get out was to pull another car into the attached two-car garage, crawl into the backseat, and let someone else drive past the mob at the end of her driveway.

They reached the hotel at half-past nine Nashville time. The driver waited with the car while Tanya headed straight for the fitness center.

A guest pass was waiting for her at the reception desk. She checked her coat in the locker room and quickly changed into her bathing suit. The attendant offered her a terry-cloth robe that bore the Opry Land Hotel monogram.

"Thank you," said Tanya as she slipped it on. "Just looking for the hot tub."

"Straight through that door," the attendant replied.

She paused to collect her wits, then pushed open the door.

The room was small, but the mirrored walls on all sides made it seem bigger. Granite tile surrounded the octagon-shaped hot tub. The sun streamed in through the skylight, making the bubbles glisten atop the churning water. Tanya could feel the heat rising from the tub, but the sight of Buck LaBelle still gave her chills.

"Come on in," he said. He was submerged to his armpits, his thick neck rising from the waterline like an old stump from the swamp. His arms extended out languidly along the ledge. His head was cocked back comfortably, resting against a rolled-up towel at the base of his neck.

Tanya stepped to the edge of the tub and removed the robe. Her bright yellow bathing suit was a bit more revealing than she would have liked under the circumstances. She caught him gawking in the mirror, like a pimple-faced teenager peeking into the girls' shower.

"Guess you work out a little, huh, Tanya?"

She ignored him, lowering herself into the tub and glaring at eye level across the foamy water. "Okay, I'm here. What's this about?"

The lecherous grin faded from his face. "Your father told me about your conversation last night.

I don't know what you think you heard us saying, but you obviously misunderstood."

"I know what I heard. There's no misunderstanding. You used Mitch O'Brien to create a phony scandal about adultery, and now you're out to silence him before the FBI can find him."

"All your father meant was find him and talk some sense into the man."

"I don't believe you."

"Well, you'd *better* believe us."

She looked at him coldly. "Or what, Mr. LaBelle?"

He pulled himself from the water and sat on the ledge. His body was red from heat. His face was even redder, compounded by his anger. "Listen, you may be General Howe's daughter, but let's leave that out of this. The bottom line is, you threatened us—your father, me, the entire campaign. Now, it's my job to respond to threats."

"Is he involved in the kidnapping, Mr. LaBelle, or isn't he?"

"Where in the world would you get the idea that he is?"

"A lot of little things. And they all add up to one thing. My father would do anything to be elected president."

"That's absurd. If that was true, why hire somebody to kidnap his granddaughter? Why not just hire somebody to blow Allison Leahy's brains out?"

"Too obvious, for one thing. People might immediately suspect his campaign was behind it. And even more important, if you know my father, you know he doesn't want a meaningless victory over a dead opponent. He wants a mandate. He wants to be *elected* president, even if it means killing his own granddaughter—anything to win, so long as it *appears* that his victory was fair and square."

"You're psycho, you know that, girl?"

"Maybe. But if my daughter isn't home by tomorrow morning, this psycho is going on television to tell everyone what she thinks *really* happened."

His eyes blazed. "It's just like your daddy said. You're nothing but a troublemaker."

"I didn't make this. You did."

"Horseshit. You took one conversation out of context and used it to blackmail your father into doing whatever it takes to get your daughter home before the election. He should have taken you out back and slapped the shit out of you. But he's such a decent man, his only response is to agree to pony up a million-dollar ransom. That's a generous move on his part. And maybe it will even help get Kristen back. But let me tell you straight. You and your threats are hurting a lot of people other than your father—people who, up until now, may have been feeling pretty sorry for you and your daughter. You fuck with us, we may not be feeling so charitable."

"Don't you dare threaten my daughter."

"I'm not," he said with an icy glare. "I'm threatening *you*." He leaned back and flipped off the power switch, stilling the waters between them.

Scores of commuters had come and gone in the several Metro stops between Judiciary Square and Forest Glen station. Allison hadn't moved from her seat on the right side of the aisle, third seat from the rear. She had a clear view of the entire car. A few empty seats, but most were taken. It was the typical mix of Washington riders. Shoppers with parcels from the downtown stores. Teenage boys clad in baggy clothes listening through headphones to what was undoubtedly rap music. Businessmen and women reading the *Washington Post* or the latest tell-all bestseller by a fallen Washington star.

Allison watched discreetly from behind her sunglasses. She wasn't sure which of the riders she might need to remember. She made it her job to remember them all, noting for each a distinguishing feature—the cleft on the chin, the wart on the hand. In the end, however, her eyes drifted back to the far end of the car, toward the homeless guy wearing a tattered army coat, asleep in the seats reserved for the handicapped.

She figured by now the FBI was somewhere on the train, definitely all over the Forest Glen Station. The two-way radio, however, had been out since boarding. Too far underground, she guessed. Or maybe Harley had just stopped trying, fearful that if he kept changing frequencies he might hit one the kidnappers could easily intercept.

The speeding train was somewhere between stations in the long, dark tunnel. She checked the subway map posted above the window. Forest Glen was the next stop. The deepest station in the Metro system, according to Harley. They were going down. She could actually feel the descent. Twenty-one stories beneath the surface. Seventy meters of earth and cement. A million-dollar ransom in the suitcase beside her. A kidnapper waiting at the station ahead. A killer maybe in the seat beside her.

They killed Reggie Miles, she reminded herself.

She clutched the suitcase and quietly held her breath.

One of the teenage boys rose from his seat. The pant legs of his baggy jeans dragged around the expensive Nike high-top shoes. The long sleeves of his bulky jacket covered his hands. A Georgetown Hoyas cap was backwards on his head. He strutted down the aisle, eyeing Allison as he approached.

She watched cautiously, avoiding eye contact, hoping he'd pass. *A scraggly mustache*, she noted, the kind worn by teenage boys who had never shaved in their life.

He stopped beside her. Her pulse quickened. *Big for his age,* thought Allison. Like a basketball player.

"You're in my seat," he said.

She didn't look up, stared straight ahead.

"Lady," he said, this time leaning forward, staring down at her. "I said, you're in my seat."

"You're in my face," she said. "Get out."

He scoffed, gyrating with some rhythmic motion that, with a little more animation, could have passed for dancing. "You think I'm in your face? This ain't nothin', bitch." He arched his back, raising his crotch toward her. "How about you open real wide and I stick it *right* in your face. I bet you'd like that, huh?"

"Leave her alone." It was the businessman seated across the aisle.

The punk glared. "This ain't about you, asshole."

"Just leave us alone," he said, though with slightly less conviction.

Another punk strutted down the aisle, backing up his buddy. He wore exactly the same outfit.

Gang attire. "What's this?" he scoffed, towering over the man. "The accountant cops an attitude?"

"Look," said Allison. "Everybody just calm down, okay?"

The punk raised his voice. "Calm down, you say? You want *me* to calm down? Just get the fuck outta my seat, I'll calm down."

Allison went rigid. The car was silent, no one moving. The homeless guy in the handicap seat was mumbling in his sleep. Allison moved slowly and said, "All right, I'll move." She rose, taking the suitcase firmly in her hand. Halfway across the aisle, the punk grabbed it.

"Hey!" she shrieked, fighting him off.

"Leave her!" said the accountant as he intervened.

A third punk raced down the aisle. The homeless guy leaped to his feet, shouting something, no longer mumbling. "Now!" he cried.

The train screeched on the rails, sliding to a halt. Passengers flew into the backs of the seats in front of them. Allison tumbled hard to the floor. The suitcase flew straight up the aisle, halfway up the car. One of the gang members rolled after it, grabbed it.

"My bag!" cried Allison.

The homeless guy braced himself on a pole and pulled out a pistol. Allison gasped. Passengers screamed and scurried for cover.

"FBI!" he shouted. "Freeze!"

The punk hurled the suitcase at him. His buddy pulled out a gun. The homeless guy fired, hitting him in the chest. Blood splashed onto Allison's coat as he fell in the aisle beside her. She dove toward him and pried the gun from his fingers. She looked up. The disguised FBI agent had the other two under control, pinning them on the floor at gunpoint.

The wounded one looked up at her, choking for his life. *Just a kid*, she thought. But her pity waned as she suddenly thought of Kristen, the plan gone awry, and the kidnappers turning violent when they didn't get their money.

"You screwed everything up!" she shouted, wishing she could help him and kill him at the same time. "You idiot! What the hell were you doing?"

His body trembled. His eyes were rolling back into his head. She shook him, reviving him. "Who are you?"

He didn't respond.

"Who *are* you?"

He was breathing loudly, sucking for air. His eyes briefly seemed to focus. He was struggling to speak, nearly strangling on his words. "Shit, lady. Just wanted the fucking suitcase."

"Who? *Who* wanted it?"

His lips quivered. His eyes began to drift.

"Damn it, tell me! Who sent you? Who wanted the suitcase!"

His head rolled to one side.

Her grip tightened on his jacket, but his body was dead weight. A sick feeling swelled inside her, a rising bitterness in her throat. She rose slowly from her knees, oblivious to the hot blood staining her hands and clothes. She turned toward the FBI agent guarding the other two punks. Her eyes filled with rage.

"I want to talk to those boys," she said through clenched teeth.

46

It took nearly twenty minutes for the FBI to bring the two surviving gang members up from the subway. That the train had stopped midway in the tunnel between stations only made the task more difficult. Forest Glen station had been closed and roped off as a crime scene, which forced the media and other onlookers to wait outside the chain-link fence surrounding the parking lot. Allison was hoping to rush to the FBI van without being recognized, but other passengers on the train had already confirmed her involvement. The media erupted as she emerged from the station, zooming in with their camcorders from thirty yards away and snapping her picture through telephoto lenses. Reporters shouted an endless string of questions, but it was pure cacophony.

Allison quickly disappeared into the lead FBI van. A second carried the suspects and arresting agents. A team of police motorcycles with sirens blaring led the entourage back into the district toward FBI headquarters. Allison watched on a portable TV set in the back of the van as aerial shots of the speeding motorcade flashed live across the country. Her heart sank as the coverage shifted to the just-recorded footage of her exit from the station. Her hair was a mess. Splattered blood was clearly visible on her coat. She looked like a refugee from an air raid. The television camera froze on that image as the anchorman announced a station break.

"When we return, more of our continuing coverage of the Kristen Howe kidnapping and the failed rescue effort that has resulted in the unconfirmed death of at least one teenage boy. Stay tuned."

The network switched to a commercial. Allison closed her eyes in despair. They might as well have said that she had personally put a gun to the head of a Boy Scout and pulled the trigger. She turned off the set and removed her bloody coat, passing it to the agent in the front.

"Here," she scoffed. "Exhibit A at my congressional lynching."

She grabbed the phone and called Peter back at the Justice Building basement just to assure him she was unhurt. As she'd expected, he'd watched it all unfold on television.

"Do you still have the money?" were his first words.

"Yes," she answered, a little dismayed by his priorities. "And by the way, *I'm* fine, too."

"Sorry, honey. You looked fine on television. I just didn't see the suitcase."

"The FBI recovered it along with the suspects. We're all heading to headquarters now."

"That's right across the street. I'll meet you there."

"Peter, I think you should just stay put for now. There's a mob of reporters outside the Justice Building. I don't want you to have to deal with that."

"All right, I'll wait here. Love you."

"I love you, too." She hung up and dialed

Harley Abrams at the Op Center. They spoke as the FBI van raced through the red lights along Georgia Avenue, toward the heart of the district.

"If Nashville was strike one, Harley, this is definitely strike two."

"I'm sorry, Allison. I just thank God you're okay. You sure you don't want to go to the hospital or something? Or I can have a doctor check you out when you get here."

His concern for her safety took some of the bite out of her reply—but not all of it. "I'm fine, really. I just want to know what the hell happened down there."

"Don't know yet. When I lost radio contact with you, we flooded the train with undercover agents—seventeen boarded at various stops. I need to talk to all of them to piece things together."

"Who stopped the train?"

"We did. The agent posing as the homeless guy in your car was in contact with the control car. The radios worked between points in the same tunnel. It was the surface-to-tunnel communication that we were having trouble with. When things looked like they were getting out of control, our agent gave the word to stop the train."

"Any leads on those idiots who hassled me?"

"Nothing promising as yet. We faxed their fingerprints right from the Metro station. They all have records. Two have been charged before as adults. Small-time stuff. Drugs, car theft."

The vans entered the FBI garage. Heavy metal doors rolled down, shutting out the pursuing media. The phone crackled with interference from the thick cement walls. "We're here," she said. "Meet me at the interrogation room."

"I hope you're not entertaining thoughts of interrogating the suspects yourself."

"No, but I want to observe. Or at least listen."

She watched as the suspects were taken from the van and rushed inside. The two boys looked confused, overwhelmed.

She grimaced, still speaking into the phone. "You know, these kids don't look at all like the savvy criminals who would plan a kidnapping. They look more like the five or six people on the planet who still haven't heard that Kristen Howe has been kidnapped."

"We won't know until we question them. Looks can be deceiving."

"The one thing that has me really curious is something one of them said—the leader, the one who attacked me and grabbed the suitcase. Before he died, he said something like 'Just wanted the suitcase, lady.' Somebody had to tell him there was money in the suitcase. Why else would they target it? Why else would they spring their attack right before the Forest Glen station, where the kidnapper told me to drop the money?"

"We'll get into all that in the interrogation. We'll get the answers."

"I know you will," she said. "Unless the only one with the answers is the kid we shot on the train."

Harley didn't reply. She switched off the phone and entered the building.

Tanya Howe listened in disbelief to the live radio broadcast from Washington, alone in the backseat of her mother's town car. She felt paralyzed, wanting desperately to know what it all meant for Kristen but far too afraid to consider the possibilities.

The driver had said nothing during the trip

back from the hotel. She could only imagine his thoughts. The tips of her fingers were still pruned from the hot tub. Her skin smelled like chlorine. Her wet bathing suit was soaking through her overcoat. She had rushed from the hotel fitness center after the threat from LaBelle, too sickened and shaken to shower and change back into her clothes.

She peered through the town car's tinted windows as they neared her driveway. Remarkably, the media presence had expanded on the street and sidewalk. Twice as many vans. Many more reporters and cameras. The usual sit-around-and-wait mode was over. They had sprung into action with live reports from Tanya Howe's residence, filling airtime even though they had nothing to report.

The car radio suddenly regained her attention. The announcer had mentioned her father's name—something about his arrival at Washington National Airport.

"Turn it up, please," she told the driver.

The volume increased. The voices were jumbled, like shouting traders on the floor of the New York Stock Exchange. Her father was reportedly at the airport, but it sounded like he was being mauled. Slowly the background noises filtered away. A reporter had apparently gotten a microphone in the candidate's face. He spoke in a controlled but angry voice.

"I'm in no position to make a statement at this time," said Howe. "However, I would like to express my sympathies to the family of the young boy who was killed in this morning's shoot-out. I have no idea what our suspended attorney general was trying to accomplish. My only hope is that her rash and irresponsible actions do not result in further loss of life. Thank you," he shouted over the follow-up questions. "I'll have more to say later today."

The announcer was back on the radio, but Tanya's attention was turning to the mob blocking the entrance to her driveway. The car forged ahead like a wedge, splitting the crowd into two camps. The garage door opened. The car rolled in, and the door closed behind them. Tanya jumped from the backseat and ran to the kitchen door, eager to turn on the television. Her mother was waiting at the kitchen table. One of the FBI agents was across from her. The television on the counter was tuned to CNN's coverage of the subway debacle. The volume was low, almost inaudible, as if her mother could bring herself to watch but not listen.

Neither Natalie nor the agent said a word. Her mother's sullen eyes drew Tanya's attention to the large brown envelope on the table.

"What's that?" asked Tanya.

"It came by courier while you were out," said Natalie.

"Who's it from?"

"It doesn't say."

"What's in it?"

"I didn't open it. It's addressed to you."

The agent said, "We took it down to the field office. Our lab scanned it, had the dogs sniff it. No poisons or explosives. We brought it back for you to open."

Tanya started to remove her coat, then realized she was still wearing her bathing suit. With her coat on she sat at the table, beside her mother and across from the agent. She reached for the envelope, but the agent stopped her.

"Let me open it," he said. "If there are fingerprints or other physical evidence, we don't want to lose them."

Tanya nodded, acquiescing.

The agent pulled on a pair of thin latex gloves. Carefully, he slit open the envelope on the bottom, not the top, so as not to destroy any traces of saliva the sender may have left behind when licking the flap. With a large pair of tweezers he removed a flat piece of cardboard about the size of a legal pad. He held it up at the edges without touching the surface, the way an artist might hold a still-wet masterpiece.

The agent seemed to freeze.

Tanya trembled at his reaction. He was holding the cardboard square at eye level. She could see the back side as he examined the front. She shuddered at the message scrawled in blue ink: PIG'S BLOOD THIS TIME. NEXT TIME IT'S KRISTEN'S. KEEP THE FBI OUT OF THIS.

The agent lowered the cardboard and looked straight at Tanya. "It's a photo," he said. "It's Kristen. I don't think you should see it."

"It's phony blood," said Tanya. "Read the message on the back."

The agent flipped it over, careful not to let Tanya see the photo. He glanced back at the front side, taking an even closer look at the photo. He seemed relieved, but he was still firm. "I still don't think you should see this. This is a very cruel psychological ploy."

Tanya shook. "You mean the message or the photo?"

"The sender obviously intended for you to see the photo before you read the message. He's one heartless and manipulative son of a bitch."

"Is Kristen okay?"

"I believe so," said the agent. "That's what the message implies. But the photo was obviously staged to make you think otherwise."

"Show me," said Tanya.

"That's not a good idea."

"*Show me,*" she said.

The agent drew a deep breath. Slowly he turned the cardboard, revealing the Polaroid snapshot to her.

Tanya gasped—like she wanted to scream but had no voice. She only looked for a second. That was all it took. Anyone else would have needed time to confirm that beneath the blood-soaked clothing the girl in the bathtub was indeed Kristen Howe. Tanya knew that face in an instant—even splattered red. She closed her eyes and looked away, instinctively burying her face in her mother's bosom.

Natalie stroked her daughter's head, her voice shaking. "It's not real, Tanya. It's phony blood. Kristen's still all right."

The agent laid the photograph face down on the table. "I do believe it's staged," he said.

Tanya lifted her head and wiped a tear from her cheek. She glanced at her mother. It was an awkward moment, as if Tanya suddenly remembered that she and her mother needed a good talk to sort out the threat from Buck LaBelle.

"There's more in here," said the agent. With tweezers he removed another envelope from inside the larger envelope. It was sealed separately. On the front was scrawled another message: PERSONAL AND CONFIDENTIAL, it read. DELIVER TO ALLISON LEAHY.

The three of them read it simultaneously. The agent looked at Tanya. "I guess I'll take this."

Tanya grabbed his hand. "No you won't."

"Excuse me," he said. "The message says it's for Allison Leahy."

"It came in a package addressed to me. The instructions told me to leave the FBI out of this."

"I don't think it wise to follow those instructions."

Tanya glanced at the television on the counter. It was still tuned to the subway coverage. One of the frightened passengers from the train was being interviewed. She glanced back at the agent. "I think I'll take my chances without you guys. Give me the envelope."

He grimaced. "It says it must be delivered to Allison Leahy."

She snatched it from his hand. "I'll make sure she gets it."

47

From the small observation tank adjacent to the FBI interrogation room, Allison watched in solitude as Harley Abrams and another agent debriefed the two surviving gang members. The audio was fed to her through a small speaker. A one-way mirror allowed her to see all without being seen.

Harley had been working hard on the younger one—the one who had seemed most determined to steal Allison's suitcase. The teenager was seated in a folding chair, slouching irreverently in the center of the yellow room. Harley stood directly in front of him, firing questions. The other agent sat at the small table against the wall. When they'd first brought him in, the kid wouldn't talk. His tune quickly changed when Harley made it plain that he'd better start explaining if he didn't want to be the number-one suspect in the Kristen Howe kidnapping.

Allison had watched his reaction carefully. He'd seemed genuinely shocked—as if Harley's accusation was the first he'd ever heard of a possible link to a larger conspiracy. Twenty-five minutes later, the kid was still babbling.

He rolled back his head in response to another question, seemingly bored by the repetition. "Man, I told you five times already. I don't know nothing about no kidnapping. All I know is that some dude paid Jessie a thousand bucks for us to follow the bitch in the blue coat onto the Metro at Judiciary Square."

"And then what?"

"I *told* you."

"Tell me again," he said, pressing for inconsistencies in his statement. So far, there were none.

"We was just supposed to wait. If the bitch was still on the train between Sandy Springs and Forest Glen, the deal was we'd grab the suitcase. We'd get another five grand if we get him the suitcase."

"Get it for who?"

"I dunno. Jessie know who."

"Jessie's dead."

"That's *your* fucking problem, isn't it?"

Allison lowered her head. Harley had been over this same line of questioning several times. The answers were always the same. She could tell the kid wasn't lying. They were just punks—sacrificial lambs sent by a kidnapper who *knew* the FBI was waiting in the wings. The only thing she disputed was the part about Jessie's death. It wasn't Harley's problem. It was *hers.*

The phone rang in her purse—the private phone that only a handful of people ever rang. She answered quickly.

It was Tanya Howe.

"I'm sorry, Tanya. I promised I wouldn't let you down, and I did. I'm still trying to figure out what went wrong."

"The FBI—*that's* what went wrong. Somehow the kidnappers know when they're involved. I don't know if they're tipped off, or if the kidnappers are just savvy enough to sense when law enforcement is around. Either way, if I don't keep the FBI out of it, Kristen's going to die. That's their final word."

"Have you heard something?"

"Yes. I got a package this morning—after your disaster. A picture of Kristen. We think she's still alive. A warning, too. No more FBI."

"Tanya, this may be hard for you to swallow in light of everything that's happened. But I personally don't believe that you're better off without the FBI. Trust me. You need them."

"Forget it! It's my call now. You can come with me or stay behind. But leave your army at home."

"I don't know what to say. Let's assume the kidnapper gives us another chance. Let's say Kristen's alive, and they want me, personally, to deliver the ransom—just like before. I can't say I'm eager to do it without the protection of the FBI."

"Well, maybe you won't have to do it."

"Time will tell."

"It may not take as much time as you think. I have a package here for you, too. It came with mine."

"What's in it?"

"I haven't opened it. It simply says that I'm to deliver it to you. Where do you want to meet?"

"We don't have time to meet. Just get the FBI to open it."

"No."

"Tanya," she said sternly. "It's my package. Do as I say."

"It's my *daughter*," she said in a shrill, shaky voice. "It's time *somebody* does what *I* say. So listen to me. Your package came inside my package, and my package said to keep the FBI out of this. I'm keeping the FBI out. Period."

Allison sensed it was futile to try to change

Tanya's mind—and part of her sensed that maybe Tanya was right. "Okay, Tanya. We'll do it your way. But we don't have time to meet. Somebody has to open that package and tell me what's inside."

"I'll open it."

"Too dangerous," said Allison. "Could be booby-trapped."

"The FBI scanned it already, when they scanned mine. It's clear."

"All right," said Allison. "Then you open it. But be careful not to get your fingers all over it. I know you don't want the FBI involved, but someday we may want the lab to analyze it."

"I watched the FBI agent open my package. I'll be just as careful."

Over the phone, Allison could hear the envelope tearing open. She held her breath and waited.

"It's open," said Tanya. "It's a photograph. A young girl. Blond hair. Fair complexion. She's wearing a plaid jumper, like a school uniform."

"How old does she look?"

"I don't know. Maybe eight or nine."

Her excitement swelled. "Where is she?"

"Can't really tell. Looks like there may be a school in the background. Like somebody took the picture from across the street while she was on the playground. She's definitely not posing for the picture. It looks more like somebody took it without her even knowing it. There's another photograph here, too."

"What is it?"

"It's another picture of the same girl, only a lot more close up. It really zeroes in on the side of her face. Not her cheek, but the part that's closer to the ear. Like where a man would have sideburns."

Allison swallowed hard. "What do you see?"

"Just her profile. Same happy expression, just like the other picture."

"Which side of her face is it?"

"The left."

"Do you notice anything? Birthmarks, moles, anything like that?"

"Yes, actually. She has four little moles right in front of her ear. Fairly distinctive. If you took a pencil and connected the dots they'd form a perfect little square box—like the markings on a pair of dice."

Allison went cold. Her eyes welled with tears as she brought a hand to her mouth. She could barely speak. "Dear God in heaven. It's Emily."

Part 5

48

Harley entered the observation room without knocking. On reflex, Allison stuffed her cellular phone back in her purse. From the look on his face, she could see the interrogation had gone as far as it was going to go. She sucked back her emotions, struggling to make her own face a little less revealing.

"What's wrong with you?" he asked.

Her eyes were moist. She knew she had to say something to explain her distraught appearance—something short of the truth, since she'd just promised Tanya she'd exclude the FBI. "Oh, I don't know," she said as she dabbed her eye with a tissue. "I guess I'm starting to feel a little sorry for myself. That's all."

He closed the door and leveled a suspicious look. "I don't buy it. Allison Leahy doesn't sit around weeping, feeling sorry for herself. What's wrong?"

She checked her runny mascara in her pocket mirror. "Wrong? Nothing. A botched ransom delivery. A dead seventeen-year-old on the subway. All in a day's work."

"Look, we all feel lousy. But it's not like these punks were innocent bystanders."

"Those kids had no idea the guy who hired them was Kristen Howe's kidnapper. They were set up, just like we were."

"That's probably true. The kidnapper was smart enough to know that *whoever* went into the subway to get that suitcase wasn't going to walk out with a million dollars. He knew you would disobey his orders and have FBI protection—at least on the first run. These punks didn't know it, but they weren't hired to retrieve a suitcase. They were hired to walk into a trap and teach you a lesson: next time, leave the FBI at home."

Harley paused, expecting a response. Allison didn't even seem to be listening. Something other than the subway had to be bothering her.

He glanced at the open cellular phone sitting at the top of her open purse. "Who were you talking to on the phone?"

She looked down. The power was still on. The flip cover was open. No use denying it. "None of your business. That's who."

"Is that what upset you?"

"Damn it, Harley. I said it was none of your business."

Her tone forced him back a step. "I'm sorry. I'm just concerned, that's all."

"We're all concerned. It's a miracle Kristen is still alive." She kicked herself, realizing what she'd just given away.

Harley pounced on it. "So you *have* heard from Tanya. You know about the photo and the message on the back."

She grimaced. A slip like that wasn't like her, but after eight years of hoping and waiting, she was still shaking from the news about Emily. "Yes, yes. I just spoke to Tanya, if you must know."

"Did she tell you what was in that second envelope—the one the kidnapper addressed to you?"

"Yes. And that's between me, Tanya, and the kidnappers."

He shook his head. "I guess I can understand that reaction from Tanya. But I'm not sure I understand it from you."

"I'm totally committed to getting Kristen back alive."

"So am I. But that doesn't mean I'm willing to cut myself off from the FBI and take marching orders from the kidnappers."

"Maybe I don't have a choice."

"Or maybe you're reacting more like a mother than an attorney general."

"Kristen is not my child."

"No. But Emily is."

Allison glared. "What do you know about Emily?"

"Nothing. But I do know you. The tears. The sudden willingness to shut out the FBI. You wouldn't be acting this way if your own personal stake hadn't risen."

"You think I'm that self-centered?

"No. It's just human nature. There's a limit to what we'll do for someone else's child. There's no limit to what we'll do for our own." He stepped closer and leaned across the table, looking her in the eye. "There was something in that envelope about Emily, wasn't there?"

She stared for a moment, then looked away. "I really can't discuss that now," she said as she rose and gathered her purse.

Harley touched her forearm, stopping her. "I want you to know something, Allison. If you were to share any information with me in total confidence, it wouldn't leave this room. You have my word on it."

She gave him an assessing look. He seemed sincere, but she saw no reason to commit now. "Why don't you keep the ransom money here in the vault. I'll be in touch." She started for the door.

He stopped her again. "Allison, please. Don't take this guy on alone. The kidnappers may have seemed a little disorganized at first, but all that's changed. Even the voice on the phone has changed. It's as if somebody new has taken charge. He beat us in Nashville. He beat us again this morning. He's not winning because the FBI is stupid. He's winning because he's one smart son of a bitch."

She looked him in the eye. "Then I guess I'll just have to be smarter." She opened the door and hurried out, leaving Harley alone in the room.

The crowd outside the FBI headquarters grew larger every minute. The onslaught had begun just as soon as television coverage showed Allison's caravan disappearing into the FBI garage. First on the scene was the pack of reporters who had been waiting outside the Justice Building, unaware until the broadcast that Allison had sneaked out of her office through the Marilyn Monroe escape route. They simply moved their traveling ambush across Pennsylvania Avenue, from Justice to FBI. Hordes of others were just minutes behind the initial wave of media—hapless latecomers in an industry that increasingly operated on real time.

Cameras were trained on every known exit to the building. Allison knew the FBI could still get her out undetected, but she didn't want another stealth exit. The whole world knew she was inside. If she didn't face the cameras, she'd be branded a coward. After a year of campaigning, "coward" was a label she couldn't accept, not even in a campaign that may have already made the move from bleak to hopeless.

Her team of FBI escorts met her in the lobby of the employee entrance. Roberto, the one who'd served her the longest, spoke for the group. "Mr. Abrams said you might not want us anymore. At least let us get you out of the building. You'll be mauled without protection."

She glanced through the window. The sidewalks were packed. Members of the media stood shoulder to shoulder along both sides of Pennsylvania Avenue. Mounted police and barricades kept pedestrians from spilling into the street. Police officers argued with media van drivers whose illegally parked vehicles were blocking traffic. It looked like the parade route on inauguration day, only everyone was a journalist.

Allison shrugged helplessly. Tanya might well see her on television surrounded by FBI escorts, and she might infer that Allison had broken her promise to cut out the FBI. But she would just have to understand. "Okay," she told her escorts. "Get me out of here."

Vincent Gambrelli stood calmly behind the yellow barricade, unfazed by the media hoopla around him. Reporters rudely shoved from both sides. Cameras poked him in the back. His feet didn't budge from the sidewalk.

He wore a long wool coat and rubber-soled shoes that resembled a businessman's wing tips. A convincing brown wig covered his bald head. His eyesight was perfect, but the tortoiseshell eyeglasses with plain glass enhanced the disguise. Tinted contact lenses turned his blue eyes brown. Stage makeup added fleshiness to his nose. He had staked out a prime spot facing the ground-floor Pennsylvania Avenue entrance for employees and guests. The small lobby looked out on a brick courtyard with a fountain, park benches, and a bronze plaque in honor of J. Edgar Hoover.

"That's her!" someone shouted.

Gambrelli peered through the lobby windows, all the way inside to the elevators. His gaze fixed on the blond woman moving toward the door, coming briskly toward the crowd. His right hand slipped casually into his coat pocket, a split second away from his Glock-17 pistol.

So easy, he thought. *It would be so damn easy.*

The door swung open. Out stepped Allison Leahy.

The crowd surged forward. One of the crowd-control barricades toppled over. A cameraman went down hard on the sidewalk. He and his equipment were promptly stampeded.

Gambrelli stood fast as the frenzy intensified. Leahy was barely out the door before the mob stopped her progress. Microphones were thrust into her face. Reporters nearly leaped over one another for the lead position. Boom microphones swung in from overhead. She was surrounded in confusion—hysterical strangers just inches away from her unprotected head and torso. It was impossible to discern which hand was connected to which body, which microphone belonged to which reporter.

Too easy, he thought. *Where's the challenge?* Even his nephew could have pulled this off—Tony the fuckup who was barely qualified to hang back at the house and baby-sit Kristen Howe while his uncle went out.

Leahy was talking now, issuing a short statement to the media, fielding a few questions. Her expression was serious. Smart. Attractive. A very impressive package. A most attractive target.

Gambrelli's smirk faded. The fantasy was over. As appealing as it might seem, he reminded himself this was not a hit. Not today, anyhow.

He watched as she waved off any further questions. Her brief statement was over. Four men in dark suits were clearing a path for her. She and her escorts inched across the sidewalk, nearing the curb. They were FBI, it was plain. Four FBI agents surrounding the attorney general—despite his warning.

His face flushed with anger. Hadn't she received his message? Was she *ignoring* his instructions?

He watched, furious, as her entourage crossed the street and headed toward the Justice Building. Open defiance. That's what it was. There was no other explanation. He'd warned her to keep the FBI out of this. The setup in the subway should have made it clear that he wouldn't tolerate disobedience. Her response was a veritable parade across Pennsylvania Avenue with an FBI escort. Did she still think he was bluffing? Was she betting that he lacked the guts to act on his threats?

Arrogant bitch.

He hurried away from the crowd. Simply unacceptable. It was time to make it clear that he meant what he'd said.

49

Allison didn't have time to rush off to Nashville in response to Tanya's call. With a little cajoling, however, Tanya had agreed to scan Emily's photograph on her home computer and send it over the Internet via e-mail. Although scanning could possibly smear any latent fingerprints the kidnapper might have left behind, Allison was striking a balance. On the one hand, it didn't seem likely that the kidnapper would be so careless as to leave any prints. On the other, her heart would surely burst if she didn't see her little girl immediately.

Allison could barely stand still as the old Justice Building elevator carried her up five floors. Barring a technological glitch, she knew Emily's picture was waiting on her computer in her office suite. She felt a mild tinge of guilt, knowing that Peter was still waiting for her in the basement, abiding by her instructions. Surely he'd understand.

The elevator doors opened to her suite. She rushed to her private office and leaped into her desk chair in a dead run. It rolled across the plastic carpet protector, landing her in front of her credenza, facing the computer terminal. She switched on the power, watching nervously as it booted.

"You've got mail," the computer-generated voice announced.

She clicked her mouse on the mail-center icon. Scores of unanswered messages were waiting. For each, the mailbox listed the date and time delivered, and the screen name of the sender. She scrolled down to the most recent one.

It was from Tanya Howe.

Allison clicked on the electronic envelope for the "THowe" listing. The text of Tanya's message appeared on the screen. DEAR ALLISON. I HOPE THIS IS WHAT YOU THINK IT IS. I PRAY WE'LL BOTH HAVE SOMETHING TO SMILE ABOUT. GOOD LUCK. TANYA.

The postscript read, PHOTO ATTACHED.

Allison's heart was in her throat as she clicked with her mouse. The screen flickered. The attached photographs were downloading to her hard drive. She clicked her mouse again. Slowly, from top to bottom, the photograph was coming into focus on her computer screen.

She could see sky at the very top. It was blue—the photo was in color. The bottom nine-tenths was still a blur. A few more lines came into focus. A redbrick building emerged in the background—the school Tanya had described on the phone.

Her heart skipped a beat. She could see the crown of a little girl's head. Blond hair. Just a little more and she'd be able to see the face.

Her body shivered. The eyebrows—the eyes! Children never think they look anything like their baby pictures, but their mothers can always see it. Allison grabbed the photo of Emily she kept on her credenza. She was just four months old. It had been a long eight years, but the resemblance was plain. The curve of the eyebrows, the shape of the eyes.

More came into focus. Her whole face was visible. The nose was a little different, more grown up. But the pouty lower lip was most definitely Emily.

Tears were clouding Allison's vision. She brushed them from her cheek and clicked on the second attachment—the close-up photograph of the telltale markings on the left side of Emily's face. The four little moles that formed a perfect square were the distinctive markings she had mentioned to the police to help identify her baby. She watched in disbelief as the image filled the screen. Too much to bear. She closed her eyes. Excited. Frightened. Overwhelmed.

"Emily," she said in a soft, lonely whisper.

She stared at the image, her thoughts whirling. The resemblance couldn't possibly have been any stronger. Emily was prettier than she'd ever imagined. And she was out there somewhere—*alive* and totally happy! Totally unaware of how much Allison Leahy loved her. Totally oblivious to the man hiding in the car or the bushes who had followed her to school and secretly snapped her picture.

The thought suddenly sickened her.

It took all her remaining strength just to click with her mouse one last time. She hit the print button for hard copies of the photos. She fell back in her chair, emotionally exhausted, as the color printer cranked out the images.

Her phone rang in her purse, stealing her moment of catharsis.

Tanya again? she wondered. Or perhaps Peter wanted to know where the hell she's been. "This is Allison," she answered.

"One last chance," came the angry reply. The

voice was muffled, as if the caller were speaking through a handkerchief for a makeshift disguise.

She was suddenly erect in her chair. "Who is this?"

"I told you to lose the FBI. You didn't. You defied me."

"I had to get across the street."

"The only thing you *have* to do is listen to me."

"Okay. I'm listening."

"The subway was purely a test. You flunked. The FBI was all over the place. That stunt is going to cost you."

"Please, just don't take it out on the girl."

"I won't, so long as you don't double-cross me again. When I say no FBI, I mean *no FBI.*"

"All right, we'll do it your way. What do you want?"

"The newspaper says your campaign has a big party scheduled tonight at the Renaissance Hotel, and that you're going to be there."

"That's right."

"Do whatever is necessary to make people think that's where you'll be. Have someone get a room in your name, send your husband there, whatever it takes."

"Where do you really want me to go?"

"The Grand Hyatt. There's a room in the name of Emily Smith. Go there, but do not be detected. Wear a disguise if you have to. Pick up the key from the front desk. I'll contact you in the room at nine o'clock."

"How do you expect me to walk into a hotel and pick up a key for someone named Emily Smith?"

"How about a wig and some phony identification, genius?"

"That would be a whole lot easier to come by if you'd let me use the FBI."

"Bullshit. In this city, the only thing easier to buy than a fake ID is a United States congressman. You don't need the FBI. Stop stalling."

"I presume I should bring the money."

"Put it in a Spartan 2000 large metal security briefcase. You can buy it in any spy shop on Connecticut Avenue. It easily holds two million dollars."

"Two million? You mean one million."

"I mean *two* million. The price has gone up. A million for Kristen. A million for Emily."

She gasped at the mention of Emily's name. "Where is Emily?"

"She's fine. You'll never find her without my help."

"You bastard. Do you have her?"

"I can have her anytime I want. I know exactly where she lives. You don't even know her name anymore. There's absolutely nothing you can do to protect her—except follow my orders."

"Don't you dare hurt her."

"That's up to you. All you got to do is pay the money."

Her throat tightened with emotion. "If I pay, you have to tell me where Emily lives. I have to find her. I just *have* to."

He snickered, mocking her. "It's only natural."

"That you'll tell me?"

"No," he said coldly. "That you need to know."

She slumped, then shot up from her chair, emboldened by her anger. "Don't taunt me, you creep. If you deal with me, you deal in good faith. If I give up the FBI, you give me Emily. And I can't get you another million dollars by nine o'clock.

So here's the deal. Kristen and Emily. One million dollars. No FBI. *That's it.*"

The line was silent, but she could tell he was still there.

She pressed, "Do we have a deal. Or don't we?"

"Yeah," he said flatly. "We got a deal. But if I see just one FBI agent at the hotel, Emily is the first to go. Slowly. Painfully. Then Kristen. Understood?"

"Yes. Understood."

The line went dead in her ear. The caller was gone.

She closed her eyes, collecting herself. She knew she was right to play hardball—to make sure that if she gave up something she got something in return. But being right didn't loosen the knot in her stomach.

The printer cranked out the second photograph. She took one more look—the first look in eight years at the daughter she'd lost. She grabbed her attaché from beside the desk, stuffed the photocopies inside, and rushed to the elevator.

50

"It's suicide," said Harley. "By shutting out the FBI, your wife is committing suicide." He watched Peter carefully, gauging his reaction.

Allison's traffic-stopping exit had given Harley the diversion he'd needed. He'd left headquarters through a side exit and reentered the Justice Building through the back entrance, then down into the basement. Peter and the other FBI agent were still there, waiting for Allison. It took him only a few minutes to bring Peter up to speed. Harley knew any husband would have been worried sick. He was hoping to enlist Peter to talk some sense into his wife.

"Funny," said Peter. He seemed detached, philosophical. "That's exactly what I told her a year ago, when she said she wanted to run for president. It's suicide."

"It doesn't have to be."

His eyes turned accusatory. "It's General Howe, isn't it? I'll bet Howe hired those punks to snatch the ransom away from her and screw everything up. I saw him on television this morning, criticizing Allison, expressing his sympathies to the families of those juvenile delinquents. He *wants* Allison to fail."

"He may want her to fail," said Harley, "but I don't think he thwarted the plan. I doubt he has anything to do with the kidnapping at all, actually."

"How can you be so sure?"

"Nobody knew that the kidnapper was going to send Allison into the subway until that last phone call. From that point on, things were moving too fast for anyone but an insider to thwart the plan. Those punks had to be hired by someone who knew she was going down in the subway *before* she was actually down in the subway."

"Which only confirms it. General Howe knew she was going down in the subway because *he* sent her there."

"That's certainly where that line of thinking takes you. But I'm not so sure that's the right theory."

"What other theory is there?"

The elevator door opened, breaking their conversation. Allison stepped out. She looked first at Peter, then at Harley.

"What are you doing here?" she asked Harley.

Peter said, "Mr. Abrams was just explaining his latest theory of the case."

She glared at Harley. "Mr. Abrams should know that if the FBI can't talk to me, they can't talk to my husband."

Harley said, "Just because you're cutting yourself off from the FBI doesn't mean the FBI has to cut itself off from you. One way or another, I'm going to let you know what I'm thinking and doing. Otherwise, you're going to get yourself killed."

"He's right," said Peter. "Let's hear what he has to say. Continue, Detective."

He was about to say he was a special agent, not a detective, but so long as Peter was on his side and enjoying his role as Sherlock Holmes, why alienate him? "Allison won't confirm this," said Harley, "but I'm quite certain that the kidnapper's latest contact conveyed some information about Emily's whereabouts."

Peter shot her a look. "Is that true?"

"Peter," she groaned. "Later, okay?"

Harley gave her a sobering look. "There is no *later*, Allison. If he told you something, you should tell me. If he gave you something, we should have the lab analyzing it right now."

She paused. His latter point about the lab made sense. Reluctantly, she dug in her purse for the photos and handed them to Harley. "The kidnapper sent these to Tanya to pass along to me. These are reproductions from my computer. I'm ninety-nine percent certain it's Emily. The birthmarks on her cheek are the clincher. Still, it might not hurt to have one of the FBI face-agers examine it, just to verify."

Harley examined them. "This makes me more convinced than ever of a connection between Kristen and Emily. And as I was explaining to Peter, the more this connection becomes apparent, the less likely it is that General Howe is involved."

"Why?" asked Peter.

"Because eight years ago, when Emily disappeared, General Howe probably didn't even know who Allison Leahy was. And even if he did, he had absolutely no reason to steal her baby."

Peter asked, "So who does that leave as your suspect?"

He glanced at Allison. "Mitch O'Brien. I know he's a sore subject between you two, but it's time we all addressed it."

"Mitch?" she said. "Kidnapping? I don't think so."

"You're defending him now?" Peter snapped.

"I'm not defending him. I'm just testing the theory. He *was* pretty upset when I broke our engagement. And he did get pretty weird when he showed up two months ago."

"And now we can't find him," added Harley. "Nobody can find him."

"You think he's bitter?" asked Peter.

"Bitter eight years ago because Allison broke their engagement. Bitter today because she rejected his efforts at reunion." He looked at Allison. "He could be a sick puppy who's out to destroy you."

Peter sighed, as if blown away. "Fine. O'Brien. What does this mean? What should Allison and I do?"

"I already know what I'm going to do," said Allison.

"Here's what I'd *like* you to do," said Harley. "I'd like you to go back to those files you have on Emily's abduction. If I'm right about the connection between Kristen and Emily, I'd like you to review whatever videotapes you have of the crime scenes, tapes of news coverage, anything like that. Mitch would have had to hire someone to kidnap Emily, since he was talking on the phone when it happened. Or maybe I'm missing something and Mitch has nothing at all to do with this. Either way, it's fairly common for abductors to insinuate themselves into the investigation. They sometimes even help with the search for the child, just so they can keep tabs on how close the police are to solving the crime. You should study those tapes very carefully. Look at every single person standing in the background. See if you recognize anyone. Try to recall if you've seen any of those people recently—

say, in the last six months. Maybe they showed up at a political fund-raiser or a rally. Maybe they even work on your campaign staff. If you find that person, I'd *love* to talk to him."

Allison showed no reaction, but she didn't refuse. "Okay. And while I'm at home with my videotapes having a Blockbuster afternoon, what are *you* going to do, Harley?"

He glanced at Peter, then back at Allison. "Find O'Brien."

Lincoln Howe went straight from Washington National Airport to the Mayflower Hotel, where he and Buck LaBelle would hammer out the wording of his final pre-election statement on the kidnapping. Howe was certain it would be highly critical of Allison Leahy and her subway disaster, but he wanted to strike the right tone. Downtown was the proper setting, he was sure of it. Possibly on the steps of the Justice Building or the FBI headquarters. Maybe even in Lafayette Square with the White House in the background. The way time was flying, however, he feared he might end up delivering it right at the hotel.

Two Secret Service agents took him up the elevator to Suite 776. Howe knew the room number was no accident. LaBelle always stayed at the Mayflower in Suite 776, the room in which President Roosevelt had written: "We have nothing to fear but fear itself." LaBelle had never said it, but it clearly tickled him to orchestrate a Republican campaign from the very room in which the greatest Democrat president had penned his most famous line.

"Come in, come in," LaBelle said hurriedly.

The general left his Secret Service escorts waiting in the hall and stepped into the spacious suite. Early American antiques and carved walnut wainscoting gave the sitting area a dark but elegant feeling, though the crystal chandelier was cranked to full power for maximum lighting. Reams of papers and a bottle of Makers Mark bourbon rested on the floor beside the couch. Heavy silk draperies covered the windows—completely covered them, ensuring privacy.

LaBelle pushed the notebook computer aside, shuffling through scattered papers on the coffee table. "Here's the latest quick and dirty poll, General. Not very scientific, given the immediate turnaround. But even with a huge margin of error, it looks as if Leahy's screw-up in the subway may be the last straw. Even female white baby boomers are beginning to bail out on her."

Howe leaned back in an armchair, examining the one-page summary. He seemed unimpressed. "What about Tanya's threat?"

"What about it?"

"She made it pretty plain. If Kristen isn't home by tomorrow morning, she's going on television to tell the world that she thinks I'm responsible for the kidnapping. That could change everything."

"We just have to brace ourselves," said LaBelle. "Reinforce public opinion, and hope that her accusations come too late in the game to change anyone's mind."

He made a face. "A daughter is going to accuse her own father of kidnapping. How do you brace public opinion for *that*?"

"You make it impossible for them to swallow, that's how. We've surveyed this." He shuffled through another stack of papers, then handed up another summary.

Howe waved off the paper. "Just tell me what it says. I'm tired of reading this shit."

"Yes, sir. Right now, only one in ten Americans think it's even remotely possible that Lincoln Howe might have planned the kidnapping of his own granddaughter. Among that ten percent, eighty-five percent would be less inclined to believe that Lincoln Howe was behind the kidnapping if he were to reconsider his position on the payment of a ransom and meet the kidnappers' demands."

"I can't reverse my position. I'll look weak."

"You've already done it privately, General. The FBI knows you're willing to pay a ransom. Now it's time to tell the American people that you've changed your mind."

"The press will annihilate me. I'll be labeled President Flip-Flop Howe before I'm even elected."

"Ordinarily, I'd agree with you. But Leahy's bumbling has given you the perfect excuse. You're not changing your mind; it's a change of heart. You have to do something to counteract her meddling and save your grandchild."

"I don't know," he groaned.

"General, you have to go with this. It's what the polls are telling us to do."

Howe rose and walked away from the mess of papers. "All this polling and public opinion stuff. Can't I ever just make an intelligent decision based on what *I* think?"

LaBelle looked up from his computer, his face deadpan. "Sir, every politician I've ever served has at some point lodged that same complaint. And after the election, they all told me I was right. If you're going to be a successful president, you have to stop thinking like the hard-charging soldier and start operating like the tactical sailor. A good sailor understands that if you want to sail across the bay, you can't just go straight across. You have to see which way the wind is blowing. You tack to the left, then to the right—back and forth, until eventually you get across. Politics is the same. The wind is public opinion. You don't just hoist your sail and go wherever it takes you. You don't buck it, either, and end up crashing on the rocks. You study it and tack accordingly. Eventually you land wherever it is you want to go."

"A flawed metaphor," Howe quipped. "A sailor can't create his own wind. But a president *can* shape public opinion."

They looked at each other in silence. A thin smile crept onto LaBelle's face. "You're learning, sir. You are definitely learning."

The general returned the smile, then turned serious. "All right. I'll make you a deal. I'll announce my so-called change of heart on the ransom. But before I do, you have to find that O'Brien character. It's bad enough I may be blown out of the water by my own daughter. But I don't want Mitch O'Brien coming back to haunt us, too. We can survive one hit. Not two."

LaBelle shook his head, frustrated. "I've already put my best investigators on it. They can't find the guy."

"Then get better investigators."

"I don't think it will make a difference."

Howe moved closer, his voice booming. "That's not what I want to hear, Buck."

He nearly cowered. By this stage of the game, he knew when an order was not to be questioned. "Yes, sir. We'll find him."

51

It was a political first, she figured—a presidential candidate ducking the press a day before the election. But the last thing Allison wanted was another wrestling match with the media outside her front door. Peter took one of her assistants back to the townhouse to pack her a bag for her trip to Chicago and to box up the old videotapes Harley had suggested she review. She made some phone calls while waiting at her office, starting with her campaign strategist.

"I'm through campaigning, David."

"*What?*" His voice was shrill, beyond urgent.

She considered telling him the truth, but it was too complicated. "My life's in grave danger. The Secret Service has advised me to cancel my appearances."

His long pause confirmed that she'd hit the right nerve. Self-preservation. Self-interest. Those were motivations a hack like Wilcox could appreciate.

"Forget the public appearances. We just need a media response. You have to explain what the hell happened in the subway. A teenage boy is dead. The speculation is that you botched the ransom delivery—that Kristen Howe is as good as dead."

"She's not dead."

"You *were* delivering the ransom, weren't you?"

She struggled, preferring not to say too much. "I can't get into it, David."

"You *have* to get into it. If we play it right, the spin can be extremely positive. You risked your life for someone else's child. You were altruistic enough to use your own money for the ransom. For God's sake, Allison. Even if it's just a written statement, we have to say *something*."

She grimaced. David was right, politically speaking. But if the kidnapper sensed she was making political mileage out of this, she might never see Emily. "David, I just can't focus on that right now."

"When can you?" he scoffed. "*After* the election?"

"Tonight, at the hotel."

"So you are still going to the party?"

She made a face, heeding the kidnapper's warning that she lead everyone to believe her plans were unchanged. "Yes, I'll be there. But if I issue any statement on the kidnapping, it has to be late. Some time after nine o'clock."

"That's no damn good. We need something for the early evening national news."

"Can't do it."

"Why the hell not?"

"David, it's literally a matter of life and death. And I'm not exaggerating."

"I'm not exaggerating either. The ten and eleven o'clock news is too damn late. By that time, the only thing that could possibly turn this election around is if you personally drop off the kidnappers at the county jail, then drive Kristen Howe home safely to her mother and tuck her into bed."

If all goes well . . . she thought. "We can talk more later."

"But—"

"See you at the hotel," she said, then switched off the phone.

Allison's assistant returned to the office at 1:15 with the suitcase and videotapes Peter had packed for her. The plan was to stay at the hotel in Washington tonight and then fly to Chicago in the morning, so that Allison could vote in her hometown. Peter had decided to stay back at the townhouse until it was time to leave for the party.

Allison ordered a sandwich from the Justice cafeteria and ate alone in the small conference room in her office suite. The box of videotapes lay on the rectangular table. The television and VCR were on a metal stand, facing her. She was trying to be selective, knowing she didn't have near enough time to view each one from start to finish. She started with the videotape of the scene outside her house on the night Emily was taken. Eerily, the police had recorded it for the very reason she was now watching it: Abductors have been known to return to the scene, even to assist in the search.

Chills hit her spine as the camera panned the late-night hysteria. It started at the street and crept steadily toward the house. Police cars with swirling lights had pulled onto the sidewalk and front lawn. Friends and neighbors were pulling up, concerned and curious. Police kept them behind the yellow crime scene tape. In the center of it all she saw herself—standing on the front porch, talking to an officer. She looked numb, in shock. She leaned against the door, barely able to stand. Her robe was torn at the hem. Leaves and twigs dangled from the sleeve, remnants of the bushes she'd charged through in her frantic search for her baby.

The conference room began to spin. She stared at the television, watching herself, the numbness returning. The voice-over on the tape startled her. It had been eight years, but she recognized the voice as that of one of the officers on the scene. "Date: March thirty-first, nineteen-ninety-two, twelve-thirty-five A.M. Location: nine-oh-one Royal Oak Court. Subject: Emily Leahy, white female, four months old. Case Number: nine two–one zero one three seven."

Allison felt her heart flutter. The night that had changed everything. One minute, Emily was a sleeping angel in her crib. For the next eight years, she was Case Number 92-10137.

Draining as it was, Allison made it through the entire tape—and more. The crime scene tapes, the search tapes, the neighborhood Crime Stopper tapes, recordings of the local news coverage—she screened each one, carefully examining each person lurking in the background. Some tapes she watched on fast-forward to get through more quickly. As she finished with each one, she dropped it into another box on the floor. In between sips of Diet Pepsi she jotted a few notes on her yellow legal pad. Ninety minutes of viewing, however, had failed to produce a suspect along the lines that Harley had hoped for. She didn't see anyone in any of the tapes who had suspiciously returned into her life.

It was almost three o'clock when her phone rang. She hit the PAUSE button on the video remote and answered it.

"It's me, Harley. I know you don't want FBI

protection, but I have something you should know—with or without us."

"Did you find O'Brien?"

"No. Still no sign of him. But we finally got the DNA results back from the lab on the traces of saliva we found in the lipstick on your scarlet letter photograph."

"What's the verdict?"

"Negative on Diane Combs—you know, that woman we found dead in Philadelphia, who I thought might be connected to the kidnappers."

"What about Natalie Howe?"

"Negative on her, too."

"Where does that leave us?"

"Process of elimination is leading to Mitch O'Brien."

She scoffed. "Unless Mitch has *really* changed in the last eight years, I don't think he wears lipstick."

"No. But you do."

"What are you talking about?"

"We verified the brand of lipstick that was used to scrawl that letter *A* on your forehead. It's Chanel."

"That's my brand."

"I figured. I want you to get a DNA sample to the lab. I'm willing to bet the saliva on the lipstick is yours."

"Which means what? I sent the marked-up photograph to myself? We've been down this road before, Harley. You're going in circles."

"Don't you see? It's one more link to O'Brien. He probably swiped a tube of lipstick from your purse when he saw you at the hotel in Miami Beach, or maybe at that gala in Washington."

Allison fell silent.

"Allison?" he asked. "You'll get us that DNA sample over to the lab, right?"

She didn't respond.

"Allison?"

"Sure, Harley. I'll get it to you. Just as soon as I can."

"This is very important."

"You have no idea," she said flatly. "I'll talk to you later." She hung up, staring blankly into the middle distance. Harley definitely had her thinking. She dug into the box of tapes on the floor—the tapes she'd already viewed. There was one thing, in particular, she needed to see again.

Now that her eyes had been opened.

52

Warm Florida sunshine glistened on the blue-green chop of Biscayne Bay. Sailboats skimmed by the Port of Miami, whose berths were emptied of cruise ships that had set out to sea. To the south, Miami's glass and granite skyline towered above the bay and river. To the north and east, the island of Miami Beach stretched between the Atlantic Ocean and the mainland. In between lay some of world's most expensive real estate—a string of small residential islands, connected by bridges, dotting the bay like huge stepping-stones. It was here that many of Miami's well-to-do called home, a veritable showcase for more Mediterranean-style mansions than the Mediterranean itself boasted. Many were merely winter homes that sat empty until Thanksgiving. Every so often, Marine Patrol would check the docks behind vacant houses for illegally moored boats.

On Monday morning, they found one of interest to the FBI.

Special Agent Manny Trujillo of the FBI's Miami field office answered the call with his partner and a team of forensic experts. Trujillo was the South Florida supervisor of a search that stretched from Key West to Palm Beach. The discovery of Mitch O'Brien's sailboat was the hard-earned payoff of an exhaustive multi-agency effort.

Marine Patrol had already confirmed that the boat was empty before the FBI arrived. Trujillo secured the boat and dock as a crime scene. The forensic team spent the rest of the morning checking for fingerprints and collecting evidence that might lead to Mitch O'Brien. After lunch, he called Harley Abrams from the boat with an update.

"Any signs of foul play?" asked Harley.

"Nothing obvious. To be honest, I approached the boat expecting to smell rotting flesh, but there was nothing. Marine Patrol said it was pretty stuffy when they opened the cabin, as if it had been closed up for a quite a while. We scoured the galley and sleeping quarters. No sign of struggle. The whole place has a very sterile feel to it. It's almost *too* clean. Smells like industrial-strength cleaning solvent in a few spots."

"Doesn't sound like O'Brien is living there, hiding out. Is that what you're telling me?"

"That's exactly what I'm saying."

"You think someone whacked him and sanitized the place?"

"Can't say for sure. Boat owners use all kinds of concoctions to clean off the salty residue. It's conceivable that O'Brien is just one of those neatnik sailors who keeps his boat spic-and-span. Maybe he was hiding out here after he heard the FBI was looking for him, then just abandoned ship when we started closing in."

Harley tapped a pencil eraser on his desktop, thinking. "I need a quick answer on this, Manny. Try a chemical reagent wherever you detected that cleaning solvent odor. See if you pick up any traces of blood."

"Now?"

"Yeah. I'll hold."

Trujillo tucked the portable phone under his chin and called over his forensic expert, Linda Carson. "Abrams wants to try the Luminol. Will it work in this environment?"

"Not outdoors. Too sunny."

"What about below, where we smelled the cleaning solvent?"

"Should be dark enough below if we pull the drapes. I've got some in my bag. Let me get it." She jumped from the deck to dry land, pulled a spray bottle of Luminol from her duffel bag, then jumped back on board and ducked into the cabin.

Trujillo followed. "How reliable is this stuff?"

"Luminol? As good as any of the reagents on the market. Picks up blood residue even where the quantities are too small for lab analysis. If there was any blood down here at all, we should see a pale blue glow wherever I squirt it."

The cabin was four steps down, half below and half above the deck. A small cooking galley and dining table were on the left. A long bench-seat that converted into a sleeping bunk was on the right. Toward the bow were the head and main sleeping quarters.

Carson pulled the drapes shut. The cabin darkened, save for the shaft of sunlight streaming in through the companionway door behind Trujillo. She crouched on the floor beside the dining table, where they had detected the strongest odor of cleaning solvent.

"Ready?" asked Trujillo.

She aimed the squirt bottle at a section of the floor, then nodded. Trujillo closed the door. The cabin went completely dark.

The sound of three quick pumps of the squirt bottle hissed in the darkness. Almost instantaneously, a bright pale blue smear glowed on the floor.

"Bingo," said Carson.

She squirted another area. Another explosion of blue light. She squirted the table. Same result. The wall. More traces of blood. She kept spraying. The cabin was aglow with a pale blue horror story.

Trujillo drew a deep breath, then brought the phone to his mouth. "Harley, you still there?"

"Yeah. What did you find?"

He was staring in disbelief, sweating in the hot, stale air. "I think we may have figured out what happened to O'Brien."

Allison stared at the television in quiet disbelief. The realization had come to her slowly, perhaps even subconsciously at first.

She clicked the rewind button on the VCR remote control. She hated to bring Harley back into this, but she needed a second opinion—someone to tell her she wasn't misreading the videotapes. Or, hopefully, someone to tell her she was. She called him from the conference room.

"It's me," she said.

Harley hesitated. "How weird. I was just about to call *you*. We found O'Brien's boat. Doesn't look good. Bloodstains in the cabin."

Her eyes closed in sorrow. "Poor Mitch," she said, fearing the worst. "But that's exactly where my thinking was headed."

"What do you mean?"

"Up until a few hours ago, I was nearly convinced that General Howe was behind Kristen's kidnapping, figuring he'd do anything to win. Then you shifted my focus, with your suggestion that Mitch was bitter about our breakup. Bitter about the way I'd rebuffed him in Miami. Possibly even bitter enough to send me the marked-up photograph a couple months ago with my own lipstick."

"It seemed plausible."

"On the surface, yes. But the more I thought about it, the more contrived it seemed. Mitch had problems when he drank, that's for sure. But even dead drunk he was too smart and too afraid of jail to send threatening mail to the attorney general. It was as if someone were trying really hard to make it look like Mitch. And that's when it hit me."

"What?"

Her voice filled with concern. "Remember that night General Howe went on television to speak to the kidnappers? The night he declared war on child abductors?"

"Of course."

"Remember afterward, how you were so suspicious because he never referred to Kristen by name. You said it was like a case you had before, where the father killed his baby girl and then in interviews referred to her as an 'it,' rather than using her name or at least saying 'she.'"

"Right. Psychologically, it was his way of distancing himself from the crime. Using the word 'it' depersonalized the victim, made it easier for him to deal with what he'd done. I thought Howe might be doing the same thing."

Allison turned her attention back to the videotape on the television, still speaking into the phone. "I have a videotape from two days after Emily's abduction. Just to give you a little background, Peter and I had been dating about seven months at the time. He was really in love, but I honestly wasn't. I had even told him I wasn't looking to get married and was perfectly happy raising Emily on my own. Still, he was unbelievably supportive after Emily was gone—right from the start. He even went on the news to say that he was offering a half-million dollars of his own money for information that would lead to the arrest of Emily's abductors. Listen to what he said."

She hit the PLAY button and held the phone close to the television speaker. Peter's recorded voice boomed, "We will find the baby. It will never be forgotten. Allison and I will do everything humanly and financially possible to find it."

Allison trembled, barely able to hit the stop button as she spoke into the phone. "In three sentences he called her 'the baby' once, 'it' twice. He never used Emily's name."

"Well, that's just one tape."

"It's like that in *all* the tapes, Harley. I've been keeping track in my notes. Twenty-three times he referred to Emily as an 'it.' Never did he call her by her name."

Harley was silent.

"Are you still there?" she asked.

"Yes," he answered. "I think I should see the tapes. I can be there in fifteen minutes."

"I'll have them ready."

Allison hung up the phone. Her hands shook as she stared at the screen and the frozen image of Peter speaking to the press.

"My God. Peter."

53

Peter was in the bedroom packing a suitcase for Chicago when his telephone rang. It was the phone on the nightstand on his side of the bed, the private line that he used primarily for business. He dropped the Armani suit on the bed and answered it.

"Hello."

He heard a click, then a message. "You have e-mail." Another click. Then the dial tone.

He laid the phone in its cradle, staring at it in confusion. The voice was familiar. It was that standard, recorded voice that plays automatically whenever you turn on the computer and there's e-mail in your mailbox—the "personal" touch in an impersonal world, like that mysterious woman from the long distance company who jumps in after you dial with your credit card and says, "Thank you for using AT&T."

Peter stood still for a moment, mulling it over. The message was clearly for him, not Allison. The call had come on his own line—no one ever called Allison on that line. Obviously, they wanted him to check his computer. He walked cautiously toward his briefcase on the other side of the room. He removed the notebook computer and plugged the modem into the phone jack. He dialed his office in New York, watching the screen as his notebook computer interfaced with his business computer in New York.

"You have e-mail," said the computerized voice—the same recorded voice he'd heard on the phone. It unnerved him at first. He couldn't help feeling as though the caller had recorded *his* personal message. But he knew that 40 million people subscribed to his same Internet carrier, all of whom received the same "You have e-mail" message. It wasn't like someone would have had to access his personal computer to record it and play it back to him over the telephone.

The computer screen blinked on. Scores of unanswered e-mail messages appeared in his mailbox. Each specified the date and time received. All but one identified the sender. The most recent one, received today at 3:54 P.M., had an unintelligible entry next to the "Sender" designation. The sender, Peter realized, had managed to scramble his screen name to protect his identity.

Peter clicked his mouse on the most recent e-mail. The typewritten message flashed on the screen. He stared at it carefully, reading it once, then again.

CHANGE IN PLANS. MEET ME IN ROCK CREEK PARK AT THE WATER FOUNTAIN EAST OF THE OLD PIERCE MILL. 5:00 P.M.

His pulse quickened. There was no signature, of course, but the postscript indicated an attachment. He clicked his mouse again, downloading the attachment to his computer. He clicked once more and opened the file. A photograph slowly emerged on his screen. Bright red everywhere, splattered on white. The image came into better focus: a young girl in a bathtub, covered in blood. The focus sharpened further: The girl was plainly Kristen Howe.

Peter closed the file, wiping the photograph from the screen. The original message popped back on the screen—MEET ME AT ROCK CREEK PARK. He sighed deeply, collecting his thoughts.

Rock Creek Park bordered on Georgetown. He had jogged there hundreds of times. He knew exactly where the meeting spot was.

He also knew the handiwork—the girl in the bathtub covered in animal blood. It was as good as a signature. Vincent Gambrelli.

He switched off his computer and placed it back in his briefcase. He stepped to the window and peeled back the bedroom drapes. Below, a few members of the media were still waiting outside the townhouse, but the crowd had thinned greatly. Most had apparently inferred that Allison wasn't coming back when they saw her assistant leaving with her suitcase.

Peter checked his watch—4:15. Even if he took a few circuitous turns to shake the media, he could easily make it to Rock Creek Park in forty-five minutes. He put on his jacket and grabbed his car keys, then stopped, turned, and disappeared into the closet. Down on one knee, he peeled back the carpeting in the corner, uncovering the floor safe. With three quick turns of the combination dial, it opened.

A semiautomatic pistol lay inside.

He checked the ammunition clip to make sure it was loaded. It was. He tucked it inside his jacket and closed up the safe, then quickly headed for the door.

*   *   *

A foggy mist clung to the city as dusk turned to early evening darkness. City lights glistened on the glossy-wet streets and sidewalks, though there were still a few dry patches beneath the urban trees and storefront overhangs. Some rush-hour commuters had popped their umbrellas. Others seemed oblivious to the precipitation, *sans* weather gear, rushing through crosswalks and heading for the Metro as on any other day. It was the meteorological version of classic Washington ambiguity—raining, but not really raining.

Moisture gathered steadily on the taxicab's windshield as Peter rode alone in the dark rear seat. The wipers were on intermittent speed, clearing the windshield about every half-block along Q Street. Peter looked ahead to the next intersection. Streetlights grew brighter as the gray sky darkened into night. The fog began to swirl in the beaming headlights of oncoming traffic. Like searchlights, thought Peter, hundreds and hundreds of them. He drew a deep breath and shook off the paranoia.

The taxi stopped at the red light, and Peter glanced out the rear window. He couldn't be absolutely certain that no one had been tailing him, but he had been riding around Georgetown for the past twenty minutes and was now on his fifth cab. Had someone been following, he figured he would have noticed.

"This will do, driver," he said as he passed up a five-dollar bill. "Keep the change."

He opened the door and stepped onto the sidewalk. He was standing at the P Street entrance to Rock Creek Park, eighteen hundred acres of remarkably preserved green space right within the district—the smaller Washingtonian version of New York's Central Park. It was a year-round home to deer and other wild fauna, as well as a cool summer oasis for D.C. residents. Picnic areas dotted either side of Rock Creek, the babbling waterway that snaked through the meadows and scattered groves of dogwood, beeches, oak, and cedar. November, however, was not the most beautiful time to visit, and the darkness made the woodlands seem nearly impenetrable. Still, after four years of coming here, Peter knew his way around the miles of bicycling routes and hiking and equestrian trails.

He checked his watch. Almost 4:45. The park would close in fifteen minutes. Not that it mattered; in this weather and at this time of year, the park would be virtually empty at any time of day. He tugged at his jacket and checked his gun, then entered the park and headed south along the creek, toward the old Pierce Mill.

The sounds and lights of the city faded into the background as he headed down the trail. He could hear the creek nearby, the soothing sounds of moving water against the rocks. Still, he was tense. What was the change in plans? he wondered. What did Gambrelli want? Money, Peter figured. With Gambrelli, it was always about money.

He stopped near the old Pierce Mill. It was the park's major tourist attraction, a restored nineteenth-century gristmill powered by the falling water of Rock Creek. The sign said it was closed on Mondays and Tuesdays, so the area was even more deserted than Peter had expected. In fact, it was *totally* deserted.

He stood by the water fountain and waited, as instructed. He hadn't smoked a cigarette in years, but he suddenly felt the urge. He checked his watch. Two minutes before five o'clock. Gambrelli was the punctual type. When he said five o'clock, he meant exactly five.

"Hello, Peter."

He wheeled at the sound of a woman's voice. He squinted in the darkness. She was wearing a hooded raincoat, barely recognizable in the foggy mist. But he knew that voice, that face.

"Allison?" he said nervously. Their eyes locked. His face was ashen. "What are you doing here?"

She stepped from beneath the shadow of the oak tree. "I'm the one who sent you the invitation. What are *you* doing here?"

She could see in his eyes that he was scrambling for an explanation. He was breathing nervously, audibly. His eyes darted as the words stumbled out. "I, uh, I thought I could catch these guys. I thought I would ambush them."

"All by yourself?" she asked incredulously.

He was sputtering, speaking fast but barely coherent. "Yes. I—just. Yes. By myself. I would come and, you know, when they got here I would, like, arrest them."

Her eyes flashed with rage, then pity. "Stop the lies, Peter."

"I'm serious. I was going to arrest them. I even brought my gun." He pulled a pistol from his pocket.

Allison stepped back. "Put the gun away."

He smiled pathetically. "Don't worry. I would never hurt you. I love you. All I've ever done is love you."

She grimaced, bewildered and disgusted. "You call this *love*? Did you honestly think that hiring someone to kidnap Kristen Howe would help me win the election?"

His eyes darkened. The voice filled with bitterness. "No, darling. I thought it would make you lose."

Allison shuddered. "Make me *lose*?"

"It was the only way to save us."

"Save us from what?"

He froze, as if debating whether to say more.

"Peter," she said sternly. "Save us from *what*?"

"I can't say it."

She stepped closer. "Damn it, Peter, you're *going* to tell me. Or I'm calling in the FBI right now and you can tell it to them."

He lowered his eyes. "We can get past this, Allison. You and I can get past anything."

"I can't get past it if I don't know what it is."

He looked up, speaking softly. "I overheard you and your old fiancé talking that night at the gala, two months ago—you and Mitch O'Brien."

Allison stiffened, recalling the mysterious footsteps in the hallway.

He continued, "I saw the way you looked at each other. I watched you duck out to the hall. I saw him follow. So I followed, and I listened. I heard what he said about how you met him in that hotel room in Miami Beach."

"Mitch was talking nonsense. We never shared a hotel room."

"Then why did you refuse to answer the adultery question at the debate?"

"That was purely a matter of principle."

"Don't patronize me," he said sharply. "I know you fucked him. Maybe others, too. There would only be more after you were elected. All the men presidents had lovers. Why would the first woman be any different? I'd be a laughingstock. Not just among our friends. Not just in our hometown. The entire world would know that Peter Tunnello couldn't satisfy his wife. I couldn't let that happen to us. I *wouldn't* let that happen to *me*."

Allison glared. "Mitch is dead, isn't he? That's why no one can find him."

"Who cares? He was a drunken slob who couldn't keep his hands off my wife."

"You sent me that photograph with the lipstick—the one with the scarlet letter on it."

"It was just to scare you, Allison."

"Is that why you hired someone to kidnap Kristen—just to scare me?"

"I did it for *us*, Allison. If you won the election, I knew I would lose you."

"God! You should have just killed me. I *wish* you had just killed me."

His expression changed again, sweeter now—deranged. "*Kill* you? I *love* you, Allison."

She cringed. "How could you hurt an innocent child?"

"I swear, I never planned to hurt her. For a hundred thousand dollars they were supposed to keep her until the sympathy threw the election in Howe's favor, and then let her go. But they got greedy, I guess, and demanded a ransom. When Howe refused to pay, they wanted *me* to cough up the million dollars. When I said forget it, they called and demanded the ransom from you. What could I do then but pay it? You have to believe me, Allison. The thing just snowballed. Once I pushed the button it was too late to reel these guys back in."

Her glared tightened. "What about Emily?"

He looked away, then back. "If you can forgive me, I promise I can help you find her."

"*Forgive* you?" She took a half step closer, her

voice shaking. "If you know where Emily is, you are going to tell me."

A silent projectile whistled past her ear. Two quick thuds pounded on Peter's chest. He fell backwards, landing in a twisted heap on the asphalt trail.

"Peter, no!"

She ran to him and fell to her knees at his side. His chest was soaked in blood. Frantically, she looked toward the mill to gauge the line of fire. She saw no one.

"Peter, talk to me!"

She checked his pulse. Nothing. She lifted him by his jacket, but his head dropped back against the pavement, lifeless. She held him with all her strength, shocked, refusing to believe. Tears streamed down her face as she released her grip. His body slipped away.

She looked up, startled by the sound of approaching footsteps. Two men were running toward her. She pried the gun from Peter's hand and jumped to her feet.

"FBI!" they shouted.

She shook the lead agent by the jacket, nearly knocking him over. "I told you not to follow! Why did you shoot! Why!"

"We didn't shoot!"

Allison froze as the agent spoke into his headset.

"Civilian down, Rock Creek Park at Tilden and Beech Drive. Possible sniper. Need back up immediately at all park exits. Request K-9 and helicopter search support."

The agent kept talking, and the rain was falling harder. Her hair and coat were soaked. Peter lay motionless in a puddle. The adrenaline flowed and emotions surged at the sight of her dead husband—gone, though he was never the man she'd thought he was. She knelt at his side, her voice shaking as the cold rain pelted her lips.

"Don't," she said softly. "You bastard, don't take Emily with you."

54

Vincent Gambrelli slashed through the forest at a dead run. Low-hanging branches slapped his face. He slipped on wet leaves and mosses. His lungs were burning. Over the years, he had kept his lean body in excellent condition, but he wasn't twenty-five years old anymore. He stopped when he reached an isolated trail. He leaned forward, hands on his thighs, catching his breath.

"Shit," he muttered, seeing he'd stepped in horse dung. Then his eyes brightened at the sight of even more droppings all along the trail. A good thing, he thought—he had to be near the Equestrian Center. He jogged ahead and stopped. The stable was dead ahead. *A horse!*

He sprinted another fifty yards down the trail, slowing as he reached the stable. A light burned inside. He pulled the pistol from his jacket, reattached the silencer, and peered through the open stable door. An old man was grooming one of the horses in his stall. He appeared to be alone.

Gambrelli concealed his weapon in his sleeve and walked inside. The sound of the falling rain pattered on the roof. His footsteps were silent on the cement floor. One of the horses snorted as he passed, but the old man was too absorbed in his work to notice. Gambrelli stopped at the lighted stall.

The old man was standing beside the gelding, whistling some made-up tune as he combed through the black tangled mane. The whistling stopped when he noticed the stranger. "Sorry, mister. I'm closed."

"Permanently," said Gambrelli. He raised his arm and fired a muffled shot.

The old man clutched his chest and fell to the ground. He lay motionless at the horse's hoof. Gambrelli rushed inside the stall and saddled up the horse. He put one foot in the stirrup, then stopped. This was suicide, he realized. No way could he ride out of this park like the Lone Ranger. The FBI would surely see or hear him galloping away.

A thin smile creased his lips. He had a better idea.

He jumped down, grabbed the old man, and threw him in the saddle. He tied his feet in the stirrups with leather straps. A long leather lunge line was hanging on the post. He snatched it and tied the old man's torso around the horse's neck. He looked like a jockey leaning forward in the homestretch.

"Come on, boy," he said as he led the horse from the stall, then out the stable door. They stopped at the trail. Gambrelli looked up and listened. He could hear helicopters in the sky.

Perfect, he thought.

He aimed the horse toward the meadow, then laid the barrel of his gun flat on the horse's hind quarters. It was grazing the skin, so the animal would feel the burn and the flesh wound without serious injury. He fired once. The startled horse screeched and took off. In seconds, the mysterious night rider was galloping across the meadow at full speed.

Gambrelli ran in the opposite direction, through the woods. He felt stronger now that he had a plan. He ran at full speed, reaching for every bit of long-distance stamina. He ran along the side of the creek—upstream, figuring the FBI might expect him to be swimming downstream toward the Potomac. He ducked beneath the bridge at the north end of the park, continuing right through, quickly covering another hundred yards on the other side, where he noticed the impressive granite monuments. He leaped over one, never losing speed. Headstones, he realized. He'd reached Oak Hill Cemetery. The terraced cemetery overlooked the park, making the climb like a giant staircase. Gambrelli reached the top terrace before he finally turned and looked behind him.

Helicopters with searchlights were circling over the meadow. He smiled to himself. The diversion had worked.

He turned away, toward the city lights and the street beyond the cemetery wall. He gave an extra burst of energy for the last hundred yards, then hopped the fence and landed in the bushes on the other side. He brushed himself off and walked to the sidewalk, giving one more quick glance over the park. The choppers were hovering over the meadow. It looked like SWAT members were swooping down on ropes. In a few seconds they'd realize their mistake—a few seconds too late.

He checked traffic and crossed the street, hailing a taxi in front of a restaurant. The cab pulled up to the curb, and he jumped in the back.

"Where to?" asked the cabbie.

"Downtown," he said as he burrowed into the backseat. "And hurry."

* * *

Allison stared into her steaming cup of black coffee. She was in the passenger seat of a parked FBI van, her body wrapped in a blanket to keep off the wet chill. The rain sounded like golf balls bouncing off the metal roof. Her chin dropped. She tugged at the microphone clipped to her sweater. Harley Abrams opened the driver's side door and jumped in the seat beside her.

She stared out the windshield, into the inky darkness of the park. "He's going to get away, isn't he?"

Harley didn't respond.

"It's my fault," she said. "I'm the one who got the bloody photo from Tanya Howe. I sent Peter the message. I'm the one who told you not to follow me. If you hadn't put a tail on Peter after I called you, the FBI wouldn't have even been in the neighborhood when this happened. I might have been killed."

"It was a good plan, Allison. Just because something goes wrong doesn't mean it was the wrong thing to do."

"Now I just wish I hadn't picked such an isolated meeting spot."

"Peter had to believe he was meeting with the man he hired. If you were a hit man, you'd pick an isolated spot, wouldn't you?"

She unclipped the microphone from her sweater and handed it over. "You heard it all, I assume."

He nodded, not sure what to say. "Yes. I'm sorry."

Her voice filled with sadness. "Part of me still doesn't want to believe it. The whole time I was waiting in the park, ready to spring the trap, I kept hoping I was wrong. That it wasn't Peter. Then there he was. And I knew."

"I guess I can't even imagine how that feels. To be searching all these years. Then to find out it's your husband."

She looked up. "You want to know how it feels? Think of the first time you walked into the National Center for Missing and Exploited Children. The walls are covered with photographs of happy, innocent kids. It gives you a sick feeling to think that every single one of them is in a place very different from where their picture was taken. Then you walk down the hall, and there's another wall with more photos. But this time the sign above the children doesn't say 'Missing.' It says 'Recovered.' You can't help but feel a rush of relief and excitement. Until you realize that 'Recovered' doesn't necessarily mean recovered *alive*.

"Multiply that feeling—that letdown—by a factor of about ten thousand. *That's* how I feel right now."

"Allison, after something like this, it's natural for you to go through the full range of emotions. But guilt shouldn't be one of them."

"Too late," she scoffed. "I've already told myself about a hundred times that if I hadn't let Peter into my life, Emily never would have been abducted. And maybe if I hadn't been campaigning all over the country, I could have seen the warning signs in Peter. Maybe I could have gotten him some help before it came to this."

"Don't do that to yourself. It's like blaming a woman for marrying a perfect man who turns out to be a child abuser. Look, Peter was smart. He hid his problems not only from you, but from the media, your own political party, Lincoln Howe's campaign sharks, the FBI, and everybody else who vetted the guy when you got involved in national politics. There's no reason you should have known."

She nodded, knowing he was right. But she still felt nauseous. "Do you think the shooter followed me here, or Peter?"

"Definitely you. If he had followed Peter, he probably would have noticed the agents who were tailing your husband. He would never have pulled the trigger if he thought the FBI was around."

"What do you think set him off?"

"He's tailing you, probably to make sure you're heeding his warning to stay away from the FBI. You lead him out to the park, he sees you meeting your own husband. What else could it possibly look like? He probably thought Peter called you out here to get the two of you away from the FBI and everybody else—so he could confess in total privacy, no eavesdroppers. He couldn't just stand by and let Peter tell you who he hired. So he wastes him."

"How would he have heard what we were saying?"

"He didn't have to hear a thing. One look at your face probably told him you weren't out here bird watching."

Allison shivered, recalling Peter's words. "I still don't totally understand it. He said he could help me find Emily. Why would he have taken my four-month-old daughter?"

"As I recall, you said he fell in love with you pretty quick, and you weren't exactly responding the way he wanted. I mean, adopting a baby and telling a guy you're not interested in marriage doesn't give him much encouragement."

"Yeah, but steal my daughter?"

"Maybe his plan was supposed to be just like the Kristen Howe thing. He hired somebody to take Emily away for a few days. Just long enough for him to step forward like a hero and offer a reward with his own money. All the courageous things that eventually made you fall in love with him."

"Then why didn't he give Emily back to me?"

"Maybe he got to like things the way they were. A strong, beautiful woman who's been reduced to a basket case. She needs him, depends on him, can't get through the day without him. Bringing Emily back would have destroyed all that."

She grimaced. "That's sick."

"It's psychopathic. But it happens every day. Some men beat their wives. Some men strangle prostitutes. Some men burn their girlfriend's high school yearbook and photo albums. Domination and control. It's what drives them."

Allison massaged her throbbing temple.

Harley said, "If you look back at your relationship with Peter, I'll bet he was happiest and most loving when you needed him. When you had a crisis. When things were tough at work. When someone close to you was sick or dying."

"When I was losing an election," she added.

Their eyes met. Each could tell the other was suddenly thinking of Kristen Howe. Allison's phone rang in her purse, breaking the silence. Harley nodded. Allison answered.

"Hello."

The response was cool, cocky. "Did you know that in the last eight years only a hundred and nineteen infants under the age of six months have been abducted in the United States?"

"What do you want?"

"Did you know that of those abductions, a hundred and ten were recovered? Most within a few days."

Allison's hand shook. She said nothing.

"Your Emily was one of the nine they never found. *Nine*. Have you done the math on this, Allison? Nine babies in the whole United States in eight years. Over four million births each year. What are the odds of being on the short end of *that* stick? But, of course, you're used to beating the odds, aren't you? How many women have been attorney general? How many women have run for president?"

"What's your point, jerk?"

"My point?" he scoffed. "I'd say fate has found you, Ms. Leahy. For better. *And* for worse. See you at the hotel. Nine o'clock. Or both kids are dead."

The line clicked.

55

Tony Delgado was moving as fast as he could, cursing his Uncle Vince for leaving him to do the grunt work. The temperature inside the garage was no more than fifty degrees, but sweat had soaked through his shirt at the armpits. In half an hour, he had completely loaded the van through the double rear doors. He shoved the last of the plastic five-gallon buckets into the cargo hold, then stood back to admire his work from behind the van. Fifty buckets in all, forty pounds apiece. They were stacked four-high, floor-to-ceiling, along each side of the van. The center was open from front to back, like a long narrow aisle.

He turned and lifted a large black trunk. It was light, empty. He slid it into the open space and opened it, like a casket.

"Good job, Tony boy," he told himself.

He walked back into the house, stopping at the kitchen sink for a glass of water, then continuing to the back bedroom. The door was closed, but he opened it without knocking.

Kristen Howe was sitting on the floor, dressed and ready to go. She was blindfolded. Her mouth was taped. Her hands and feet were bound. Her body stiffened at the sound of approaching footsteps.

Tony unlocked the handcuffs that secured her

to the bedpost. "Time to go," he said. "Get up."

She rose slowly, obediently. He untied her feet, then faced her toward the door. "Walk," he said.

She took small steps. Her world was black from the blindfold, making each step a leap of faith. She could feel her captor's hand on her shoulder, leading her across the room and down the hall. She heard a door open. Colder air hit her face. A step down. The floor now felt like cement. *The garage?*

"Be still," he said.

She cringed as he lifted her off the ground.

"In you go," he said. He laid her in the trunk long ways, front to back. He checked her blindfold and the tape on her mouth. He readjusted the plastic cuffs on her hands and bound her ankles. All secure. He slid the trunk forward as far as possible, leaving a small space in the back by the doors. Finally he loaded the last bit of cargo into the van—a carpet cleaning machine, hoses, and a big canvas tarp.

The doors slammed shut. The sign on the back read, CAPITOL CITY CARPET CLEANERS.

He opened the driver's door and jumped behind the wheel. The engine rumbled with a turn of the key. He turned around to check his cargo. The air holes on the sides seemed sufficient. She lay perfectly still, no trouble at all.

"You want to go home, don't you?" he asked.

She nodded.

"You want to be safe, right?"

She nodded once more.

"Then lay there on the floor like a good girl. Don't twitch an inch. Don't make a sound." He lowered the lid and covered the trunk with the canvas tarp, glancing at the buckets stacked all around her. "And whatever you do," he said with a smirk, "don't light a match."

By six o'clock, the media vans were streaming into Rock Creek Park for live on-the-scene reports. With SWAT personnel leaping from helicopters and speculation running wild on police band radio, the story was breaking fast.

Allison and Harley were still in the FBI van when the SWAT leader radioed with more bad news about the murdered stable manager. She felt a tinge of sadness for the old man, followed by anger and more than a little fear. It chilled her to think she had just talked to the old man's killer. He'd sounded so calm and incredibly cool—utterly remorseless for the taking of another's life.

Harley and Allison scurried beneath the rain from the van to an unmarked car. They were headed down Massachusetts Avenue before the media mob had even confirmed her involvement in the park.

"Where to?" she asked.

Harley slowed as they approached DuPont Circle. "We need some time to regroup before nine o'clock. I suggest we go to the field operations center we've set up for tonight. It's just a block away from the hotel where you're supposed to drop the ransom. The place still looks like a vacant retail outlet, so no one knows it's there. Right now, it's probably the one place in Washington you can visit without being noticed."

"How are you going to get the ransom to me so I can deliver it?"

"It's in a vault back at headquarters. I'll have someone bring it to us once we get to the field operations center."

She nodded.

Harley said, "It's going to be difficult to keep this story quiet. You've got park rangers, metropolitan police, the medical examiner's office, FBI. Lots of opportunities for leaks. I'm sure the press already knows two people are dead. Within the hour they'll know one of them's your husband—no matter how tight we try to screw on the lid."

"I didn't expect to keep it quiet."

"What *are* your expectations?"

"I expect to find Emily. And to get Kristen Howe home safely."

He nodded. "I was thinking about that last phone call. Kind of interesting that after all that just happened in the park, the kidnapper still wants you to stick to the plan and go to the hotel."

"What do you mean, 'interesting'?"

"It just leads me to believe that he must have a pretty elaborate plan. No matter what happens, he won't change the venue. You *have* to meet him at the Hyatt at nine o'clock."

"Is that good or bad?"

"Cuts both ways. On the one hand, it gives us time to check things out. We have agents posed as hotel employees. They've been discreetly inspecting the hotel and surrounding area, making sure all is secure. No bombs, booby traps, what have you. On the other hand—well, he must have *some* reason for picking that particular place."

"Are you trying to tell me yet again that this is too dangerous for me?"

He stopped the car at the traffic light, glancing her way. "He did authorize you to wear a disguise, Allison. That makes it easier for us to use a double, if you want."

She shook her head. "Now, more than ever, this

is my responsibility. Even if it's true that Peter told the kidnappers to return Kristen unharmed, the fact remains that he hired them. It's like that example they teach you in law school—you can't fire a bazooka into a crowd and say, sorry, folks, but I didn't really intend to hurt anybody."

He shook his head, not quite comprehending. "So you feel compelled to risk your life for Kristen Howe because it turns out your husband is a psychopath?"

"Partly," she said. "But mostly because Emily is still my daughter."

The traffic light changed. Harley hit the gas. "You know, Allison, only two people heard Peter's confession. You and me. The media may find out your husband was killed. But I don't see any reason for them to know your husband was behind the kidnapping. I mean, we'll have to file a report. But that doesn't have to be tonight."

"Thank you. But there is one other person who is going to hear it tonight."

"Who?"

"Tanya Howe," she said, staring at the raindrops on the windshield. "It's time I told her who kidnapped her daughter."

56

General Howe reclined in his leather seat the moment the pilot switched off the FASTEN SEAT BELT sign. The mood was festive among his staff in the back of the campaign jet, but Howe was in his restful mode. He switched off his reading light and glanced out the window to enjoy the view. Washington was in lights, beautiful from above. Looking down from the sky made him feel almost godlike. In just a few hours, he'd own this town.

The air-telephone rang in the seat beside him. He answered quickly. It was his strategist.

"This is big," said LaBelle.

He sipped his Dewars and water. "What do you got, Buck?"

"It's just hitting the wires now. Apparently, Leahy had another go-around with the kidnapper around five o'clock this evening. This time at Rock Creek Park."

He stiffened in his seat. "What the hell is going on with that woman?"

"Thankfully, another disaster. Kidnapper got away. Some old man who runs the equestrian center got whacked. Another guy is dead. It may be Allison's husband."

"Her husband?"

"Yes. No confirmation yet, but that's the rumor."

"That's terrible," said the general.

"No shit. It could swing the sympathy factor right back in her favor."

Howe bristled. The way LaBelle had so quickly reduced his opponent's loss to political terms had taken him aback—but only for a moment. "What can we do, Buck?"

"Now more than ever we have to get you on television to reverse your position on the payment of the ransom. We have to keep people thinking about your granddaughter. Sure, what happened to Allison's husband is bad. But let's keep reminding them that a little girl's life is still at stake."

"I told you I would do that just as soon as you found O'Brien. It makes me nervous that the FBI is looking for him."

"Sir, I understand that. And I don't know why the FBI is looking for him. But nobody can find him. My investigators tell me that Marine Patrol may have found his sailboat with some traces of blood on it. Could be foul play or even attempted suicide. I don't know. All I *do* know is that O'Brien has nothing to do with your decision to pay a ransom."

Howe lowered his voice so no one could overhear. "Damn it, Buck. We have to think about appearances here. Look at the series of events. First, O'Brien comes to us and tells us he slept with Allison Leahy. Then he flunks a lie detector test. Then he disappears. Now you're telling me there's blood on his sailboat. It's starting to sound like somebody killed him."

"Possible, I guess."

"What if the people who killed him are the same people who kidnapped Kristen? What if all this comes out in a few weeks or months? What will the American people think if I suddenly say I've changed my mind one hundred and eighty degrees and now I *am* willing to pay these dirty bastards a million dollars?"

"I don't know what they'll think."

His voice was shrill but still a whisper. "They'll think I masterminded some idiotic Oliver Stone conspiracy, that's what they'll think. They'll think the million dollars was last-minute hush money or a payoff. At least that's the kind of nonsense those bastards over on Capitol Hill will lead them to believe. I don't want my entire first term tied up in congressional hearings."

"General, if you don't make that speech tonight and offer to pay the ransom, you may not have a first term."

The general paused and sipped his drink. "You honestly believe that, Buck?"

"I honestly do. You have to keep the sympathy factor in your camp, General. Because if it turns out that dead guy in the park really is Allison Leahy's husband, I may just feel sorry enough to vote for her, myself."

He sucked an ice cube, then crunched it in his teeth. "All right, damn it. I'll give the speech."

Time constraints made it impossible for Allison to sit down face-to-face with Tanya Howe and explain everything. It was only a twenty-minute car ride to the operations center, but Allison didn't want to wait another minute before making the phone call. She recalled at least two prior occasions when Tanya should have been the first person she'd called, but Tanya had been forced to call her. She wasn't going to be embarrassed like that again. Harley continued driving across the district as she placed the call on her encrypted cellular phone.

It took only a few minutes to deliver the news. Tanya had listened without interruption, without making a sound.

"Tanya?" she asked after several seconds of silence. "Are you okay?"

Tanya sat alone on the edge of her bed, staring at the photograph of Kristen on the nightstand. She blinked repeatedly, as if returning from a hypnotic state. The last thing she had expected to hear was that Allison Leahy's husband was behind the kidnapping. "What am I supposed to say?"

"I know this can't be much of a comfort, but I was probably even more surprised than you were."

Her mouth quivered. "I guess I should respect you for telling me. But I'm not sure what I'm feeling."

"You have every right to hate me," said Allison.

"No. I don't hate you. That would be like hating my mother because she's married to my father."

Her voice suddenly tightened. "Oh, my God. My father."

"What about him?"

"I honestly thought he or one of his cronies was responsible for the kidnapping. The other night, I told him that if Kristen wasn't back by the time the polls open, I'd go on television and tell people exactly what I thought."

"Hopefully, she will be back by then."

"But he's going to screw everything up. He's scrambling, trying to get her back. My mother just told me he's planning to go on television tonight to say he'll pay the ransom. If the kidnappers hear that, who knows what they'll do?"

Allison was calm but firm. "You have to stop

him. For the next few hours, no one should say anything publicly about the kidnapping. Especially not anything about a ransom."

"How do you expect *me* to get my father to shut up?"

"There must be something you can do."

The response was slow in coming, but Allison could almost feel the energy flowing on the other end of the line.

"I can think of only one thing," said Tanya.

"What?"

"That's between me and my father."

Allison paused, but after the pain Peter had caused her, she was in no position to second-guess. "Good luck, Tanya," she said sincerely.

"Thank you," she replied, then hung up the phone.

Tanya dug an address book from her purse, opened it to the right page, and laid it on the bedspread beside her. She opened the nightstand drawer. Loose change and costume jewelry were arranged neatly in little plastic organizers. A metal strongbox was in the back. She lifted one of the plastic organizers, exposing the key. She unlocked the strongbox. Inside was a Dictaphone. She removed it, closed the box and the drawer, then laid the Dictaphone on the nightstand beside the phone.

She checked the number in the address book one more time. She drew a deep breath, then dialed the number. On the third ring, she got an answer.

"Mr. LaBelle, please." She winced at the response, then said, "I don't care what he's doing. Tell him it's Tanya Howe, and he has one minute to get on the line. Or he loses the election."

She waited, checking her watch. In twenty seconds, LaBelle was on the line with his mouth in high gear.

"Tanya, I'm well aware that we're closing in on your deadline. Your father is doing everything possible to get Kristen back safely by tomorrow morning. In thirty minutes he's calling a press conference to announce that he will pay the ransom. A million dollars. What more can he do?"

"All I want is for my father to shut his mouth. He is to say nothing of Kristen or the kidnapping unless I say so. That also means no attacks against Allison Leahy for the way she is handling this."

"That's not possible, Tanya. You see, you don't run your father's campaign. I do."

She reached for the Dictaphone. "I have something here I'd like you to listen to, Mr. LaBelle. Remember that little meeting we had in the hot tub back in Nashville?" She held the Dictaphone closer to the telephone, then hit the PLAY button.

Tanya's recorded voice was first: "Don't you dare threaten my daughter." LaBelle's sharp reply followed: "I'm not. I'm threatening *you*."

Tanya switched off the recording and came back on the phone. "The whole conversation is on tape. I've kept it in a safe place for an occasion like this, just in case I ever needed to bust your ass. Would you like me to send this over to the networks?"

"That's a fake," he barked. "You spliced it together."

"It's completely genuine. I recorded it myself, word for word."

"That's impossible. You were in the hot tub. You were underwater."

"But my robe was laying right on the floor next to me, and the Dictaphone was tucked into the pocket. Maybe if you hadn't been so busy ogling my body you would have been more alert."

His tone turned more conciliatory. "Tanya, please. You may think you're hurting me. But it's bigger than that. The real person you're hurting is your father. Not just your father, but your mother, too. You're hurting your whole family."

She smiled thinly. "I'm not threatening my family, Mr. LaBelle. I'm threatening *you*."

The line was silent.

Tanya said, "I will expect no further comment from the general until *I* give you the approval. So cancel that press conference. Do we understand each other, Mr. LaBelle?"

"Yes," he grunted. "Perfectly."

"Good," she said smugly, then hung up the phone.

Tony Delgado parked the Capitol City Carpet Cleaners van behind the hotel, at the service and delivery entrance. He stepped out and pulled on a pair of green coveralls. He pulled the painter's cap down tightly, almost to his eyes. He cinched up the particle mask worn by workers who were in danger of breathing dangerous chemicals, then carried a bucket in each hand to the hotel entrance and rang the buzzer.

A security guard came to the door. He was dressed like a police officer, but Delgado noted he had no weapon. "Yeah, what is it?"

"Carpet cleaners. We're supposed to clean the second floor."

"Tonight?"

"That's right."

"Nobody said anything to me about this."

"Got a work order right here." He handed him a convincing phony.

The guard studied it, his face scrunched with skepticism. "This seems strange. Hold on a second, okay? Let me check with the night manager."

"No problem. But hey, buddy. Could you give me a hand here first? One of my buckets of cleaning solvent is leaking all over the back of my truck. I need to push some things around and get it out of there before it ruins everything."

The guard paused.

Delgado flashed a rolled-up twenty. "It'll just take a second."

The guard cracked his gum, taking the money. "Yeah, sure. I can help you out."

Delgado smiled with his eyes, talking as he led the guard to the van and unlocked the rear doors. "I guess I must have made a turn a little too fast or something. Knocked the damn bucket right over." He opened the door. "See it over there?" he said, pointing.

The guard leaned forward. Delgado snatched a pipe from his pocket and crushed the back of the guard's skull. His body landed with a thud, half inside the van, half out.

Kristen stirred inside the trunk.

"Quiet, girl," he said.

He shoved a half-dozen buckets forward, clearing space. He snatched the guard's walkie-talkie and key ring, then stuffed the body inside. With one foot on the bumper he reached atop the van and removed the dolly. In seconds, he loaded the trunk onto the dolly and pushed it up the loading ramp.

He checked his hat and mask once more, then

inserted the guard's key and entered the building. The freight elevator was just inside. He hit the CALL button and wheeled in his cargo. With a confident flick of the wrist he punched the button for the second floor.

The doors closed, and the elevator began its ascent.

57

Allison and Harley reached the surveillance post in less than twenty minutes. It did look like a vacant storefront, just as Harley had promised. The front windows were whitewashed and covered with signs that said, THIS SPACE FOR RENT. A padlocked security gate made the main entrance impassable. Harley brought her around to the rear entrance off the alley.

Inside, three thousand square feet of open retail space had been converted into a miniature operations center. Power cables snaked across the floor and dangled from the ceiling, each leading to a different piece of computer or electronic surveillance equipment. A dozen clocks hung on the wall. At least two dozen agents were stationed around the room, monitoring equipment, sipping coffee, or splicing wires. An entire wall of television screens made the joint look a little like a discount appliance warehouse.

Harley explained, "This was the advantage I was telling you about, Allison. The fact that the kidnapper told you in advance to meet at the Hyatt has given our technical agents time to set up. Each of those television screens will give us a different view of the hotel, inside and out. Some are connected to hotel's regular surveillance cameras, some are fed by the additional cameras we installed today. So long as you're in a public place, we'll be watching you."

"That makes me feel a little better."

"Come on. Let's get you wired up and into your disguise." He led her to a back room. Two female agents were inside, one about Allison's age, the other much younger. Harley made the introductions. "This is Agent Scofield," he said of the older, "and Agent Parker. Scofield will suit you up with a Kevlar vest that should stop anything the kidnappers might fire at you. She'll also hook you with a two-way radio so I can communicate with you."

The younger one stepped forward with a wig in each hand and a voice filled with attitude. "And I'm the lucky female agent who gets to play the all-important role of hair stylist and makeup artist. Redhead or brunette?"

Allison lowered her voice, as if sharing a secret, though she knew the others could overhear. "If I have any authority at all as attorney general after this is over, I promise to get you off the makeup detail."

"Thanks a lot," she said.

Allison glanced at Harley. "Before we get started, can I have a minute to make one more phone call?"

"Sure," he said as he led the other two agents out. "We'll be right out here."

Allison closed the door and dialed David Wilcox.

"I'm so sorry about Peter," he said.

"Thank you. I didn't realize you knew yet."

"Everyone knows. No confirmation from anyone yet, but all the networks are reporting it. I've been calling all night, but you haven't returned my calls."

"Sorry. I haven't been taking anyone's calls."

"I presume you want to cancel the party at the Renaissance. Doesn't seem appropriate to be celebrating tonight."

She paused, recalling the kidnapper's instructions not to change a thing. "Don't say anything about the party. Just leave everything as it is."

"You're kidding."

"Just do as I say. I'll explain later. I have to go now." She hung up and looked through the rectangular window on the door. Harley was on the phone across the room. He hung up and came toward her. Allison let him in. His face was solemn as the door closed behind him.

"Got the lab results on that blood on Mitch O'Brien's boat."

"And?"

"Definitely his."

"Any chance he lived through the attack?"

Harley shook his head. "From what I understand, there was blood all over. It wasn't a clean hit, like a gunshot to the back of the head. Looks like the attacker may have tortured him, possibly trying to extract some information before killing him."

"Like whether he'd recently slept with Allison Leahy?" she suggested.

"That would seem consistent with what Peter told you in the park."

She looked away, speaking through the lump in her throat. "Peter did it, you suppose?"

"He wouldn't be the first jealous husband to kill the man he thought was sleeping with his wife. But I think it's more likely he hired someone to do it."

"The same guy he hired to kidnap Kristen?"

"And to kidnap Emily," said Harley. "I doubt your husband had more than one contact in this business. It's not like you just look them up in the Yellow Pages."

She sighed, thinking. "Peter had lots of different bodyguards over the years. They followed him like Secret Service on business trips to countries where Americans aren't well thought of. He always used reputable corporate security firms. Mostly retired cops, former FBI. Still, I felt like some of these guys had acquaintances I wouldn't want to meet."

"That could easily be the way he found his hit man. But it wasn't a hired gun who put these ideas in his head. This was Peter's plan. His need to control you."

She slumped in the desk chair, shaking her head in amazement. "Mitch O'Brien, the drunken stalker. Peter Tunnello, the jealous psychopath. Guess my taste in men could use a little work, huh?"

"Work is good. Just don't give up on all of us."

She looked up, finding comfort in his eyes. He didn't look away.

"So what do *you* think?" she asked, breaking the silence.

"About what?"

She grabbed the wigs laying on the table, putting on the exaggerated and affected voice of a ditz. "Should I be a brunette," she joked as she held out the red wig, "or a redhead?" she said, holding up the brown one.

He could see the pain behind her smile. Humor was certainly one way of dealing with a husband's ultimate betrayal. "Surprise me," he said, then left the room, burdened with the thought that today was only the second worst day of Allison's life.

* * *

Brass chandeliers brightened the long majestic hallway of the St. George Hotel, the old granite landmark across the street from the Grand Hyatt. Antique oil paintings in gold-leaf frames brightened the silk-covered walls. Ninety of the grand old hotel's five hundred rooms were on the second floor. As usual, all seven floors were filled to capacity.

Vincent Gambrelli walked with eyes dead ahead, his footsteps cushioned in the rich red carpeting. He dug into his coat pocket for his stack of room key-cards. Five altogether, for five different rooms. He'd rented them over the past two days, each time using a new name, a new disguise, and a different clerk at the reception desk. Four bags went to each room. They all contained the same thing. None, as yet, had been unpacked. They were waiting for him now in the respective rooms, all on the second floor, according to plan.

He stopped at Room 205 and removed the DO NOT DISTURB sign. He checked the hall. Seeing no one, he inserted the magnetic key-card and stepped inside.

The room was exactly the way he had left it twenty-four hours ago. A king-size bed, neatly made. Full-length draperies, drawn shut. Extra towels and linens on the couch. Four suitcases resting at the foot of the bed.

He knelt down beside the largest suitcase and unlocked it with his key. Inside were a dozen plastic jugs, exactly the way he had packed them. He removed one of the jugs, unscrewed the cap, and poured the contents onto the bed. It soaked the mattress. He put his nose to the wet spot and inhaled.

He smirked. Wood alcohol. Virtually odorless—but highly flammable.

He opened another jug, then another, dousing the couch, draperies, furniture, and finally the carpet. It took only a few minutes to soak the entire room. When he'd finished, the empty jugs and suitcases lay scattered on the floor. He unlocked the door, opened it slowly, and checked the hallway. No one. He stepped out and closed the door. He checked to make sure it was locked, then reattached the DO NOT DISTURB sign to the knob.

He continued down the hall at normal walking speed. His hand slipped into his pocket, fishing for the key to the next room on the floor, the next target on his list. Just three more to go.

And then Kristen Howe's room.

The money arrived at the field operations center at 8:30, locked in a large metal briefcase. Allison's disguise was complete. Her short blond hair was now shoulder length and brown. Contact lenses turned her hazel eyes brown. Makeup darkened her fair complexion. She wore designer jeans and a short-waisted jacket for a younger, less businesslike look. A silk scarf and leather gloves covered the neck and hands—the two spots that, short of cosmetic surgery, would give away anyone's age.

"Has anybody seen Allison?" asked Harley.

"Very funny."

"Quick picture," said Harley. "We need a photo ID."

"For what?"

"The kidnapper said the room at the Hyatt is registered in the name of Emily Smith. We need to make you Emily Smith so you can pick up the room key. We got a Maryland driver's license all ready for you. Just need a picture."

"Smile," said the photographer. The flash blinded her. He yanked out the film and handed it to another agent. In thirty seconds, she had a driver's license.

"I wish it had been this easy when I was sixteen," she said as she tucked it into her wallet.

Harley smiled, then turned more serious. "Remember. I'll be in radio contact at all times. Hit the panic button the instant you see something you don't like. We have agents posted everywhere along the route and in the hotel. Help will never be more than two or three seconds away."

"Got it," she said. "Where's the cash?"

Another agent presented a black leather bag.

Allison grimaced. "The instructions were specific. He wants it in a Spartan 2000 large metal security briefcase."

Harley said, "It's inside the bag. The metal briefcase didn't mesh very well with your disguise. This is far less conspicuous."

Allison slung the bag over her shoulder, then took a deep breath. "What about a gun?"

"You didn't say anything before, but I brought a SIG Sauer P-228, if you want it."

"Just because I'm for gun control doesn't mean I don't believe in self-defense. I'm trained to use a gun. If ever I was going to arm myself, this seems like the time."

Harley unzipped the leather bag and tucked the gun into a side pocket. "That's a good place for it. Leave it there, unless you absolutely need it."

She nodded. "Okay. Let's go."

Harley walked her to the rear exit, stopping her at the open door. "Don't be a hero, you hear?"

She raised an eyebrow. "Don't be a pain in the ass. You hear?"

He forced a smile. She gave him a look that said don't worry, then started down the alley toward the street.

The rain had stopped, but the streets and the sidewalks were still wet, and the fog had yet to lift. It was too warm for her breath to steam, but the dampness made it feel colder than it was. She walked at a steady pace, oblivious to the noise of passing cars or the sight of the homeless curling into doorways for the night. Traffic was heavy on H Street, which came as a relief. Carrying a million dollars, she somehow felt safer around pedestrians than she would have felt on a totally isolated street.

The earpiece buzzed. "Testing," said Harley. "Pain in the ass calling hero."

She spoke in a normal voice, as instructed. The microphone was clipped inside her jacket collar. "Go ahead, pain in the ass."

"Everything seems to be working just fine. I'll be listening. Let me know when you reach the room."

She stopped at the traffic light at Tenth Street. The Grand Hyatt was straight ahead—her meeting place. She crossed the street, passing under the carport. Valet attendants hustled past her. Bellboys helped arriving guests with their bags. Allison walked right past them, straight into the lobby.

She did a double take as she entered. It was a modern hotel, but entering the lobby was like stepping onto a 1930s movie-musical set. Rooms were arranged like a Mediterranean hillside village rising around a courtyard. A gazebo, curved lounge, and dining areas encircled a blue lagoon fed by waterfalls. In the center lay a small island on which a pianist in black tuxedo played Cole Porter tunes on a white grand piano.

She scanned the crowd, then turned her focus toward the long registration counter. A battery of clerks in red uniforms were busily checking in guests. Allison made a beeline for the young guy with the confused expression on his face. He looked new, clueless—the least likely to give her a hard time.

"I'm sorry," she said. "I locked myself out of my room. Could you please give me another key. Emily Smith is the name."

He tucked the telephone under his chin, seemingly overwhelmed. "Could I see some identification, please?"

She presented her phony driver's license.

He glanced at it, then checked the computer. The name EMILY SMITH flashed on the screen. He handed over the key. "Here you are, ma'am."

She turned away quickly, relieved that the disguise was actually working—at least among idiots under the age of twenty. The key-card didn't have a room number on it, but the little pouch that held it did—Room 511. She boarded the elevator and rode to the fifth floor. The sign on the wall directed her to the right. She followed the arrows down the near hallway and stopped in front of her door.

"I'm here," she said softly into the microphone.

Harley responded, "Stand to one side when you insert the key and open the door. If it's rigged, I don't want you in the direct line of fire. And once you're inside don't say anything to me, even if I speak to you. He may have the place bugged, and I don't want him to hear your voice and figure out that you're wired. Good luck. And be careful."

She checked the hallway. All was clear, save for the room service waiter a few doors down. It was reassuring to know he was actually an FBI agent. She stepped to one side of the door, then inserted the key. The tiny light on the electronic lock changed from red to green. She paused, gathering her nerves. With a gentle push, the door swung open. She cringed and waited.

Nothing. No explosion, no trip wires. She moved into the doorway. Harley's voice was in her ear once more.

"Don't turn on any more lights than you have to," he said. "They could be booby-trapped."

She almost spoke, then caught herself, remembering his warning that the room could be bugged. She reached around the door frame and switched on the main light. The room brightened—but nothing else happened. She sighed with relief and stepped inside.

Harley spoke again. "Leave the door open, if you can."

The door started to swing closed automatically. She grabbed a towel from the bathroom and stuck it in the doorway to keep it ajar, then stepped further inside. It was a standard hotel room. Dark wood furniture. Two double beds. A fox hunt portrait hanging over the dresser.

Allison checked her watch. Exactly nine o'clock. The telephone on the nightstand rang.

Harley could hear it over the microphone. "Answer it," he said.

She lifted the receiver. "Hello."

The voice on the line was familiar but disguised. "Take a cab to the St. George Hotel. Go to the Independence Bar on the second-floor lobby. Sit down at one of the little round tables closest to the brass railing and wait."

The line clicked. Allison dropped the phone and hurried from the room. She spoke to Harley as she walked toward the elevator. "You heard?"

"Yes. I don't like it, Allison. We've scoured the Hyatt and everything around it. But the St. George is almost twenty blocks away. It wasn't within our prescreening perimeter. We won't know what you're walking into."

"Are you telling me not to go?"

"I'm telling you it's dangerous. More dangerous than I'd hoped."

"I have two words for you, Harley."

"What?"

"I'm going," she said as she stepped into the elevator.

58

The freight elevator opened to the second floor of the St. George Hotel. Tony Delgado wheeled out his dolly and carpet cleaning machine. Five buckets—twenty-five gallons—were stacked on the dolly. It was his third trip, and his "cleaning" job was nearly finished.

He pulled the dolly into the storage room at the end of the hall. He opened the tank to the carpet cleaning machine and poured from the bucket. It was supposed to hold five gallons of nonflammable cleaning solvent. Tonight it held wood alcohol.

Delgado wheeled the cleaning machine back into the hall, plugged it in, and switched on the power. The cleaning brushes turned quietly in a circular motion, working the alcohol deep into the carpet. He looked down the hall, then checked the room number on the nearest door. He couldn't remember exactly where he had left off before going down to the van for more alcohol. He shrugged. Didn't matter, he figured, so long as he laid a flammable path connecting each of the rooms on his uncle's list.

He pushed the machine forward a few more feet, then stopped. Someone was coming out of Room 235. A silver-haired man wearing an expensive pinstripe suit. Looked like a distinguished congressman. The disguise fooled him at first, but he soon recognized his uncle.

"Evening, Senator," he said with a smirk as they passed in the hall.

"Evening," Gambrelli replied.

Overstated elegance described the decor at the historical St. George Hotel. Fluted columns of green Brazilian marble rose three stories in a lobby as spacious as a Broadway theater. Leather couches, oriental rugs, and plenty of brass and mahogany accents gave sitting areas the look of old English men's clubs. Glittering chandeliers hung like clouds from the mirrored ceiling.

Still, the hotel was past its prime, in a state of decline. Paint was peeling from some of the crown moldings. The silk wall coverings were beginning to yellow. Allison was reminded of Venice as she crossed the lobby—beautiful from a distance, but don't scrutinize the canals.

Allison didn't feel all that out of place in her casual clothing. Some guests were sharply dressed, many of them addressed by name by the courteous staff. Others were obviously here to take advantage of the discount rooms that hadn't been refurbished since Truman was president. The mix covered the spectrum, and it made for a lively and bustling lobby.

Allison headed straight for the grand staircase. She climbed to the mezzanine level, where the Independence Bar overlooked the main lobby. The bar wasn't a room per se. It was more like a terrace area that had been separated from the traffic lanes by a row of potted plants and velvet rope hanging from brass poles. A long mahogany bar stretched across the far end. Small cocktail tables dotted the seating area. Two Japanese businessmen were smoking cigars and sipping wine. An old couple was staring into space and munching on mixed nuts, nothing left to talk about. Allison spotted the small round table closest to the brass railing—the one the caller had mentioned. It had a reserved sign on it.

Allison approached the bartender. "Excuse me, can I have that reserved table over there?"

"Are you Emily Smith?"

She caught herself, remembering her alias. "Yes."

"It's reserved for you."

"Who reserved it?"

He gave her a funny look, as if she should have known. "White-haired guy in a suit. Gave me twenty bucks to hold the table for Emily Smith. Didn't catch his name."

She wanted to press for details, but Harley's voice was in her earpiece. "Don't push it, Allison. You'll raise suspicions. Just take the table."

The bartender asked, "Can I bring you a drink?"

"No, I'll wait," she said, then saw herself to the table.

It was a choice table, as far as bar tables went. It was right against the polished brass railing, like sitting on a balcony. She could see the entire main-floor lobby below, the staircase, the elevators. At the mezzanine level, she could see down the hall to the restaurant and to the double doors that led to the second-floor guest rooms. The table was more secluded than most, surrounded on three sides by leafy green plants in huge floor pots. Allison sat in the leather chair with her back to the bar. Her eyes shifted from the lobby to the staircase, back and forth.

The bartender brought a telephone to her table. "For you, miss," he said.

She waited for him to get back behind the bar, then answered. "Yes?"

"Check the potted plant closest to the rail. There's a thirty-six-inch cable bicycle lock."

She turned around discreetly and checked. "Yes, I see it."

"Take it out. Wrap it around the briefcase and through the handle. But don't lock it."

She did it. The cable fit neatly around the briefcase. "Okay, done."

"Now put the briefcase at your feet under the table and lock it to the railing."

"I'm not leaving a million dollars here in the bar."

"Lock it. No one can open or remove it but me."

"How do I know you won't take it away before I get the girls?"

"Because you're not going anywhere. You're going to sit right there and watch it. Now stop stalling. Lock it to the rail."

Chills went down her spine. What was his plan—to sit down across the table from her?

She lowered the briefcase below the table, slipped the loose end of the cable around the rail and snapped the lock shut. "Okay. It's secure. Now when do I get the girls?"

"One at a time. Kristen first."

"What about Emily?" she asked, her voice hardening.

"Kristen will tell you how to find Emily."

"Where is she?"

"Sit tight," he said, "And watch the staircase."

59

Tony Delgado clutched the silent beeper in his hand. *Really* clutched it. Timing was crucial. He had to react the instant the beeper started to vibrate—the moment his uncle gave the signal.

He stood at an intersection in the second-floor hallway near the elevators and stairway. The cleaning machine rested at his side. One eye was on the door to the stairwell. The other peered down the hallway. The silent beeper suddenly pulsated in his hand—the signal.

He struck a match and dropped it.

Blue and yellow flames raced across the alcohol-soaked carpeting like wind over a wheat field, scorching a path down the hall to the detonation rooms. It hit Room 205 first, then 217, then 235—each one quietly erupting in flames like a fiery game of dominoes. Delgado watched with an arsonist's curiosity, impressed by his own work. In seconds, the heat was unbearable. More fire than he'd anticipated, moving faster than he'd expected. Too much alcohol.

The hallways were laid out like a square doughnut, all interconnecting, with rooms on the outside facing the streets and an open courtyard in the center. The flame zipped down one hall, turned left, down another, turned left, down the third leg, turned left.

Delgado suddenly felt heat at his back. He turned. The wall of flame had come full circle. He hadn't been *that* careless. In a split second, he knew: His own uncle had toasted him.

"Oh, shit!"

His eyes widened as the flames overtook him. His machine exploded, propelling him down the hall in a massive fireball.

Allison leaped from her seat. The explosion shook the entire building. The lights flickered, then went out. Emergency lighting switched on as the fire alarm sounded. Panicked guests screamed and ran in every direction. Thick smoke poured from the second-floor hallways and was filling the lobby.

Allison tugged at the briefcase. The cable lock was secure, leaving no way to free it. She tried opening it to take the money, but the cable was wrapped too tightly around it. That was no accident, she realized, since the kidnapper had selected the briefcase and supplied the cable. The pungent smoke thickened and choked her lungs. Her eyes were burning. She'd just have to leave it. She grabbed a cloth napkin from the table to cover her nose and mouth. Her leather bag was empty save for the gun. She tucked the pistol inside her jacket and left the bag.

Harley's voice was in her ear. "Allison, what's going on!"

"Fire!" she said. "They've started a fire."

"Get out."

"Not without the girls."

"Allison, just get *out*!"

Allison ignored him. She leaned over the railing to check the lobby. The emergency lighting was spotty and getting worse with the smoke. An emergency sprinkler was soaking a corner of the lobby near the entrance, but most weren't activated. The second floor was completely dry.

"They must have vandalized the sprinklers," she told Harley. "Only a few are working."

Below, excited mobs were fighting to squeeze through the revolving doors, slipping in the darkness on the wet marble floors. Others tumbled down the stairs in the race to safety. Two men jumped over the mezzanine railing to avoid the traffic jam. In the midst of the confusion, Allison saw one person moving *up* the staircase, fighting against the flow. It was a young girl. Even in the dim lighting, she knew that face.

"*Kristen!*" she shouted.

The girl looked up, kept coming.

"Kristen, come this way!"

The noise from the crowd and the pulsing alarm was deafening. She feared Kristen couldn't hear her. She could barely even hear Harley's voice, which was right in her ear.

"Do you see Kristen?" he asked—or she thought that was what he'd said.

"Yes. The staircase. They've released her!"

Allison ran for the staircase, but the crowd wouldn't let her pass. Flames shot from the hallway behind her. Staff carried out guests who had been overcome by smoke. Allison kept her eye on Kristen. Strangely, the girl seemed to be heading up the stairs on her own initiative, not in response to Allison's calls. It didn't make sense, thought Allison—unless the kidnapper had promised Kristen that her mother would be waiting for her upstairs, a cruel ploy to send the child to a fiery death right before Allison's eyes. Allison pushed toward the lobby, forcing her way down the crowded staircase one slow step at a time.

She could see the top of the girl's head, just a few steps below. "Kristen!" she shouted, but the words barely made it from her mouth. The smoke gagged her. She surged forward, forcing her way past the man blocking her way. Just a few steps and a few dozen bodies separated them. She reached as far as her arm would stretch but couldn't quite get there. She made one final push, one last stretch, closing the gap—and she had her! She had her by the arm!

Their eyes met for an instant, then Kristen screamed and wiggled free—lost as quickly as she was found.

"Kristen!" she shouted. "It's okay, come back!"

Kristen had turned in the opposite direction. She was moving with the flow down the stairs, away from Allison, frightened and confused—she'd obviously expected her mother or someone she knew.

Allison gave chase. "The disguise," said Allison, not sure if Harley could even hear her anymore. "The whole world knows what I look like, but Kristen doesn't recognize the disguise."

Harley said something in reply, but it was just a painful screech in her ear. "Harley, I'm disconnecting. Too much static." She pulled it from her ear and continued down the stairs. The smell of smoke filled the lobby. Allison could hear sirens blaring outside the hotel. Hysterical guests fled from the halls, restaurants, and bars—from every direction.

Frenzy, she thought. *Total frenzy*.

The crowd thinned at the base of the staircase. Kristen ran for the revolving door. Allison sprinted and caught her, wrapping her arms around her.

Kristen fought out of fear, but Allison held on, taking the blows.

"It's all right. Your mother sent me. I'm Allison Leahy."

Kristen froze. She examined the face, looking past the disguise. A glimmer of recognition came to her eyes, then her face scrunched with disapproval.

"What in the world did you do to your hair?"

Allison smiled cathartically and hugged her with all her strength. Then she whisked her away. "Come on."

They slowed only for a moment at the bottleneck at the entrance. Together they spilled onto the sidewalk outside with the rest of the crowd, stepping over fire hoses that crisscrossed the wet sidewalks. Cool, fresh air cleared their lungs, causing them to cough. Fire trucks and firefighters were all over the street. Police officers and paramedics helped staggering guests into ambulances and emergency vehicles. Allison recognized an FBI agent at the curb between a police car and fire truck. She took Kristen to him.

"I'm Allison Leahy," she shouted above the noise. "This is Kristen Howe. Get her in one of these ambulances!"

The agent took her hand, but Allison stopped her. She got down on a knee and looked Kristen right in the eye.

"Kristen, do you know where Emily is?"

"Who?"

"The other little girl. The kidnapper said you would know how to find her."

"I don't know anything about another girl."

Her heart sank. She turned to the other agent. "Take her. I have to find Emily."

The agent hesitated.

"Take her!" she shouted. She touched Kristen gently on the cheek. "It's okay. Go with him."

The agent lifted her off the ground and carried her to the ambulance. Allison put the receiver back in her ear and spoke into her microphone. "Harley, are you there?"

The response was pure static. She glanced at the squadron of emergency vehicles around her. Probably a thousand other radios were operating. Then she heard something, a broken response.

"Allison, one of our agents has Kristen."

"You don't say."

Injured guests staggered by her. The swirl of emergency lights gave everything an orange and yellow cast. A hook and ladder moved noisily into position overhead. Firefighters were carrying stranded guests down from the higher floors.

Allison shouted into her microphone. "Harley, I spoke to Kristen already. She doesn't know anything about Emily."

Allison pressed the earpiece, straining to hear. After a brief pause, she heard his response. "I'm sorry, but don't lose hope. We have agents working on those pictures the kidnapper sent. Maybe something will turn up."

"Turn up?" she shouted. "In eight years nothing has turned up!"

Static crackled over the line. She couldn't hear his voice. Her eyes welled as she stared back into the burning building. Kristen was safe, but that was only half the deal. A million dollars for Kristen *and* Emily. *That* was the deal.

And now the money was burning in a stupid building.

Or was it? she wondered.

She scanned the mayhem around her, and her sadness turned to anger. It was all a big diversion—that's *all* it was. In any kidnapping, the exchange of the child for the money was always where the plan came unraveled—it was where kidnappers were so often captured. This was the perfect way to handle the exchange—mass hysteria. While everyone was rushing from the building, Emily's kidnapper was happily making off with the money in a briefcase *he* had specifically requested and that was undoubtedly fireproof.

She tweaked her microphone. "Harley, I'm going back inside."

"Allison, don't!"

He said something more, but Allison couldn't hear. She adjusted the microphone to improve the reception—then someone grabbed her arm.

It was a cop. "Lady, you can't stand here."

"Please, I'm the attorney general."

"Yeah, and I'm the Duke of Earl."

"Let go," she said, wrestling free. Static rattled in her ear. She pressed her earpiece again. "Damn it, Harley, I don't want to go inside without radio contact, but I can't hear you!"

The cop grabbed her again. "You're with the press, aren't you?"

She ignored him. "Harley, are you there?"

"Damn media sharks," the cop groaned. "Get your bony reporter's ass behind the police tape." He ripped the microphone from her ear. The radio went completely dead.

"You idiot!" she screamed.

He grabbed her with one hand. His walkie-talkie was in the other. It squawked, giving Allison an idea. She wrestled free and grabbed his walkie-talkie.

"Hey!" he shouted.

Allison ran off.

"Lady, stop!"

She kept going, disappearing into the crowd. She pushed against the flow and made it back into the lobby. The smoke was beginning to clear below, but it was still clouding from the second floor. She pushed the button on her walkie-talkie.

"I don't know who I'm talking to, but this is Attorney General Allison Leahy. I need to reach Special Agent Harley Abrams of the FBI immediately." She left it on, hoping for a response.

Firefighters in full gear had replaced the hysterical guests in the lobby. Black soot and cinders covered the walls and floor. The chandeliers were dark. Emergency spotlights were the only source of light. Traces of smoke irritated her eyes, even though the fire was under control and the smoke had diminished. Most of the firefighters were wearing masks, but it wasn't absolutely necessary. Allison could breathe without one.

She hurried inside and stopped at the base of the stairwell. The lighting was spotty, but she could see up to the mezzanine and the charred Independence Bar. A lone fireman was crouched by the table where she'd left the money. He wore a complete set of firefighting gear, including a self-contained breathing apparatus, like a scuba diver. Dressed like that, he could walk through any cloud of smoke. And, she realized, he could walk right out of the building without being detected.

As he rose from his crouch, Allison could see it—he had the money in hand. Their eyes met briefly at a distance, him from above and her from below. The man froze. Allison didn't flinch. His face was barely visible behind the clear fireproof mask, but Allison could have sworn she saw him smile. In one swift motion, he snatched the briefcase and ran for the guest rooms.

Allison charged up the stairs, past the bar, heading at full speed toward the guest rooms. The smoke was thicker upstairs, though not impenetrable. The carpeting had completely burned away. The exposed floorboards were still hot from the flames.

Allison turned down the hall to the second-floor rooms. Glass crunched beneath her feet. The windows facing the inner courtyard had shattered in the explosion. Some interior walls had burned away completely. Others were charred but still standing. An emergency light shined through the smoke like a lone headlight beaming through fog. She was closing on the man in the fire suit. He was struggling beneath the weight of his gear.

He stopped suddenly, turned, and pointed his gun. On impulse, Allison ducked into an open room just as the bullet whizzed by her. She took her pistol from inside her jacket and peered out the doorway. He was running down the hall again. She ran after him.

He fired another shot on the run, but it was erratic. He seemed to be having trouble shooting with the thick fireproof gloves on his hands. Allison kept coming, though the floor was getting weaker. Some boards were completely burned away. She watched her step but refused to stop. She was just twenty feet behind him when the floor gave way beneath his feet.

Allison stopped as he plunged up to his waist in the fire-eaten floor. In his struggle to save the briefcase his gun fell through the opening in the floor. Allison assumed the police stance and pointed her gun at him from behind.

"Freeze!" she shouted.

He kept struggling. He was like a man who'd fallen through the ice and couldn't pull himself up. Each time he groped for a firm piece of flooring, it broke away beneath him. Flames from below were lapping at his heels. He was barely hanging on—but he was getting away.

"Freeze!" she said again.

He kept inching away from her, though the heavy equipment and air tank were clearly slowing his movement. Finally he reached firm flooring, leaving a gaping hole in the floor between him and Allison. He wobbled to his feet. He started to run, but he'd hurt his leg in the fall. He limped away with the money.

Allison took aim, but she couldn't shoot. Not without answers about Emily. She aimed lower, for his legs, but under the smoky conditions she feared her shot would come in high. An erratic bullet in the compressed air tank strapped to his back would unleash an explosion that would silence him forever—particularly with tanks that had been heated by the raging fire. She lowered her gun and charged forward, stopping at the hole. It was like gazing into hell—a long way down, nothing but flames.

The hole was slightly off-center. She walked along the intact ridge of flooring near the wall. The charred boards creaked beneath her feet, but she knew she weighed less than the man in all that gear. Her feet slid an inch at a time, one step at a time. Heat shot up from the open hole; it was like standing over a volcano. She moved faster, then leaped the last three feet to more secure flooring.

The kidnapper was just ducking into a room at the end of the hall—unarmed, she assumed, though she couldn't be certain he didn't have another weapon. She raced down the hall, gun in hand. The floor was still weak in spots, but she didn't slow down. If he could make it wearing all that gear, she could surely make it. She stopped in the doorway and pointed her gun.

The man leaped from behind the door and knocked her backward, across the hall. She crashed through the remnants of a charred French door, but she fell only ten inches before the balcony caught her. Behind and below her was the hotel's central courtyard. Staring at her from across the hall was Vincent Gambrelli.

Still on her back, she aimed her gun. "Stop right there," she said.

He was framed in the doorway across the hall, fifteen feet away. He pulled off his mask and tossed it aside. He looked huge in his gear, especially with the breathing tank bulging behind him.

"Stop the charade," he scoffed. "I know you're not going to shoot me."

She rose to her feet and stood on the balcony, aiming right at his face. She glanced at the courtyard behind her, fifty feet below. It was a maze of English gardens surrounded by wrought-iron fences with sharp-pointed pickets. The fear of falling forced her forward, but only a step. "I'll kill you if you come any closer."

"And where would that leave you? Peter is dead. I'm the only man alive who knows where Emily is."

"You son of a bitch. Where is she?"

The walkie-talkie crackled in her coat. This time, the voice was familiar. "Allison, it's Harley Abrams. Where are you?"

"Don't you dare answer that," said Gambrelli.

She had two hands on the gun, taking aim.

Gambrelli said, "I'm in control here, Allison. Not you. Not Abrams. Only I know where Emily is. You can't kill me. You know you can't kill me."

The walkie-talkie crackled. "Allison, this is Harley. Where are you?"

Gambrelli heard it. She heard it. Allison didn't move. He took a step toward her.

"Stay right there!" she shouted.

"Or what?" he sneered. "You're not going to kill me. You won't even tell the FBI where you are because you're afraid *they* might kill me. You come up here all by yourself, trusting no one else to do the job. You know that if I'm dead, you'll never find Emily."

Her hands shook. She wanted to kill him—the man who had sneaked into her house and taken her sleeping baby right from her crib. But she knew he was right. She couldn't kill him. Not if she ever hoped to find Emily.

Gambrelli took another step. "Now be a smart broad and give me the gun. You and I are going to walk right out of here."

Her finger twitched on the trigger. Her face cringed with agony. She couldn't give him the gun. She couldn't let herself become a hostage. But she couldn't give up on Emily.

The walkie-talkie crackled once more. "Allison, if you can hear me, those photographs gave us a lead. We found Emily. She's alive and well in New York."

Her eyes brightened.

Gambrelli's face filled with panic.

In desperation he leaped toward her to grab the gun. Allison fell right back onto the balcony, much harder this time. The weight of Gambrelli's equipment made him like a high-speed train, completely unstoppable. On her back, she felt him tumbling right over her. She yanked his coat with all her strength to keep his momentum going forward. In a split second he was flying over her head, flying over the rail, flying off the balcony, and screaming like a wounded banshee. She turned as he fell to the courtyard below, into the maze of walkways surrounded by wrought-iron fences with sharp-pointed pickets. He was falling face up, leading with his breathing tank. He landed squarely on the iron fence. The sharp picket punctured the tank, releasing an explosion of fire-heated compressed air that rocked the balcony fifty feet above. Allison covered her head from flying debris, then looked down. Shreds of the tattered firefighting suit lay strewn across the courtyard.

Vincent Gambrelli was gone. *Completely* gone.

Allison shivered as she peered over the railing. "That was for Emily," she said from above.

Epilogue

Flames lit up the late Monday evening newscasts across the country, though the fiery loss of the St. George Hotel was just a footnote to the breaking story on the night before the election. Kristen Howe was safe, and Allison Leahy had rescued her. That was as much as Harley Abrams and Tanya Howe would tell the press. It was the kind of headline that had Lincoln Howe empathizing with a certain Republican governor named Dewey who'd gone to bed on election night thinking he'd defeated Harry Truman.

It was a half-truth Allison couldn't let stand.

At 11:15 P.M. eastern time, she issued a brief statement to a packed pressroom back at the Justice Building. "With great shame and personal regret," she told the American people what they deserved to know—that her late husband was behind Kristen Howe's kidnapping.

Stunned silence fell over television audiences across the country, followed by an immediate outburst of questions from reporters. Allison answered none of them. Exhausted, she retired to the sleeping loft in her office suite, leaving it to Tuesday's voters to decide whether she was a hero, a victim, or something else altogether.

She rested only a few hours. At 5:00 A.M. the Justice Department's Sabre jet flew her to New

York. Harley Abrams went with her. She didn't have to force him. He seemed unwilling to have it any other way.

At 8:00 A.M. they were on their way to Ellington Prep School. It had been the school—the redbrick building in the background of Gambrelli's photograph—that led the FBI to Emily. The analysts in the lab had picked up something invisible to the naked eye—a plaque dedicated to the school's founder posted by the door. Once they had the school, they had Emily.

The sedan stopped directly across the street from the schoolyard. Brownish grass and bare oak trees stretched beyond the chain-link fence surrounding the yard. Mothers and fathers led their children down the sidewalk to the school gate, sending them off for another day. Harley parallel-parked near the crosswalk, then shut off the engine. Allison sat quietly in the passenger seat, gesturing with her hands, engaged in a silent and imaginary conversation.

"Who you talking to over there?" asked Harley.

"Huh?"

"Who you talking to?"

Her head rolled back as she sighed with anxiety. "Oh, jeez. I was just explaining to Emily—" She stopped herself. "Her name's not even Emily. It's April. April Remmick. The only child of Henry and Elizabeth Remmick. Two decent, hardworking people who had no idea the little girl they were adopting eight years ago hadn't come from Russia but was stolen from me." She grimaced, as if suddenly in pain. "They're a family, Harley. What right do I have to upset that?"

"You're her mother, that's what right you have."

He got out of the car. Allison stayed put. She watched through the windshield as he walked around the front. She locked the door as he reached for the handle.

He tapped on the window. "Allison, get out of the car."

She shook her head.

"Allison, we're right here."

"But if I see her . . ." Her voice trailed off. Her eyes shifted toward the schoolyard, forty yards away. The children were lining up to go inside—young boys and girls, all wearing the school uniform. One, however, seemed to stand out in Allison's line of sight. It was as if she were wearing a different uniform. As if she were alone in the yard.

Allison unlocked the door and got out of the car. She crossed the street slowly, one step at a time, drawing closer. Her gaze never left the little blond-haired girl with the pink barrette and red knee socks, third in a line of twelve youngsters arranged from shortest to tallest. She stopped at the fence and grasped the chain links with both hands, still staring, just thirty yards away.

Harley's footsteps clicked on the sidewalk behind her.

She couldn't look away. "That's her," she said.

"Looks just like her picture."

"Somehow, I think I would have known it was her. Even without the picture. I feel something inside. A connection. Can you understand what I'm saying?"

Harley nodded.

"She looks so happy. A little shy, but happy." She looked at Harley. "April. That's a pretty name, too, isn't it?"

He smiled with his eyes. "You know, lots of kids have two sets of parents. Some kids who are adopted even get to know their biological mother. It's not unheard of, I mean."

She looked at Emily—April—then back at Harley. "Honestly, if you were her parents, would you let her get anywhere near me?"

"Why wouldn't I?"

"Because these special kind of arrangements are hard enough when you have two sets of *normal* parents. Win or lose today's election, I can never offer anyone a normal life. It's like the kidnapper said—fate has found me. Any family I touch will be instantly dysfunctional."

"That's crazy, Allison. *Every* family is dysfunctional. No, I take that back," he said, raising a finger for a case in point. "The Addams family. Now there's the one family that was not dysfunctional."

"The Addams family?"

"You know—Gomez, Morticia, Uncle Fester. The only family in the history of the world where everyone just accepted each other for exactly what they were."

She smiled. "Never thought of it that way."

"You should. All those people in Washington who keep trying to define the perfect American family should, too."

"So, do you think Emily's—I mean April's—parents are like Gomez and Morticia?"

He laid his hand on his heart, smirking. "We can only hope."

She smiled, then glanced back at April. The children were filing inside.

Harley turned toward the car, offering his arm. "Come on, Allison. Let's go talk to Mr. and Mrs. Remmick. You might be surprised."

She paused, then took his arm. There was a spring in her step as they crossed the street.

"Allison?"

"What?"

"You're on *my* arm, and you're leading."

She didn't break stride. "Harley?"

"What?"

She pinched his ribs. "Don't be a pain in the ass."

Part 1

June 1999

1

Amy wished she could go back in time. Not *way* back. It wasn't as if she wanted to sip ouzo with Aristotle or tell Lincoln to duck. Less than a fortnight would suffice. Just far enough to avert the computer nightmare she'd been living.

Amy was the computer information systems director at Bailey, Gaslow & Heinz, the premier law firm in the Rocky Mountains. It was her job to keep confidential information flowing freely and securely between the firm's offices in Boulder, Denver, Salt Lake City, Washington, London, and Moscow. Day in and day out, she had the power to bring two hundred attorneys groveling to their knees. And she had the privilege of hearing them scream. Simultaneously. At her.

As if I *created the virus*, she thought, thinking of what she wished she had said to one accusatory partner. He was miles behind her now, but she was still thinking about it. Driving alone on the highway was a great place to put things exactly as they should have been.

It had taken almost a week to purge the entire system, working eighteen-hour days, traveling to six different offices. She had everyone up and running in some capacity within the first 24 hours, and she ultimately salvaged over ninety-five percent of the stored data. Still, it wasn't a pleasant experience to have to tell a half-dozen unlucky lawyers that, like Humpty Dumpty, their computer and everything on it was DOA.

It was a little known fact, but Amy had witnessed it first hand: lawyers *do* cry.

A sudden rattle in the dashboard snagged Amy's attention. Her old Ford pick-up truck had plenty of squeaks and pings. Each was different, and she knew them all, like a mother who could sense whether her baby's cry meant feed me, change me, or please get grandma out of my face. This particular noise was more of a clunk—an easy problem to diagnose, since torrid hot air was suddenly blowing out of the air conditioning vents. Amy switched off the A-C and tried rolling down the window. It jammed. Perfect. Ninety-two degrees outside, her truck was spewing dragon's breath, and the damn window refused to budge. It was an old saw in Colorado that people visited for the winters but moved there for the summers. They obviously didn't mean *this.*

I'm melting, she thought, borrowing from *The Wizard of Oz.*

She grabbed the *Rocky Mountain News* from the floor and fanned herself for relief. The week-old paper marked the day she had sent her daughter off to visit her ex-husband for the week, so that she could devote all her energy to the computer crisis. Six straight days away from Taylor was a new record, one she hoped would never be broken. Even dead tired, she couldn't wait to see her.

Amy was driving an oven on wheels by the time she reached the Clover Leaf Apartments, a boring collection of old two-story red brick buildings. It was a far cry from the cachet Boulder addresses that pushed the average price of a home to more than a quarter million dollars. The Clover Leaf was government-subsidized housing, an eyesore to anyone but penurious students and the fixed-income elderly. Landscaping was minimal. Baked asphalt was plentiful. Amy had seen warehouse districts with more architectural flair. It was as if the builder had decided that nothing man-made could ever be as beautiful as the jagged mountain tops in the distance, so why bother even trying? Even so, there was a four-year waiting list just to get in.

A jolt from a speed bump launched her to the roof. The truck skidded to a halt in the first available parking space, and Amy jumped out. After a minute or two, the redness in her face faded to pink. She was looking like herself again. Amy wasn't one to flaunt it, but she could easily turn heads. Her ex-husband used to say it was the long legs and full lips. But it was much more than that. Amy gave off a certain energy whenever she moved, whenever she smiled, whenever she looked through those big grey-blue eyes. Her grandmother had always said she had her mother's boundless energy—and Gram would know.

Amy's mother had died tragically twenty years ago, when Amy was just eight. Her father had passed away even earlier. Gram had essentially raised her. She *knew* Amy; she'd even seen the warning signs in her ex-husband before Amy had. Four years ago, Amy was a young mother trying to balance a marriage, a newborn, and graduate studies in astronomy. Her daughter and course work left little time for Ted—meaning too little time to keep an eye on him. He found another woman. After the divorce, she moved in with Gram, who helped with Taylor. Good jobs weren't easy to find in Boulder, a haven for talented and educated young professionals who wanted the quintessential Colorado lifestyle. Amy would have loved to stick with astronomy, but money was tight, and a graduate degree in astronomy wouldn't change that. Even her computer job hadn't changed that. Her paycheck barely covered the basic living expenses for the three of them. Anything left over was stashed away for law school, which was coming in September.

For Amy, a career in law was an economic decision, not an emotional one. She was certain she'd meet plenty of classmates just like her—art historians, English literature majors, and dozens more who had abandoned all hope of finding work in the field they loved.

Amy just wished there were another way.

"Mommy, Mommy!"

Amy whirled at the sound of her daughter's voice. She was wearing her favorite pink dress and red tennis shoes. The left half of her very blond hair was in a pigtail. The other flowed in the breeze, another lost barrette. She peeled down the walkway and leaped into Amy's arms.

"I missed you so much," said Amy, squeezing her daughter tightly.

Taylor laughed, then made a face. "Eww, you're all wet."

Amy wiped away the sweat she'd transferred from her cheek to Taylor's. "Mommy's truck has a little fever."

"Gram says you should just sell that heap of junk."

"Never," said Amy. Her mother used to own that heap of junk. It was about the only thing she'd managed to come away with in the divorce.

That, and her daughter. She lowered Taylor to the ground. "So, how is your dad?"

"Fine. He promised to come visit us."

"Us?"

"Uh huh. He said he'll come see you and me at the party."

"What party?"

"*Our* party. For when you gradgy-ate law school and when I gradgy-ate high school."

Amy blinked twice, ignoring the sting. "He actually said that?"

"Law school takes a long time, huh Mommy?"

"Not that long, sweetheart. It'll be over before we know it."

Gram came up from the behind them, nearly panting as she spoke. "I have *never* seen a four year old run that fast."

Taylor giggled. Gram welcomed Amy back with a smile, then grimaced. "For goodness sakes, you're an absolute stick. Have you been living on nothing but caffeine again?"

"No, I swear I tried taking a little coffee with it this time."

"Get inside and let me fix you something to eat."

Amy was too tired to think about food. "I'll just throw something quick in the microwave."

"Microwave," she scoffed. "I may be old, but it's not like I have to rub two sticks together to heat up a late lunch. By the time you're out of the shower, I'll have a nice hot meal waiting for you."

Along with a month's supply of fat and calories, thought Amy. Gram was from the old school of everything, including diet. "Okay," she said as she grabbed her suitcase from the back of the truck. "Let's go inside."

The threesome walked hand-in-hand across the

parking lot, with Taylor swinging like a monkey between them.

"Home again, Mommy's home again!" said Taylor in a sing-song voice.

Amy inserted the key and opened the door. Home was a simple two-bedroom, one-bath apartment. The main living area was a combination living room, dining room, and play room. Gram sometimes said "the girls" had turned it into one big storage room. Bicycles and roller blades cluttered the small entrance; the small ones were Taylor's, the big ones were Amy's. There was an old couch and matching arm chair, typical rental furniture. An old pine wall unit held books, a few plants, and a small television. To the right was a closet-size kitchen, more of a kitchenette.

Amy dropped her suitcase at the door.

"Let me get started in the kitchen," said Gram.

"I help!" Taylor shouted.

"Wash your hands first," said Amy.

Taylor dashed toward the bathroom. Gram followed. "Your mail's on the table, Amy. Along with your phone messages." She disappeared down the hall, right on Taylor's heels.

Amy crossed the room to the table. Two week's worth of mail was stacked neatly in piles: personal, bills, and junk. The biggest stack was bills, some of them second notices. The personal mail wasn't personal at all—mostly that computer-generated junk written in pre-printed script to make it look like a letter from an old friend. In the bona-fide junk pile, a package caught her eye. There was no return address on it. No postage or postmark, either. It appeared to have been hand-delivered, possibly by a private courier service. For its size, it seemed heavy.

Curious, she tore away the brown paper wrapping, revealing a box bearing a picture of a crock-pot. She shook it. It didn't feel like a crock pot. It felt like something more solid was inside, as if the box had been filled with cement. The ends had been re-taped, too, suggesting the crock pot had been replaced with something else. She slit the duct tape with her key and opened the flaps. A thick plastic lining encased the contents, some kind of water proof bag with a zipper. There was no note or card, nothing to reveal the identity of the sender. She unzipped the bag, then froze.

"Oh, my God."

Benjamin Franklin was staring back at her, many times over. Hundred dollar bills. *Stacks* of them. She removed one bundle, then another, laying them side-by-side on the table. Her hands shook as she counted the bills in one stack. Fifty per stack. Forty stacks.

She lowered herself into the chair, staring at the money in quiet disbelief. Someone—an anonymous someone—had sent her two-hundred-thousand dollars.

And she had no idea why.